JESUS AND THE TIME TRAVELERS

R. J. MASON

PublishAmerica
Baltimore

Hardcover 9781462659319
Softcover 9781462668137
eBook 9781462671397
PUBLISHED BY PUBLISHAMERICA, LLLP
www.publishamerica.com
Baltimore

Printed in the United States of America

PROLOGUE

Time was up and the portal to his daydream abruptly closed as the classroom door slammed shut, waking him back to reality while he was sitting at his desk waiting for class to begin. During David's high school years, he became the lunchroom topic of the teachers because he could learn complex mathematical concepts and excelled in his other class subjects. In 1981, during his senior year, Mr. Zwirko, his calculus teacher, asked David to come to his classroom when classes were over for the day. He didn't have a clue why Mr. Zwirko wanted to meet with him and thought it was because math tutors were needed to help other students. After his final class, he proceeded to Mr. Zwirko's room, not knowing what the meeting would be about. He arrived at his teacher's office and noticed an older man holding a piece of white chalk in his right hand, staring at the chalkboard. The blackboard had a mathematical equation written on it.

Mr. Zwirko approached David and introduced him to Mr. Kramer, a friend and theoretical mathematician in the field of quantum physics who taught at the Massachusetts Institute of Technology (M.I.T.). David was humbled to be in the presence of such an intelligent man and was at a loss for words while introducing himself. So Mr. Zwirko took over and told Mr. Kramer that David was a gifted mathematics student. Mr. Zwirko said, "I truly believe that David's intellectual gift should be allowed to fulfill its potential and to achieve greatness, which ultimately will help future generations." He then told David why Mr. Kramer was in his office, explaining that certain students are given the opportunity of a lifetime to attend prestigious universities in the United States and abroad through academic scholarships at schools such as M.I.T., Harvard and Cambridge Universities. "I invited him here to meet you and to test your mathematical abilities. If he believes you are a gifted student, he has enough influence at M.I.T. to recommend that you be accepted into the university and given a full scholarship."

"Professor Kramer has written a mathematical problem on the chalkboard and would like you to solve it," Mr. Zwirko said.

David stared at the complexity of the equation and thought that the formula was not solely calculus, algebra, trigonometry or finite mathematics, but also included advanced physics. As David approached the chalkboard and began solving the problem, the two teachers smiled in approval at his approach.

When David had finished the final portion of the equation, Professor Kramer said, "Please interpret the meaning of your results."

David looked at the M.I.T. professor with a puzzled expression on his face and said, "I'm sure you know the answer, sir. We don't have the technology or knowledge to travel in time."

"Yes, that's true, young man," said the professor, and then he smiled at Mr. Zwirko and told him he had to leave for his next appointment. As he was walking out of the classroom, he said, "David, you'll be hearing from me soon."

After he left the room, David asked, "Is Mr. Kramer upset with me?" His teacher said, "Oh, no. He's a busy man, and his time is very valuable. I'm sure he'll call me in a day or two," and then they both left the school for their homes.

CHAPTER 1

The year was 2010 and Professor David Solomon was home in the library with the fireplace roaring, reading a science fiction novel as it started to snow. David Solomon is forty-eight and has a fair complexion with brown hair and brown eyes. He is a single father of a still-growing fourteen-year-old boy with blond hair and blue eyes named Luke. He was married to Miriam before she died while giving birth to Luke at the hospital. The death of his wife had a traumatic psychological effect on him that took a year of grief counseling to resolve. He is a spiritual man and belongs to the local Catholic parish, where on Sundays he and Luke attend church and pray. Annually, on Mother's Day, they visit the cemetery to pray and leave a bouquet of flowers on Miriam's grave. The inscription on her headstone reads, "If I could travel in time, I would bring you back."

As a boy, he was always intrigued by the novels he'd read and the movies he'd seen that used sci-fi technology. He wondered if these machines and devices would one day become a reality. While reading a novel, David glanced at the television as the weatherman was announcing that Boston and the North Shore should brace for a snowstorm. The snow would accumulate up to eighteen inches with a temperature of twenty degrees and continue for the rest of the week. While continuing to read his novel, he began to wonder if M.I.T. would cancel classes. Being a tenured professor at his alma mater, he thought about calling the school's president's office for an update when the telephone suddenly rang. It was the school's president's secretary announcing that due to the snowstorm, classes would be canceled for the week. He worried about his students not knowing of the announcement, afraid they would show up for his lecture. He taught astrophysics and theoretically applied engineering techniques, one of the most sought-after classes. There was only one week left before each student would begin to work in the school lab on a thesis that would form an important part of their final grade for a master's degree.

The front door opened and a blast of cold air caused the fire in the fireplace to jump. "Is that you, Luke?" David asked.

"Yes, Dad."

"Is the snow sticking to the ground?"

"No. It's just blowing around," Luke said while taking off his coat and heading up to his bedroom.

Over the years and as a hobby, David had been an avid inventor trying to perfect some of his theories in his basement lab. The focus of most of his experiments involved time travel. He always dreamed of being the scientist to make it a reality—to right the wrongs done by man in the past and save the human species from destroying itself and the planet. The idea of traveling in time had become stuck in his mind ever since the day he met Professor Kramer in Mr. Zwirko's office because an intellectual was also interested in the same subject and it was the first time that he'd seen a time travel equation. David's favorite TV series was *Star Trek* and he always wondered if an invention could someday be created like the transporter on the Starship *Enterprise* to make it possible for humans to be transported from one place to another without destroying their molecules.

Since it was late Sunday afternoon, he decided to go to the local church to pray for some good things to happen in the world and talk to God. He put on his winter coat and walked out the front door and into the cold with snow blowing around, which was now beginning to stick to the ground.

The local Catholic Church on Jefferson Avenue is named Saint Peter's and is a fifteen-minute walk from his home. The church is one of the oldest in New England, with two tall steeples in the front and two large oak doors at the main entrance. As David approached the church, he could barely see in the swirling snowstorm. When he reached the main entrance, he tried to open the huge doors, but they were locked. He walked to a smaller door to the left, but found it locked too. He was about to leave when he remembered a side door that provided an entrance near the altar. Thankfully, that door opened and David entered with a sigh of relief and instantly felt the warm air surround him.

David looked around for other parishioners, but saw none. The lighting was dim and there were candles burning near the Lord's Table that provided the only other light. David approached and knelt before the marble altar, making the sign of the cross, and began to say a prayer for Luke and his late wife, Miriam. He also prayed for the storm to pass and for the safety of his students and the homeless. After saying his prayers, he looked up and focused on the large cross with Jesus on it and thought about the suffering Jesus endured leading up to and during his crucifixion. He bowed his head and thanked God for all he had been given and for sacrificing himself so the gates of heaven would be open for all to enter.

As he finished praying, he saw a sixty-something-year-old priest with gray hair wearing black pants and shirt with a white collar around his neck walking toward him from behind the altar where he had earlier seen a light. The unfamiliar priest asked why he was in the church in the middle of a snowstorm. David said, "Father, I live only fifteen minutes from the church and come here often with my son to pray. I've been a member of this parish for many years, and I do not recall your face."

"What's your name?" the priest asked.

"David Solomon."

"Hello, David. I am a new resident of Salem. The Vatican has sent me here to serve the parishioners. I'm Dominick Carlucci. Please call me Father Carlucci."

"It's a pleasure to meet you, Father. How are things going in Rome?"

"The church is still defending priests wrongly accused of past sins and punishing those who have been found guilty. I would prefer that we change the topic. We must support our church and help the people who are in need of our assistance."

David said, "Amen. Do you have a few minutes to talk about what Jesus might say in today's extraordinary times?"

"What's on your mind?"

"Well, Father, I turn on the television and see terrible events occurring all over the world. I listen to the radio and hear the same bad news. Then there are shows on TV contradicting the New Testament, discussing the lost Gospels of Mary Magdalene and of Judas Iscariot, along with others recently found in the Middle East desert. We see televised Christian programs advocating in the name of Jesus. After watching them I start to question my faith. I begin wondering if the Bible is correct and whether instead discovered lost Gospel writings are true. Was the New Testament written to meet only the needs of the church at that time?"

Father Carlucci began to answer David's questions by saying, "Christians today are allowed to question their faith, and it's not held against them. In much older times, if you questioned the Bible it was considered blasphemy. Case in point, Galileo Galilei. He discovered a fourth moon orbiting Jupiter, but the Holy Scriptures states only three moons orbited the planet. And, Professor, you know what happened to Galileo."

"Yes, Father. He did discover a new moon in 1610 and published his discovery, which contradicted the beliefs of the time that said the Earth was the center of the known universe. He was eventually summoned to Rome to appear before an inquisition of the Catholic Church. Galileo was sentenced to recant his view that the sun was the central point of the solar system or be tortured. He recanted, but knew he had told the truth, even saying so on his deathbed."

"Today the church is more tolerant of new ideas and welcomes archeological evidence supporting events mentioned in the Gospels," Father Carlucci said.

"But, Father, we have Christian leaders on television professing daily their faith in the name of Jesus and then asking for donations from the viewers. The TV audience gives blindly, believing their donation will go to a needy cause."

"The Catholic Church does the same, but not on TV. We pass a basket during each Mass hoping for voluntary gifts to support the church. Can you see behind you on the wall the wood box beyond the confessional booths? That is for donations. Our parishioners give blindly, believing we will help the people in need," Father Carlucci said.

"Yes, Father. I get your point. What do you believe Jesus would say if he were here today? I mean physically, not spiritually."

The priest looked up at the cross and stared for a moment, and then he said, "David, that's a very difficult question to answer. We've all been waiting for Jesus to return, and we pray constantly for that to happen. We also pray for a sign proving God's existence—not only Christians, but practitioners of all religious faiths. We all would like to witness a miracle," and after pausing, he said, "David, in today's times we could use a man like Jesus again to unify all religions and bring peace on earth."

"Father, I agree. If Jesus were here today, even for a short time, the world would become a better place for all its inhabitants. Well, Father, I must leave now. It was a pleasure meeting you, and I hope to see you again."

"I know our talk was brief. Please drop by any time. I enjoyed our conservation. I'll say a prayer for you and your son," the priest said.

"Thank you for your time, Father. It was a pleasure meeting a priest directly from Rome," David said, and then he exited the church the same way he had entered.

CHAPTER 2

As David exited Saint Peter's Church, he was hit by a blast of cold Arctic air and thought of the warmth in the church. He began his short trek home in the snowstorm, which had become even stronger. While walking, he started to think about his brief conversation with Father Carlucci. The idea of Jesus returning would fulfill the written scriptures and be considered a miracle for every religion on earth. The thought of time travel raced through his head again as he got closer to his home, making him oblivious to the storm brewing all around him. He kept thinking about what would happen if he could go back in time and bring Jesus to the present for all to see and hear.

David was engulfed in his thoughts and not even aware of walking past his house until a neighbor hollered out to him from across the street. He stopped and waved hello. He turned around and, after entering his house, he called out to Luke to announce that he was home. Luke didn't respond, so he went to his bedroom to check on him. Luke's door was slightly open, and David saw him still asleep on his bed, and then he went to the kitchen to make a cup of hot tea.

He turned on the stove and soon the teapot started to whistle. The cell phone, which was in his winter coat, began ringing, so he went to the hallway and retrieved it while wondering who might be calling him. He answered and said, "Hello. David speaking."

At the other end was Brian Soranno, a former undergraduate student of his. Brian was finishing his final year at Harvard University after which he would obtain a Ph.D. in quantum physics. "Hi, Professor. It's Brian. How are you today, sir?"

"I'm fine, but a little cold. I just arrived home and I'm about to drink a cup of hot tea."

"That sounds very good, sir, considering how chilly it is outside. The school's lab is closed until the storm eases, which won't be until the end of the week. Could I use your basement lab to work on my experiments?" Brian asked.

"Yes, but you can't use the lab today because of the snowstorm. I wouldn't want a guilty conscience if something happened to you while trying to get here from Boston. You can come by tomorrow. I will be home all day," David replied.

"Thank you, Professor. I'll be at your house around 8:30 a.m., and I'll use the backdoor entrance."

"That will be fine. The key is in the usual spot, so let yourself in."

"Thanks, Professor. Enjoy your hot tea. Bye," Brian said, ending the conversation.

David poured his tea and sat at the kitchen table and began thinking about his own experiments with time travel over the years. He always seemed to be missing a variable in perfecting his time machine.

He recalled the U.S. government's secret experiment in 1943 based on Albert Einstein's unified field theory. The theory describes the natural forces of electromagnetic fields and gravity. The experiment was called the Philadelphia Experiment and it used Einstein's prediction of a solid object moving through space and time. The U.S. government denies to this day that experiments were conducted. The eyewitnesses who participated in the test swear that the U.S.S. *Eldridge,* an escort ship for a destroyer, disappeared briefly with all its crew on board and reappeared a short time later in Norfolk, Virginia, only to vanish again and reappear in Philadelphia, Pennsylvania.

He started to wonder if the U.S. government really had transported an object the size of a warship back and forth in time and to different locations. If so, then why couldn't a human move through the space and time continuum to a predetermined location, considering that a person has only a fraction of the mass of a battleship?

After David finished drinking his tea, he decided to go down to the basement and make sure the lab equipment was still functioning properly. He didn't want to disappoint Brian once he'd trekked to his home in such a storm. The components he built and acquired were mostly new and performed various types of controlled experiments. The lab was equipped with an airtight six-foot-high, four-inch-thick walk-in glass chamber and had a small, solid lead chamber for radiation tests, which could also be used for other toxic materials, plus lasers, glass beakers, burners, chemicals and scientific meters and measuring devices that he had acquired over the years. He went to each machine and turned on the power to make sure it was working.

David walked to a specially designed PC, named Eve, built with the help of his two best engineering students. The computer interfaced with a mini supercomputer to perform complex mathematical calculations in minutes that would take ordinary PCs days to solve. The mainframe was stored in a locked gray metal cabinet against the rear wall of the lab. He walked to the cabinet and unlocked the doors and booted up Eve.

After David had successfully completed testing his lab equipment, he then powered down each machine. After turning off the devices, he walked to the mainframe of Eve and marveled at its blinking lights. After staring for few moments, he began thinking of all the intellectual geniuses who created the components needed to assemble such a machine. He turned off the computer and locked the cabinet doors. He then proceeded to turn off the large monitor on the wall and also the PC on his desk.

As he was about to shut off the lights in the basement, he paused and turned around and stared at the gray cabinet housing his mini supercomputer. After a moment, he walked toward it and said, "It's time to return to the drawing board and finish the job." David took his wallet from his pants and removed a small key in a special pocket and inserted it into a keyhole in the top rear of the metal cabinet. The key and lock were specially designed to hide what was behind the wall. He turned the key and four tumblers clicked, freeing it from the steel locking mechanism that was firmly attached to the basement's cement wall. He gently rolled the gray cabinet to the left on hidden wheels he had drawn and built to protect the computer and his secret room.

David bent over and ducked his head to pass through the opening. When he was inside the room he reached for the light switch and turned on the lights. The hidden room was illuminated and larger than the basement's lab and was equipped with more advanced testing equipment that he had diagramed and built. Over the years, he had invented and produced his own components to test and prove his theories. He decided any invention he created having the potential to change the world would remain in his own lab and not be shared with other scientists. He scanned the room looking at all his equipment as he went to a workbench that had the master plan for his time machine, which he called StellaPort. After turning a few pages of the blueprints, he stared at the seven-foot-high enclosed glass chamber with a door that was connected to four five-foot-tall control panels. He called the unit Stella. He began talking out loud while looking at the transportation chamber and said, "The time has come to achieve my lifelong dream, but if I fail, I will know I gave every ounce of my intellect trying to succeed."

He glanced around the room one last time before exiting his secret lab and then turned off the lights. He gently swung the metal cabinet into its locking position and turned the key, which made the four tumblers click again. He tried moving it, but it was now fastened to the wall, and then he shut off the lights as he was leaving the lab.

Back in his living room and sitting on the sofa, he began thinking again about his brief conversation with Father Carlucci concerning his thoughts on what Jesus might do in today's times. He had a mental flash and thought, "The only way of knowing would be to invent a time machine and invite Jesus to this time period. I'll restart my work where I stopped."

CHAPTER 3

David's bedroom radio alarm clock came on at 6 a.m., announcing the local news, and the weatherman was reporting a continuing cold snap with more snow on the way as he went to the bathroom for a shower. While in the shower, David thought of Brian, who would be driving in bad road conditions this morning to use his lab. After showering, he got dressed and then stopped by Luke's bedroom and saw him using his computer. "Good morning, Luke," David said, standing in the doorway.

"Good morning, Dad."

"What would you like for breakfast?" David asked.

"I'll have scrambled eggs, bacon, toast and orange juice."

"Okay," David said, and then he left for the kitchen.

While David was cooking, he began to think of his past experiments and remembered one specific experiment using his time machine. The object he had placed inside the machine briefly disappeared and then reappeared. David decided that after breakfast he would review his notes about that test.

Luke entered the kitchen. While he poured a glass of orange juice, David said, "Pull up a chair, young man."

"It smells delicious, Dad."

"I hope you like the chef's special of the day," David said.

When they had finished eating, David asked, "Luke, what do you have planned for the day, since your classes are canceled?"

"I have a history project due next Thursday. I have to write a report about the Revolutionary War and why the thirteen colonies rebelled against England."

"Do you know that Lynn, Massachusetts, had a shoe industry supplying the boots worn by the Colonial soldiers? There's a lot of material at the public library, but I'm sure it's closed today. You can use the Internet to research information," David said.

"Good idea, Dad. That's what I'll do. What are you going to do today?"

"I'll be in the library researching," David replied.

"On what subject?"

"Einstein's theory of relativity and the space and time continuum."

"Sounds interesting. Albert Einstein was intelligent. I'll bet you're as smart as he was."

"I wish I were. His mathematical theories are still being used today to give insight into the world of atoms using quantum physics. Do you know that an atom is a basic unit of matter consisting of a dense, central nucleus surrounded by a cloud of negatively charged electrons?"

"No. That sounds complicated."

"Oh, Brian will be stopping by this morning around 8:30 to use the lab," David said.

"I like Brian. He's a cool guy and smart. I'm going to my room now and work on my history paper. Later today I'll go to the store to buy batteries for my radio and flashlight, just in case the power goes out."

"Good thinking," David said.

Brian would be arriving soon, so David cleaned up in the kitchen. Then he went to his library to find books on the theories of electromagnetic fields. The electromagnetic field extends indefinitely throughout space and can be viewed as the combination of electric and magnetic fields and David thought that traveling faster than light might be possible if one ignored Einstein's theory of special relativity. Traveling beyond the speed of light would be considered moving backward in time. David had acquired many physics books about various topics over the years that were useful for his experiments and had cataloged all his books in the library for quick reference. David opened the side drawer to his cherrywood desk and retrieved his list of books. After reviewing the list, he noticed five books of interest and went to the bookshelf and got them.

David heard a noise at the back door of his house and looked at his wristwatch. It was 8:40. He thought it must be Brian. Brian is twenty-nine years old, six feet tall, has brown hair and eyes, a muscular build, and an olive complexion. David set the books down onto the desk in the library and went to the back door to greet Brian.

"Hey, Professor," Brian said, as he entered.

"Hi, Brian. How was the drive from Boston?"

"I left my home at 7. I had to drive slowly even though there weren't many cars on the road. The snow is getting heavier and the plows are everywhere trying to keep the roads cleared."

"I'm glad you made it here safely. You know where things are in the lab."

"Thanks, Professor."

"I'll be in the library if you need me. Please feel free to help yourself to some hot tea," David said.

"Thank you, Professor. Maybe later."

Brian was familiar with the basement lab and the equipment because he would occasionally use it. He thought of David's lab as if it were his own and enjoyed having a professor nearby to get a second opinion and to help with his experiments. Brian's thesis was on black hole forces as you approach the speed of light and the effect on the molecular structure of an object entering it, with an emphasis on the skin tissue and internal organs of the human body. He was developing a theory of how long it would take to reach the other side of a black hole while traveling faster than light. Brian was also interested in knowing if something exiting a black hole would eventually stop, slow down or just travel at a constant speed through the universe. His first objective was to achieve the goal of traveling at or beyond light's speed using a laser in combination with electromagnetic waves.

Brian went to the desk and set his backpack down beside it. He turned on the PC and then the power to the laser. He returned to the desk and pulled out his notebook and began turning the pages to review his notes. He then went to where the laser was and adjusted the small mirrors that would be used to reflect the light. The mirrors were attached to sensitive electrodes and connected to a machine that could accurately measure the speed of the light and send the results to the PC. Brian turned on the laser and a white light reflected off the mirrors. After thirty seconds, he shut off the unit and, just as he'd predicted, the outcome was the same as his prior experiment—186,285 miles per second, the speed of light—and was now ready for his next experiment of combining electromagnetic waves with a laser. Brian believed the attempt would be a first and wanted David to witness it.

David was in the library sitting at his desk and skimming through pages of a book titled *Traveling Faster than Light, the Possibilities*. He was intrigued by the theory and thought it could become a reality with the right combination of physics applied in one overall theory. However, what a challenge it would be—like trying to duplicate the recipe of Kentucky Fried Chicken. He imagined sitting at a table with eleven herbs and spices on it and trying to select the correct spices and the exact amounts.

David sighed and closed the books on his desk. As he was going to the lab, Luke came downstairs and asked, "Dad, is Brian here?"

"Yes, he's in the lab. Do you want to say hello?"

"Of course," Luke answered, and they headed for the lab.

When Luke entered the lab, he saw Brian and said, "Hi, Brian."

"Hey, dude. What's up?"

"Nothing. I haven't seen you in awhile."

"Yes, I know. I've been busy with my work," Brian said.

"I know how that can be," David said.

"How old are you now?" Brian asked.

"I'm fourteen. Do you still own Murphy?"

"Yes. I'll bring him by one of these days."

"That would be cool. I'm leaving for the store now to buy some batteries just in case the power goes out."

"That's smart thinking, dude."

"I'll see you later today," Luke said, and then he left the lab.

"Brian, how are things going? Any major discoveries to report?" David asked.

"Well, Professor, I just completed one basic experiment, verifying the speed of light using a laser. I was waiting for you before conducting my second experiment. It could be a breakthrough in quantum physics research."

"Sounds exciting. What kind of test is it?"

"My idea is to use one source of nature and magnify it on another source to see what the effect will be. I'll be using light and electromagnetic waves. I plan to introduce the waves with a laser to possibly increase the speed of light."

"This seems to be an intriguing idea and will rock the world of physics if proven true," David said.

"Sir, will you review my papers to verify my equation and solution?"

"Sure. I value dearly your trust in me," David replied.

"Professor, I would like you to help. I trust only you. You're a true friend."

"Thanks for the trust. I'll take a look at your paper. In the meantime, you can help yourself to a cup of hot tea and anything else you'd like in the refrigerator," David said.

"Thank you, Professor. I think I'll have a cup of tea and maybe a sandwich," Brian said, and then he left for the kitchen while David sat at the desk analyzing Brian's paper.

CHAPTER 4

Brian was in the kitchen making tea when he began to get hungry and thought of how a nice hot pastrami sub with mustard would satisfy his empty stomach. He knew the local sub shop would be closed because of the snowstorm, so he went to the refrigerator to see if there were any ingredients for making a sandwich. Brian found lunch meat, lettuce, tomato, mayonnaise and bread and he carried all the items to the kitchen countertop. When he set down the ingredients, a tomato rolled off the edge of counter and landed on the floor. Brian picked it up, rinsed it off and then made his sandwich. The water in the teapot was now steaming hot, so he made a cup of tea. While sipping his tea, he thought about the tomato falling to the floor and how the force of gravity pulled on it.

David was still at the desk carefully going over the equation Brian had developed for his theory and found a flaw. Brian did not account for the gravitational forces interfering with the movement of an object.

Brian also came to realize that he had omitted the invisible forces of gravity on matter and went to David's library to find a book on the subject. As he was going to the library, the front door in the hallway opened and Brian felt a rush of cold air and got a quick chill as Luke entered. "Hey, dude," Brian said.

"Hi, Brian. It's still chilly outside and snowing."

"Did you find a store open so you could buy your batteries?"

"Yes. There's a store that's open 24 hours five blocks from here."

"I hope you don't have to use them."

"Me too," Luke said, and then asked, "Who's taking care of Murphy?"

"Nobody. Murphy is now old enough to stay out of trouble," Brian replied.

"Please bring him the next time you visit. He's a cool dog."

"I will, dude. If the weather weren't so lousy, I'd have brought him today."

"I have to go now and continue working on my history class assignment. I'll talk to you later. Bye," Luke said as he left for his room.

Brian continued to the library to find information on gravitational forces exerted on an object. In the study, he saw on the desk a catalog listing all the books on the bookshelves. The inventory listed a book by Albert Einstein titled *The Theory of General Relativity*, which he had developed from 1907 to 1915. The idea addresses the force of gravity on an object and rays of light bending in a gravitational field. He went to the bookshelf to get the book, but it was not there, so he continued looking, thinking it might be misfiled, but he still couldn't find it. He returned to the desk and noticed three books stacked on top of each other. They were about electromagnetic fields, quantum electrodynamics and traveling faster than light, and the book he was looking for was also on the desk. He began wondering why Professor Solomon had pulled them out. Was the professor interested in the same idea of traveling beyond the speed of light? Or was he searching for new material to introduce to his students for his lectures on astrophysics and theoretically applied engineering techniques?

David had come to the conclusion after reviewing Brian's equation that he hadn't accounted for the invisible forces of gravity. It would not be possible to travel at or to increase the speed of light even with electromagnetic waves added into the formula. He thought there might be the possibility if gravity could be neutralized, thereby allowing an object to travel through the space and time continuum. He thought again of his failed experiment using StellaPort when attempting to move an object in time. The test had consisted of using a laser and electromagnetic waves, but did not include the idea of neutralizing the forces of gravity. He then mumbled, "Brian might have something here that could be worked into my theory for making time travel a reality."

Brian left the library for the lab with the book about Einstein's theory of general relativity. When he entered, he saw David still at the desk skimming through the pages in his notebook. Brian went to David and said, "Hi, Professor. So what do you think of my theory?"

"Well, Brian, after carefully analyzing it, the math does not support it. A major flaw I found was that gravity was not being considered."

"I just realized that when I was in the kitchen. A tomato rolled off the countertop and hit the floor. I went to your library to find information on gravitational forces and selected this book about Einstein's theory of general relativity. I hope you don't mind. I found it on the desk and brought it with me for reference."

"Not at all, Brian. I'm interested in your idea of combining electromagnetic waves with a laser. I'd like to witness your experiment now, if you don't mind. I'd like to know the electromagnetic frequency that you'll be applying."

"I'll need a few minutes to set up the equipment for the experiment," Brian replied.

"Take your time. We're not going anywhere for awhile because of the snowstorm. While you're preparing for the test, I'll look at Einstein's theory of general relativity again," David said.

Brian began to connect the laser to one end of a six-foot-long, four-inch-thick glass cylinder. The cylinder was made of tempered glass and could withstand temperatures of up to 450 degrees. It opened from the top and was similar to a pressure cooker. At each end of the cylinder were mirrors, which he aligned, and then he closed and sealed the lid. The mirrors still had the electrodes attached to them and were linked to the PC. He then attached a black cable to one of the protruding nodes on the cylinder and the other end to an electric current oscillating (E.C.O.) machine that would be used to introduce the electromagnetic waves during the experiment.

Brian was now prepared to conduct his test even though it would not achieve the desired results. "Professor, I'm ready to start the experiment," Brian announced.

"Okay, I'll check the computer. It's working fine. Let the show begin," David said.

Brian turned on the laser and then the E.C.O. machine, which had a digital meter to measure the electrical voltage flowing through the cable to the electrode that was connected to the cylinder. As he gradually turned the dial to the right, they noticed the white laser light's diameter expanding in circumference, and when he moved the dial in the opposite direction to shut off the equipment, they saw the light returning to its original width. Brian and David looked at each other with an expression of surprise. They were anxious to view the results of the experiment, but knew it would take a few minutes for the computer to process the data and reveal the results. "That was interesting. I have never seen anything like that!" Brian exclaimed.

"Me neither. I've never seen the diameter of a laser light increase as an electric current was being introduced along its path."

"I'm hoping the results will be just as exciting," Brian said.

Brian's cell phone began playing the theme music to *Mission Impossible*, and he said, "Excuse me, Professor. I need to answer this. Brian here. Hi, Martha. Where are you? I'm visiting my former professor who teaches at M.I.T. He's letting me use his lab because Harvard's is closed. I'm sure you're aware of that by now. Well, I don't know. I'll ask him. I'll call you back. Adios, señorita. Sorry for the interruption. That was my girlfriend. Her name is Martha Valdez and she's from Bogota, Colombia. Martha received her undergraduate degree in astronomy and physics at the University of Arizona. After graduating from the U of A, she applied for graduate school at Harvard University and was accepted in the field of astrophysics. She's finishing her final semester for a master's degree in astrophysics."

"She sounds like an intelligent young lady. What's her thesis on?"

"It's on finding the coordinates of a location by using celestial bodies for creating a fixed point to navigate through the solar system. She's developing a computer program to display accurately the stars in the night sky. Her program will calculate the exact location of an object in space using two stars as reference points."

"That seems like a very complicated project, knowing that planets rotate and orbit around a sun," David said.

"Professor, Martha asked if she could come with me tomorrow and use your lab too. As you know, the lab at Harvard is closed."

"I don't see why not. She seems to be a bright young lady and I would like to meet her."

"I'll call her and let her know that it's okay with you. We'll come by tomorrow around 9 a.m. Thank you, Professor."

The PC completed the analysis of the experiment and displayed the results and, just as predicted, they were the same. David pointed to the graph on the monitor and said, "There seems to be an abnormality at this point."

"Most likely when the electromagnetic waves were being introduced," Brian said.

"That would be my assumption too. We should test again to make sure it's not a fluke," David said.

"I have two remaining experiments to conduct if time permits."

"What are they?"

"One is combining electromagnetic waves and a laser to learn what the effects will be when combining both forces on a liquid and then on a solid. My other experiment concerns the effect on the molecules after the experiment," Brian answered.

"Sounds like good science to me," David said.

"Professor, I must leave at 3. I have a dinner date with Martha tonight, and driving on the icy roads is slow going."

"I'll be in the library if you need me, Romeo."

"Okay. Thanks, Professor."

CHAPTER 5

After David left the lab for the library, Brian began reviewing his notes before conducting his next experiment. His experiment would be the same as the one he had just completed, but would include a solid object, a pig's foot he'd bought at a local supermarket. He grabbed his backpack and unzipped a side pocket and removed a clear plastic container with the foot inside it. The specimen would be used to test the effect on solid matter when using a laser and electromagnetic waves at the same time.

David was in the library at the fireplace starting a fire. After the oak logs were burning, he went to his desk and sat watching the flames dance. He started to feel the warmth from the fireplace as it began providing heat to the room. Leaning back in his chair, he thought about what he'd seen in the lab and wondered if it would be possible to travel beyond the speed of light if the invisible gravitational force did not put a drag on matter. His mind raced trying to recall if experiments had ever been conducted to clock light's velocity outside of Earth's gravity. He remembered a TV special about NASA's *Apollo* missions to the moon in the 1960s and 1970s. The program mentioned an experiment NASA had performed using a laser beam. For that test, the *Apollo* astronauts positioned a mirror on the Moon, and a laser beam was sent from Earth 238,000 miles to the moon, passing through our atmosphere and the invisible gravitational force to its target. He tried to recall if an experiment had ever been done using one of the labs in the International Space Station and then leaned forward in his chair and mumbled, "Maybe in a weightless environment."

Brian was now ready to conduct his experiment. He placed the pig's foot in the center of the glass cylinder on an inverted drinking glass, then closed and locked the lid. He switched on the laser and the beam of light did not reflect off the mirrors. He then turned the dial slightly on the E.C.O. and the white light now encompassed the entire foot and reflected off the mirrors. As he gradually increased the electricity going into the machine, a hazy, grayish fog began to form above the pig's foot. While he was increasing the electrical energy, he suddenly saw the fog begin to move and become a gray-and-black cloud. As he continued to turn the dial ever so slightly, the cloud became a mini vortex, and the foot began to shake on the glass. Brian twisted the dial a bit more and the miniature tornado started moving in a circular motion with increasing speed. He decided that was enough and quickly shut off the E.C.O. As soon as he did, the fog and vortex disappeared. He didn't understand what had just happened because he'd never seen anything like that being created in a lab or heard of a scientist harnessing nature's forces. After unlocking the cylinder, he removed the foot and used a scalpel to remove a sample of the skin tissue. He placed it under the lens of the microscope and didn't see damage to the tissues.

"Wow, that was something," Brian thought. He was still in awe of what had just happened and believed the results were a first as he prepared for his final experiment using water, the pig's foot and a laser along with the E.C.O. He opened a door under the sink and got a long hose and connected one end to the faucet and put the other end into the glass cylinder. Then he turned on the water until it rose above the laser's lens. He shut off the water and then closed and locked the lid and went through the same steps as before, increasing the electrical current to the E.C.O. He didn't see anything new.

While the water was being drained from the cylinder, he jotted down notes in his notebook while the results were still fresh in his mind. Brian used the PC to print graphs of his three experiments and, after analyzing the printouts, he noticed that the first chart was identical to the third, but the second graph, toward the end of the experiment, caught his attention. There seemed to be an anomaly on the diagram. He knew that was where the vortex had formed.

Brian organized his working papers and placed them along with the pig's foot in the plastic container in his backpack. As he was about to leave, he used his cell phone to call Martha Valdez. Martha is twenty-six years old, five feet, six inches tall, with brown hair and eyes, and a light-tan complexion. Martha answered and said, "Martha speaking."

"Hi, Martha. This is Brian."

"Hi, Brian. How are your experiments coming along?"

"I think I'm onto something new in the field of physics."

"That sounds promising. Are we still on for dinner tonight?"

"Yes, I'm leaving now and should be home soon. I'll call you when I get in."

"Okay, give me a ring and drive safely. Adios, amigo."

Brian turned off the computer and the lights to the lab and then went to the library to say bye to David. When Brian entered, he saw David bent over in front of the fireplace stoking the fire and said, "Hi, Professor. I've completed all my experiments for the day and I'm ready to go home now."

"How did your tests go? Were the results what you expected?"

"I experienced an odd result during one of them. I'll try to duplicate it tomorrow so you can see what I mean."

"Now you have me curious. I hope I can sleep tonight," David said, smiling.

"I'm hoping it's not a fluke. I'm leaving now. Please say bye to Luke for me. Oh, and I'll bring Martha with me tomorrow."

"Okay, drive carefully. The main streets should be cleared of snow by now," David said.

After Brian left, David walked to the picture window that was facing the street and watched Brian get into his 2006 gray, two-door Ford Mustang for his drive to Boston. The snow was tapering off as though it was going to stop. The streetlight poles and powerlines had icicles hanging on them because of the extreme cold temperature, but he was warm from the fireplace.

David heard Luke coming down the stairs and walk toward the study. "Did Brian just leave?" Luke asked when he entered the library.

"Yes. He'll be here tomorrow to use the lab."

"I hope he remembers to bring Murphy. He's a cool dog. I came downstairs hoping to say bye. I'm going to get something to eat and then continue with my history report."

"When you finish your report, I want to read it."

Okay, Dad, but you can't give me a grade. You're not my teacher," Luke said with a laugh, and then he headed for the kitchen.

David was now alone and sitting on the maroon leather sofa with a book about gravitational forces and their effect on nature. He found a chapter on gravity and its effect on light, but the author discussed only Einstein's theory of relativity and stated that reaching the speed of light was impossible. David thought that may be true on Earth, but would his idea still be true in an antigravity environment? He put the text down on his lap while gazing at the flames dancing in the fireplace and dozed off.

David awoke from his nap and thought about what Brian said concerning his second experiment and was now curious, so he decided to go to the lab to try to duplicate Brian's test. David turned on the lights to the lab, the PC and the equipment to be used. Brian had left the laser in its position, and the cable was still connected to the node on the glass cylinder. David closed and locked the lid and was now ready to begin his test. He switched on the laser and the white beam reflected off the mirror at the opposite end of the cylinder and returned to the one that was angled near the lens of the laser. He then turned on the computer monitor on the wall so he could view the test as it was happening. He was now ready to add electromagnetic waves using the E.C.O. Slowly increasing the electric current as the laser beam expanded, he glimpsed at the monitor and noted the point on the graph where the spike occurred. It was the same place as before. David continued increasing the electric current, which sent the waves through the cable. While increasing the current, the laser beam's diameter did not change. The outcome was identical to the one before and he wondered why Brian became so excited if only the light's width had expanded.

When Brian arrived home, Murphy, a three-year-old male golden retriever with tan fur, came prancing up to him, wagging his tail. After playing with and feeding his dog, Brian went to his answering machine, where three messages were waiting for him. The first message was from his mother inviting him to Nantucket for dinner and to spend time with his family. The next was from Harvard's Graduate School of Science announcing that the school would be closed for the rest of the week and classes would resume on Monday morning. The last message was from Martha, saying she'd be running late because she was finishing work on her thesis project and should be ready about 8 p.m. Brian called her, but she didn't answer, so he left a message stating he was on his way to pick her up.

Martha lives in Cambridge and shares an apartment with a female student who also attends Harvard University. It usually took fifteen minutes to drive from his residence to hers, but because of the driving conditions, the travel time would be longer. He planned to have dinner in the Prudential Tower on the 52nd floor in the Top of the Hub restaurant on Boylston Street in Boston. The top level of the restaurant is where the patrons dined and allows for a 360-degree panoramic view of Boston and its suburbs. He knew Martha would be impressed.

Brian put on his coat and headed out the door, leaving Murphy behind. He arrived at her apartment a little after 8 and knocked on her door. After Martha opened it, she said, "Hi, Brian. Come in and have a seat. I'll be with you in a few minutes," and then she went to her room to finish putting on her makeup. After a brief time, she returned to where Brian was sitting and asked, "Brian, are you ready to go?"

"Yes. Let's go. I'm hungry."

"Me too," Martha said while putting on her coat in the hallway, and then they left.

Brian parked his car in the garage across the street from the Prudential building. The restaurant was on the top floor in the skyscraper. They entered the building and went to the elevator and pressed the button for the 52nd floor. "Where are we going?" Martha asked.

"You'll soon see," he replied.

When the elevator doors opened, Brian led Martha to the restaurant. She was impressed with the view of Boston from such a great height.

When they were at the entrance to the restaurant, Brian approached the hostess and said, "I have a reservation for Brian, for two."

The hostess reviewed the reservation list and saw his name, and she said, "Please follow me." She escorted them to their table next to a window with a panoramic view of Boston and its surrounding suburbs.

"Brian, I'm impressed. This is a beautiful restaurant. I can see many tourist attractions from here. Look, there's Bunker Hill, the U.S.S. *Constitution* and over there is a baseball stadium."

"That's Fenway Park where the Boston Red Sox play baseball, and there's Kenmore Square," Brian said.

The waiter came and took their orders and returned with their beverages. While waiting for their main entrées, Martha said, "Tell me about your experiments today. You seemed very excited."

"I still am. For my first experiment, I used a laser to determine if the speed of light could be increased, but it couldn't. I invited Professor Solomon to observe my second experiment because I introduced electromagnetic waves hoping to increase light's speed, but what caught our attention was that the laser light's diameter expanded."

"That's not something to write home about," Martha said, smiling.

"I know, but it gets better. Professor Solomon left the lab for his library, leaving me to work on my final two experiments. For my next experiment, I used a pig's foot to test what happens to skin tissue when applying a laser and electromagnetic waves. As I increased the electrical current, a grayish fog suddenly appeared above the foot. I continued increasing the current, and then a vortex appeared. I got nervous and quickly turned off the equipment, and the fog and vortex immediately disappeared."

"What do you make of it?" Martha asked.

"I'm not sure. I plan to duplicate my experiment tomorrow, so you and Professor Solomon can be a witness to the results."

"That sounds interesting. I'm looking forward to seeing it."

"The professor thinks your research is interesting. He was impressed when I explained your thesis to him."

"I'm looking forward to meeting him. He must be an intelligent man to be teaching at M.I.T.," Martha said.

"Yes, you'll like him. His wife died while giving birth to their son, Luke. He's fourteen years old and a good kid," Brian said.

The waiter arrived and served their meals. While Brian and Martha dined, they enjoyed each other's company and the exquisite view of Boston and its suburbs. After eating, Brian said, "Martha, would you like to visit Faneuil Hall? We can mingle with the tourists."

"Sure. I like going there. It has such a nice atmosphere and the experience is always pleasant."

Faneuil Hall is known as the Cradle of Liberty, a place where the colonists met to protest the unfair policies toward Massachusetts and which eventually became the origin of rebellion against the British government.

After walking and holding hands for awhile, Brian and Martha decided to end their date and go home. When they arrived at Martha's place, she gave Brian a kiss before leaving the car, and then he said, "I'll call you tomorrow morning around 8."

"I'll be waiting for your call. Adios, señor," Martha said. Then she went to her apartment and Brian drove home.

CHAPTER 6

It was Friday morning. David and Luke had finished eating their breakfast when David asked, "Luke, what are your plans for today?"

"I'm going to the theater with two friends to watch the movie *2012*. The kids at school are saying the video is scary because that's the year when the world is supposed to end."

"The movie is only fiction. It's just a writer's imagination that's based on a theory of why the Mayans and other ancient civilizations' calendar cycles all stop in the same year," David said.

"Do you think the world will end in 2012?" Luke asked.

"Well, Luke, the dinosaurs died due to a catastrophic event and scientists today are still theorizing what caused their extinction. Some believe an asteroid hit the planet and others theorize that they evolved into birds or were killed off by a plague. We know for a fact that dinosaurs did exist on the earth, so, back to your question, yes, it's possible for all life to end on Earth. Will that happen? I hope not. It would be nice to travel into the future to know if the human race still exists."

"Traveling in time would be cool. I could be an adult," Luke said.

"Yes, that would be wonderful," David said with a smile.

"Please call me when Brian and Murphy are here. I'll be in my bedroom working on my history paper," Luke said.

Luke went to his room while David entered the library and put a log on the fire. He then began searching for another book on gravity.

Brian woke up at 7 a.m. and went to the kitchen for a cup of hot brewed coffee and to feed Murphy. He opened a can of dog food and fed Murphy, drank his coffee and then took a shower. After he got dressed, he called Martha to tell her that he would be coming by to pick her up at 8:30. He put on his coat and attached a leash to Murphy's collar before he left his apartment. After walking Murphy, Brian returned home and checked his telephone for messages, and there were none. He went to the refrigerator and removed the container with the pig's foot and put it into his backpack along with his notebook and papers and left his home with Murphy for Martha's apartment. When Brian arrived at Martha's place, he beeped his car horn and Martha came to the car carrying her tote bag that contained her laptop computer. She opened the passenger door and got in, leaned over, gave Brian a kiss and said, "Good morning, Brian."

"Good morning," he replied.

"I had a wonderful time last night," she said.

"I'm happy to know you enjoyed our date. I did too. We'll have to do it again soon," Brian said as they headed for Salem. The driving conditions had improved. It had stopped snowing and the roads had been plowed and cleared of snow.

David was in the study when the doorbell rang. He went to the door and opened it just as Luke came down the stairs. David said, "Hello, Brian."

"Hi, Professor. This is Martha, the person I was telling you about yesterday, and you know Murphy."

"Hi, Martha. Please come in and get out of the cold," David said.

After they entered David's home, Luke began playing with Murphy and said, "Thanks for bringing him. He still remembers me."

"Of course he remembers you, dude. Luke, this is my girlfriend, Martha."

"Hi, Luke. Brian told me you're an intelligent young man, one of the brightest students in your class," she said.

"My father is smart. He helps with my homework. I just try hard to pass my classes," Luke said and then asked, "Martha, do you go to Harvard?"

"Yes, I'm attending graduate school."

"You and Brian are smart and so is my dad," Luke said.

"If you keep studying and pay attention to your father, you'll have the opportunity to attend Harvard too," she said.

"Luke is going to the movies this afternoon with his friends. They'll see the movie *2012*. Luke, go check if Murphy's thirsty and afterward you can play with him in the backyard, if that's okay with you, Brian," David asked.

"Fine with me. Have fun, dude."

"Oh, and Luke, make certain the gate is closed before you let Murphy outside. We don't want Murphy running around the neighborhood looking for Brian," David said with a chuckle.

David invited his guests to the library. When they entered, he said, "Please make yourselves comfortable. I'll be back shortly with tea." After David left for the kitchen, Brian sat on the sofa while Martha was walking around the room looking at the books on the shelves, the paintings on the walls, and the pictures on the fireplace mantel and on the library desk. David returned and, while serving tea to his guests, said, "I hope it's hot enough."

"Thank you," they replied.

Martha was still standing when David said, "Martha, please have a seat," and then she sat next to Brian on the sofa while David sat in the leather chair next to them. After everyone was seated, David asked, "How was the drive from Boston this morning?"

"Much better. The snow has stopped falling and the main streets are cleared now," Brian answered.

"That's good to hear. Brian mentioned that you're from Colombia and attending graduate school at Harvard University," David said.

"I'm from Bogota and I'm pursuing a master's degree in astrophysics. My undergraduate studies were in astronomy and physics at the University of Arizona, where I had a double major."

"Why did you select the University of Arizona?" David asked.

"U of A is a major university in the field of astronomy and is a vital player in NASA's space programs such as the Hubble Space Telescope, the Mars Landers and other big projects that are in the pipeline. Also, Kitt Peak National Observatory is located thirty miles from Tucson."

"Brian also mentioned that your thesis is on finding the coordinates of a fixed location in space using the stars as a point of reference."

"Yes. May I tell you about my work?" Martha asked.

"Of course. Please do," David replied.

Martha began to explain her thesis, which she titled Starbase, and she said, "I envision a handheld device giving the coordinates of a fixed location in space by using celestial bodies in the Milky Way Galaxy as points of reference. I'm creating a computer program to identify the stars and constellations in our own galaxy. The program will show their positions on any given day. I have accumulated many star maps for building my database of known planets and stars, and I'm also writing another software program to account for the tilting of the Earth's axis at any time of the year and its rotation. The two applications will work in unison to become one functioning program."

"Sound's complicated, but how would you find the coordinates of a distant planet?" David asked.

Martha answered, "When both programs are completed, I'll need a specially designed device that is the size of a handheld calculator for loading my software into. The unit, which I call Starbase, will have three laser lights for locking onto two fixed stars, one to the left and one to the right of the destination point. The third laser will lock onto the arrival site, and the person holding Starbase will be at the home base. You need to picture the letter V, and where the two lines meet is home base. At the top of each line forming the V are the fixed stars that were selected. So if you were traveling between planets, Starbase would give you the coordinates of your destination. For example, if you traveled from Earth (home base) to visit a planet in the Alpha Centauri star system, you would select two fixed star points from Earth, and Earth now would become your home base. You'd then pick the planet (destination point) in the star system as your destination and lock onto it. The planet in the Alpha Centauri solar system would now become the middle point between the two fixed star points. My software program would then calculate the distance to be traveled.

For the return trip home, the two previously selected fixed stars that you locked onto would continue to be your two fixed star points. The destination planet in the Alpha Centauri star system would then become your home base, and Earth would be your arrival planet. You would need to imagine an inverted V (^), and where the two lines meet would be the Alpha Centauri planet."

"Your idea sounds remarkable. Do you have a prototype or drawings?" David asked.

"No. I was hoping you could help me design something using nanotechnology. The device will require laser technology and a mini computer to perform the needed calculations and to accommodate my software programs. To make this a reality, I would need someone with your engineering experience and knowledge to build the unit to my specifications."

"You have a wonderful concept. Building a handheld device is not a challenge. The challenge will be having your two programs working together as you envision."

"Would you be interested in working with me to create Starbase?" Martha asked.

"I believe I can acquire the parts from my lab here and at M.I.T.," he replied.

"Awesome. Thank you so much. You've made my day," Martha said.

Brian was pleased to hear that David would work with Martha on her project. Brian then asked, "Professor, can we go to your lab now? I would like to show you and Martha something."

"Yes. You had me curious since you left here yesterday. I would like to see what you discovered."

After they finished drinking their tea, David escorted them to his lab and turned on the lights. Brian went to the desk and set his backpack on the floor and booted up the computer. Martha followed him and set her tote bag beside the desk while David turned on the equipment. After turning on the machines, he joined Brian and Martha at the desk as Brian was removing his notebook and working papers from his backpack. Brian placed the three graphs of yesterday's experiments onto the desk and pointed to the spot on the graph showing the anomaly. He said, "Professor, after you left, I used a pig's foot for my next experiment to examine the effects on tissues of a laser combined with electromagnetic waves. I was stunned at what I saw when I gradually increased the electric current during the test."

"Why did you use a pig's foot?" David asked.

"Because the anatomy of a pig and a human is similar. Both are mammals that receive nourishment through an umbilical cord before being born. Basically, the internal cavity of a pig is almost like a human's, but smaller. The heart is located at the same place between the lungs, liver and gall bladder, like in humans. The pig's whole digestive tract is similar and the skin of a pig has hair follicles and is thinner than a human's. My theory is that if skin cells are damaged when traveling through a black hole, then the internal organs will have the same fate."

"I understand your logic. You would need a live animal to test the circulatory system and organs, but my lab is not equipped for such in-depth biological experiments," David said.

"I believe studying the tissue of a pig's foot will give me a basis to move forward with my research," Brian said.

"That sounds like solid science," David said, and then he asked, "What were the results of yesterday's experiment?"

"I'll show you," he answered.

The equipment was in the same position in which Brian had left it. He removed the container with the pig's foot from his backpack and then went to the glass cylinder and placed the foot on an inverted drinking glass. He closed and locked the lid while David turned on the PC monitor on the wall. Brian was ready to begin his experiment, so he switched on the laser and the light and, just as before, it did not pass through the pig's foot to the mirror. He turned the dial slightly on the electric current oscillator and the white light from the laser now encompassed the foot and reflected off the mirrors. "Watch. It gets better," Brian said, looking at David.

Brian continued to gradually increase the electric current, and now a hazy, grayish fog formed above the pig's foot. When he increased the energy, they saw the fog become a moving gray-and-black cloud. David leaned forward for a closer look at what was happening. Brian continued to turn the dial ever so slightly and then the cloud became a mini vortex while the pig's foot started moving on the glass. Brian moved the control a bit further and the small cloud spun in a circular motion with increasing speed. He decided that was enough and turned off the E.C.O. The fog and vortex immediately disappeared, and the laser light did not reflect off the mirrors, which ended the experiment. Brian unlocked the glass cylinder and removed the foot to examine the skin tissue. After taking samples, he placed them under the microscope and didn't see any damage—just healthy cells.

David went to the PC monitor on the wall and stared at the graph being displayed and compared today's result with yesterday's, and they were the same.

"Martha, please look at the skin tissue. I would like a second opinion," Brian said.

Martha studied the tissue for a few minutes and said, "All I see is healthy skin tissue too. No damage is present," and then they went to the desk where David was busy studying the results.

"Professor, have you seen anything like that before?" Brian asked.

"Yes, to be honest with you," he answered.

Suddenly, Murphy came running into the lab panting and went to Brian and then Luke entered. While Brian was petting Murphy, he asked Luke if he'd had fun with him.

"I sure did. I brought him here because I'm leaving now for the movie theater. I hope to see you guys when I return," Luke said.

"Depending on the time it takes to conclude our remaining research, we could still be here. If not, we'll see you tomorrow, and I'll bring Murphy with me," Brian said.

"Thanks, Brian. I enjoyed meeting you, Martha."

"Don't let the pretty girls distract you from the movie," she said.

"We're going to meet a few girls from our school before the show starts and maybe sit with them," he said.

"It sounds like a date to me, dude. You'll have to tell me about the flick. I've heard good reviews about it," Brian said.

"I have to leave now. I don't want to be late meeting my friends. Bye," Luke said, and then he left for the theater.

CHAPTER 7

After Luke left the lab, David said, "Brian, you asked if I had seen anything like that before. Well, I have. What I'm about to tell you must remain here in this room and not be repeated. Do you agree?"

They nodded their heads and said, "Yes, of course, Professor."

David began by saying, "When I was a boy, and which continues to this day, I always dreamed of and believed that one day traveling through time would become a reality, and I would be the scientist who would make it possible. I met an M.I.T. professor named Sebastian Kramer, who was a theoretical mathematician while I was in high school. Eventually he became my mentor. He used his influence to get me into M.I.T., and during my undergraduate years, I'd assist him with his research. He was convinced he could make time travel a reality and not just science fiction.

Professor Kramer suddenly became ill and was told by his doctor that he had six months to live. He called me soon thereafter and asked if I would come by for a visit and he mentioned that he had something to show me. During the evening I met with him, he led me to his basement, which was quite large. He took me to another room, and there was this machine in the center of it with a circular vertical glass chamber looking like something you would see in a science fiction movie. My first thought was that he'd invented a cancer curing machine to rid his body of the disease. I asked him what the machine was for and what it would do. The professor said it was a time machine, and then he turned it on and explained how it worked and the purpose of each component. I was awestruck and asked him if he had tested it. He said it was not ready yet. He turned it off and offered to give me his time machine, knowing I had the same interest. I told him I was honored and would continue with his research, then we made arrangements to have the machine moved. Sad to say, Professor Kramer is no longer with us. He died four years ago."

They didn't know what to make of his story. Brian asked, "Professor, where is your time machine now?"

"It's hidden in a safe place."

"Can we see the machine?"

"Yes, but first you both must promise me that you will not mention or discuss what you're about to see with anyone. Do I have your word?"

They nodded their heads yes and Brian said, "Professor, you can trust me. I will not tell a soul."

"Professor Solomon, I know you just met me and do not know my character, but Brian can vouch for me. I am a woman of my word. I'll not discuss what you have told us or what you're about to reveal, I promise," Martha said.

"Okay. I'll show you StellaPort," David said.

They looked at each other and Martha said, "StellaPort?"

"Yes. StellaPort is what I call my time travel machine. When completed, it will transport a person backward or forward in time," David said, and then he led them to a gray metal cabinet that contained his very powerful computer.

"Is this the StellaPort?" Brian asked.

David laughed and answered, "No," and after opening the cabinet doors, he said, "Meet Eve, a mini supercomputer."

"Wow, you have your own supercomputer? I thought only the U.S. government and very large corporations owned them," Martha said.

"I know a computer engineering scientist and told him that I needed a computer to solve complex mathematical equations quickly for my work in the fields of nanotechnology and quantum physics. He suggested we build one with a parallel central processing unit. Eve can perform at a speed one hundred percent as fast as a supercomputer. I believe you need the government's permission to obtain an already assembled one, but you don't if you create your own for personal use."

David turned on the computer and Eve's many colored lights on the control panel started flashing. Then the lights stopped blinking and stayed on. David removed his wallet and got the small key from the special compartment and inserted it into the keyhole at the top rear right corner of the cabinet. When he turned the key, four tumblers clicked, freeing the cabinet from the cement wall. He gently rolled the cabinet on its wheels to reveal a hidden room.

David bent over slightly and entered the room. After turning on the lights, he invited Brian and Martha to join him. "Be careful. Watch your head," he said as they entered the room. After entering the room, they stared in awe, gazing at the time machine.

"This is StellaPort, the life-long dream of Professor Kramer and me."

Martha and Brian stood in front of the seven-foot-high circular glass chamber with a door and five round platforms proportionally spaced. There were small lights at even intervals along the inside edge of the transportation chamber making a complete circle. The ceiling of the chamber was identical to the floor except for a circular indentation in the center. Brian and Martha felt as though they were looking at technology from another planet. "Professor, how does it work?" Brian asked while he and Martha were still staring at the time machine.

"StellaPort is based on quantum mechanical physics, using nanotechnology to build the machine. My time machine works like this: First, you determine if you want to travel backward or forward in time, and then you enter the year, month, date, time, and the longitude and latitude into this component. The platform reflectors on the floor and on the ceiling in the glass chamber are constructed of space-age materials. They will help accelerate the traveling speed of a person, and the speed is displayed here in this window. I call the reflector Mollie because it identifies the molecule structure of the person and will reorganize them in biological order. You can think of the acceleration process like a super ball that you played with as a kid. After throwing the ball at a hard surface, the velocity increased exponentially on its own. Then electromagnetic waves are used at a precise frequency and displayed in this window's meter. When the electric current is increased, a vortex, or portal, will appear, which allows entry into the space and time continuum. While the person is standing on Mollie, which is connected to Eve, they begin working in tandem to calculate the person's mass. Eve will arrive at the exact amount of energy needed and send the requirements to Mollie. Mollie relays the calculations to Stella to recalibrate the power required to open a portal. When the green light appears in this window, you turn this dial and the person will disappear quickly and be sent to the date, time and coordinates selected and reappear there."

"Professor, how do you know the individual is unharmed and at the chosen location?" Martha asked.

"What we learned from Brian's experiment is that the pig's foot skin tissues were not harmed, which you verified. I'm sure you will agree further tests are needed to determine if the energy used is safe. The answer to the second part of your question would be tested and confirmed by using your software program and its database of star maps. Your program can be loaded into Eve for arriving at the precise longitude and latitude of a past or future location anywhere on the planet based on the star's alignment on that date."

"Professor, how does the person return home?" Brian asked.

"Good question. We wouldn't want them lost in space, now would we," David chuckled and then said, "The coordinates entered into Stella along with Eve's calculations will keep a constant fix on a person. The invisible electromagnetic wave stays connected just like an umbilical cord attached between a mother and her baby. As long as the power is being constantly supplied, the individual will stay connected to Stella. Imagine it as a computer monitor that, if not in use for a certain time period, will automatically go into hibernation but stays linked to the PC. I had solar panels installed on the roof two years ago that are connected to a generator for back-up power. When you have decided that the subject should be returned home, you turn this dial either forward or backward. Stella will come out of hibernation mode and begin the return process. Mollie will request that Eve recalculate the energy needed for the transportation process. Stella will transmit the required electromagnetic waves, and a vortex will appear above the person, and then the person disappears, following the wave through the space and time continuum, and then they will reappear in the transportation chamber."

"What will be the effect? Would they age quickly?" Martha asked.

"Martha, this is a transportation machine, not an aging machine. The individual is transported instantly, and their body would age normally during the whole time. The person traveling back in time will not become younger, but can see the reverse aging of family members to their nonexistence. A person traveling to the future would notice the aging of their family until death."

"Professor, what would happen if someone were sent back in time to see themselves?" Brian asked.

"If a person just observed and did not interfere with past events, there wouldn't be a change to their destiny. However, if a person were transported back in time with the intent of altering their past or civilization's history, such as informing Adolf Hitler of the Allies' June 6, 1944, D-Day invasion battle plans to change the outcome of WWII, there would be. Also, because of their action, the person could not return from the past if a time machine hasn't been invented, and if they did come back, the world would be a much different place from when they left."

"What would happen if someone goes back in time and dies?" Brian asked.

"Good question. Keep in mind that the molecules that make up an individual are being transported through the space and time continuum. The person's deoxyribonucleic acid (DNA), which is the blueprint for all living organisms, is created when they are conceived. When a person dies, their existence ends, be it in the past, present or future. My time machine does not allow for immortality. For example, if a person is sent today to the date of July 2, 1863, and arrives in the middle of the battlefield at Gettysburg, Pennsylvania, during the Civil War and is killed, the deceased person's body would still be transported to the present time because it's constantly linked to the time machine until the connection is severed. If somebody died while using the time machine, I would have a lot of explaining to do."

"I have one last question. Can two or more people travel in time using StellaPort?" Brian asked.

"StellaPort is designed to accommodate up to five people and each person must stand on a Mollie in the transportation chamber. Then Mollie and Eve will go into action calculating each individual's mass."

"Sorry, Professor. I have one more question," Brian said.

"Sure. What is it?" David replied.

"What happens if somebody touches or clings to a person while they are being transported?" he asked.

"Another good question," David replied. "If a person, let's say, is holding the hand of an individual, Stella will treat them as one and transmit the data to Mollie, and then Mollie will ask Eve to recalculate the energy needed to transport them both. Stella will send the required electromagnetic waves, and a vortex will form above them, and then both will disappear, following the wave through the space and time continuum to the transportation chamber."

"Professor, may I recap what you just explained?" Martha asked.

"Yes, please do," he answered.

"Stella is the control panel consisting of many components to process all the information needed to transport a person. It's basically one big processor that can calculate and produce the energy to make time travel possible. StellaPort is the overall name of your time machine. The glass chamber is where the person enters and a vortex, or portal, is created above them while they are standing on Mollie. Mollie identifies the molecular structure of the person and will organize them in biological order. Eve performs the complicated computations for the precise amount of energy needed. The calculations from Eve are sent to Mollie and then to Stella to start the transportation process. The person in the transportation chamber will experience a vortex above them while their molecules are being organized. The vortex will rotate in a counterclockwise motion if traveling into the past and spins in the opposite direction for the future."

"That pretty much sums it up," David said, and then he said, looking at Martha, "After you have completed writing your software program, I'll load it into Eve so when the year, month, date, time, longitude and latitude are entered, Eve will calculate the precise arrival site based on the stars in the sky on that date." David looked at Brian and said, "With your research on black holes and human cell structure, we would know if a person can withstand the energy force being applied and survive the ordeal."

"Professor, that all seems logical, but is the machine operational?" Brian asked.

"Not yet, but I believe I figured out a solution to travel beyond the speed of light. My theory is that light's speed on Earth travels at a constant rate of 186,000 miles per second because of the gravitational force creating a drag. We can't touch or measure the force because it's invisible. However, I plan to invent an antigravity device to test my theory in a weightless environment, and I'll also build Martha's Starbase device."

"How long will it take you?" Martha asked.

"It shouldn't take long. I should be able to gather the components from my labs here and at M.I.T. The most complicated task will be miniaturizing a computer processor that will have enough power and memory to accommodate the size of your software programs. I would estimate one month's time."

"I believe with the help of Eve, I could have my program completed in two weeks," she said.

"Professor, it will take me longer. I need to continue working on my experiments," Brian said.

"Seems we all understand what needs to be done, so let's get started," David said.

CHAPTER 8

Brian and Martha were working Saturday afternoon in David's lab while David was busy in the other room building Martha's Starbase device and his antigravity machine. While Martha was using the PC, she mumbled, "Finally." Martha went to Brian, who was looking through a microscope examining the tissue on the pig's foot and said, "Brian, I've completed my software program. Let's tell Professor Solomon."

When Brian and Martha entered the room, they saw David at his workbench working on an electronic component. Brian asked, "Professor, may we interrupt you for a few minutes?"

"Sure. What is it?"

"Martha has some news to report and wants to share it."

"Professor, I just completed the work on my Starbase software program, and I'm now ready to test it," she said.

"That's good news. You can load your software into Eve and test for any bugs in the application. How were you able to complete it so fast?"

"I used a scanner to load all my star maps into one database. I then created another database for the longitude and latitude on Earth while using the Gregorian calendar and accounting for a leap day every four years. I applied the extra day to the last month of the year like the ancient Egyptians did and linked both databases to my software program," she answered.

"Very good. Let's test your application," David said. They went to the PC, where Martha opened her just completed program and pointed to the monitor while explaining what they were looking at.

"See those empty dialog boxes with the headings year, month, date, time, city and country? They are for entering the criteria and then the program will do the rest and display the longitude and latitude, including the star formation in the sky on that date. Professor, since you were so gracious to allow me to use Eve, I would be honored if you made the selection for this maiden test," she said.

"I consider it a privilege. I'll pick three dates using the same city to confirm the accuracy of your program. I have a city in mind, Jerusalem in Israel, and the dates are January 1, 2010, January 1, 1000, and January 1, 0001."

"Professor, is there a specific reason why you picked those dates?" Brian asked.

"There's been much written about Jerusalem throughout history, and we should be able to verify the accuracy of Martha's program," David replied.

"Please, Professor, key in your selection and push the enter key," Martha said with excitement.

Her program was designed to process one request at a time. David entered the first date, January 1, 2010, 12 a.m., Jerusalem, Israel, and then he pushed the enter key. The latitude of 31'47N and longitude of 35'10E appeared in the dialog boxes and the formation of the stars was also displayed. Martha pointed to the star map on the monitor and said, "This is how the night sky would have looked on that date at their location."

David then requested a computer printout of the results and did the same for the two remaining dates. He arranged the printouts by the oldest to the most current year and pointed out how the longitude and latitude had slightly changed and so did the stars' alignment. David then said, "Martha, your program is working, but you'll need to confirm the accuracy of the results."

"Yes, Professor. I'll go to Harvard's library, which has an extensive collection of literature on ancient astrological maps. I've been there numerous times. Some books are very old and cannot be checked out, but photocopying is allowed."

"I'll drive you there. I've finished my work for today," Brian said.

"Thanks, Brian. With your help the research will be faster. This is so exciting."

"We should be back in a few hours," Brian said.

"Fine. I believe I'll have Martha's device ready by then," David said. After they left for the library with the computer printouts of the star map, David returned to his workbench to work on Starbase and was impressed with her program. As he was assembling the device, David wondered if five hundred gigabytes of memory would be sufficient to accommodate and process her software, including the two large databases. He was pleased with himself because he had miniaturized the unit that included advanced technological features with the three laser lights for locking onto stars and planets. David removed a dome-shaped device with five pointed antennas from under his workbench, and then he opened and tested the component using an electrical voltage meter to verify that it was working properly. The unit was fine, so he reassembled it and left the device on his workbench. David then went to his antigravity machine, which was also on the bench, and began working on it.

Brian and Martha arrived at Harvard's library and headed for the astronomy area on the third floor, which contained astrological maps. Martha was familiar with this section of the library because of the time spent researching stars and constellation systems for her thesis. She led Brian to a room having hundreds of books about astronomy. They entered and were the only ones in the room. Martha removed the PC printouts from her tote bag and set them down onto a table and said, "Brian, I'll search for information on ancient Egyptian astrological maps and the book titled *The Almagest* by Ptolemy. He was the first Greek astronomer, in 50 BC, to make a map having longitude and latitude coordinates. You can help by looking for a book by Abd al-Rahman al-Sufi titled *Book of Fixed Stars*. He drew an accurate star chart in 964."

"We can compare our findings to the star charts made by ancient Egyptian astronomers," Brian said.

"That's what I'm thinking too. We should have two different maps with the identical star alignments. After we return to Professor Solomon's lab, we can search on the Internet for a star chart over

Jerusalem for January 1, 2010," she said, and then they began searching for the books.

David was still at his workbench testing the motor for his antigravity machine. He had combined the physics of quantum mechanics and general relativity for building the device. The antigravity force being created would neutralize the gravity on the Earth and a person in the antigravity field would experience the same weightlessness that astronauts encounter beyond Earth's atmosphere.

Brian was across the room opposite Martha when he said, "Here it is." He pulled the book from the shelf and sat in a chair at the table while Martha continued searching. Brian began turning the pages and found the map that Abd al-Rahman al-Sufi had drawn in 964. He showed it to Martha and asked, "Is there a photocopy machine on this floor?"

"Yes, down the hall and near the stairway."

"I'll be right back," Brian said, and he left the room for the photocopier.

Martha continued searching and found the volume of books by Ptolemy titled *The Almagest* and retrieved volumes seven and eight about stars and constellations. Then she stood at the table and began turning the pages. While scanning the books, she found the map she was looking for and continued her search for a book on star charts by ancient Egyptian astronomers. After Brian returned with the photocopy, he asked, "How are you doing in here? Did you miss me?"

"I'm having a difficult time locating an old star chart for or near the year AD 1," Martha replied.

Brian picked up the book from the table and asked, "Do we need to make a photocopy of the pages in this book?"

"Yes."

"I'll be right back to lend you my research skills."

After Brian left, Martha continued searching and was beginning to get frustrated because she was scanning row by row but wasn't having any luck. When Brian returned with the photocopies, he asked, "Have you found it?"

"No, not yet. Let's see your research skills in action and help me find something."

"I'll give it a shot," Brian said, and then he started searching on the side of the room opposite Martha. They were quiet while looking intently for a book with a star map for the year AD 1.

Suddenly, Martha broke the silence by saying, "If I'm correct, there is an Egyptian sculpture called the Dendera Zodiac in the Louvre Museum in Paris. The Dendera Zodiac has been dated to 50 BC and was dedicated to Osiris in the Hathor Temple at Dendera and contains the Zodiac images of Taurus the bull and Libra the scales. We'll go to the first floor and look there for a book with pictures of the art exhibits in the Louvre Museum, and hopefully we'll find it."

"Good idea. Let's file these books and see what we can find on the first floor," Brian said.

On the first floor, Martha asked the woman librarian where she could find information about the Louvre Museum in Paris, France. After the curator escorted them to an area that had many books on European museums, she said, "You can find some material on the museums here. If you need further assistance, please let me know."

"Thank you. You were helpful," Martha said, and then she looked at Brian and said, "I'll search for books containing illustrations of the Louvre Museum exhibits, and you look for texts with pictures of artifacts in the Cairo Museum."

"I hope there are only a few books. I know an easier and faster way. We can use the Internet."

"Brian, we have all these books in front of us. Let's search here first, and if we're not successful, we'll try the Internet," she said.

The literature was filed alphabetically by country, and then by museum. Martha quickly found France and the Louvre Museum. She pulled the first book from the shelf and skimmed the section on Egyptian artifacts and had no luck. She removed another book, with the same results, but the third book she took from the shelf had a clear image of the Dendera Zodiac sculpture. Martha went to Brian and said, "Here it is. Let's make a photocopy of it."

After photocopying the image of the sculpture, Martha gestured to Brian by pointing to signal that a table with chairs was vacant. They went to the table and sat down. Martha set down the two PC printouts and placed them next to the photocopies for comparison. Brian said, "Martha, the maps of the stars seems to align exactly with each other, but for the Dendera Zodiac we'll need to change the twelve Zodiac signs into star formations."

"It seems like both star maps agree," Martha said. Pointing to the star map created by Ptolemy and then to the Zodiac symbols on the sculpture, she said, "When we convert the Zodiac symbols on one map to the star formations on the other map, the two star maps are the same."

"Seems like all your efforts paid off. I'm sure Professor Solomon will be impressed. We should head back to his lab and show him our results," Brian said.

"I hope he's completed my Starbase device."

"Me too. I'd like to see it in action," Brian said while collecting the papers from the table.

CHAPTER 9

David decided that now was the perfect time of the day, before the sun set, to attach the electromagnetic wave transmitter and receiver to the brick chimney on the roof of his house. The weather was fine and all the snow had melted and the temperature was fifty-five degrees. He went to his garage and removed a ladder from the rafters and placed it on the right side of his house. After making sure the ladder was in a safe position for climbing, he went to the lab and got the unit and a screwdriver and the metal band for fastening it to the chimney.

David brought the equipment and tools to the ladder and climbed, toting the electromagnetic wave transmitter and receiver to the roof. When David was on the roof, he carefully walked up the slight incline and securely fastened the transmitter and receiver to the chimney with the metal band. As David was about to climb down, he saw Luke holding it, and when he was back on the ground, he said, "Thanks for keeping the ladder steady for me."

"Dad, what were you doing up there? You should have hollered for me to help you."

"I didn't know you were home. I've been working in the lab all day," David said, and then he pointed to the chimney while saying, "See that transmitter and receiver with the antennas? I just attached it."

"What's it for?" Luke asked.

"It's for one of my experiments that will transmit and receive electromagnetic waves. Do you want to help me? I could use somebody with muscles."

"Sure. I'm not doing anything. I was watching TV."

"In the garage there are two spools of black cables on the floor near the door. Please bring them here. Oh, I also need the roll of blue tape and the box of tacks next to the spools."

While Luke went to the garage to get the supplies, David looked at the device once again with its antennas sticking up well above the rim of the chimney. When Luke returned with the supplies, David said, "Thanks, kiddo. Now I have to climb to the roof one more time and connect each cable to the transmitter and receiver unit."

David climbed the ladder while holding onto each end of the black cables. After connecting them to the unit, he held the power supply cable over the edge of the roof where Luke stood. While wiggling it, David said, "Luke, please put a piece of the blue tape on this cable because I need to know which one is supplying power to the unit."

After Luke put the tape on the cable, David said, "How about demonstrating what kind of arm you have? Throw the box of tacks up here."

Luke picked up the tacks from the ground and, pretending to be a baseball pitcher, threw them to David. When David caught the box, he said, "Strike. You're out." David tacked the cables to the roof so the wind wouldn't blow them around and damage the unit.

When David was back on the ground, he stepped back from the side of the house to examine his work. He asked, "Luke, what do you think? Are they secure enough for a wind storm?"

"Yes. Only a tornado could move those cables now."

"A tornado would probably blow the roof off the house. Please use your muscles and carry the ladder inside the garage, and when I have time I'll put it up in the rafters," David said, smiling.

When Brian and Martha entered the backyard, they saw David standing next to the spools. Brian said, "Hi, Professor. We finished our research. We'll show you our findings in the lab."

"Professor, do you need any help?" Martha asked after looking at the spools on the ground.

"No," and then he pointed to the electromagnetic wave transmitter and receiver and said, "I just completed connecting two cables to that unit."

When Luke returned from the garage, he said, "Hi, Brian. Hi, Martha. Did you bring Murphy?"

"He's still home chilling out," Brian answered.

"Brian, the next time you come by, please bring him with you," Luke requested.

"Sure thing, dude. I'll bring him by tomorrow."

"Let's go to the lab and discuss what you discovered," David said, and they went to the lab.

When they arrived, Luke said, "The metal cabinet has been moved," and he quickly went to it. David had forgotten to push it against the wall before leaving the lab to attach the electromagnetic wave transmitter and receiver. Luke saw the hidden room and entered it, and they heard him say, "Wow!"

Brian and Martha looked at David, and he said, "Yes, now the four of us know," and when entering the room, they saw Luke staring in awe at the transportation chamber.

"Dad, what is this?" Luke asked.

"A time machine I call StellaPort."

"Can I try it?"

"No, it's not quite ready to be tested with humans. You must promise me you will not tell anyone about this. It's confidential. Only we four know about it."

"Dad, I swear on Mom's grave, I'll keep your time machine a secret."

"Thanks, kiddo."

"How does the machine work?" Luke asked.

"Briefly, a person will step into the glass chamber and stand on one of the five platforms. The person will then be transported in time and eventually be brought back," David answered.

"Excuse me, Professor. Can we show and explain our findings to you?" Martha asked.

"Yes, let's do that."

"Dad, can I stay here and look around?" Luke asked.

"Okay, but don't touch anything."

"Thanks, I won't."

At the desk, Martha removed from her tote bag the PC printouts along with the photocopies made at the library and placed them onto the desk. She then paired the photocopy with the printout. While pointing at the first set of copies for the year 1,000, she said, "This star map was drawn in AD 964 by Abd al-Rahman al-Sufi. We photocopied the map from the book titled *Book of Fixed Stars*, and my map agrees with his. Now for the year AD 1, this map was drawn by Ptolemy in the year 50 BC and is from book seven of *The Almagest*, and both maps also agree. We found another map for the same year that was sculptured in sandstone on the ceiling of a temple in Egypt called the Dendera Zodiac and dates to 50 BC." Martha then pointed at the photocopy of the sculpture and said, "The Egyptian astronomers would observe the night sky and map where the constellations were. They plotted their formations using zodiac symbols instead of individual stars. If we substitute each Zodiac symbol with their star constellations, both maps should agree. The Dendera Zodiac depicts the night sky of 50 BC, and when we compare it to Ptolemy's star map, see, they agree. We now have two ancient star maps that are identical to my map."

"I'm impressed that you could find two maps for the same time period to validate your program," David said.

"Professor, have you completed building my device?" Martha asked.

"Yes. I'll go get it."

Luke was still in awe looking at the time machine. After David entered the room, he said, "Seems as though this machine has piqued your curiosity."

"Yes, Dad. It looks so cool."

"Luke, I need your help. I must connect the two cables that are on the spools to Stella."

"Who's Stella?" Luke asked.

"This big panel is called Stella. I'll explain more about the machine later," David said, grinning and touching the control panel of his time machine.

"Okay, I'll go outside now to find a spot on the house for the cables to go through," Luke said.

"Thanks, kiddo," David said, and then he went to his workbench to get Martha's device.

Brian was looking at the computer monitor while Martha was surfing the Internet seeking a website that would show star formations. She found a site that had star maps and clicked on the date January 1,

2010, and a map appeared. She said, "This star map also agrees with mine," and printed it.

When David returned to the desk with Martha's device in his hand, he said, "Starbase is ready for testing," as he handed it to her.

"The dimensions are exactly what I had envisioned—small enough to hold in your hand. How were you able to make the device so tiny?" Martha asked.

"I used nanotechnology to miniaturize all the components so they would fit into an area the size of a handheld calculator. The only concern I had while building the unit was having enough memory for processing the data and to accommodate the two large databases. I'm hoping five hundred gigabytes of memory will be sufficient. Martha, do you know the size of the memory that is required for operating your software program and databases?"

"No. I use a secure website to store and work on my program. The website allows unlimited storage and is password protected," she answered.

"The only way of knowing is to download the software application and both databases into Starbase," Brian said.

Martha then removed a USB cable from her tote bag and connected it to the PC and to her device. She logged on to a website and gained access to her program and files and began downloading them to Starbase while a progress bar was displayed on the monitor indicating the percentage of files remaining to be transferred.

"It looks like it's going to take awhile. I'll be outside checking on Luke. I gave him something to do," David said, and then he left the lab to see how Luke was doing.

Luke was outside standing next to the spools looking for a spot on the house to run the cables through the wall to be connected to Stella. David approached him and asked, "Any luck, kiddo?"

"No, but I was thinking we could drill a hole in the wall here."

"Drilling into a concrete wall would take some time to complete," David said.

"That's what the cable TV guys do," Luke said.

"I understand, but kiddo, were not cable guys. How about if we run the cables through each bottom corner of the basement window that's near the metal cabinet, and then we can run them to Stella."

"Yes, that's a much better plan than mine," Luke said.

"Luke, please get the battery-powered drill and the wood drill bits from the garage."

After Luke returned with the tools, David drilled a hole in each corner of the wood window sill and when he was done, he said, "Luke, I'll go inside and open the window now. After I do that, I want you to pass the spools to me."

David entered the basement and went to where Brian and Martha were talking. He glanced at the progress bar, which read 55% complete, and said, "We still have awhile to go," and then he went to the windowsill he'd just drilled and opened the window. He motioned for Luke to hand him the spools and he did.

"After I close this window, I want you to tack the cables to the frame, and when you're done, put the tools back into the garage," David said, and then he closed and locked the window without a problem.

David went to the PC and glanced at the progress bar on the monitor, which was now displaying 80% complete. He said, "Brian, while we're waiting for the download to be completed, I could use your help to run two cables to be connected to Stella."

"Sure thing, Professor. Are you done remodeling?"

David grinned and said, "Yes, we need to run each of these cables along the wall and under the metal cabinet," and then he began releasing the cables from the spools as he walked along the basement wall and into the room that housed Stella.

"Brian, please push the metal cabinet to the wall and pull as much cable as you need to run it along the bottom of the wall."

"Okay, Professor, I'm finished," Brian said.

David retrieved the wire cutters from his workbench and cut the two cables from their spool and handed them to Brian, saying, "I need you to push the metal cabinet against the wall and slide the cables under the cabinet so the wheels are free to roll."

"Professor, what else can I do?" Brian asked after he had pulled the cables to the wall.

"That's it for now. After I connect these cables to Stella, I'll join you and Martha at the computer."

After David finished working on Stella, he joined Martha and Brian in the other room. The progress bar on the monitor displayed 99%. "The download should be finished any minute now," Martha said, and then the status bar read 100%. "There seems to be more than enough memory space," she said while logging off the Internet.

"After it becomes dark outside, we'll give your device a test run," David said.

Brian looked at his wristwatch and said, "It's 7:30. We should be able to view the stars in an hour."

"Since we have some time to kill, let's go and get something to eat," Martha said.

"There's a sub shop down the street called Mario's, a fifteen-minute walk from here. Luke can show you. He's a regular there," David said.

"I know Mario. He's the owner and cook," Luke said.

"Professor, will you be coming with us?" Martha asked.

"No, I'm not hungry. I need to test the cables I just connected to Stella. I'll be here when you return," David replied, and then they left the lab for Mario's.

David was now at Stella's controls and he turned on the machine. The green light beside the subject tracking display window was on, indicating acknowledgment by Stella. The window was designed to show the coordinates of each person and is capable of tracking up to five people at once. The reading in the window was 0 for both the longitude and the latitude because a person had not been transported. David was pleased to know that the subject-tracking equipment was working properly.

Luke, Brian and Martha returned from the sub shop while David was still working on Stella. David heard Luke's voice when he entered the lab with Brian and Martha, so he turned off Stella and joined them in the other room.

"Professor, how was your test?" Brian asked.

"Good so far. I have power to the electromagnetic wave transmitter and receiver, and Stella has acknowledged it. I'd like to test it, but I'll wait, because to do that, I will need a test subject."

"When do you think you'll be ready to go?" Brian asked.

"I'm hoping soon, if I don't run into any problems."

David looked at his wristwatch and said, it's 8:30. Let's go to the backyard and test Starbase."

In the backyard and looking up at the night sky, they saw many stars twinkling. David asked, "Martha, may I have Starbase so I can explain its features to everyone?" Martha handed him the device and David said, "Luke, please turn on the outdoor garage lights for some light."

After Luke returned from the garage, David held the black plastic unit so they could all see it. Starbase was the size of a handheld calculator, but thicker. David began by pointing at the controls of the unit and said, "The three laser lights are in the front with one at each corner for locking onto a fixed star and one in the center for your destination or home base planet. Above the three lasers are these four display windows and below the windows are buttons for scrolling up or down to find a star or planet and for locking onto a celestial body. The three windows in the middle of the unit will display the destination selected, including the home base planet, and the distance traveled. This larger window in the top center of the device will show a map of the star system selected, and after making your selections, a V for the home planet appears and an inverted ^ for the arrival point is displayed. The intersecting point of the V's will either be your home base or destination point. Now below the star map are these three dialog boxes to enter the country, city and address and these two windows will show the longitude and latitude of the location selected. As you can see, there is a keypad, giving you the option to scroll for or manually enter the data into the unit. The button at the lower right is for power. I installed a solar panel to recharge the battery and to save energy. I included a USB port here at the bottom for uploading and downloading data, which Martha has already used. I hope it meets your expectations. Any questions?" David asked, looking at Martha.

"Thank you very much, Professor. You have built Starbase as I had envisioned it to be, and now hopefully my software program will work as intended. The only way to know is to test it," she answered, and then David handed Martha Starbase.

Martha, Starbase in hand, said, "I will select two fixed stars that are in what are called circumpolar constellations because they are visible year round." She used the scrolling feature to find the two stars for the left and right corners of the device.

"I'll pick Polaris, better known as the North Star in the Little Dipper, for the fixed star on the left," she said, and quickly found the star and pushed the lock button. She continued, "I will now select the star Kochab that is also in the Little Dipper for the star on the right." She scrolled and found that star too and locked onto it. The distance from Earth to Polaris was being shown as 430 LY (light years) and for Kochab it was 126 LY and the distance traveled was zero. The star map window now displayed a V. The top left and right lines of the V were locked onto the stars of Polaris and Kochab, and where the lines of the V intersected was Earth.

"Now I'll select a planet as my destination point. There's a planet that was discovered around the star 47 Ursae Majoris in the year 2001 and is also located in the Big Dipper. Since we can't see the planet without a high-powered telescope, I will lock onto that known star instead," Martha said. She located the star in the database and locked onto it, and the distance to be traveled read 51 LY. The map now displayed a V and an inverted ^ above the V. She continued, "Where the two lines of the V's intersect are the home base and destination points." Martha was pleased because the Starbase was working as intended.

"Let's verify whether the longitude and latitude are working. We can use Professor Solomon's address for the test," Brian said.

"Great idea," Martha replied. She entered David's address, and the longitude displayed was -70.909912 and the latitude was 42.5044405. "Professor, can we verify the coordinates by finding a longitude and latitude website on the Internet?" Martha asked.

"Okay, sounds good," David answered, and then they went to the PC in the lab. Martha logged on to the Internet and started surfing for a longitude and latitude website and found one. She entered David's address and the same coordinates appeared. After David saw the results, he said, "Very good. All your hard work has paid off."

"Thanks, Professor, but without your help creating Starbase, it would still be a dream," she replied.

"Well, it was a pleasure to help. Mankind can benefit from a device like yours," David said.

"It's getting late. We should continue our work tomorrow," Brian said.

"Sounds like a good idea. We can end the night on a positive note. I'm planning to test Stella tomorrow," David replied.

"Brian, please bring Murphy with you," Luke said.

"Will do, little dude," Brian said, and then they left the lab for the evening.

CHAPTER 10

It was 7 a.m. and David was in his lab standing in front of the chalkboard analyzing the part of his equation about the mass, weight and volume of an object and the energy that was needed for time travel. His theory now accounted for electromagnetic waves along with gravitational forces on matter and, after studying the formula, David came to the same conclusion that traveling at or beyond the speed of light could not be achieved. He decided to rework his theory by eliminating the force of gravity and replacing it with antigravity. As David was rewriting his equation on the chalkboard, he realized that by substituting gravity with negative gravity and increasing the electromagnetic waves, it would be possible to travel faster the speed of light. He wrote the following equation:

$$E = mc^2 + F^{12} = G\frac{(-m^1)m2}{r^2} r^{21} = G\frac{m^1 m^2}{r^2} r^{21} = -F^{21} + {}^\wedge V = C + \Delta^2 - VE\frac{\partial 2}{\partial T2} B$$

$$= O + I = \frac{\Delta q}{\Delta t} = nqAvd + A = \frac{Q}{M} \quad E = T \text{ and } T = \sqrt{1 - \frac{V2}{C2}}$$

David became excited because he believed he had discovered a breakthrough and now needed to test his theory within a negative gravity field.

David rolled out his antigravity machine, which was behind his workbench, and laid it down on the floor in front of StellaPort. He plugged the power cord of his machine into an electrical socket on the wall. David scanned the room looking for something to place on the antigravity machine and saw Einstein's book on general relativity on his workbench. He put it onto the center of the wheel-shaped unit and turned on the machine. The book began to rise and float freely in the air. After watching the book float for a few minutes, he shut off the machine.

David realized that the antigravity machine was now a critical part of StellaPort. He removed the bottom rear panel of the glass chamber and unfastened the support braces and removed them. He slid the antigravity machine under the transportation chamber and reattached the panel. David placed the book on a Mollie and then turned on the antigravity machine and, just as before, it floated. He turned off the machine and the book rested on the Mollie. David was now ready to prove his theory that traveling at or beyond the speed of light was possible within an antigravity field.

Luke entered the lab and saw David staring at the chalkboard, and he said, "Dad, you're up early. What are you doing?"

"I had to perform an experiment before Brian and Martha arrive."

"What kind of experiment?" Luke asked.

"I just tested my antigravity machine, and it works."

"Where is it?" Luke asked.

"I just installed it under the transportation chamber. I can demonstrate how it works. See that book in the chamber?" David said as he turned on the antigravity machine. The book began floating in the air.

"Wow, it's working. Can I try it? I've never floated," Luke said.

David shut off the machine and said, "Okay, but only for a few minutes. I have other things to do. Please go and stand on a Mollie."

Luke picked up the book and held it while standing on a Mollie. David asked, "Are you ready?"

He nodded his head yes. David turned on the antigravity machine and Luke began to float in the air. "Dad, this is so cool. I'm lighter than a feather."

"I might have to tie a string to your foot so you don't float away," David said, smiling.

"Yes, like a balloon," Luke said, laughing. David turned off the machine and Luke was now standing on Mollie again.

Brian, with Murphy in his car, picked up Martha at her apartment. Martha got into the car and said, "Good morning, Brian," and then gave him a kiss.

"Good morning, señorita," Brian said, and then he drove to Harvard to get a lab mouse that David had asked for. Brian parked his car outside the science building and told Martha he would be right back. Brian entered the building using his card key and went to the science lab room. Entering, he looked around the lab for something to put the mouse into and saw a shoebox on a counter. After Brian got the box, he went to a cage with mice and put a mouse inside the shoebox, and then left the lab for David's home.

It was 9 a.m. when Brian, Martha and Murphy arrived at David's home. When they entered the lab, Brian said, "Hi, Professor. I brought the mouse you requested."

"Thanks, Brian. He'll become useful later today. Please put the shoebox on the workbench."

Luke went to the bench and opened the box, saw the white lab mouse and asked, "Can I keep him?"

"We plan to use him for our experiment. If he survives, you can keep him," David replied.

"Cool. Bye, Harry. See you later," Luke said, naming the mouse, and he placed the lid back onto the shoebox.

"Hi, dude. I brought Murphy."

"Thanks, Brian, I was just floating in the air," Luke said.

"No way. Impossible," Brian said.

"It's true. Dad invented an antigravity machine that works."

Grinning, David said, "Luke was lighter than a feather for a few minutes. I demonstrated how the machine works using him as a test subject."

"Where's the antigravity machine?" Brian asked.

"I installed it under the transportation chamber."

Martha asked, "Will you demonstrate it for us?"

"Kiddo, do you want to be weightless again?" David asked Luke.

"Sure. Can I bring Murphy too?"

"Brian, is it okay?" David asked.

"Okay, dude. Go ahead. Take him with you." Luke opened the door to the transportation chamber and called Murphy, who came prancing in.

"Are you ready?" David asked.

Luke glanced down at Murphy and said, "Yes."

David turned on the antigravity machine, and they floated in the air. After a few minutes, David shut off the machine and their feet and paws were back on the floor. Brian opened the chamber door, and Murphy pranced out. Luke followed. "You and Murphy looked cool floating in the air. I wish I'd brought my camera. Professor, can I check Luke's vital signs?" Brian asked.

"Yes, please do."

In the other lab room, Brian checked Luke's blood pressure, pulse and heartbeat, which were all normal. After his checkup, Luke said, "Brian, I'll take Murphy upstairs to see if he's thirsty."

Brian returned to the room containing the time machine and saw David explaining to Martha his equation on the chalkboard. Brian went over and said, "Professor, Luke's vital signs were normal."

"That's good to hear—no side effects. While you were checking Luke, I was pointing out to Martha where I had made a change in my equation to include electromagnetic waves and antigravity. The next step is to prove my theory using a laser light in an antigravity field and, if successful, then with a live subject to determine if a human could survive the transportation process."

"When will you perform the experiment?" Martha asked.

"I'm planning on doing it later today."

"Professor, what can we do to help?" Brian asked.

"Martha, please disconnect the PC and reconnect it here so we can download your files into Stella."

"No need, Professor. I brought my laptop," she said.

"Good. You can start downloading your files now." Martha went to her tote bag and removed the laptop computer and USB cable and connected them to Stella and logged on to the Internet and started transferring her files. While her files were being downloaded, David said, "After Martha's files are downloaded, the subject tracking unit will be fully functional, allowing Stella to keep a constant lock on a subject and give us their precise location."

When the progress bar for the download displayed 100%, Martha said, "Professor, the program has been successfully downloaded to Stella."

"Good. Now we're ready to check each component of Stella's control panel."

"How does the antigravity machine come into play during the process?" Brian asked.

"After the laser lights are turned on, I'll turn on the machine. There are two specially made alloy discs that will spin at more than 6,000 RPM, creating a magnified electromagnetic force. The energy being generated flows through the copper coils that form a ring around the outer edge of the machine and are connected to an energy transference unit. When the antigravity machine is on, the area within the ring becomes a weightless environment. The machine resembles the rim of a bicycle with spokes and an axle. The axle is where the motor is and contains the space-age discs, and the spokes are the conduit for the energy being transferred from the discs to the coils, neutralizing gravity."

"The machine does work and that's a proven fact," Martha said.

"Yes, let's hope it continues working as intended," David said.

Luke returned to the lab with Murphy as David was about to turn on Eve. Luke said, "Dad, I didn't know we had a machine in this cabinet. What's it for?"

"It's a small supercomputer that is more powerful than the PCs sold in stores."

"Cool. Can I use it for my math homework?" Luke asked.

"No, Eve's for sophisticated mathematical computations," David answered, and after turning on Eve, he switched on Stella's control panel, and all its lights came on. "I'll now begin testing each of Stella's components to make sure they're working properly."

David went to his workbench and removed the lid from the shoebox and said, "This little guy will be the first time traveler." He placed the lid back on the box and left it on the bench. Stella was operating fine and the speed of light meter on the control panel was lit, indicating that the unit was working. David turned on the lights along the outer edge of the ceiling in the transportation chamber, and they immediately ricocheted off the reflectors on the floor. The meter read 186,000 miles per second (mps). There wasn't a change in the velocity of light. "We are at the speed of light. I will now introduce a negative gravity field and, if my calculations are correct, we'll witness an increase in light's speed to 266,000 miles per second."

David turned on the antigravity machine and all eyes were on Stella's speed of light meter. Just as he'd predicted, the meter read 266,000 mps. He kept the machine on for a few more minutes to see if the speed would increase, but it didn't. David turned off the antigravity machine and the laser lights.

"Wow! That was something. We just witnessed a major breakthrough in physics. Let's test the time machine using Harry, and if he survives, I'll examine him to determine the effect on his body. Then we'll know if time travel is safe for a human," Brian said.

"I'm ready, but I don't know if Harry is. I'll transport him here one hour into the future," David said.

David was now using the keypad on Stella to enter the longitudinal and latitudinal coordinates of his home and today's date. He looked at his wristwatch. It read 10:35, so he entered 11:35 a.m. as the time of arrival. Then he said, "Brian, please put the shoebox on a Mollie."

Brian opened the door to the transportation chamber and placed the box onto a platform, and then Mollie and Eve went into action. The amount of energy required for the transportation process was being calculated by Eve and transferred to Mollie. The numbers in Mollie's display window on Stella stopped changing and then a green light appeared beside the window, indicating that the calculation for the amount of power needed for transporting Harry was complete. David turned on the lights in the transportation chamber and the many colored lights on Eve and Stella made a spectacular sight. David switched on the antigravity machine, and the shoebox rose. He introduced the electromagnetic waves using a dial on Stella and then turned the transport dial to the forward position. A vortex now appeared at the ceiling of the glass chamber. The cloud began moving in a clockwise rotation with increasing speed. Suddenly Harry and the box disappeared. David shut off the antigravity machine, the laser lights and the electromagnetic wave inducer, and the room immediately became less illuminated. The subject tracking unit signaled that it was locked onto a subject, but the longitude and latitude display window read zero because Harry was still in transit. They waited nearly an hour.

"It's 11:30. Harry should be arriving anytime now," Martha said.

Luke was in the library playing with Murphy. He threw a green tennis ball and Murphy chased it out of the room and into the hallway and then began barking. Luke went to find out why Murphy was barking and saw a shoebox on the floor that looked like the one that Brian had brought this morning.

David, Martha and Brian heard Murphy barking, and then Martha said, "It must be Harry."

They glimpsed at the longitude and latitude on Stella, and David's home coordinates were now being displayed. They quickly went to where Murphy was growling and saw Luke holding the shoebox.

"Somebody forgot to return Harry to the lab," Luke said.

"Luke, please give me the box," David said. Luke gave the box to David, and after he removed the lid, he saw Harry moving about and appearing fine.

"Professor, Harry seems fine, but I'd like to test his blood and vital signs," Brian said.

"Yes, please do. I'm curious to know if there are any side effects," David said as he gave Brian the shoebox.

Brian returned to the lab and withdrew a sample of blood from Harry. Examining it under a microscope, he didn't see any abnormalities. He then looked at Harry's skin tissues, and they were normal, as were his vital signs. "I can't find anything wrong with him. He's a healthy little mouse."

"Excellent news. We'll transport Harry backward in time and return him to our time," David said, and then he went to Stella and turned off the subject tracking unit because Harry was now in the present time. "I'll now send Harry to the year 2005, the year after I bought this house, and use the same coordinates."

David entered the coordinates for his home again and the date of March 22, 2005, and time of 7 a.m. into Stella. Brian placed the shoebox on a Mollie in the transportation chamber and said, "Harry, what you are doing is a noble cause for all of humanity and rodents. Harry is ready," and then he closed the door.

"Shall we pack him a toothbrush for his trip? We should give him a bon voyage party," Martha said, smiling.

"Before we send Harry, I'll write a note to myself so when I find and open the shoebox, I'll know the reason why Harry had come to visit," David said.

David went to the desk and wrote a message to himself that read, "My name is David Solomon. I just performed an experiment, and I am sending Harry to you along with this note. You must write the date, time and location you found Harry and keep the message in the key compartment of your wallet. Harry, including the note and shoebox, will soon return to the year 2010. David, looking at Martha and Brian, said, "I hope I follow these instructions."

"We'll soon find out," Martha said.

David went inside the transportation chamber and put the note into the shoebox. He returned to Stella's control panel to begin the process, but this time, to the past. When the vortex appeared, David turned the transport dial to the backward position, and then it rotated counterclockwise faster and suddenly the shoebox vanished. They looked at the subject tracking window and saw the coordinates for David's address displayed in the window. Harry was now in David's house, but in the year 2005.

CHAPTER 11

David, now in the past, was five years younger and walking down the hallway in his home. He saw a shoebox on the floor. He picked up the box and felt something move inside it. David removed the lid and saw a white mouse and a note. He read the message and paused for a moment. David went to his library and set the shoebox down onto the desk and got a pen and paper and wrote a note per the instructions and then folded the paper and placed it into the key compartment of his wallet. David put the note into the box and then sat on the sofa with many thoughts racing through his mind. Staring at the shoebox, he thought, I'm the only one who knows about the key compartment in my wallet. I must have invented a time machine and, after staring at the box for some time, David went to the kitchen for a drink of water. When he returned to the library, the box was gone.

The shoebox was now in the transportation chamber. Brian entered the chamber, removed the shoebox and carried it to the workbench. After David opened the box, he saw Harry move while he removed the note from the box.

"Dad, is there a note in your wallet?" Luke asked.

"Yes," David said as he took his wallet from his pants pocket and removed a folded piece of paper from a compartment. David continued, "I've carried this note I had written to document what I had experienced five years ago," and then he read the message out loud, which said, "On March 22, 2005, at 7 a.m., I found a shoebox in the hallway of my home containing a white mouse along with instructions for me. I was asked to write a note about what had just happened and to keep it in the key compartment of my wallet. "I remember that day clearly, and I always kept the paper waiting for the day to reveal it."

"Professor, after Harry returned, you remembered that you had a note in the key compartment of your wallet. It seems the space and time continuum changed for you," Brian said.

"It's true, Professor. After the mouse came back, you recalled seeing him and the note with instructions to yourself," Martha then said.

David looked at both notes and said, "There seems to be a mental and not a physical effect."

Murphy was in the lab sniffing the shoebox with Harry still inside. "Brian, are you game for one more test for today?" David asked.

"Sure, Professor. What do you have in mind?"

"I would like to transport Murphy with a miniaturized video recorder attached to his collar to a time when you were a child. Dogs have a keen sense of smell and Murphy should be able to recognize you even as a boy. We'll send Murphy to a place that is outdoors such as a birthday party, a park or playground. The video camera will record the meeting between you and Murphy to prove that time travel is possible."

"It's fine with me. Harry is healthy, and I'm sure the time machine would be safe for Murphy too. I'm curious to watch the interaction between us. The encounter should be something to see. Do you have a video recorder small enough for his collar?"

"Yes. It's in the lab's desk drawer. I'll go and get it." After David returned with the miniature camera, he said, "I'll attach the recorder to the top of Murphy's collar." The collar had a metal dog tag with Murphy's name and Brian's address engraved on it, just in case he got lost. Brian gave the collar to David and he fastened the video camera to it.

"We should test the recorder to make sure it works," Martha said.

"I'm sure it works, but it's better to be safe than sorry. I'll start recording now. Luke, please bring Murphy to the backyard and have him chase you for a few minutes. We want to see if the camera will stay attached to the collar and is recording," David said.

Luke called for Murphy, and they ran from the lab to the backyard. After a short time playing outside, Luke returned with Murphy prancing behind him, panting. "Luke, please bring Murphy to the desk. Martha, can we use your USB cable?" David asked.

Martha went to her tote bag and got the cable and handed it to David. He connected it to the PC and downloaded the video from the camera on Murphy's collar. After the video was transferred, David played the recording, and it was okay with no obstacles in the way of the lens. They saw Luke running from the lab and in the backyard. "The camera is working just fine," David said, and then he deleted the video.

They went to the room that housed StellaPort and there David asked, "Brian, can you recall a time and place when you were at a park or playground as a child?"

"I remember a birthday party when I turned nine years old. The party was at Christopher Columbus Park on Atlantic Avenue in Boston, and there were about fifteen kids and adults who attended. The celebration was from noon to 4 p.m."

"Brian, what's your date of birth?" David asked.

"It's June 27, 1981," he answered.

"We'll send Murphy to June 27, 1990, at 1 p.m., and longitude -71.0527111 and latitude 42.3610355," David said.

David entered the date, time and coordinates into Stella while Brian led Murphy into the transportation chamber and positioned him on a Mollie and commanded him to sit, which he obeyed. Brian exited the chamber and closed the door while Murphy kept staring at him, still obeying his master's command. David started the transportation process again and Eve transferred to Mollie the amount of energy required to transport Murphy. The numbers in Mollie's display window stopped changing, and a green light appeared to indicate that the amount of energy needed had been calculated. David turned on the lights in the transportation chamber and then the antigravity machine. He turned a dial on Stella that added the electromagnetic waves and moved the transport dial to the backward position. The vortex above Murphy started moving in a counterclockwise rotation with increasing speed. Suddenly Murphy vanished. David shut off the antigravity machine, the lights and the electromagnetic wave inducer.

Stella signaled that it was locked onto a subject, and the longitude and latitude coordinates of Christopher Columbus Park were displayed in the tracking window.

"Murphy must be at the park. I hope he can find me," Brian said.

Murphy was now at Christopher Columbus Park and seemed confused because he was suddenly outdoors in a strange park. He started sniffing the air and followed a scent that was luring him to the center of the park, where a group of people were on the grass enjoying a picnic. Murphy began walking toward them and would stop and sniff the air. The scent of Brian was becoming stronger as Murphy approached the people and recognized Brian playing with his friends. Murphy, wagging his tail quickly, pranced to Brian and sniffed his pants. Brian, while petting Murphy, said, "Good boy. Where's your owner?" and then he looked around for his new friend's owner, but didn't see anyone and thought the dog must be lost. Brian checked the dog tag on the collar and saw the name Murphy and an address. "Your name is Murphy and you live at 1516 Storrow Drive, Boston, Massachusetts, 02114. I'm sure you're hungry," Brian said. He led Murphy to his picnic table and fed him hot dogs. After feeding Murphy, Brian went to his dad and said, "Dad, I'm going to the waterfront with Murphy."

"Who's Murphy?"

"The dog I just found."

"He's a handsome golden retriever. Okay, but not far, and not too long. I want to keep an eye on you."

"Thanks, Dad." Brian went to the picnic table and got a green tennis ball and he ran toward the waterfront with Murphy.

The park had a beautiful view of the harbor. Brian threw the ball and Murphy retrieved it. While Brian was playing with his new friend, a park ranger approached him. The ranger said, "Son, you must keep your dog on a leash or I'll have to give you a fine. Who are you with?"

"Murphy, sit," Brian said, and he obeyed his command. Brian said to the park ranger, "I'm with my dad, mom and friends. Today is my birthday, and we are celebrating it with a picnic."

"It's a beautiful day for a birthday party. How old are you?" the ranger asked.

"I'm nine years old today, sir."

"Happy birthday. I have a boy your age. Since today is your birthday, I'm going to give you a present by not giving you a fine, but you must keep your dog on a leash while in the park."

"Thank you, sir. I'll go put him on one now."

"What's your name?" the ranger asked.

"It's Brian."

"Brian, I enjoyed meeting you," the ranger said.

Brian was holding onto Murphy's collar as he led him back to his picnic table. At the picnic table, he looked toward the waterfront but didn't see the park ranger. He then looked at Murphy and said, "That was close. You might have ended up in doggie jail."

The table had a large cloth covering it which extended to the ground on both sides. "Murphy, I don't want you to go to jail, so you'll have to hide under the table for now," Brian said.

Murphy was now hidden and safe from the park ranger's view. Brian left him there and joined his friends to play a game of wiffle ball.

David was in the lab monitoring Stella's components while Brian and Martha chatted to kill time when Luke asked, "Dad, do you think we should bring Murphy back now?"

David glanced at his wristwatch and said, "It's been an hour and a half. He should have located Brian by now."

David turned the transport dial forward, and the green light on the subject tracking unit shut off, indicating that Murphy had returned. Murphy suddenly reappeared, lying down on a Mollie in the transportation chamber. Brian opened the door and Murphy got up and pranced out, wagging his tail. Brian said while petting Murphy, "If you could only talk, you would tell us what it was like to travel through time."

"Yes, Brian, that would be cool, but we have a video of his experience," Martha said.

"How do you feel? Are you physically and mentally okay?" David asked.

"I'm fine. I'm happy knowing Murphy was not harmed," Brian replied.

"Please remove Murphy's collar and bring it to the desk so we can download the video file." Brian removed Murphy's collar and gave it to David. After downloading the video, he jokingly said, "Okay, who wants popcorn before the main feature?" and he played the movie.

The beginning of the recording showed static interference and suddenly Christopher Columbus Park was seen on the PC monitor. Murphy was slowly walking and stopping, which allowed for the park's features to be identified. Brian said, "I remember that day. It was my ninth birthday, and I was playing when a golden retriever came up to me wagging his tail and sniffing me. The name on his dog tag was Murphy. I almost got into trouble that day with a park ranger, but was given only a warning because it was my birthday."

David stopped the video and said, "Please continue recalling that day."

"I remember that after the ranger warned me, I hid Murphy under the picnic table, and I went to play with my friends. When I returned to check on him, he was gone. I always wondered what happened to that dog. He seemed to know me. Ever since that day, I'd always ask my parents if I could have a dog, and they would say no. So I decided when I moved out of my parents' home I would buy a golden retriever and name him Murphy."

Brian started petting Murphy and said, "You're my best friend, right boy?" and Murphy barked.

"Brian, before we sent Murphy to your ninth birthday party, you didn't remember encountering him," David said.

Martha and Luke both nodded their heads and then Martha said, "It's true. You didn't remember meeting him, but as soon as he returned, the event became part of your memory."

"Brian, I'll replay the part of the video where you look at Murphy's dog tag and read his name and address. If we listen carefully, we will hear you say his name and address," David said, and then they listened intently, as young Brian said, "Your name is Murphy and you live at 1516 Storrow Drive, Boston, Massachusetts, 02114."

"Wow! That's my address and I've been living there for one year," Brian said.

David continued playing the video and suddenly there was static interference again and then the lab appeared. After David stopped the video, he said, "It seems safe, but if somebody traveled back in time and created an event that hadn't occurred, our history as we now know it would be altered. We should stop working and meet here tomorrow to discuss our concerns about the machine."

"Sounds good, Professor. We'll come by tomorrow morning," Brian said.

"Okay, here's an easy assignment. I'd like everyone to think of an event in history you would like to witness or a person you want to meet. I'm just curious to know what we all come up with," David said.

Brian, Martha and Luke said, "Okay," and then Brian and Martha left the lab with Murphy to go home.

"Dad, I'm going to my room to think about what my choice will be."

"I have to turn off all the equipment. I'll join you upstairs shortly," David said, and then Luke left the lab while David shut down the machines.

CHAPTER 12

David was up early on Saturday morning as usual, while Luke was sleeping, and he decided to go to Saint Peter's Church and pray. He was also hoping to meet Father Dominick Carlucci again because of the pleasant conversation they had had the last time they met. He put on his spring jacket and headed out the door for the church. As he approached the church, he recalled how the front doors had been locked during the big snowstorm, so he decided to go directly to the same side entrance as before. After David entered the church, he saw parishioners sitting, kneeling and praying on their cherrybark oak pews. He knelt and blessed himself before entering the first-row pew in front of the altar. After David entered, he knelt and made the sign of the cross again and said prayers. When David was finished praying, he sat on the bench and noticed Father Carlucci lighting candles near the altar.

David sat watching the priest perform his duties, and then the father disappeared from view as he walked toward the rear of the church. A few minutes later, the priest reappeared at the right side entrance to the altar, and when he recognized David, the father went to him and said, "You are an M.I.T. professor, correct?"

"Yes, Father. We met last month during that terrible snowstorm. I'm David Solomon."

"I remember the face, but the name eludes me. Sorry, my son."

"Father, please sit and join me," David said, and the priest sat next to him.

After sitting, the priest said, "I recall from our last conversation that you had asked me what Jesus might say in today's time of turmoil. I thought about the question for days after you left and came to the conclusion that Jesus would have to return as prophesied. However, if Jesus appeared today in the flesh, there would still be skeptics, as there were in his time."

"I was wondering what it would take to convince a doubter to believe that a man is indeed the Lord," David said.

"I don't know. Maybe a miracle. But then there would still be those believing that any divine act is a magician's trick."

"What would the pope think if a man approached him, saying, 'I'm Jesus'?" David asked.

"I think he would believe the man was off his rocker."

"In your opinion, what act or event would persuade the pope to believe Jesus had returned?" David asked.

"I believe the pontiff wouldn't need to witness a divine act to convince him that Jesus had returned to us from heaven as written in the scriptures. The charisma of a man to captivate an audience and renew their belief in the glory of God's kingdom, as Jesus did, would definitely be viewed as a miracle in today's time. We are always searching for an exceptional leader, a person who is charismatic and ignites the dormant soul of an individual for making a difference in the world."

"I couldn't agree more," David said. He looked at his wristwatch and noticed that an hour had passed by quickly, and he said, "Father, I must leave now, but I'm sure we'll meet again."

"It was a pleasure seeing you again, David. I hope to see you at my 9 a.m. Sunday sermon."

"I've been busy lately, and when things settle down, I'll attend your Sunday Mass with my boy, Luke."

"There's always time for God, whether in church, home or any other place you decide to talk to him." Both men shook hands, and David left Saint Peter's for his residence.

Martha was at the local coffee shop near her apartment building in Cambridge waiting for Brian to arrive. They had made plans to have breakfast together. Martha had arrived at the restaurant first and was sitting in a booth. When Brian entered the restaurant, he saw Martha and went to her and said, "Good morning, señorita," and then he gave her a kiss and sat across from her.

"I arrived just a few minutes ago," Martha said.

The waitress came to them and asked if they would like something to drink. They both said, "Coffee."

"Do you serve Colombian coffee?" Martha asked.

"Yes, we do."

"I'll have a large cup, please."

"Me too. She's related to Juan Valdez," Brian said, smiling.

After the waitress had left with their order, Brian said, "That was something yesterday in Professor Solomon's lab."

"Yes, I know. I was thinking about Harry and Murphy all night. I believe it's true what the professor said about how his time machine could become dangerous in the wrong hands," Martha said.

"Do you think Professor Solomon would let us use his machine to become rich and famous? We could use the machine to travel into the future to learn in advance how stocks performed and know the winning lottery ticket numbers and the final score for college and professional sports. We would be loaded!" Brian said.

"I don't think the professor intended to invent a time machine so we could get rich," Martha replied.

"It's just an idea. Have you thought about the question he asked us yesterday?" Brian asked.

"Yes. I was up all night. I had so many thoughts racing through my mind, like attending a gala hosted by France's Queen Marie Antoinette in the year 1770. I imagined watching the Egyptian Pharaoh Cleopatra in 41 BC applying makeup so I could learn her beauty secrets. I also thought about going to the year 1192 to see Helen of Troy, the Greek face that launched a thousand ships to start the Trojan War, which lasted from 1194 BC to 1184 BC. And finally to 1526 to meet the explorer Francisco Pizarro from Spain to ask him why he was so brutal to the native populations of South America."

"Last night I was thinking about whom I'd like to meet and what I wanted to see. My first choice is witnessing the building of the Pharaoh Khufu's pyramid in Giza, Egypt, in the year 2575 BC. I would be the guy to solve the mystery of how the Giza pyramids were built," Brian said.

"Yes, Brian, you'd be the man," she said jokingly.

"My next choice is sitting in the Roman Colosseum in the year AD 81 to watch gladiators fight all day, and my final selection would be meeting John the Baptist, the cousin of Jesus. I would go to the Jordan River to be baptized by him and also witness John baptizing Jesus."

"That would be awesome to see."

"I've been wondering why Professor Solomon asked the question. Does he have something in mind?"

"I guess we'll soon find out," Martha replied.

The waitress returned with their coffee and took their breakfast order. After eating, they drove to David's home.

Luke was awake and lying in bed thinking about his dad's question. His first thought was traveling back in time to the year 1995 to be with and talk to his mother, but he knew he would be with her in heaven after he died. Luke then imagined meeting George Washington in 1795, the year before he died, because George Washington was the first president of the United States and the commander of the Continental Army, who defeated the British Army to win independence from England for the thirteen colonies. Luke also considered going back in time sixty-five million years to witness what really killed the dinosaurs. But then he decided against that because whatever killed the dinosaurs would likely kill him too. Luke narrowed his selection between seeing and talking to his mother and George Washington. He decided it would be General Washington because of his history report, and he pictured himself eating apple pie baked by Martha Washington while interviewing George to get answers for his questions about the Revolutionary War.

When David returned home from church, Luke heard the front door close and he got out of bed to find out who it was. Luke went to the top of the hallway stairs and saw David hanging up his jacket. He said, "Hi, Dad. Where did you go?"

"I was at church saying prayers. Take a shower and then get something to eat for breakfast. Brian and Martha will be here soon."

"Okay, I'll be down in a few minutes."

David went to the kitchen to make a cup of hot tea. After the teapot whistled, he poured the water into his cup and sat at the kitchen table to drink his beverage. While sipping his tea, he started to think of a person he would like to meet or a historical event he'd like to witness. He thought of meeting Plato in the year 360 BC to ask him if Atlantis was a real city or just a story and, if it existed, then where was it located. For a moment, he envisioned being the discoverer of the lost city of Atlantis but quickly came back to reality. David then pictured himself in the Vatican's Sistine Chapel watching Michelangelo paint the ceiling in the year 1511. The painting of the chapel's ceiling took four years to complete, from 1508 to 1512. David also thought about traveling five hundred years into the future to check if mankind was still alive and colonizing other planets. But he was more interested in the great achievements of men before his time.

Martha and Brian arrived at David's home and knocked on the front door. "I'll get it," Luke hollered. After opening the door, he saw Brian and Martha. Luke said loudly so David would hear him, "It's Brian and Martha."

"Hi, dude. No, I didn't bring Murphy today. I'm letting him rest. He had a big day yesterday," Brian said.

"Hello, Luke," Martha said.

"Hi. Dad's in the kitchen waiting for you guys," Luke said. They went to the kitchen and saw David sitting at the table sipping his tea.

After David stood, he said, "Good morning. Please sit and join me for a hot beverage," and he offered Brian and Martha tea or coffee. They both preferred tea since that's what David was having.

While they were sipping their tea, Luke said, "Dad, I have someone in mind I would like to meet."

"Who might that lucky person be?"

"George Washington."

"Why do you want to visit George Washington?"

"Because he was the leader of the Continental Army and defeated the British Army and then became our first president."

"Are there any other reasons?" David asked with a grin.

"Yes. I have a history report due next week, and it's about him as a military general and I want to interview him. I could get valuable information from him that's not in my history book. My teacher would be impressed, and I would get an A for the class."

"Dude, sounds cool, but if it's not in the textbook, your teacher will think you made it up. The instructor might flunk you," Brian said.

"I didn't think of that, but it still would be cool to drink tea and eat apple pie with him," Luke replied.

Martha, looking at Brian from across the kitchen table, asked, "Brian, what's your choice?"

"I came up with two choices. The first is sitting in the Roman Colosseum watching gladiators battle all day, and the other is observing the Egyptians build the Giza pyramids. I would be the guy who solved the mystery of how the pyramids were built."

"Brian, they might enslave you like they did the Israelites," Luke said laughing.

"Luke has a good point. The Egyptians required a large labor force to build those pyramids, and you, being a strong, healthy male, would be a prime candidate to join their involuntary workforce," Martha said.

"How about for a quick peek and then I'm out of there," Brian said, smiling.

"Martha, have you made a choice?" David asked.

"I'd like to meet Cleopatra to see how beautiful she really was. Cleopatra had two powerful Roman leaders, Caesar and Mark Antony, who fell in love with her. I also thought about meeting Francisco Pizarro, but after listening to Luke and Brian, I wouldn't want to end up as a slave. I would prefer to meet Cleopatra and learn some beauty secrets."

"That sounds cool, but you'll probably come back with a craving for makeup," Luke said with a laugh.

"I already have. I will not leave home without my mascara," she replied with a smile.

David then stood up from his chair and stepped back from the kitchen table. He said, "All those choices are worthy of a visit, but as you know from our discussion, traveling in time could be dangerous to your health. The event or person we would like to meet is risky because in those days it was a time of conquest. Wars were being fought all over the world, tribe vs. tribe, army vs. army, country vs. country and gang vs. gang. The same is taking place today, but at a much smaller scale. Conflicts are now regional and then slowly diminish and a new one arises. I would like to meet a true unifier of all people. A person speaking for all, an individual that can eliminate barriers such as race, color, sex, religion, etc., and bring harmony and peace throughout the world."

"That's a tall order, Professor. Who do you have in mind?" Brian asked.

"To find a person like that would be a miracle," Martha said.

"What do you think about bringing Jesus here? We could introduce him to the pope so he could reinvigorate his message of love, peace, family and the worship of God. The Vatican is the perfect world stage for Jesus to convey his message to the world. As you know, the scriptures tell us of Jesus returning to the Temple Mount in Jerusalem. We could bring Jesus here before his planned day of coming back to our world," David said.

"Professor, in today's time, if a man claimed he was Jesus Christ, he would be locked up in a psychiatric hospital," Brian said.

"But what if Jesus had a small following that grew rapidly into a very large audience? The pope would have to meet with him."

"That sounds interesting, Professor, but would Jesus want to visit us, and if he did, wouldn't Jesus be disappointed at what he sees and hears?" Martha asked.

David returned to his chair and said, "There's only one way to find out and that would be to ask him. The Bible talks of the missing years of Jesus' life, where he is not mentioned in the New Testament for eighteen years. The Gospels, written by Matthew, Mark, Luke and John, mention Jesus from birth to the age of twelve and are silent until the age of thirty, when he starts his church. We could travel back in time before his thirtieth birthday and before he begins ministering to invite him here to the year 2010. The history about Jesus would not change as long as he was returned to start his ministry. The missing years are as if Jesus had vanished from the face of the earth. Biblical scholars only hypothesize about where he was and what he was doing during those years. As of today, there has been no written or archeology evidence to account for them."

"If he agreed to travel with us, how would we bring him here?" Martha asked.

"Do you recall the umbilical cord example of a mother and her newborn baby when I explained how the subject tracking unit works? The unit can track the movements of up to five people at a time because an electromagnetic wave is continuously connected to them. To bring Jesus here, one must hold his hand, and Eve will compute the mass for both people and send the data to Mollie, who will remember the molecular structure for each person and then transmit the data from Mollie to Stella with the energy needed for the transportation process. For example, if you were to meet Jesus and John the Baptist, and they were willing to come with you, I could transport both because Mollie and Eve are designed to account for the mass of a person (host) plus two additional people (guests). Each guest must hold a hand of the host during the transportation process so Eve and Mollie can determine the combined mass and the required amount of energy. A third guest would not be included in calculations because both hands of the host would be occupied."

"Dad, if I were holding Jesus' hand, Eve would treat us as if we were one person. So if Jesus held the hand of somebody else and my hand at the same time during the transportation process, the person holding one of Jesus' hands would not be transported because Mollie would account only for Jesus and my molecules?" Luke asked.

"Exactly," David said, smiling and looking at Brian and Martha.

"You're a sharp dude. You cleared that up for me," Brian said.

"Yes, you're an intelligent young man," Martha said as she smiled at Luke.

"Thanks. I got my brain from my dad," Luke said proudly.

David stood again and moved to the center of the kitchen floor. Looking at them, he said, "Shall we try to transport Jesus to the 21st century?"

"Yes," all three answered.

"Dad, can I go and invite him?"

"Sorry, Luke. This is a task for adults. It's a lot more complicated than just inviting Jesus here. We must locate him and then approach him at the most opportune time."

"Professor, I'd like to become the first human time traveler. I would be the only person in history to meet Jesus in the flesh after AD 33," Brian said.

"Are you sure you want to go?" David asked.

"Oh, yes, Professor. I'm sure," Brian answered.

"Dad, can I go with Brian? He's an adult."

"No, not this time, kiddo."

"Professor, I would like to go too, just in case Brian needs somebody to bail him out," Martha said.

"What kind of help would I need?" Brian asked, looking at Martha.

"I want to keep an eye on you so you don't get into trouble. I'll have to protect you from all the pretty women," she said, smiling.

"Let's go to my library and talk more about your trip to the Holy Land," David said.

Martha and Brian were sitting on the leather sofa in the library and David sat in the chair next to them. Luke was seated at the library desk. David, looking at Brian and Martha, then said, "We must research the first century AD to get a better understanding of the people and their culture and customs. We should know what they ate, the styles of clothes worn and how they lived."

"Brian will have to grow a beard to blend in with the men," Martha said.

"She's correct, Brian. Many of the men during the time of Jesus had beards and wore tunics with belts, robes and sandals. The women also dressed the same, wearing tunics and belts, veils, sandals, and head scarves. The men and women in that part of the world had tanned complexions with black or brown hair. You and Martha should have no problems blending into the population. Brian, how long does it take for you to grow a beard?"

"One week," Brian answered.

"Good. That will give us plenty of time to research the customs and traditions practiced during the time of Jesus. It will also give us time to learn about the everyday life of people in the first century AD," David said.

"I have a friend attending acting school in New York City. I'll call her and ask where we can rent or buy biblical clothes," Martha said.

"There should be stores in Boston or in the surrounding area selling or renting costumes," Brian said.

"Okay, then. Brian and Martha, you can start searching for your wardrobe, and Luke and I will research the customs and traditions of everyday life for that time period. We'll meet here next week to discuss our progress."

"I'm hoping to be sporting a bushy beard by then," Brian said.

"I'm thrilled. Please excuse me while I call my friend," Martha said, and then she used her cell phone and called Marisol Fernandez, who was from Bogota, Colombia, and grew up with Martha and was now living in New York City. "Hi, Marisol. Martha here. Please call me when you get this message. Thanks mucho and besos."

"Marisol is not answering. So I left a message for her to call me."

"We'll meet you both here next week," David said, and then Brian and Martha left for Boston to begin their search for clothes to wear in the Holy Land.

CHAPTER 13

Luke was sitting at the desk in his bedroom surfing the Internet for information about the time of Jesus. He was curious to know how the people dressed, looked and what they ate. Luke was having a difficult time finding the information he wanted and was getting frustrated because his search results were only about Jesus and his life, not on the culture and traditions of the people. So Luke decided he would have better luck at the local library in Peabody and knew he could ask the librarian for assistance.

David was in his study thinking of a place in Judea to send Brian and Martha that would increase their chances of finding Jesus in a matter of days and not weeks. When Luke entered the library, he said, "Dad, please give me a ride to the Peabody Library. I want to do my research there."

"I need to research too. Would you like to accompany me to the Salem State University library?" David asked.

"Yes, but you don't teach at that school."

"I have influence there and I think I can sneak you in," David said, jokingly.

"That library is way bigger than Peabody's public library. We should be able to find what we're looking for there," Luke said, and then they left.

After leaving David's home, Brian and Martha decided to go to Harvard's library to research the style of clothes worn during the time of Jesus. As they neared the campus, Martha's cell phone rang. It was Marisol returning her call. Martha answered and she said, "Hello. Martha speaking."

"Hi, Martha. It's Marisol. I received your message. I haven't heard from you in awhile. How are you?"

"I'm fine. I've been very busy with my classes and with my thesis. How are you?"

"I'm okay. I will be graduating from acting school by the end of this summer and will return to Colombia, where I plan to audition for Latin American soaps. Colombian soap operas are now very popular in Central and South American countries and also in the United States."

"I know there's an English version of *Betty, la fea* being shown in the U.S. The reason I called was to ask you if you know of a character supply store for actors in Boston. I'm interested in costumes as worn during the time of Jesus."

"Are you auditioning for a play?" Marisol asked.

"Oh, no. My friend is researching the styles of clothes the ancients wore in the Holy Land during the biblical days," Martha said, after she laughed.

"There's a store in the theater district on Boylston Street in Boston. I can't recall the name of the shop, but I'm sure you'll find what you're looking for there. How soon do you need a costume?"

"By Saturday."

"I can definitely get you something down here in New York City. We have many theater supply shops on Broadway."

"Thanks, Marisol. I'll try your suggestion first, and if I can't find a store, you'll be hearing from me. Love you, besos, adios," and then Martha ended the call.

"Marisol thinks we can find something on Boylston Street," Martha said to Brian.

"Let's research the styles during the time of Jesus. We wouldn't want to start a new fashion trend."

"I know. It would be embarrassing. Imagine what could happen to us while trying to explain where we got our clothes."

Luke sat in the passenger seat of David's car, a 2010 black four-door Buick LaCrosse, as they drove to the Salem State University library, which was a short drive from David's home. David parked his car on the campus, and they entered the library and went directly to the reference desk, where David showed his M.I.T. credentials. "Hi, Professor Solomon. I haven't seen you here in weeks," Mary, the librarian, said.

"Hi, Mary. I know. I've been busy lately."

"Who's this young man with you?" Mary asked, smiling.

"This is Luke, my son. Luke, say hi to Mary."

Luke bashfully said, "Hi. I'm with my dad."

"I can see that. How old are you?"

"I'm fourteen, almost fifteen."

"You look like you're sixteen. Professor Solomon, if you need anything, please see me."

"Thank you, Mary. It was nice seeing you again. Oh, Mary, where can I find literature on ancient customs and traditions such as dress styles, food, religions and cultures of primarily Middle Eastern countries?"

Mary went to the computer on the reference desk and entered David's request. She said, "The material you're interested in is on the second floor, east side, near the religious books section. Do you need me to show you where those books are shelved?"

"No, thank you. I should be able to find my way. Thanks again for your help."

"You're welcome," she said with a smile.

Brian and Martha were in Harvard's library when Brian said, "Martha, let's ask the librarian where we can find books on ancient dress styles," and then they went to the reference desk and saw the librarian who had helped them before.

"Hi. You look familiar. How can I help you?" the librarian said.

"You showed us where we could find information about world museums," Martha said.

"Yes, now I remember. Did you find what you were looking for?"

"Yes, thank you. Now we're searching for information concerning ancient dress styles and the materials used to make clothing during the first century AD," Martha said.

"You'll find that information on two floors. On the fourth floor, there's a collection of books on ancient cultures, and on the second floor, you will find literature about fabrics. I'll show you. Please follow me," and the librarian led them to the information about old cultures on the fourth floor. Gesturing toward a section on the bookshelf, she said, "This area has books about world civilizations and their cultures. I'll now show you where you can find literature on ancient fabrics. Please follow me." The librarian escorted them to a section of books on the second floor, and there the librarian said, "These books are about fabrics and textiles."

"This looks like a good place to start, and there are fewer books here," Brian said.

"If I can be of further help, please visit me on the first floor. I hope you find the information you're seeking."

"Thanks again. You were very helpful," Martha said.

David and Luke were on the second floor, walking along the aisles and reading the category labels identifying the literature on the shelves, when Luke said, "Dad, this title says religion."

"Good job, kiddo. I missed that one. The information we're looking for should be in this area, according to Mary."

"Dad, what kind of books are you looking for?"

"I'll know when I see them." David located an area of books that caught his eye, and he began sliding his index finger along each book hoping to find a title of interest.

Brian and Martha were searching for books on ancient fabrics when Brian said, "We should definitely find something here."

"Imagine our being sent to the Holy Land in formal wear—you're in a suit and tie, and I'm wearing a gown," Martha said with a smile.

"The people would want to know who our tailor is," Brian said, also with a smile.

"We could start our own fashion shop called Martha and Brian's formal dress," Martha said with a laugh.

Brian, looking at a section of books, said, "I found one. The title is *Fabrics of the Ancients in the Time of Jesus.*" He removed it from the shelf and placed it onto a table near the bookshelf. He then began flipping the pages and saw a section that explained the type of fabrics used in the time of Jesus with illustrations of the dress styles.

David took a book from the shelf titled *Everyday Life in the Time of Jesus* and noticed a volume of books that were titled *Antiquities of the Jews,* which was written in AD 94 by Josephus, a first-century Jewish historian.

The name Flavius Josephus, as he was referred to after becoming a Roman citizen in AD 71, was because Flavius Vespasian and his son Titus captured him and made him a prisoner in AD 67. Josephus was released from prison in AD 69 and eventually was taken to Rome, where he did all his writing. The twenty volumes frequently mention the history, laws, culture and traditions of the Jewish people from the beginning of creation to the twelfth year of Nero's rule in AD 66.

David pulled volumes fourteen through sixteen from the shelf, which mention Herod the Great, and set the books down onto a nearby table with chairs. He returned to the area from where he just removed the texts and began searching for literature by Rabbi Yehudah HaNasi, who was also known as Judah the Prince. The book he was looking for was titled *The Mishnah* and was compiled in the second century AD. *The Mishnah* consists of sixty-three volumes and describes six major topics concerning the everyday life of Jews during the first century AD. He hoped to locate a book that was a condensed version of the book, but could not.

"Luke, I found what we're searching for. I'll skim through a few books to find what we need. I would like you to research the money being exchanged during the time of Jesus." David knew the shekel was the most common coin used at that time, but wanted to give Luke something to do so he wouldn't get bored.

"Okay. Where do I start?" Luke asked enthusiastically.

"With Mary at the reference desk. I'll be reading, and when you have found a book, please bring it here so we can both review it," David answered, and then Luke left to find Mary on the first floor.

Luke was in line at the reference desk waiting to ask Mary his question. When it was his turn, Mary said, "Hi, Luke. How can I help you?"

"I'm looking for a book with information about money used in ancient times."

"Let me guess. You're interested in the currency being exchanged by people during the time of Jesus."

"Yes. Do you know where I can find a book?"

"I'll check my database. Hmmm. Here's one that seems promising. The book's title is *Ancient Coins of the Middle East*, and it's on the second floor near the section about religion."

"I can find it. I found the religious books section for my dad," Luke said.

"Good for you. If you need my help, you know where you can find me," Mary replied with a smile.

Luke returned to the second floor and went to David. He said, "Dad, the information we want is in this area. I'll try to locate it."

"Good luck, kiddo. The book I'm reading is very helpful. When you find one about ancient money, bring it here."

"Will do, Dad," Luke said, and he walked three rows from where David was sitting and began searching until he found the book titled *Ancient Coins of the Middle East* and removed it from the shelf. He opened it and saw photographs of old coins discovered during archeological excavations. After Luke brought the book to the table and set it down, David said, "That was quick work. Let me have a look at what you've found," and then he began looking for a section in the book for coins dating to the first century that were used to pay for goods and services.

"There they are," David said, as he pointed to a photograph of a gold and silver shekel, and then said, "These are the coins that were frequently exchanged during the time of Jesus. The Greek silver drachma and the Roman silver denarius were also common coins exchanged in that time period."

Brian and Martha were on the second floor of the library and had completed their research on fabrics. The fabrics used in the time of Jesus were wool, cotton, goat and camel hair, and silk made from a plant called flax. The ancients would also make dyes from animals, plants and vegetables for coloring their clothes.

"Let's go and search for the styles of dress that were worn in those days," Brian said. They went to the fourth floor to where the librarian had taken them earlier and began searching for clothing styles in ancient times. They each found a book and started looking for the dress styles of biblical days.

"Women wore a loincloth under their tunic, a mantle and a braided belt with tassels that was tied around their waist. The women also used sandals for footwear and a piece of cloth to wrap their hair in or to mask their face, and if the weather was cold they would wrap themselves in a shawl or blanket. They wore jewelry, and their clothing was more colorful than men's. They had to cover their arms and legs," Martha said.

"The men dressed the same, but with less color. Men would wear jewelry around their necks and rings on their fingers and used wool cloaks. We should make photocopies to use as a reference when selecting our clothes. We need to be stylish and wear the fashion of the day," Brian said, smiling.

"Good point. I don't have a thing to wear," Martha said with a laugh.

"If we don't find something, we can call your friend Marisol, and hopefully she can send us clothes."

"It might be better to have clothing made by a tailor. All we would need is a pattern design and the wool material. It shouldn't take long to make our clothes. They're basically robes and nightgowns," Martha replied.

"You're right. Let's go and make our photocopies on the first floor, and afterward we can ask the librarian where we can find ancient clothing patterns."

They carried their books to the elevator. When it arrived, they headed for the first floor. When the elevator doors opened, Brian and Martha headed to the photocopier. After making their photocopies, they placed the books in a bin to be filed and went to the librarian's desk.

"Hello again. How can I help you?" the librarian asked.

"I'm looking for a book on wardrobe patterns during the first century," Martha answered.

The librarian went to her computer and entered Martha's request. After looking at the search results, the librarian said, "You're in luck. The books about world patterns are on this floor. I'll take you to them," and then the librarian showed them to a room having information on dress styles from ancient to modern civilizations.

"Thank you again. You were very helpful," Martha said.

"If you need further assistance, please see me," the librarian said.

Martha removed the binder that had first-century patterns from the shelf and set it onto a table in the center of the room. "For backup, you and I will need to select a pattern and make a photocopy of it," she said, turning the pages.

"Hmm. What style goes with your pretty hair and eyes?" Brian said.

"Let me see. We need a style to enhance your sexy ankles. I hope your ankles won't turn the girls on," Martha said.

After making photocopies of their selections, Martha placed them into her purse, and they exited the library for the theater district on Boylston Street to find a shop selling or renting biblical clothing.

In the Salem State University library David and Luke were discussing what they had just learned. Luke asked, "Dad, what will Martha and Brian use for money? They don't have ancient coins."

"They'll use the international currency of the world."

"What's that?"

"Gold. Brian and Martha will take pieces of gold with them and trade them for coins to pay for the things they need."

"For silver shekels. Am I right?"

"Yes, of course, for silver shekels," David said, smiling.

"Dad, do you think we could have found the same information on the Internet?"

"I don't know, but we just learned what the people during the time of Jesus used for money. We need to file these books before we leave. We don't want Mary to think we're lazy," David said as he smiled at Luke. After Luke returned the books to the shelf, they left the library for home.

Brian and Martha were walking on Boylston Street in the theater district in Boston looking for a costume supply store. While walking,

Martha noticed a theater supply shop across the street with a sign in the window advertising for props and costumes. She said, "Brian, look, there's a shop on the other side of this street."

Crossing the street, they stood in front of the shop looking at the posters of past theater performances such as the *Phantom of the Opera*, *Les Misérables, Fiddler on the Roof* and more. Also in the window were mannequins dressed in costumes for the renaissance period. "This shop seems promising," Brian said.

When Brian and Martha entered the shop, they saw many props and mannequins wearing clothing depicting various historical periods. The mannequins were dressed in themes representing the Colonial days, medieval times, ancient Romans, Greeks and more. Brian went to the mannequin dressed as a gladiator and was admiring the costume when the shopkeeper approached him. The gentleman was wearing a gray suit and red tie, and he said, "I see you like this costume. It would look good on you."

"Thanks, but we're interested in a costume typical of the time of Jesus."

"The costumes for the nativity scene are stored in the basement because that theme has passed. The clothes being displayed are requested throughout the year."

Brian asked Martha for the photocopies in her purse, and she gave them to him. "Thanks, Martha," he said after receiving the copies. Brian then turned to the shopkeeper and showed him the photocopies, saying, "Sir, we are interested in these styles of ancient tunics and mantles. Do you have them to rent?"

"Yes, but as I said, the clothing is packed in boxes and stored in the basement."

Brian, pointing at the photocopies, said, "We would like to buy these two styles."

"The costumes are not for sale, only for rent."

"How much is it to rent them monthly?"

The shopkeeper answered, "Each costume will cost seven hundred dollars per month."

"Please bring them up from storage so we can try them on," Martha said.

"I must search for them in the basement, and that will take time."

"Fine. We'll come back. Is there a coffee shop nearby?" she asked.

"Yes. Two blocks down on this side of the street."

"Thank you. We'll return in a half hour," Martha said. Brian and Martha left the shop for a cup of coffee while the shopkeeper went to retrieve the costumes.

David was in his lab using the PC to search the Internet for additional information on everyday life during the time of Jesus. He entered his search phrase for biblical caves and found a link to a story titled "Cave in Israel Linked to John the Baptist." David became curious and clicked on the link taking him to the article. After reading the story, he sat back in his chair and thought, "We now have an arrival site for Brian and Martha." David believed that if they located John the Baptist, the cousin of Jesus, he could lead them to Jesus or tell them where they would find him. His mind was racing with excitement because a historical site had been discovered dating to the time of Jesus. He printed the article for Martha and Brian to read.

When Brian and Martha returned to the theater supply shop, they saw the shopkeeper in the back of the store taking costumes out of boxes. They went to the shopkeeper, who gave Brian a manila folder and said, "This folder contains photographs of models wearing our biblical clothing."

Brian opened the folder and said, "Martha, look, this style for men is exactly like the photocopy," and after turning a few more pages he said, "The style for women is also the same."

"These costumes are authentic styles worn at the time of Jesus. I'm sure you understand theaters are profitable only if they sell tickets," the shopkeeper said, and then asked, "How long do you plan to rent them?"

"One month," Brian replied.

"Fine. That will be fourteen hundred dollars for both costumes, and I'll throw in the accessories for free, sandals, belts, head scarves and robes, etc. I usually charge twenty-five dollars per month for each costume's accessories, but since you're renting two costumes for a month, there'll be no extra charge."

"Can we try them on?" Brian then asked.

"Sure. We have dressing rooms in the back of the store. Please follow me," the shopkeeper answered. Brian and Martha followed him. At the dressing rooms, he gave them their garments to try on. They entered their rooms and after a short time Brian and Martha came out wearing their costumes. Martha's tunic was white and her wool mantle was a turquoise blue. Brian's tunic was a dirty white, and his mantle was a sandy color.

"It appears the clothes are a little loose on you both, but don't worry. We have a tailor who works for the shop. I'll drop off the costumes today, and they should be ready by 3 p.m. tomorrow," the shopkeeper said.

The shopkeeper used yellow chalk to mark the areas on the garments that needed adjustments, and when he was done Brian and Martha returned to the dressing rooms and changed back into their clothes. After coming out of their rooms, they gave the man their costumes and Martha said, "We'll see you tomorrow afternoon," and they left the shop.

CHAPTER 14

It was 3 p.m. the next day when Brian and Martha entered the theater supply shop. The shopkeeper greeted them and said, "Your garments are ready. Please come with me so you can try them on."

When they were at the dressing rooms, the shopkeeper gave Brian and Martha their clothing, and then they entered their rooms to try on their garments. After they came out of the rooms, Brian and Martha were modeling their costumes for each other.

"You both look like a couple from the time of Jesus," the shopkeeper said.

"Sir, you made my day," Brian said with a smile.

Martha was smiling too and said, "These costumes are perfect. We'll take them. Brian, please pay the gentleman."

After Martha and Brian changed their clothes, they handed the costumes to the shopkeeper who then put the garments and accessories into boxes. The shopkeeper said, "Please follow me to the cash register," and at the register the man said, "That will be fourteen hundred dollars, please."

Brian gave him his credit card and the transaction was completed.

"Thank you for your business. I'll see you in thirty days," the shopkeeper said after giving Brian back his credit card.

After leaving the theater shop with their costumes, Martha called Marisol to tell her that she had found the costumes she needed and thanked her again for the suggestion.

"Martha, can I use your cell phone? I'd like to call Professor Solomon to tell him that we have our wardrobe," Brian said after she was done talking with Marisol.

Martha gave Brian her phone and he called David. He answered, "Hello. David here."

"Hi, Professor. Brian here. I'm with Martha on Boylston Street. We're in the theater district. We just left a theater supply shop with two authentic-looking costumes, including accessories. It's 4:30 now. Will you be home? We want to model our garments for you and get your opinion."

"I'll be here. Please come by."

"Okay, we're on our way." After returning Martha's cell phone, he said, "Thank you. Professor Solomon is expecting us," and then they went to Brian's car and put their boxes into the trunk and drove to David's house.

When Brian and Martha arrived at David's home, Brian knocked on the front door. David was in his library and hollered, "I'll get it." Opening the door, he said, "Hi, Martha. Hi, Brian. Please come in. We'll go to my study where we can chat."

Luke came down the stairs, entered the library and sat in the chair at the desk and said, "Brian, you grew a beard fast."

"Yes, I know. I could pass as a hippie, and if I were wearing sunglasses, you might not recognize me."

"Hi, Martha. His beard must tickle your nose when you kiss," Luke said.

"No, not really. I just sneeze a lot. I prefer him without hair on his face. He's more handsome," Martha said, smiling.

"Hey, handsome. Please sit so we can brief each other on what we've accomplished since our last meeting," David said.

Martha and Brian were sitting on the sofa, each with a box resting on their lap that contained their costumes. "Professor, we have our clothes," Brian said, and then he opened his box and removed the garment, and so did Martha. Brian and Martha stood and placed their garments against the front of their bodies, and he asked, "Do you have a room where we can change into these costumes?"

"Yes. Luke, show Martha where the spare bedroom is, and Brian can use your room," David answered.

Luke led them upstairs and showed them to their rooms. Then he said, "I'll be in the library with Dad."

Brian and Martha entered their rooms and changed clothing. Afterward, they appeared in the library wearing their tunics and mantles. Martha was wearing a white tunic and a turquoise blue wool mantle with a braided brown wool belt around her waist with tassels and a light tan shawl covering her head. Brian wore a dirty white-colored tunic and a sandy-colored mantle with a tan wool belt tied around his waist. They both wore tan-colored sandals.

Luke was standing next to David and said, "Wow, you guys look like the people from the Bible, just like in the Christian movies."

"The shopkeeper who rented us these costumes said they were authentic dress styles and that actors and actresses rent them to play the roles of people during biblical days," Martha said.

"I agree with Luke. You both will have no problem blending into the population," David said.

Brian and Martha stood in the center of the library and slowly turned around so David and Luke could view their clothes from all angles. David said, "Good work. You look as though you are from that time period. Please have a seat. Today, Luke and I visited the library at Salem State University to research the everyday life of the people during the time of Jesus."

"I know the money they used in those days. It was the silver shekel," Luke said.

"Luke was helpful today," David said with a smile.

David, who was still standing, went to the leather chair and sat next to the sofa where Brian and Martha were now sitting while Luke sat in the desk chair. David said, "Luke and I have some facts we would like to share with you. The people ate bread, berries, chicken, eggs, figs, fruits, vegetables, grains, fish, beef, goat and mutton. Jewish people were forbidden to eat meat from animals with split hoofs such as pigs."

"I guess BBQ pork will not be on the menu. Professor, do you think the water will be safe to drink?" Brian asked.

"Yes, their drinking water came from underground wells, but you should prefer beverages made from boiled water such as tea so you don't risk being infected with cholera. The people who lived in the desert used tents made of goat hair. They also lived in small stone-walled homes with wood or dirt floors that had a flat roof, and the poor used caves for shelter. The main occupations were shepherds, farmers, fishermen, craftsmen and begging. The clothes worn at that time were basically the same for men and women. They wore a loin cloth under their tunic and a mantle over the tunic and wore a belt around their waist and sandals on their feet. The people observed the Sabbath, a day of rest, on the seventh day, which starts on Friday at sunset and lasts until Saturday at sunset. The Jews celebrate their freedom from slavery in Egypt during April, and the Exodus was led by Moses. It's called Passover and it's most celebrated. The coins commonly used to pay for goods and services were the Jewish silver shekel, the Greek silver drachma and the Roman silver denarius."

"How will we pay for food or a place to sleep? Shekels, drachmas and denarii are in museums or owned by coin collectors," Brian asked.

"I'm glad you asked that question. Martha and you will use the international world currency. Luke, what is that?"

"It's gold."

"Very good, Luke. You'll bring pieces of gold jewelry to pay for the things you'll need."

"Wouldn't it be dangerous to carry gold with us when most people were poor in those days and bandits roamed freely? We would definitely be robbed and possibly killed," Martha said.

"I considered that possibility and came up with a solution. You and Brian will need to have pockets with zippers sewn into the underside of your mantles that will be used to hide and store your gold and some dried foods."

"I'll bring gold necklaces and earrings," Martha said.

"I can donate a few gold chains to take with us," Brian said.

"I have two chains that you can sell," David said.

"Professor, when we're done here, we'll stop at a fabric store to buy the material for making pockets with zippers. I'm sure we can find a seamstress on the way home," Martha said.

After David had finished with some facts of everyday life during the time of Jesus, he said, "I have a plan to find Jesus in a matter of days instead of weeks. As I was searching the Internet for more information about Jewish life in the first century AD, I discovered a link to an article titled 'Cave of John the Baptist found.'"

David then gave Brian and Martha a copy of the story and said, "When you both have time, please read the article. It's very informative and could be helpful. We now have the coordinates for your arrival, and hopefully John the Baptist will be there or nearby. He will be your first lead in finding Jesus. If John is not at the cave, he most likely will be at the Jordan River baptizing. The people in the first century didn't have a surname, so they addressed each other by their given name, then by family members or by occupation. For example, after you arrive at John the Baptist's cave, if he is there, you will ask him this question: Are you John the son of Zechariah, a priest, and your mother is Elizabeth, the cousin of Mary from Nazareth? After he has replied yes, you will then ask: Do you know where I can find Jesus from Nazareth, the son of Joseph the carpenter and whose mother is Mary, the cousin of your mother?"

"I understand how to use a phrase to find people. It shouldn't be that difficult," Brian said.

"The only loose ends remaining are the pockets to be sewn inside your mantles and gathering up the gold jewelry." David stood from his chair and said, "I would like to take you both and Luke to a Middle Eastern restaurant in downtown Boston on Massachusetts Avenue named Scheherazade's. I'll make the reservations for tonight at 9. Consider it a bon voyage dinner party before your trip."

"That sounds wonderful, Professor," Martha said.

"We'll meet you there, but now we must change our clothing and find a fabric store and seamstress," Brian said.

After Brian and Martha changed their clothes, they said bye to David and Luke and then left with their mantles. While driving in Salem, Martha saw a handcraft store and said, "Look, there's a store selling fabric. Let's go and check out the colors and materials."

They entered the store and found the textile section and located the exact color of the fabric for their mantles. Martha took two rolls of the fabric and went to the checkout counter, where a store clerk was helping customers. When it was Martha's turn for service, she set the materials onto the counter and said, "Hi. I need one piece of cloth of each color to make two pockets with zippers for two garments."

"How much material do you need?" the clerk asked.

"I would like one square foot of both fabrics," Martha answered.

After the material was cut, the clerk asked, "Is there anything else?"

"Yes. I want to buy these four zippers. Does this store provide a sewing service?" Martha asked.

"We have a seamstress for our customers. She works in the back of the store. Do you want me to get her?" the clerk asked.

"Yes, please," Martha replied.

The clerk left the counter and quickly returned to the checkout counter with the seamstress. The woman asked, "How can I help you?"

"Hi. We would like two pockets with zippers sewn onto the underside of each garment," Martha answered.

"Do you have the garments with you?" the woman asked.

"I'll go and get them," Brian said, and then he left the store for the mantles and quickly returned and gave them to Martha.

"We need two pockets, six inches by six inches, sewn on the inside of these two garments," Martha then said.

"That shouldn't be a problem. I'll have them ready by 10 tomorrow morning," the seamstress said.

"Thank you. That will be fine," Martha said, and then she paid the clerk.

It was 8:45 p.m. when David and Luke entered the Middle Eastern restaurant in downtown Boston. David approached the hostess and said, "Hi. I made reservations for a party of four for 9 in the name of David Solomon."

After the hostess reviewed the reservation list, she said, "Yes. Here's your name. Please follow me." David and Luke followed her to their dinner table, which was in front of the dance floor. The hostess said, "Please have a seat. The show will start in one hour."

"What show?" David asked.

"Tonight there will be belly dancers performing from 10 to 11," she answered.

"Thank you," David said.

"Enjoy your dinner and the show," the hostess said.

Brian and Martha entered Scheherazade's and went to the hostess. Brian said, "Hi. Do you have reservations for a party of four, made by David Solomon?"

"Oh, yes. I just seated him and a boy. Please follow me." She escorted Brian and Martha to the dinner table where David and Luke were waiting for them.

At the table, Martha said to the hostess, "Thank you." They sat next to each other facing Luke and David across the table. After Martha looked around the interior of the restaurant, she said, "Professor, this is a beautiful place. The décor is truly Middle Eastern."

On the walls, there were paintings of nomads in the desert riding on camels, ancient Persian palaces and sheiks receiving gifts, to name just a few. In the restaurant were small Aladdin-type oil lamps lit on the walls that provided light between the oil paintings of flora and fauna. The restaurant had a red carpet with gold-colored designs of date trees, tents, camels and elephants woven into the rug and a polished wood dance floor. The floor had randomly placed large genie lamps and woven reed snake baskets with a flute leaning against each basket.

"I'm pleased you like it. There will be a belly dancing show tonight at 10," David said.

"That should be fun," Martha replied.

"I would rather watch a snake charmer use his flute to make a cobra dance," Luke said.

"Dude, we're sitting too close to the dance floor. Imagine if the snake decided to make a break for it. I wouldn't want to be rushed to a hospital because of a cobra bite," Brian said.

The waiter came to the table and took their orders. David requested the grilled lamb dinner and falafel as an appetizer. Luke and Martha asked for the lamb shish kabobs with lentil soup. Brian ordered beef shish kabobs and a Middle Eastern salad. When the server left, Martha said, "Professor, tomorrow morning we'll pick up our mantles with the pockets and zippers sewn into them."

"Great. After picking up your garments, you and Brian should come to my house."

"We brought the gold jewelry that we'll take with us," Brian said, and he removed from his shirt pocket three fourteen karat gold necklace chains and set them down onto the dinner table. Martha removed from her purse two sets of earrings and three necklaces, also made of solid gold and which weighed fourteen karats each, and placed them onto the table too.

David picked up each piece of jewelry and quickly examined them. He said, "They look fine. You shouldn't have a problem exchanging them for shekels. I have two gold wrist chains you can have. I'm sure you can sell the two chains for close to twenty-six silver shekels each. I'll use a digital scale in my basement lab to break up some of this gold jewelry into ounces."

David put the jewelry into the inside pocket of his sport coat as the waiter arrived with their meals. The server set their entrées and appetizers in front of them and poured hot tea into their cups and said, "Enjoy!" He then asked, "Do you need anything else?"

"We're fine for now, thank you," David said, after looking at everyone.

After finishing their meal, the waiter returned to clean the table. After he removed their dinner plates, he said, "The show will start in a few minutes."

The ceiling lights became dimmer as the dance floor lights got brighter. The belly dancing music began playing over the speakers. Two women dressed as belly dancers with veils covering their faces came onto the floor and started dancing with finger cymbals on their thumbs and middle fingers. The dancers were shaking their hips and moving their arms in a rhythmic motion, just like in movies when a sheik is being entertained in the Arabian Desert. During the middle of the show, one belly dancer began gesturing with her arms and hands toward Martha for her to join them, and Luke said, "Martha, she wants to dance with you."

"Go ahead. You can consider this practice. You might have to entertain a sheik next week," Brian said with a smile.

Martha smiled at Brian and stood and took the belly dancer's hand. The audience began clapping. Martha was now on the floor between the two dancers and was mimicking their hip and hand movements. It appeared as though she had belly danced before. She caught on quickly and the audience was clapping again. She was enjoying herself and then the belly dancers escorted Martha back to her seat and the diners began clapping once more. When the dancers finished their performance, they left the floor.

When the show ended, David said, "Luke and I must leave now. It's past his bedtime. We'll see you tomorrow."

"Martha, that was the best dance show I've ever seen. You could be a belly dancer instead of a scientist," Luke said.

"That's sweet of you to say, but I prefer to be a scientist rather than a professional belly dancer."

"We should leave too. We have a big day tomorrow," Brian said, and then they left the restaurant. When they were outside, they said goodnight to each other before going home.

CHAPTER 15

David was in his basement lab weighing the gold jewelry using a digital scale on the counter next to the sink. He divided the jewelry into one ounce and one-half ounce pieces. The total weight of the gold Brian and Martha would take was eleven and one-half troy ounces, consisting of twelve pieces. One troy ounce of gold equals 31.10 grams. David estimated that Brian and Martha should receive close to 95 silver shekels based on a silver shekel weighing 11 grams. He also considered the money changer's profit.

After David had finished weighing and dividing the gold, he went to the PC in the lab to search for the coordinates of John the Baptist's cave. The location of the cave was outside Jerusalem, Judea, and he found the cave's longitude, 35.1195, and latitude, 31.7843, the arrival site for Brian and Martha. He knew they most likely would have to travel from that location to find John the Baptist, and the only way he would know if they found Jesus or wanted to be transported home is if they reached one of the designated departure sites.

David thought that if John the Baptist was not at the cave, Martha and Brian would have to journey to the Jordan River where he performed baptisms. They would have to make their way to the river from Jerusalem traveling on the Jericho road to the city of Jericho.

According to the Old Testament, Jericho was the first city conquered by Joshua, in 1440 BC. The Bible states that God spoke to Joshua telling him to march his army around the city for six days with seven priests carrying rams' horns. On the seventh day, Joshua was to order his army to march seven times around Jericho, and the priests were to blow their horns. After Joshua's army marched for the seventh time around the walls of Jericho, the priests sounded their rams' horns and Joshua ordered his army to shout. The city walls collapsed and his army completely destroyed Jericho and killed every occupant.

If John the Baptist was not found along the Jordan River near Jericho, they would have to continue north in the direction of the Sea of Galilee. When Brian and Martha arrived today, David would explain his logic on how to find John and then Jesus.

Luke went to the lab and saw the lights on in the room housing the time machine. After entering, he saw David writing on the chalkboard below his equation and said, "Hi, Dad. What are you doing?"

"I'm drawing a map of the Jordan River Valley" and, using the chalk in his right hand as a pointer, David said, "This body of water to the north is the Sea of Galilee. This pool to the south is the Dead Sea, and the squiggle line connecting both seas represents the Jordan River. The area on each side of the river is called the Jordan Valley."

David made a small circle on the left side of the Jordan River near the intersecting point and slightly north of where the Dead Sea and the river meet. After making the circle, he said, "This is the city of Jericho." He drew two smaller circles and a larger one and then David said, "This bigger circle represents Jerusalem. The two little circles to the east of Jerusalem represent the villages of Bethphage and Bethany."

David made an X on the chalkboard to the southwest of and very close to Jerusalem, and then he said, "This is the spot that Brian and Martha will be transported to, near the village of Ein Kerem, where John the Baptist was born."

"What will they do if he's not there?" Luke asked.

"They'll travel to the Jordan River using the old Roman military road known as the Jericho Road that was a heavily traveled road connecting Jerusalem to Jericho. The river is four miles beyond the city of Jericho, and to the east is the village of Bethany in Jordan, where John performed baptisms," David answered.

David drew another small circle on the chalkboard to identify where Bethany was located, and then he added more ancient villages to the map on the western shore of the river north of Jericho and continued to the Sea of Galilee. When David was finished, he said, "We should go to the store to buy a few food items for Martha and

Brian to take with them." He turned off the lights in the lab, and they left for the local grocery store.

Brian and Martha entered the handicraft store to pick up their mantles and approached the clerk at the service counter for assistance. "Hi. Can I help you?" the store clerk said.

"Yes. We left two garments here yesterday to have pockets sewn into them, and they are supposed to be ready this morning for pickup," Martha replied.

"May I see your sales receipt?" the clerk asked.

Martha handed the employee the receipt, and after the clerk checked it, she said, "I'll be back in a minute." She went to the rear of the store and entered a room. After a few minutes, the clerk appeared with the seamstress, who was carrying the garments, and set them down onto the service counter. The dressmaker turned the mantles inside out so Martha could review her work and then said, "I have made the pockets with zippers as you requested."

Martha checked the seamstress's work by putting her hand into each pocket and making sure the seams were completely stitched and the zippers worked properly. After testing the quality of the work, she said, "Perfect. You did an excellent job. Thank you."

"You're welcome. Please come by again," the seamstress said, and then they left the store for David's home.

David and Luke were in the supermarket when Luke asked, "Dad, what kind of food are we shopping for?"

"Dried, unwrapped food products that will not spoil such as fruits, meats and vegetables. We'll buy a few items in small quantity to last Brian and Martha for a couple of days, which should give them enough time to exchange their gold for shekels."

"I see dried food products near the deli section," Luke said as they were walking in the grocery store.

"That's a good observation, kiddo. We'll buy some dried banana chips, raisins, figs, apricots, beef jerky and tomatoes," David said while they walked toward the deli. After shopping, David paid for the groceries and drove home. When he and Luke approached their house, they noticed Brian's car parked in front.

Martha and Brian had put their mantles onto the sofa in the library and were in the room that contained David's time machine, admiring the sophistication of the equipment. Martha looked away from the machine and then at the chalkboard and said, "Professor Solomon has drawn a map below his equation. It looks like a map of Judea. There's Jerusalem, the Dead Sea, Sea of Galilee, Jordan River and all these ancient villages."

"Yes, it's a diagram of where the villages are located," Brian said.

David and Luke entered their home through the front door, each carrying a bag of groceries, and went to the kitchen and set the bags down onto the counter.

"Brian and Martha must be in the lab. Let's go say hi," David said, and they went to the lab and entered the room housing StellaPort and saw Martha and Brian talking in front of the chalkboard.

"Hi. How are things going today?" David asked.

"Fine, Professor," Brian answered.

"Luke and I returned from the grocery store. We bought some dried food for your trip," David said.

"Hi, Professor. I see that you've drawn a map of the Middle East on the chalkboard," Martha said.

"Yes, I'll explain later today. Did you pick up your garments?" David asked.

"Yes, they're in the library on the sofa. We arrived about ten minutes ago, and you and Luke were not home, so we went to the lab to look at your time machine," Martha replied.

"We must formulate a plan to increase the odds of finding John the Baptist and then Jesus. Please come with me to my library where we can develop a plan," David said.

As David was leading the way, he stopped at the counter where he had weighed the gold jewelry and said, "Luke, please collect and bring the jewelry with you and set it on the desk in the library." Luke got the jewelry as David, Martha and Brian left the lab.

In the study, David asked everyone to sit. Brian and Martha sat on the sofa with their garments on their laps. Luke entered the library holding the gold in his hand and sat at the desk while David sat in the leather chair next to Martha and Brian.

"I have a plan to increase the odds of finding John the Baptist and Jesus in a matter of days, not weeks. First, I know the longitude and latitude of the cave used by John, and it's located two and a half miles from Jerusalem. The cave's location will be your arrival site and also will be one of the departure sites. Please keep in mind that Stella will be constantly tracking your coordinates as you move about in the Middle East. After you find Jesus, you must bring him to the cave or to the Damascus gate named Kisan, which is another departure site. I'll be monitoring the tracking display window on Stella, and when I see longitude 35.1195 and latitude 31.7843 for the cave or the longitude of 36.3152 and the latitude of 33.5063 for the gate, I'll know you are ready to be transported," David said, and then he leaned forward in his chair and said, "If John the Baptist is not at the cave, you must travel to the Jordan River and try to locate him there. But first you will need to go into Jerusalem and exchange some of your gold jewelry for silver shekels before starting your journey."

David sat back in his chair and then continued, "After bargaining for shekels, you'll have to purchase supplies such as flasks to hold water to drink, fruits, meat and any other things you need. After buying your supplies, you must find the road that leads to Jericho and, along the way, there are two small villages named Bethphage and Bethany, and then Jericho. The distance between Jerusalem and Jericho is seventeen miles, a one day's journey on foot. The New Testament mentions the village of Bethany as the home of Jesus' special friends Lazarus, Mary and Martha. The Gospels say Lazarus fell seriously ill and his sisters sent for Jesus. By the time Jesus arrived, Lazarus had died and was buried for four days prior to when Jesus raised him from the dead. At Jericho, you should stock up on supplies and get a good night's rest because the next day you must travel east and cross the Jordan River to the village of Bethany on the west side of the Jordan River, where the Gospels mention John baptizing. The distance from Jericho to the river is four miles and then it's a short trip to Bethany."

"Professor, what if we can't find John the Baptist? Then what?" Brian asked.

"You'll have to journey north toward the Sea of Galilee. Jesus spent much of his life in the Galilee area, where Nazareth and his favorite village of Capernaum were located. Capernaum became Jesus' base for his ministry after he was rejected in Nazareth and is where four of his apostles—Peter, Andrew, James and John—were from. Mary Magdalene also lived in the region and was from the village of Magdala on the western shores of the Sea of Galilee."

"Dad, how will Brian and Martha get there?" Luke asked while fidgeting in his chair.

"Capernaum is on the north shore of the Sea of Galilee from the mouth of the Jordan River. They can choose walking, horse, donkey, camel or boat."

"I'd choose by boat," Luke said.

"That's sound cool, dude, but we'll make the call after evaluating our options, if and when we get to that point," Brian replied.

"Keep in mind that you are searching for Jesus in a time before he started his ministry and toward the end of his missing years. My gut feeling is that if he is not in Capernaum, he will be found in Nazareth working with his father, Joseph, as a carpenter. If I'm wrong, then I would assume he's on a caravan route north of the Sea of Galilee, returning to his home village of Nazareth. The scriptures start mentioning Jesus again at the age of twenty-seven, traveling from Nazareth to the Jordan River to be baptized by John," David said.

"Professor, he could be anywhere north of the Sea of Galilee. Some scholars believe he was in India," Martha said.

"Jesus did not speak India's language of Hindi or recite Hindu scriptures from the Shruti or Smriti texts during his ministry."

"Are there any hints that would indicate he was still in the Middle East?" Brian asked.

David leaned to the right in his chair and said, "The only clues to find Jesus will be the questions you ask people who are close to him."

The room was quiet for a moment because they were thinking about where Jesus might be during the missing years and the direction he could be coming from when returning to Nazareth.

"Dad, Jesus is too young at 13 to be traveling alone. He would need an adult with him," Luke said.

"Good point, kiddo. I agree, but which adult or adults?" David asked.

"Professor, you might be onto something. It's possible Jesus was still in Nazareth working as a carpenter with his father. The writers of the New Testament just lost interest in him because Jesus was not the story. He had a daily routine that was ordinary for the people of that time," Martha said.

"Jesus and his immediate family could have moved to a distant village without telling his family and friends. The writers of the New Testament who were documenting his life did not follow him because they didn't know he had moved on. When Jesus and his family arrived at a village, the people would not know of him and would show no interest toward them. They just melted into the population," Brian said.

"That could also be a possibility, but which village? The scriptures speak only of his family moving to Egypt and returning to Judea, both times due to concerns about the safety of Jesus," David said.

"Professor, just as you said earlier, if Jesus is not in the Galilee area, he would be coming home to Nazareth traveling on a caravan route leading to Damascus. The Silk Road joins other roads that go through Egypt and the Middle East which connect to Damascus. There's a road east of the Jordan River connecting Damascus which traverses south to Egypt, and if Jesus traveled north on this road from Egypt to Nazareth, he could have been baptized on his way home. But when Jesus starts his ministry, the Gospels state, he traveled southeast from Nazareth to the Jordan River to be baptized by John," Brian said.

"Jesus might have been traveling from a location northeast of Damascus and moving in a southwest direction toward Nazareth. We could assume Jesus moved a long distance to return to Nazareth if he was passing through the area of the Jordan River where John was performing baptisms," Martha said.

"Let's go to the chalkboard in the lab and discuss the map I drew," David said. They all went to the lab. In front of the chalkboard, David removed a piece of chalk from the tray and pointed at the map below his equation. He said, "I will add more information based on what we just discussed in the library."

David, using the chalk in his right hand as a pointer, said, "This body of water to the north represents the Sea of Galilee. The water to the south is the Dead Sea, and the squiggle line connecting both seas is the Jordan River. The area on either side is called the Jordan Valley. This small circle where the Dead Sea and the river meet is the city Jericho. The X on the east side of the Jordan River is Bethany, where John performs baptisms. The two small circles west of Jericho are the villages of Bethany and Bethphage, and the larger circle is Jerusalem. The X southwest of Jerusalem is the place you both will be transported to. It's near the village of Ein Kerem, where John was born."

David was still pointing at the map with the chalk in his right hand as he said, "In this region in Galilee are the known places Jesus traveled, as written in the Gospels. The villages of Tiberias, Magdala, Capernaum, Bethsaida, Gergesa and Hippos are along the shore of the Sea of Galilee and to the southwest is Nazareth. The X north of the Sea of Galilee is Damascus and the line from Damascus going south past the Dead Sea and along the east side of the Jordan River is a caravan route. The road was a heavily traveled trade road, which continued west along the side of the river from Be'er Sheva in southern Judea to Damascus."

David was now pointing at the northeast area of the map, and he said, "Jesus would most likely be coming from this direction heading toward Nazareth to visit his mother, Mary. The best caravan route for him to take would be the one leading to Damascus and then travel on another route to Nazareth." David added another X to the map just to the southeast of Damascus, and he said, "The ideal location to meet Jesus will be here. There is one caravan road to the east that connects to the other routes."

"If or when we find Jesus on a road, we must persuade him to come with us to our time, and if he does, Damascus would be the closest departure site," Brian said.

"When you're at the Kisan Gate, it will signal that you are ready to be transported," David said, and then he drew an X on the map to indicate the location of the Kisan Gate.

"We now have an arrival and two departure sites," David said.

"Professor, you've basically covered all the details. It is a carefully thought out plan. I hope we can find Jesus in a few days," Martha said.

"You should trust nobody—only your instincts—and be careful what you do and say. You'll need to take extra precautions when you're on the road to Jericho because bandits are known to hide along it.

If my theory is correct, Mollie will rearrange your molecules in a way such that they will fit the time that you are transported into. For example, you would speak the language of the time and the culture wherein you arrived, and you would use the units of measurement used by the people of that particular place. You would say, for example, in the time of Jesus, when speaking about distance, that you could walk 140 to 160 furlongs in a day, there being eight furlongs to the mile. Or it might be that a camel costs 30 shekels. You would know the language of the people and the means of commerce in use at whatever time and place it is that you arrive.

Does anybody have any questions?"

"Dad, can I go with Brian and Martha? I want to meet Jesus."

"Sorry, kiddo. If plans go accordingly, you'll meet Jesus soon. If there are no more questions, let's get something to eat."

They went to the kitchen and David said, "I'll prepare supper. I hope you like barbecue chicken, hot dogs and sausages."

"I will make a salad and set the dinner table," Martha said.

"I'll bake four potatoes," Brian said.

"I'll get the soda and milk," Luke said.

"Now this is teamwork," David said.

After preparing their meal, when they were all sitting at the supper table, David said, "Please join me in saying the Lord's Prayer before we eat," and then they all said while holding hands, "Our Father, who art in heaven, hallowed be thy name. Thy Kingdom come, thy will be done on earth as it is in heaven. Give us this day our daily bread, and forgive us our trespasses, as we forgive those who trespass against us, and lead us not into temptation, but deliver us from evil, Amen."

"After we finish our supper, we'll adjourn to the library for a drink and to finalize our plans."

When they finished eating their dinner, David said, "Luke, please clean up in here, and when you're done, come and join us."

Luke began cleaning while Brian and Martha followed David to his library. After they entered, David asked, "May I offer you wine?"

"Yes, thank you. That would be wonderful after a delicious supper," Martha said.

"I couldn't agree more," Brian said.

David went to fetch a bottle of wine from the rack on the counter in the kitchen.

"We're going to have some wine, so when you're done in here, pour yourself a glass of soda and join us," David said to Luke.

"I'm almost done."

"Okay, kiddo. We'll see you in the study." David returned to the library with a bottle of wine and three glasses. After removing the cork from the bottle, he poured the wine into the glasses and gave Brian and Martha their drinks and then sat in the chair at his desk.

David called out for Luke, and when he entered the library, Luke said, "Yes, Dad?"

"Please bring your glass of soda here. I would like to propose a toast."

Luke quickly went to the kitchen and returned with his soda and sat in the chair next to the sofa. David stood up from his chair with his glass of wine in his right hand and extended his arm slightly up and away from his body. David said, "To Brian and Martha, the soon-to-be-first human time travelers in the history of mankind and the first to interact with biblical figures since ancient times. May God bless and guide you."

"Professor, that was a beautiful toast," Martha said with a smile.

"Jerusalem is seven hours ahead of Salem. I think it's best to arrive in the mid morning hours, say, 5 a.m., because at that time of the day, there should be less of a chance of someone seeing you suddenly appear," David said.

"I agree, Professor. The earlier the better. Five a.m. will be a perfect time to begin searching for the cave used by John the Baptist," Brian said.

"I'll transport you and Martha early tomorrow morning, after you've had a good night's rest. Luke, please bring the grocery items we purchased this morning," David said.

Luke went to the kitchen and returned with a shopping bag and set it onto the library desk. "Thanks, kiddo. Here are some dried food products that you can take. There's enough food to last a couple of days until you can exchange your gold for shekels," David said.

After David separated the gold into two small piles, he said, "When you put the food into your mantle pockets, don't forget to include the gold. I would suggest Brian carry the wrist chains because they are fashionable pieces of jewelry for men and would be worth more shekels as one piece," and then he took the jewelry from the desk and gave a pile to Brian and one to Martha. After giving them their gold, David said, "Martha, you can sleep in the spare bedroom and Brian in Luke's room. Luke will sleep on the sofa. He has a sleeping bag."

"Professor, I'll bunk here," Brian said.

"Brian, please sleep in my room. I don't mind," Luke said.

"Please, Professor. I would like to sleep on the sofa," Brian said.

"Are you sure? You should get a good night's rest because you'll have a long and probably tough day tomorrow in the Holy Land," David said.

"I'm sure. Just be sure to wake me up. I don't want to miss my electromagnetic wave out of here," Brian said with a laugh.

When they finished drinking their wine, David said, "I'll wake you both tomorrow morning at 4 a.m., and after you have showered and dressed, please go to the lab. Luke, let's leave them alone. They need to get some rest."

After David and Luke went to their bedrooms for the night, Martha said, "Brian, we should go to sleep too. I have butterflies in my stomach."

"We'll be making history and witnessing it at the same time," Brian said.

Martha gave Brian a kiss and said, "Goodnight."

David set his alarm clock for 4 a.m. before falling asleep. The alarm sounded and he couldn't believe it was already 4 a.m. It seemed as though he had just gone to bed. He got up and put on his robe and went to Martha's bedroom door, knocked on it and said, "It's time. There are towels in the bathroom."

"Thank you, Professor," Martha said.

David went to the library and gently shook Brian, waking him, and said, "You have a wave to catch."

"Thanks, Professor. I'll meet you in the lab shortly," Brian said.

David returned to his bedroom, took a shower and then got dressed. Then he went to Luke's bedroom and woke him up and said, "Brian and Martha are getting ready. Get dressed so you can say bye to them. I'll meet you in the lab." He left Luke's room and headed for his time machine.

David entered the room containing StellaPort and turned on Stella. Then he went to the metal cabinet and opened it and turned on Eve. He checked Stella's control panels to make sure all the components were functioning properly, and they were. Brian and Martha, who were dressed in their biblical clothes, entered the lab with Luke.

"You both look like a couple from the movie *The Ten Commandments*. Do you have your gold and food stored in your garments?" David asked, smiling.

"Yes," they both answered.

"I guess it's time. Luke, please use the video camera to record this historic event," David said.

Luke left the room and quickly returned with the camera and said, "Dad, I have the camcorder."

"Okay, kiddo. You start recording after they enter the transportation chamber," David said.

David, standing at Stella's control panel, used the keypad to enter longitude 35.1195 and latitude 31.7843, the location for the cave used by John the Baptist, and the date of April 30, 0029, and 5 a.m. as the time of arrival. The coordinates, date and time were now set, and David said, "Martha and Brian, please enter StellaPort's transportation chamber and stand on a Mollie."

Brian opened the chamber door. Martha entered first and stood on a Mollie. Brian did the same as Luke closed the door and stepped back and start recording. Mollie and Eve went into action. The amount of energy required to transport them was being calculated by Eve and transferred to Mollie. The numbers in Mollie's display window stopped changing, and a green light appeared next to the window, indicating that the energy required had been calculated.

"Are you ready?" David asked, and they nodded their heads yes. David switched on the laser lights, and all of StellaPort's different colored lights illuminated the room. He turned on the antigravity machine. Brian and Martha began to rise. David introduced the electromagnetic waves, and then he moved the transport dial to the backward position. A dark gray vortex appeared above Brian and Martha and started rotating in a counterclockwise motion with increasing speed. Suddenly they disappeared. David turned off the antigravity machine, the laser lights and then the electromagnetic wave inducer. The room immediately became less illuminated and the subject tracking window displayed longitude 35.1195 and latitude 31.7843, indicating that Stella was locked onto them. After Luke stopped recording, David said, "They are now in the Holy Land tasked with tracing the footsteps of Jesus."

CHAPTER 16

Brian and Martha were transported to the year AD 29, near the village of Ein Kerem, and were standing next to each other in Judea, just outside Jerusalem. As they viewed the surrounding landscape to get the bearings of their new environment, Brian asked, "Martha, how do you feel? Are you okay?"

"I'm fine. The last I remember was standing on a Mollie in the transportation chamber before I blacked out and regained consciousness, and now I find myself standing here. The professor's time machine worked. We're not in Kansas."

"I know, Dorothy. We must have been sent to the year 29 just as planned."

Martha scanned the landscape and then pointed northeast and said, "Jerusalem should be in that direction. The cave used by John the Baptist should be nearby. I remember that in the story Professor Solomon gave us to read, it mentioned a water source, and if we can find water, it will help us locate the cave."

"We should start walking east toward those limestone hills to see what's on the other side. But first we'll construct a marker with rocks, just in case we need to be transported from this location," Brian replied.

They made a two-foot-high reference point from the rocks that were everywhere by gathering and piling them on top of each other. After constructing their arrival marker, they started walking east toward the hills and found a path that looked like it was heavily traveled. They followed the beaten trail, which led to a small complex of stone structures, and there was a well for water, indicating an underground reservoir. Brian and Martha followed the path snaking to the right of the steep hills, which had crevices that could easily hide a cave. The trail split to the left in the direction of Jerusalem and also to the right along the bottom of the limestone hills. They decided to follow the path to the right and, while walking, they noticed an opening ahead of them in the side of a limestone hill. Brian said, "Look further down. That opening might be the cave."

When Brian and Martha got closer to the opening in the hill, they saw that it was a dark cave and then they heard a noise from within. Brian motioned with his hands for Martha to stop walking and to be quiet. Martha stopped dead in her tracks as Brian moved closer to the entrance, but couldn't see inside the cave. He knew he was at a disadvantage because the person or persons who were inside could see him, and he couldn't see them. Brian nervously said, "Hello, I am a friend." There was no reply, just silence. Then he said, "I'm here to meet John the Baptist. I wish to speak with him for spiritual guidance. I know you can see me. Please come into the light so we may talk. I mean you no harm."

Brian now heard the echoes of footsteps getting louder as the person or persons in the cave walked toward the opening, and then a figure began to emerge from the darkness. As a precaution, he stepped back from the entrance to allow more space between himself and the occupant or occupants. He figured if they were hostile, he would have a better chance to defend himself.

Finally, an older-looking gentleman wearing a tunic and sandals with a blanket wrapped around him emerged from the cave. "Hello, I am Brian," he said to the man and then looking at Martha, Brian said, "Her name is Martha. We came to talk with John the Baptist from the village of Ein Kerem. Are you him?"

"Oh no, my name is Elijah. John is God's chosen messenger until the Messiah arrives. I'm his humble servant, following the preachings of John. Where does the name Brian come from?"

"My name was given to me by my mother. I was born in Rome."

"Why do you seek John?"

"I would like to meet and talk with him. I know John is a wise man, and God is pleased with his work."

"Yes, John is wise. He could be anywhere spreading the message of God. He now spends his days at the Jordan River baptizing."

"When was the last time you saw John?" Martha asked.

"It's been many days now. He likes to spread God's message throughout Judea and in the Jordan Valley."

"If we traveled to the valley, could we find John?" Martha asked.

"Yes. He most likely is on the east side of the Jordan River near the village of Bethany. You'll see people traveling to or from the river who can direct you to him."

"How long does it take to get there from Jerusalem?" Brian asked.

"The distance is one hundred sixty furlongs, a one day's journey."

Brian extended his hand and shook Elijah's while saying, "You have been helpful, my friend."

"You're most welcome. If you stay on this path and follow it northeast, you will arrive at Jerusalem, and there you can ask for directions to Jericho," Elijah replied.

Brian and Martha backtracked the way they had come and at the split in the trail, they followed the one to the right, going in a northeast direction toward Jerusalem. As they were walking, Martha said, "Elijah looked like a figure portrayed in the movie *The Ten Commandments* or in a religious painting that just came to life. This is so exciting."

"That's true. We must be careful about whom to trust because strangers might try to con or possibly rob us," Brian said.

"Brian, you should remove the wrist chain from your mantle now while nobody can see your hiding place."

"Excellent idea. I'll do that now. Make sure nobody is coming," and then he reached under his mantle and unzipped the left pocket and removed the jewelry.

"Somebody is approaching from behind us," Martha said as Brian was reaching under his mantle.

Brian was quick to put the gold chain on his right wrist, and then he said, "We'll keep moving toward Jerusalem and hopefully the stranger will pass by us."

The stranger was walking very fast and was closing in on them. When the person caught up and was walking beside them, he said,

"Good morning. I'm traveling to Jerusalem to visit my cousins. And you?"

"We're going there too," Brian said.

"My name is Thomas from the village of Ein Kerem," the stranger said, who was a twenty-year-old Jew, five feet ten inches tall, with brown hair and eyes and a light-tan complexion and slim build.

"Our names are Brian and Martha. We are visiting from Rome. We hear many good things about Jerusalem and Judea," Brian said.

"This is the first time I have heard the name Brian. You must truly be from within the Roman Republic," Thomas said.

"You may walk with us since we're traveling in the same direction," Brian said.

"Yes. That would be fine. It's nice to have company while traveling. Our travel time will seem to go by faster, and Jerusalem is only 16 furlongs from here. We must stay on this path, which will lead us to a road that goes to the Jaffa Gate, which is the western entrance into the city." As they followed the path, Thomas said, "There's the road and on the other side of the hill is Jerusalem."

Brian and Martha had to walk at a faster pace to keep up with Thomas because he lived in a time when walking was the predominant way of traveling between villages. When they were at the top of the hill, the limestone-walled city of Jerusalem appeared. "Jerusalem seems smaller from the—" Brian said, and then stopped in mid sentence to catch himself. He was going to say from what he viewed on TV and in pictures, but suddenly remembered he was in a time when TV and cameras were not yet invented. Brian then continued and said, "Smaller from the drawings and stories that I've been told."

As they kept walking, Thomas said, "I am going to the Temple Mount to pray and afterward will visit my cousins."

"We are also headed to the Temple," Brian said.

"Afterward we will be traveling to Jericho," Martha said.

"I'll escort you to the Temple, since we are traveling to the same place," Thomas replied.

"Thank you. That is kind of you," Martha said.

Brian, Martha and Thomas were now walking on the Jaffa Road approaching the Jaffa Gate. The walls surrounding the city were becoming much taller as they got closer to Jerusalem. They entered Jerusalem and saw many people moving about performing their daily activities: shopping, praying, begging and walking in different directions. The city was alive and thriving with commerce. As Brian and Martha followed Thomas, they could see merchants selling many goods such as silk, furniture, woven baskets, animals, spices, fruits and vegetables, and many other items.

"Thomas, I must find a money changer. Do you know anybody?" Brian asked.

"Yes. My friend Ali is a Palestinian, and he's an honest man. He will not cheat you," Thomas said.

"Can you take us to him?" Brian asked.

"Come with me," Thomas answered and continued walking on the street on which they had entered the city.

"Martha, there's the Temple Mount," Brian said.

"We are almost at the place where Ali does business. It's further down on this street and it's near the Temple," Thomas said.

David and Luke were alone in the lab, and David was looking at the coordinates being displayed in Stella's tracking window, and they were slowly changing. "Stella is tracking them. The present longitude, 35.2275, and latitude of 31.7765 indicate that Brian and Martha are now in Jerusalem. We must keep an eye on the tracking window so we can plot their movements on the chalkboard to give us an idea in which direction they're going," David said.

"What is the longitude and the latitude for Jericho? Jericho should be their next stop," Luke said.

"That's correct. When Stella displays longitude 35.4621 and latitude 31.8554, we'll know they have made it to Jericho." David went to the chalkboard and removed a yellow piece of chalk and said, "We'll track their movements with dashes." David began making short lines from the white X on the blackboard that signified Brian and Martha's arrival site to the circle designated as Jerusalem.

Thomas led Brian and Martha to an area outside the Temple that had many money exchangers and customers. They could hear people haggling with the money changers for a reasonable price. There were merchants selling animals for sacrifice such as goats, sheep, lambs, doves and pigeons. Thomas went to a gentleman and shook his hand, saying, "Ali, I brought you two customers. I told them you are the most honest money exchanger in all of Jerusalem."

"You are kind, my friend," Ali said, and looking at Martha and Brian, he said, "Hello. I am Ali. What are your names?"

"I am Brian," he answered, and he shook Ali's hand and then Martha said, "My name is Martha."

"That's a lovely name for a beautiful woman," Ali said, and then he looked at Brian and asked, "Where does the name Brian originate?"

"Rome. My father was serving in the military in the northwest Roman client kingdoms of Britain. He returned to Rome with my mother and married her."

"Rome must be a fascinating place to live. What brings you to Judea?" Ali asked.

"I came to visit Jerusalem and travel from Judea to Damascus. I've heard many wonderful things about the Middle East from the people of Rome who have visited here."

"Yes, my friend, Judea and the Middle East are beautiful with a lot of history. How can I help you?"

"I own a gold chain that I would like to exchange for silver shekels."

"Where's the chain?"

Brian pulled up the right sleeve of his mantle and showed Ali the jewelry he was wearing on his wrist. "That is a nice-looking piece of jewelry. The craftsmanship is exquisite. I have never seen such a beautiful piece before."

"It was a gift from my father who bought it from a goldsmith in Rome."

"The Romans and Egyptians make fine gold jewelry. Please remove the chain so I may weigh it."

Brian removed the chain and handed it to Ali. Ali reached into the cloth bag at his feet and took out a small hand scale. Ali placed the chain on the scale and said, "The gold weighs three troy ounces. I'll give you 23 silver shekels. That's a good price."

Brian looked at Martha and she nodded her head approving of the transaction, and then she said, "Since we're here, let's also trade my earrings."

Martha turned her back from Ali and Thomas and reached under her mantle and removed the gold earrings from her pocket and gave them to Brian.

"I will accept your offer for the gold chain. How much for these beautifully handcrafted earrings?" Brian asked, and then he handed Ali the earrings.

After Ali weighed them on his scale, he said, "These are well crafted too and beautiful. I'll give you 12 silver shekels for them."

Brian glanced at Martha and she nodded her head in approval. Brian then said, "Okay, I will accept your offer."

Ali removed a leather pouch from around his neck containing his money and gave Brian 35 shekels. He then asked, "Do you have a pouch to keep your shekels in?"

"No," he answered.

Ali reached into his cloth bag and took out a small wool pouch with strings for closing the bag and for carrying around his neck. "I will sell this pouch to you for one half of a denarius."

"Okay," and then Ali gave him the small cloth bag after he was paid. When he received the pouch, Brian said, "Thank you, Ali. We must be going now."

"Please, my friends, let me buy you and Martha something to drink," Ali said.

"That would be fine," Brian replied.

After Ali picked up his cloth bag and put his scale inside it, they went to nearby tea vendor and ordered four cups of tea. As they were sipping their tea, Brian asked, "Ali, which gate will lead us to the road to Jericho?"

"Through the Golden Gate, Jericho is one day's journey from Jerusalem. You must be careful as you travel because bandits are known to rob people traveling alone and in small groups. It is best to travel in a large group for mutual protection."

"Thomas, have you ever traveled to Jericho in the past?" Brian asked.

"Yes, many times. I travel from Ein Kerem to the Jordan River escorting people for baptisms," Thomas replied, grinning.

"We need a guide. Would you be interested?" Brian asked after he looked at Martha.

"It will cost two shekels," Thomas answered.

"That sounds like a good price. We must buy food and flasks before leaving."

"I must visit my cousins. We can sleep the night in their home, and then we'll leave early tomorrow morning."

"Okay. We would like to be your guests in this beautiful city," Brian said after looking at Martha.

"I'll give you a tour of Jerusalem, and then we can buy food and the flasks," Thomas said, and then he thanked Ali for helping his new friends and for his concern for their safety.

Thomas was now escorting them to the Temple Mount. The Temple, according to Jewish tradition, is where the world was created and God gathered the dust to create Adam. Also, the house of prayer is the location of the first Temple (built by King Solomon in 950 BC) and the second Temple (rebuilt by King Herod the Great in AD 38), and both were destroyed.

"When we are inside the house of worship, we can pray to ask God to bless our journey and for his wisdom to guide us spiritually to his kingdom," Thomas said.

After paying a half shekel each to enter the complex, they observed many people worshiping God. They followed Thomas's lead because they did not practice the Jewish religion; they were Christians. "Please recite with me the Tefilat HaDerech prayer that is for a traveler's safe journey," Thomas said.

"I would prefer to pray silently," Martha said.

"Me too. I like praying in silence because my prayer is between only me and God," Brian said.

"I'll do the same," Thomas said, and they turned the palms of their hands toward the heavens and closed their eyes with their heads slightly tilted back and prayed.

After praying in the Temple, they went outside the complex and Brian and Martha were staring in awe because they knew this Temple would be destroyed in AD 70 by Titus Flavius Vespasianus and would never be rebuilt again.

"Follow me and I'll show you other monuments King Herod the Great has built," Thomas said, and then he showed them the Jerusalem Theatre, which was a large open-air auditorium with semicircular rows of seats where the wealthy came to watch Greeks and Romans perform drama on stage. After walking around the empty theatre, Thomas brought them to the Hippodrome, which was specially designed for chariot races. The spectators would sit on stone blocks and be entertained by chariots racing around a dirt track. Thomas then led them to the Upper City, where the rich residents of Jerusalem lived. Herod's Palace was also there, and across from the palace was the Upper Agora, a large upscale marketplace for the wealthy. The market sold luxury goods such as oils, perfumes, ivory, precious stones, gold and silver, and many different imported foods.

While at the Upper Agora, Brian said, "Thomas, we must buy three flasks for water."

"I know a merchant in the less expensive area of the city close to my cousins' house. You can buy flasks and food there and the price will be much cheaper than here," Thomas said.

They continued walking in the upper marketplace, watching the buyers and sellers interacting. The type of goods being sold and the asking prices were definitely for rich people. The wealthy lived in marble mansions with gardens and pools. The streets were laid out in grids with smooth white stone streets. The lower city consisted mostly of working-class residents living in crowed one and two-story limestone houses in noisy conditions. The atmosphere was filled with energy as people moved about at a fast pace from one vendor to another, and the aroma of freshly grilled food caught Brian's attention. He said, "Let's go get something to eat."

"I'm hungry too because of all the exercise from walking," Martha said.

"Thomas, do you know of a place that serves food?" Brian asked.

"Of course. My cousins' friend provides delicious meals, and they don't cost much," Thomas replied.

"Let's go there now," Brian said.

Thomas then began walking in the direction from which they had just come. There were many people moving about, so Brian and Martha stayed close together as they followed Thomas into the Lower City section of Jerusalem. The streets were much narrower than the Upper City and the wall surrounding the city was not visible. Thomas was walking at a brisk pace, and he had to stop so Brian and Martha could catch up to him. When they were together, Thomas said, "We're almost there. The name of the place is Mary's Hot and Cold Meals. One more street, and it's the third home on the left."

They went to the front door of a house that served food and Thomas opened it. They entered the home where Thomas was greeted by a man. "Hi, Jacob. I have two hungry guests who would like a hot meal," Thomas said.

"Thomas brought you to the right place. My wife is the best cook in all of Jerusalem," Jacob said, looking at Martha and Brian.

Jacob's wife came out of a rear room in the home and said with a smile, "Hi, Thomas. We haven't seen you in a while. How are you?"

"Hi, Mary. I've been working with my father, but the furniture business is slow right now. I brought you two hungry guests."

"Hi. I'm Mary. Welcome to our home. I would be pleased if I could serve you."

"We're hungry. What do you serve here?" Brian asked.

"Please sit," Mary said, and after they sat at one of the two tables in the dining area of the home, she said, "I have bread, lentil soup, chicken, fruits, goat's milk, wine, tea or water to drink."

"We'll have your tastiest dish," Brian said.

They were the only ones in the dining room. Mary went to the kitchen to prepare their meals and soon returned with their food.

After they had finished eating, Thomas said, "Jacob, we need to buy three liquid containers. Do you have any for sale?"

"No, but I know Joshua does, and he'll sell them to me at a good price. The price is one denarius for three flasks," Jacob answered.

"I will pay you now," Brian said, and he removed the wool pouch hanging from his neck and paid Jacob for the flasks and their meals.

After Jacob was paid, he said, "I'll return soon. Please have something to drink while you wait."

Mary returned to the table and refreshed their cups with hot tea. After eating, Martha said, "Mary, that was a delicious meal. I can understand why Jacob boasts of your cooking skills."

"Thank you, that's kind of you to say. Jacob usually sits outside the front door soliciting customers. I normally feed ten to fifteen people per day. The money helps pay the taxes and feed us. This house was passed on to Jacob after his father died."

Jacob returned with three clay flasks hanging from his neck by a cord. Each flask had a wood cork in the spout to keep its liquid from spilling out. He set them onto the table where Brian and Martha sat. After sitting, Jacob said, "These are the remaining flasks Joshua had for sale. He said many travelers were passing through and buying them."

"Thank you," Martha said.

"When a person is traveling in the desert and water becomes scarce, water will become more precious than gold," Jacob said.

"Brian and Martha, shall we leave now? I have another place to show you," Thomas said.

"Brian, where is your name from?" Jacob asked.

"My name was given to me by my mother, a Roman citizen. She was from the northwest Roman client kingdoms of Britain," Brian answered.

"I like the sound of your name," Jacob said with a smile.

"Me too," Brian said.

Thomas stood up from the table and said, "Jacob, it was a pleasure seeing you and Mary again. I'll stop by the next time I visit my cousins."

"Please stop by again. You are always welcome here," Mary said to Brian and Martha.

"You are so kind. Thank you for the food, drinks and conversation," Martha said, and then they left.

On the street, Thomas said, "I want to show you Phasael's Tower, where we can climb the stairs to the top of the tower and view all of Jerusalem and the surrounding areas."

"That would be nice," Martha said.

"Follow me," Thomas said, and he began walking in the direction of the Jaffa Gate. Phasael's Tower is located near the gate and is part of the citadel constructed to strengthen the defenses of the city. The rampart had three towers added (Phasael, Miriam and Hippicus) and was built by Herod the Great. The only purpose was to protect his palace and defend Jerusalem against invaders. The Roman military used the fortress as a base within Jerusalem. The Phasael Tower is the tallest of the three and still stands today.

Thomas was still walking at a faster pace than Brian and Martha. He would occasionally look back to determine how far behind they were. "I'd like to enter Thomas in the summer Olympic event of race-walking. He would be the clear favorite to win the race. I know one sure thing, we'll sleep well tonight," Brian said.

"He's a fast walker, and it seems so natural for him. Have you noticed the number of people that keep passing by us? The only ones that don't are old," Martha replied.

Brian said with a laugh, "I know, maybe we should hire a camel for the day."

Martha laughed too and then she said, "Yes, that's a good idea. I hope we aren't sidelined because of blisters on our feet."

Thomas stopped walking so Brian and Martha could catch up to him again, and when they did, Thomas said, "It seems you don't walk often in Rome."

"We walk short distances and travel on horseback for long journeys," Brian replied.

"There's Phasael's Tower," Thomas said, pointing.

"Can we go to the top of the tower and view the city?" Brian asked.

"Yes. I've been up there many times. We must ask for permission from the Roman soldiers guarding the entrance to the citadel. I usually give the guards figs, and one of them will escort me to the tower. I would then climb the stairs to the top and from there you can walk around a circular walkway and view all of Jerusalem," Thomas answered.

They stood in front of the citadel where two Roman soldiers guarded the entrance. The soldiers were in their early twenties and had on silver metal helmets and were dressed in red tunics, capes and white skirts, and they wore brown leather sandals. They also had black leather belts with a short sword stowed in side sleeves and they held a spear in one hand. Thomas approached one guard and asked, "May we go up the tower to see Jerusalem?"

"What are your names?" a soldier asked.

"My name is Thomas." "I'm Brian." "And I'm Martha," they answered.

"Your name is odd in this part of the world. Where does the name Brian come from?" the soldier said, staring at Brian.

Martha began to get nervous because the soldier asked with a stern voice, and if he didn't like Brian's response, he could be imprisoned. Brian was hesitant in responding to the soldier's question, and he said, "I'm from Rome. My father is a retired Roman soldier. He served under Nero Claudius Drusus and fought the Gauls about 40 years ago. He said they crushed the uprising and Claudius Drusus is a military genius. After returning to Rome, he was sent to the northwest Roman client kingdoms of Britain, serving the Emperor Gaius Julius Caesar Augustus. My mother is from Britain, where he met her while serving as a Roman soldier. My father returned home with my mother, and they got married."

The soldier looked intently at Brian and said, "I will personally escort a fellow Roman citizen to the tower. Please follow me." Martha was relieved because Brian and the guard were bonding.

The guard escorted them into the stone fortress, and they walked up two flights of stairs to the walkway along the citadel wall leading to the lookout. They climbed the stairs to the top of the tower and had a spectacular view of Jerusalem and the surrounding areas. They saw the places they visited and had a clear view of Herod's Palace and the terrain outside the city.

"The Temple Mount is where we'll exit Jerusalem through the Golden Gate and then continue east to Jericho," Thomas said.

They also saw the Mount of Olives and the Garden of Gethsemane and beyond the mountain to Jericho and the Jordan River. The Mount of Olives is a mountain ridge with three peaks which at one time was covered with olive groves, thus being known in ancient and present times as the Mount of Olives. The Garden of Gethsemane is a garden at the foot of the Mount of Olives and is the place where Jesus and his disciples prayed the night before Jesus' crucifixion.

"This view of Jerusalem is breathtaking. Thomas, thank you for sharing this with us," Martha said.

"We must thank Brian. Were it not for his father having served in the Roman army, we wouldn't be standing here," Thomas said.

"Thanks, Brian, and tell your father thank you from Thomas and me," Martha said, smiling.

"Shall we go now? I have one more place to show you before we go to my cousins' home," Thomas said.

"Okay, let's leave now," Brian said, and then they returned to the walkway where the soldier was waiting for them. When they were with the soldier, Brian said to him, "The tower allows for a beautiful view of the city."

"Yes, it does. Please follow me. You must leave now," the soldier replied.

They followed the guard to the entrance, and after exiting the citadel, Brian turned to him and asked, "What's your name?"

"Marcus from Pompeii," the soldier answered.

"When I return to Rome, I will mention you to my father," Brian said as the soldier waved bye.

"Now I'd like to show you the Tomb of King David. It's on the way to my cousin's house. King David united Judea for thirty-three years, and as a young warrior, slew the giant, Goliath, with a sling," Thomas said.

Thomas led them in the direction of the Temple and there were more people going and coming than there were in the morning. During Herod's building binge, he constructed a monument depicting the tomb of David that had a small pyramid roof unique among the surrounding structures. Thomas was already there waiting for Brian and Martha. When they arrived, Thomas said, "This tomb is to honor our most famous king, David. We can touch the outer wall of the tomb and say a prayer."

"Sure, that would be fine," Brian said, and then they went to the north wall of the monument and placed a hand against it and began to pray.

When they finished praying, Thomas said, "We will now visit my cousins, who live in the same area of the city as Jacob and Mary."

Thomas brought them back to an area of Jerusalem that was far different from the Upper City. The streets were much more congested with people because they were narrower than the Upper City. The stone homes were one and two levels that were close to each other. The people moved in many directions carrying the goods they had just bought and those to be resold. The Lower City was also booming with trade, just as the Upper City, but the difference was the quality of the products being offered and the asking prices.

They followed Thomas to a one-level home, and when Brian and Martha caught up to Thomas, Thomas knocked on the front door. An older woman opened it, and he said, "Hi, Deliylah. I came to visit for the night, and I brought two friends to stay with us."

"Please come in," she said, and they entered her single-level limestone home with a wood roof. The home's interior had a wood floor, and the furniture was made of wood. There were two separate rooms in the rear of the house with a larger room that was used for cooking, eating, entertaining and socializing.

"Deliylah, we'll leave at sunrise tomorrow morning. This is Brian and Martha. They are from Rome and visiting Judea. I'll be escorting them to Jericho," Thomas said.

"Please come in and sit," she said.

They were sitting at the table in the center of the room when two teenage girls entered with baskets in their arms. The girls were Deliylah's daughters, Miryam and Amine. Their father had died two years ago. The girls sold handwoven baskets made by Deliylah in the lower market to get by. "Say hi to your cousin. He has brought two guests, who will stay with us for the night and leave tomorrow morning for Jericho," Deliylah said to her daughters.

"Hi, Thomas," both girls said.

"We haven't seen you in awhile. What have you been up to?" Miryam asked.

"I have been busy helping my father with his furniture business. My father said I could take some time for myself and suggested I visit my cousins in Jerusalem and possibly find work in Jerusalem. So here I am, but only for a brief visit. I found work escorting Brian and Martha to Jericho. They're from Rome," Thomas answered.

"One day I wish to visit Rome and Athens. I've heard so many wonderful things about how magnificent the Greek and Roman cities are," Miryam said.

"Not me. Those cities are too far away from Jerusalem, and somebody must care for Mother," Amine said.

"Rome is a magnificent city, and it's far from here. Jerusalem is also a beautiful city with a lot of religious history," Brian said.

"Miryam, Amine and I will cook a delicious meal for you and our guests, and after our meal your cousins will perform a dance," Deliylah said to Thomas.

"That would be enjoyable," Thomas replied.

Deliylah and the girls went to an area of the big room where there was a fireplace with pots and shelves and started gathering ingredients to prepare supper. Martha went to Deliylah and asked, "Can I do something to help?"

"No, but thank you for offering. You are our guest tonight. Please sit with Brian and Thomas," Deliylah answered.

Miryam and Amine set the table with clay bowls and cups, bread and olive oil. Amine returned with a large bowl full of garden vegetables to make a salad. Deliylah requested that everyone sit at the supper table, and then she brought a pot of hot vegetable stew. After serving everyone, she sat with her family and guests. After sitting, Deliylah said, "Before we eat, I will recite the Shehecheyanu prayer. It seems fitting for this evening."

When Deliylah finished the traditional prayer, she said, "Let's enjoy our gift from God," and then they ate their supper.

After they finished eating and when Amine and Miryam had cleaned the table, Deliylah said, "My daughters will now perform a traditional dance for our guests."

Thomas asked Brian to help him move the table to make room for Miryam and Amine to dance. After the table was moved, the girls entered the big room and stood in the center and Deliylah and Thomas began to sing a traditional song. Miryam and Amine began dancing beside one other and then with each other. When the song was over, the girls stopped dancing and everyone clapped in appreciation.

"Deliylah, do we have time for one more song if Miryam and Amine are willing to dance again?" Thomas asked.

"Yes, please sing another song," the girls answered.

"Martha, would you like to join us?" Amine asked.

"Sure. I would love too," Martha replied.

Deliylah and Thomas started singing again, and her daughters started dancing with Martha while she faced them and mimicked their rhythmic motions. Martha reached out and took each girl's hand in hers, and they danced slowly in a circle. When the singing stopped, so did the dancing, and everyone clapped again.

"It's getting late and we need to rest before we leave for Jericho in the morning. Can we sleep in this room?" Thomas asked.

"Yes, it is, and yes, you may," Deliylah answered, and then she went to one of the rear rooms in the house and returned with three blankets and gave one to each of her guests.

CHAPTER 17

The sun began to rise. Thomas woke up first, and he whispered to Martha and Brian to wake them up. He was whispering because he did not want to disturb Deliylah and her daughters. Brian and Martha didn't hear him, so he went to Brian and gently pushed his shoulder, which woke him up. Thomas did the same to Martha. After Brian and Martha were awake. Thomas whispered. "Good morning. It's time for us to leave."

"Is it morning already?" Brian asked, whispering to Thomas.

Brian stood and stretched his arms and legs because the wood floor was uncomfortable and his back was stiff and sore. He was missing the comforts of the 21st century. Martha stood and whispered to Brian and Thomas, "Good morning."

Deliylah, Miryam and Amine were still sleeping as they prepared to leave for Jericho, when Thomas said, "We can fill our flasks with water at a well that's nearby. I know a breadmaker who is open for business now, and he also sells salted fish. Are you ready to leave?" Thomas asked.

"Yes," Brian answered.

Thomas quietly opened the front door, and after they were outside Deliylah's home, he said, "It's this way to the well."

After filling their clay flasks, they hung them around their necks by their cords. The streets were almost empty except for the merchants getting ready to conduct business. While walking, they saw people opening their shops and street vendors carrying their goods to be sold. Thomas led them first to a breadmaker who also sold fish. Brian bought two loafs of bread and six medium-size fish that looked like large sardines preserved with salt. After Brian paid for the food, they left the shop. Outside, Martha said, "Let's sit on the steps of the building across the street and eat our meal there before we start our journey."

They went to the building and, after eating, Brian said, "We can save the remaining food for later today." He gave the food to Thomas to store in a cloth pouch that he had taken from Deliylah's home.

"Do you need anything else before we leave Jerusalem?" Thomas asked

"No. We have enough food and water to make it to Jericho," Brian answered.

Thomas began walking in the direction of the Temple Mount because the Golden Gate was located at the eastern section of the wall and directly in front of it. At the base of the Temple's foundation was a narrow street leading to a gate, and they followed it and exited Jerusalem. When they were outside the city walls, Thomas said, "We must continue to follow this road east. The road will take us to the villages of Bethphage and then to Bethany. They are both located at the southern bottom slope of the Mount of Olives."

They began their 144-furlong trek to Jericho, and after a few minutes of walking, Brian said, "Thomas, I don't see any people. Shall we wait for a group before we go further?"

"That could take some time. It would be best to continue walking before the sun rises and it becomes warmer," Thomas replied.

"Martha, what do you think?" Brian asked.

"Thomas has a point. As the sun rises it's going to get hotter. We should keep moving and hope we catch up to a group traveling in the same direction as we," she answered.

"Well, let's get moving," Brian said.

They were now on the road to Jericho and would soon be approaching Bethphage on the left side of the road. Thomas was ten yards ahead of them when Martha asked, "Brian, do you think we should stop in Bethany to ask Jesus' close friends Lazarus, Martha and Mary where Jesus could be?"

"It's a long shot, but why not? Bethany is on the way," Brian said.

Brian then called out to Thomas. He stopped walking and waited for them to catch up to him, and when they did, Brian said, "We will stop briefly in Bethany because Martha and I want to see if our friend Jesus is there."

"Bethany is the next village on this road and is a short distance from Bethphage. We will be there soon," Thomas said.

As they continued walking east, the tiny village of Bethphage became visible on the left side of the road. Bethphage was the village to which Jesus sent his disciples to bring him a donkey for him to ride into Jerusalem as prophesied.

"This is Bethphage and the next village will be Bethany. I always pass by Bethphage and Bethany when traveling to Jericho," Thomas said.

"We will not stay long. We'll stop and ask somebody where we can find our friend Jesus," Brian said.

Bethany is mentioned in the New Testament as the village where Jesus' good friends Lazarus, Martha and Mary resided. On numerous occasions when Jesus visited Jerusalem, he would stay in Bethany with them. The village was small and the houses were made of limestone with flat wood roofs. In the center of the village was the well for water used by all the residents, and there were sheep, goats, chickens, roosters and donkeys near the homes. They also noticed a few men working with wood beside their homes, most likely carpenters making furniture. The main occupation of the men in the village was craftsmen using their hands to make a living. While walking to the well they saw a woman filling her clay pots with water. Brian approached the woman and asked, "May we fill our flasks?"

"Of course. Please help yourself," she answered, and then the woman handed Brian a wood pail with a thick cord tied to it for retrieving the water.

"Thank you," he said and tossed the pail into the well and then pulled it up full of water.

"Can you tell me which home belongs to Lazarus, Martha and Mary?" Brian asked.

"In that home," she said, gesturing with her left hand.

"Thank you again," he replied. He went to the house the woman had pointed to, with Thomas and Martha close behind him.

At the front door of Lazarus, Martha and Mary's home, Brian knocked and a man opened the door and stepped outside. The man had black hair and beard and was wearing a sandy-colored tunic.

"Hello. Are you Lazarus?" Brian asked.

"Yes. Why do you ask?"

"I am seeking Jesus of Nazareth. I know he's a good friend of yours and your sisters, Martha and Mary."

"Why do you seek Jesus?"

"I am a friend and would like to talk with him. Have you seen him?"

"No. I haven't seen Jesus for many years. The last time we met was when he came from Galilee to Jerusalem for the celebration of Passover, and he stayed with us. You may find him in Nazareth."

"How far is Nazareth from here?" Brian asked.

"It is a two-day journey," Lazarus answered.

"We're going to the Jordan River. Do you know where we can find John the Baptist from the village of Ein Kerem?" Brian asked.

"You will find John on the east side of the river," Lazarus replied.

"Thank you," Brian said, and then they returned to the well to finish filling their flasks with water.

"Are you seeking John the Baptist?" Thomas asked Brian at the well.

"Yes. Do you know where we can find him?"

"I was baptized by him in the Jordan River. We're from the same village of Ein Kerem. I remember the place where he baptizes pilgrims. It's on the east side of the river near Bethabara."

"Thomas, please escort us to where you were baptized," Martha said.

"Okay, I'll take you there. It's 48 furlongs northeast of Jericho. When we arrive at Jericho, the sun will be setting. John will have returned to his campsite in the wilderness."

After their flasks were filled, Brian said, "We should be going now," and then they left the village and were 136 furlongs from Jericho.

After walking 48 furlongs east from Bethany, they still did not see anybody on the road. Martha said, "I haven't seen anybody since we left Jerusalem."

"I know. It does seem odd. I thought this was a heavily traveled road. I guess not," Brian said.

"There's something moving along the left side of the road in the ravine," Martha whispered to Brian as they continued walking.

"Stay close to me," Brian whispered, and then he bent over and picked up a small rock that fit into the palm of his right hand and made a fist to hide it.

Brian then called out to Thomas, and when he turned to him, Brian pointed to the left side of the road with his left hand. He also put his right index finger over his lips, indicating that there was something in the ravine and to be quiet. Thomas nodded his head implying he understood Brian's warning. Brian and Martha kept walking cautiously toward Thomas, and as soon as they were all together, two men suddenly climbed out from the gully and blocked their passage east. Brian knew they were not friendly and were going to try to rob them. The two bandits were slim and one was slightly taller than the other and both were wearing dirty white–colored tunics, sandals and head scarves. Brian immediately noticed they both had daggers tucked under their thick wool belts tied around their waists. "You must pay a tax to pass," the taller robber said to them.

"The road is free for all to travel on. It doesn't belong to thieves," Thomas replied.

"This is our road and you will have to pay a tax if you want to pass," the smaller bandit said.

Brian looked at both bandits and asked, "How much is the tax?"

"How much do you have?" the taller thief asked.

"Not enough to pay you. We mean you no harm. Please let us pass," Brian answered.

"We will let you pass only after you give us all your money," the taller bandit said.

Brian asked Martha to step back and stay behind him, which she did. Martha nervously said, "We should give them our money and move on."

"The woman is wise. You should listen to her," the smaller bandit said.

"No, these thieves need to be punished, Martha. Please stay away from us," Brian said as he sized up the two bandits.

"We need to stand up to these robbers and teach them a lesson they will never forget," Brian said after he glimpsed at Thomas.

"I'm with you, Brian. I hate thieves. They steal from the ones that work hard for their money," Thomas said, looking at the bandits.

Brian was now in a fighting posture with Thomas at his side and Martha at a good distance behind them. Brian slowly moved clockwise because his plan was to position the bandits so the sun would be in their eyes, giving Thomas and him an edge. The thieves removed their daggers from their waist belts and held them out toward Brian and Thomas. The robbers moved and were now facing the sun, just as Brian had planned. He noticed the bandits were having a difficult time seeing them because of the direct sunlight in their eyes, and he said, "Thomas, use your flask as a weapon."

Thomas and Brian removed their flasks, which were three-quarters filled with water, and after Brian had removed his flask from around his neck, he saw Thomas twirling his by its cord to keep the smaller bandit away from him. Brian then threw the rock in his right hand with all his might at the taller bandit, who was standing in front of him, and hit the thief in the eye. The bandit cried out in pain and dropped his dagger and covered his face with both hands. As soon as the bandit dropped his weapon, Brian tackled him with extreme force. The crook hit the back of his head very hard on the compacted dirt road and became unconscious, and then Brian picked up the dagger lying on the ground. Thomas was still twirling his flask while Brian was standing near him in an offensive posture, moving his newly acquired weapon toward the thief in short, stabbing motions. The bandit frequently jabbed his dagger at both Brian and Thomas, but was scared because he was now fighting two armed men. Brian stepped back, still in a slightly crouched posture, and dropped his flask to the ground. He grabbed a handful of fine dirt and threw it into the bandit's eyes. As soon as the robber was blinded, Thomas used his flask to hit the thief on the side of his head, breaking the flask and knocking the bandit unconscious.

After Brian picked up the second bandit's dagger and handed it to Thomas, he said, "Good work," and then they put the daggers under their waist belts, displaying them as trophies.

"Brian, I didn't know you could fight," Martha said.

"You never asked," Brian said with a smile.

"The way you fight, you must be a gladiator," Thomas said.

"My father taught me how to fight when I was a boy, and he always said, 'There is always someone who is tougher than you.' So we should get moving before more bad guys show up. I don't want to test our luck," Brian replied.

They continued east for another 56 furlongs and decided to stop on the side of the road to eat and rest. When they were resting, Thomas said, "We have nearly 40 more furlongs to go before we reach Jericho. We should stay the night in Jericho and in the morning travel east to the Jordan River. We'll have a better chance of locating John the Baptist in daylight."

"That sounds like a good plan. We would have a full day of sunlight to find him," Martha said.

After eating and resting, they saw a group of people approaching in the distance traveling west in the direction of Jerusalem. Martha was getting nervous. She didn't know what to expect after the fight with the thieves. As the group was about to pass them, one member of the group waved and said, "Hello." Martha was relieved because they were friendly.

"Be careful. There are bandits on the road. We encountered two about 50 furlongs back and took their weapons," Thomas said to the person who had said hello.

Brian politely nodded his head toward the travelers as they were passing by and a few nodded back in response. One man in the group said, "We haven't seen any bandits so far. But we are prepared if they attempt to rob us. Thank you for the warning, and may God continue to bless your travels."

The sun was low in the sky and would be setting soon, when Thomas said, "Jericho is 16 more furlongs. I have a friend named Aaron who lives there. He'll let us spend the night in his house. When I travel this way, I always visit him, and we're from the same village of Ein Kerem. He's a close friend of my father."

"Are you sure Aaron has room for us?" Brian asked.

"Aaron is my friend. He will always accept me and my guests into his house."

"Okay. We'll stay tonight in Aaron's home. Plus, it will be dark soon and it would be best to stay in the city."

When they were at the walled city of Jericho, Thomas said, "Follow me. I'll take you to Aaron's home. It's not far from here." Brian and Martha followed Thomas through a gate and saw a city much smaller than Jerusalem, but larger than Bethany. Thomas showed them to a small limestone home with a flat roof that looked similar to the houses in Jerusalem and Bethany.

Thomas walked to a house and knocked on the front door. An older gentleman opened it and said, "Hello, Thomas. How are you, my friend? I haven't seen you in awhile."

"I've been working with my father, but business is slow now. I am with two friends, and we need a place to sleep for the night," Thomas said.

"Of course. Please come in and sit. You must be tired from your long journey," Aaron said after they entered his home.

They sat at a table with chairs in the center of the room. After sitting, Thomas said, "Yes, we are tired. We left Jerusalem very early this morning and need a good night's rest."

"What are your friends' names?" Aaron asked.

"This is Brian and her name is Martha. They are visiting from Rome. I am escorting them to the Jordan River to find John the Baptist," Thomas answered.

"Brian, what plans do you have while in Judea?" Aaron asked.

"We are traveling through Judea to know the land and its people and afterward will return to our families in Rome," he replied.

"Rome must be wealthy from all the taxes paid to the Roman governor by the people of Judea," Aaron said.

"I am not a politician and will never be one. I am not a tax collector. I obey the laws made by the politicians and, just like you, if I don't follow them, then I'm punished too," Brian said.

"I like the way you think. A Roman who is friendly toward the people of Judea and interested in experiencing the Jewish culture before passing judgment," Aaron replied.

"I like them too. They are my new friends. On the way here we encountered two bandits with daggers that tried to rob us, but we overpowered them and took their weapons," Thomas said, and then he set his dagger down onto the table for Aaron to examine.

Brian placed his knife onto the table too and asked, "Aaron, do you like this dagger?"

Aaron picked up the dagger with his left hand and then eyed both sides of the blade, saying, "Yes. This is a well-balanced knife."

"Consider it a gift to express our appreciation for allowing us to stay the night in your home."

Aaron smiled while holding the dagger, and said, "Thank you. It will come in handy. I will use this to sacrifice my animals and to butcher meat."

"When I return to Jerusalem, I'll sell my dagger to the highest bidder," Thomas said.

"You can sell it for a nice price," Aaron said.

"Aaron, is there a place to buy a hot meal?" Brian asked.

"Yes. I'll take you there," he answered, and they left Aaron's home just as the sun was setting.

It was noon the following day after Brian and Martha had been transported to the Holy Land. David was heading to the lab to monitor Stella's tracking window while Luke was already there playing a game on the PC.

"Kiddo, we need to update the location of Brian and Martha. They should have reached Jericho by now," David said after entering the lab. He went to Stella's tracking window and saw longitude 35.4621 and latitude 31.8554. "Looks like they are now in Jericho," David said.

He walked to the chalkboard and removed a piece of yellow chalk from the tray and extended the dashes from Jerusalem to Jericho. Luke said, "Their next stop should be the Jordan River and then north, right, Dad?"

"You're correct. They'll probably have to make their way to Nazareth or Capernaum to find Jesus. It's early evening now in Jericho. You can take the rest of the day off. I'll monitor Stella," David answered. Luke left the lab, while David thought about the culture shock that Brian and Martha must be experiencing.

Aaron took them to a place to eat that was in the home of his friend. When Aaron was at his friend's front door, he knocked, and an old man answered and said, "Hello, Aaron. How can I help you?"

"I brought three hungry travelers seeking a hot meal. Can you feed them?" Aaron asked.

"Yes. Please come in and sit," the old man answered, and they entered the home and stood in a large room with a table and six chairs, and they sat at a table.

"I'm Benjamin and my wife will prepare for you a delicious meal," the man said, and then he hollered, "Chana, we have travelers to feed."

Chana entered the front room and approached her guests. She said, "Hello. My name is Chana, and I would love to prepare supper for you."

"Do you serve fish?" Brian asked.

"Yes," she answered.

"We would like fish, bread, salad, figs and a cup of wine," Brian said.

"I'll prepare your meals now," she replied, and then she went to an area of the room that had a fireplace and shelves containing clay jars and pots of various sizes and cooking tools.

While his wife was preparing their meals, Benjamin looked at Brian and asked, "From where did you start your travels?"

"We started from Rome and left Jerusalem this morning."

"You must be tired."

"Yes. We had a long day, and we need to eat and rest," Brian replied.

"Benjamin, he's a Roman, but a good one," Aaron said.

"What makes him a good Roman as opposed to the others?" Benjamin asked.

Martha was getting nervous again because she sensed from the tone of Benjamin's voice he didn't like Romans.

"You don't care that much for Romans. May I ask you why?" Brian asked.

"We are not free people. Rome has imposed a king on us named Herod, and he does the bidding of Rome. While the poor become poorer, the Romans and Herod get fatter. We are double taxed, by Caesar and by the Jewish priests," Benjamin answered.

"As I told Aaron earlier this evening, I am not a politician. I don't make the laws. I have to follow them just like you do. In Rome, I must pay taxes, and if I do not, I too could be sold into slavery. I wish there was a better system, but until there is, it's the best we have. I don't believe tax collectors should get rich from the taxes they collect. The tax collector should be paid a fair wage and not become wealthy from the hard work of others. When a civil servant is caught stealing the money collected from the taxpayers, they should be sold into slavery. The message would be loud and clear that stealing the people's money will not be tolerated," Brian said.

"I can understand why Aaron likes the way you think. You are a fair and honest Roman. I wish Judea had more Romans like you, which would make this land a better place to live," Benjamin replied.

Martha gave an internal sigh of relief because Brian had defused a tense situation with Benjamin. Brian had tactfully turned a possible confrontation into a calm, sympathetic conversation.

Chana came to the table with their food in clay bowls and set them down, and then they took food from the bowls to eat. After they were done eating, Thomas said the prayer Birkat HaMazon, thanking God for the food they had just eaten and for his continued guidance to his kingdom. When Thomas finished his prayer, Brian and Martha stood from their chairs and thanked Chana and Benjamin for a wonderful supper.

"Thank you for the delicious meal, my friends. We must be going now," Aaron said after he stood up from his chair.

After leaving his friend's home, Aaron said while looking at Brian and Martha, "You must be very tired after that delicious meal and because of your long walk from Jerusalem to here."

"You are correct, my friend. I will sleep well tonight," Brian said as they were walking to his house.

After entering Aaron's home, Thomas said, "We'll sleep in the front room and leave in the morning after we have eaten. I'll wake you up before we go."

"I'll get blankets for you," Aaron said, and then he went to a room and quickly returned carrying three camelhair blankets and gave one to each of his guests. Afterward he said, "May God protect this house and its occupants. I will see you tomorrow morning. Goodnight."

CHAPTER 18

Thomas, Brian and Martha were awakened early in the morning by a crowing rooster from behind Aaron's house. After Thomas sat up, he said, "Soon we'll leave for the Jordan River."

Aaron entered the room where his guests slept for the night and said, "I hope everybody had a good night's rest. It looks like it will be a beautiful day."

"Do you have water so that I may wash my face and hands?" Martha asked.

"Yes. I'll show you," Aaron answered.

"Aaron, we need to buy a flask for Thomas and some food," Brian said, grinning, after he looked at Thomas.

"I'll take you first for water, and then to a shop for food. I know a place that sells flasks. Please come with me," Aaron replied, and he picked up the wood pail from the floor near the fireplace and a cloth rag and went to the front door and opened it. When his guests were outside his home, Aaron said, "This way," and he guided them to the center of the city, where many merchants were already conducting business. There were five wells and Aaron went to the one that wasn't being used. The wells were being used by women filling their large and small clay pots with water. At the well, Aaron dropped his pail into it and pulled the bucket up by its cord full of water and then dipped the cloth into the water to moisten it and he handed it to Martha.

"Thank you," Martha said, and then she washed her face, hands, arms and feet. Afterward, she gave the cloth to Brian and when he was done, it was Thomas's turn.

"I'll take you to a shop that sells food, but first, fill your flasks," Aaron said after everyone had cleaned themselves.

After Brian and Martha filled their clay canteens with water, Brian said with a grin, "Thomas, we'll buy you another flask. We hope you'll use it only to drink from."

"If that thief didn't have a hard head, I wouldn't need one," Thomas said with a smile.

"David slew Goliath using a sling, and you felled a bandit with a flask," Brian said, smiling.

Aaron then took them to a street with many merchants. He stopped at a shop that made and sold bread. In the store, Brian bought three loaves of bread and handed them to Thomas to keep in his cloth pouch. Aaron then led them to a merchant selling preserved fish. Brian purchased seven, and next to the fish vendor was a merchant who sold figs and nuts. Brian bought two handfuls of each and gave the food to Thomas to put into his bag.

"Brian, I see flasks two vendors down on this side of the street," Martha said, and they went to the merchant and purchased a clay flask.

"Brian, is there anything else you need?" Aaron asked.

"No. We have everything. We'll return to your home and eat before we travel to the Jordan River," Brian answered, and then they went to Aaron's home.

They were sitting at the table in Aaron's house when Thomas handed Brian his pouch. Brian removed four fish and a loaf of bread and gave each person a fish and a portion of the bread. After everyone had received their food, Aaron began to recite a prayer thanking God for the food they were about to eat.

"Aaron, are you a friend of Thomas's father?" Brian asked after Aaron's prayer.

"Yes. For many years, we grew up playing together. He's like a brother to me. We are close friends."

"We are seeking John the Baptist from the village of Ein Kerem, the same place where you were born. Do you know where we can find him?" Brian asked.

"I don't know him, but he performs baptisms along the Jordan River on the east side, not very far from here."

"Can you describe what he looks like?"

"John has long brown hair and a beard. He wears clothes made of camel hair and a brown leather girdle and a black leather belt around his waist. I believe he lives in the wilderness by himself and eats locust, wild honey, berries and other food provided by God. As you travel north along the east side of the Jordan River, you will see people at the edge of the water listening to him preach and waiting to be baptized. I'm sure you'll find him at Bethany on the east side of the river."

"Thank you for the information. You have been very helpful and kind to us. We should be able to identify John because of the description you gave us. We must leave now, my friend. Thank you for your hospitality," Brian said. He stood and shook Aaron's hands. Thomas and Martha also got up from their chairs, and Thomas reached across the table and shook Aaron's hand. Aaron went to the door with his guests and said, "If your travels bring you this way again, you are always welcome to visit."

"You are kind. Thank you," Martha said, and they left to find John the Baptist.

Thomas guided Brian and Martha to the gate. They had entered Jericho, and as they were about to leave the city, Thomas said, "The Jordan River is 32 furlongs east of here and the Dead Sea is 48 furlongs to the south. We should be at the river soon."

The Jordan River is 156 miles long and flows south from the Sea of Galilee to the Dead Sea. The length of the river has at least sixty fords (shallow water crossing points) when the water level is low. There is a ford northeast of Jericho along the Jordan River that is used by pilgrims to cross the river east to Bethany.

Thomas was leading the way for Brian and Martha. The road continued in an eastward direction, and in the distance, there was green vegetation indicating water was nearby. They saw many people traveling compared to the previous day. "Thomas, do you know why more people are traveling today?" Brian asked.

"Yes, because it was the Sabbath. I too shouldn't have traveled, but you seemed to be in a hurry to get to Jericho, and you pay well."

They continued walking and soon arrived at the west bank of the Jordan River, which provided for a greener landscape along the water's edge with palm trees, flora, fauna, reeds and tall green grass.

"We can cross at a ford north of here. It's called the Pilgrims' Crossing and the river is not deep there," Thomas said.

Brian and Martha followed Thomas north along the western shore of the Jordan River. When they were at the ford, Thomas said, "We'll cross here." After Thomas stepped into the water, he said, "Follow me," and then Brian and Martha waded into the water holding hands.

Brian, Martha and Thomas were now standing on the eastern shore of the Jordan River. Brian said, "That wasn't difficult. The river is much narrower than I thought it would be, and it has many shallow areas for crossing. I assumed a boat was needed to cross it."

"I was surprised too. Even if the water were over our heads, we could have swum to the other side," Martha replied.

"We'll follow this path north along the shore until we find pilgrims or John," Thomas said.

While they were walking, a small group of people could be seen ahead of them traveling in the same direction. "We need to catch up to that group of pilgrims. They may know where we can find John the Baptist," Brian said.

Thomas immediately began walking faster and was a good distance from them. He caught up to the group and was now walking with the pilgrims and talking with a man. Thomas and the man stopped walking and were still talking. From the short distance, Brian and Martha saw the man point north, and then the pilgrim continued walking to join his group.

When Brian and Martha caught up to Thomas, Martha said, "Wouldn't it be wonderful to be baptized by John the Baptist since we're here?"

"I'd like to do that. I had it as one of the items on my list to do," Brian replied.

"The man I just spoke with said John is baptizing further up the river," Thomas said.

As they continued walking, they saw a small group of people standing at the water's edge. A man was in the water just above his waist and preaching repentance. He wore a white tunic and had long black hair and a beard. A pilgrim entered the water and waded up to John as two other pilgrims followed. "We should get in line and wait our turn to be baptized," Brian said.

"I'll wait here. I've been baptized," Thomas said.

Brian entered the water with Martha, and they waited for their baptism. When it was Brian's turn, John asked, "Do you repent your sins and accept the heavenly Father into your soul? Do you ask God the almighty to forgive you of your sins?"

"I do. God, please purify my soul of all my sins I have committed and allow me to enter your heavenly kingdom," Brian answered.

John put his left hand on Brian's forehead and placed his right hand on the upper portion of Brian's back and submerged him backward under the water. Brian quickly emerged and moved away from John. It was Martha's turn to be baptized and John said the same words to her he had said to Brian. He then gently submerged her backward into the river and she too quickly rose up from the water.

"Thank you. Do you know where we can find Jesus of Nazareth, your cousin?" Brian asked John after being baptized.

"I don't have a cousin by the name of Jesus from Nazareth," John replied.

Brian and Martha then looked at each other with an expression of "Oops, wrong John."

"Are you from the village of Ein Kerem?" Brian asked.

"No. I am from Jericho. The John you're seeking is 16 furlongs up the river. He has chosen me to baptize pilgrims," he answered.

"Thank you," Brian said, and then he and Martha waded out of the water to the shore. When Brian and Martha were out of the water, Brian went to Thomas and said, "Thomas, you said you were baptized by John the Baptist."

"I was, but it happened a few years back. I didn't know you wanted to be baptized by the John from my village," he replied.

"An honest mistake. I'm sure John and Jesus are very common names in Judea, Samaria and Galilee," Martha said.

"Maybe the men performing baptisms should wear name tags and indicate the village they're from," Brian said, smiling.

"What if there is more than one John from the same place?" she asked.

"We should continue walking north and find John from Ein Kerem," Brian said with a laugh.

They were following the narrow path north along the shore and noticed a large group of pilgrims, in the distance, at the edge of the water looking west toward the river. As Brian, Martha and Thomas got closer, they could hear a man preaching repentance of sins, so they moved to higher ground to view the man who was preaching from the river. They saw a man fitting the description of John the Baptist that Aaron had given them that morning standing in the water up to his hips.

John the Baptist was beheaded between AD 31 to AD 33 by the order of Herod Antipas. Herod Antipas asked his step-daughter, Salome, to dance for his guests, and she agreed only if he promised to give her anything she wanted. Herod said yes to his stepdaughter's request and, after her dance, she demanded John the Baptist be beheaded.

"That's John the Baptist. I can't believe we are actually seeing a prominent figure from the New Testament," Brian said.

"I know. This is truly amazing to witness firsthand John's preaching and performing baptisms. I wish Professor Solomon could be here," Martha said, smiling.

After John stopped preaching, the pilgrims began to form a line waiting for their turn to be baptized. "There are many people here. We will have to wait awhile before we can approach him," Brian said.

"We might as well sit and enjoy the moment," Martha replied.

"I wish I had a camera to take a picture of what he actually looks like, but I guess it'll have to be a photographic memory," Brian said.

"Yes, a mental Kodak moment," she said.

"Yes, you're right. This is a special time, but without film," he said with a laugh.

As the day progressed, the number of pilgrims standing in line to be baptized was steadily decreasing. While Brian and Martha waited for an opportune time to meet John, Brian said, "We should eat now. Thomas, please hand me a loaf of bread and get a fish for you and one for Martha."

Thomas handed the bread to Brian and a fish to Martha. Brian divided the loaf and gave them each a piece. Thomas asked, "Brian, do you want a fish too?"

"No. I'll eat later today," Brian replied, and then they ate their lunch while watching John perform baptisms.

It was now late afternoon and a few pilgrims remained standing at the water's edge. Brian said, "Let's go meet John the Baptist and be baptized."

Brian stood from where he was sitting and went to the river with Martha, and Thomas followed them. When they were at the shore and standing in front of John the Baptist, who was still in the water and was now staring at them, John said, "You have come to me for answers, but first you must repent your sins and ask for forgiveness from God or his kingdom will be closed to you."

As Brian stepped into the river and was looking up at the clear blue sky while holding the palms of his hands skyward, he said, "I am sorry for the sins I have committed, and I ask God almighty for his forgiveness so that I may one day join him in his heavenly kingdom," and when Martha entered the water, she repeated what Brian had just said.

Thomas didn't join them because he had previously been baptized. John was looking at Martha and Brian and gesturing with his hands for them to get closer to him.

"Come closer, pilgrims, into God's sacred body of water. I will baptize you and absolve you of your sins in the name of the Father, God almighty," John said.

Brian and Martha were standing beside John the Baptist when John said, "I baptize you with water, but he will baptize you with a spirit of holiness," and then John submerged Brian backward into the river and afterward he emerged. Martha moved closer to John, and he said the same words to her as he had said to Brian. John submerged her backward and Martha quickly rose up from the water, and then they returned to the shore and waited for John to come out of the river. When John came out of the water, he stood facing Brian, Martha and Thomas. Brian then asked Thomas to hand him the bread and a fish from his pouch, and after he did, Brian handed John a fish and a piece of bread.

John accepted the offering and said, "Thank you. The bounty of God's harvest is everlasting," and he began to eat.

"I would like to meet Jesus of Nazareth, the son of Joseph, a carpenter, whose mother is Mary, who is your cousin," Brian said.

"Why do you seek Jesus?" he asked.

"I mean him no harm. I only want to talk with him," Brian answered.

"I haven't seen Jesus in many years. The last I heard he was in Nazareth working as a carpenter with his father, Joseph," John answered after staring at Brian for a moment.

"How far is Nazareth from here?" Brian asked.

"It's a two-day journey," he answered.

"Thank you," Brian said, and then John began walking east while eating his food.

As John disappeared from view into the wilderness, Brian said, "Thomas, John thinks Jesus could still be in Nazareth. Will you escort us there?"

"It will cost two shekels more," he answered.

Brian removed his money pouch and gave Thomas two shekels, and then he said, "Here is the money we owe. We will pay you two more shekels when we are at Nazareth."

"Thank you. I like our business arrangement. We must travel on the east side of the Jordan River to avoid going through Samaria. The people of Samaria don't like people from Judea because of our different interpretation of the Jewish religion. When we get closer to Nazareth, we will cross at a ford," Thomas replied.

"We should get going now," Brian said.

It had been two days since Brian and Martha were transported to the Holy Land. David was in his lab checking Stella's components, making sure they were functioning properly. The control panel lights were dimly lit, indicating Stella was in hibernation mode while still keeping a lock on Brian and Martha's coordinates. David went to the generator in the same room as the StellaPort and tested it as a precaution just in case of a power failure. He didn't want to risk the electricity being cut to Stella, because if it were, the electromagnetic waves attached to Brian and Martha would be severed. He would have no choice but to travel back in time to try to find them and that would be difficult to do because he was the only one who knew how to operate his time machine.

Stella's tracking window showed longitude 31.8363 and latitude 35.5526, indicating that Brian and Martha were at Bethabara (Bethany) on the east side of the Jordan River. David went to the chalkboard and retrieved a yellow piece of chalk and extended the dashes from Jericho to Bethabara on his map of the Holy Land. He knew they were now traveling in a northerly direction and wondered if they would travel to Nazareth or Capernaum next, but he would have to wait and see.

Brian, Thomas and Martha continued to follow the narrow dirt trail north, snaking along the Jordan River. While the sun was setting, Thomas said, "We should walk a little further. We might locate some pilgrims camping near the side of the road and, if so, I'll ask if we can join them."

They walked another 16 furlongs and saw a campfire in the distance. As they got closer to the campsite, they noticed people sitting in a circle around a fire. "I'll go and ask them if they will share their camp with us," Thomas said, and then he left while Martha and Brian waited for him to return.

They watched Thomas approach the group. One man stood up and greeted him while the others still sat on the ground. Thomas and the man talked, and after a few minutes, Thomas returned to Brian and Martha and said, "They are pilgrims from Galilee and are going to meet John the Baptist in the morning to be baptized. The man with whom I spoke said we can share their camp."

"We need a place to rest for the night, and we would be safer in a larger group," Brian said, and then Thomas led them to the camp.

A group of three men and two women were sitting around a fire and made room for their guests to sit with them. The men and women in the group were in their mid twenties. The men were slim and had medium-length hair and beards, and the women had long hair covered by head scarves and were petite.

Thomas said to the stranger with whom he had previously spoken, "Thank you for allowing us to share the warmth of your fire. My name is Thomas. His name is Brian and her name is Martha."

The man said, "You are welcome. I'm Daniel and to my right are Hanna, Maya, Jeremiah and Ethan. We are from Galilee and traveling to Jerusalem to visit the Temple, but before that we'll be baptized by John the Baptist."

"Daniel, how many days have you been traveling?" Brian asked.

"It's been two days, and how many for you?"

"The same, but we started from Jerusalem."

"I've not heard the name Brian before. Where are you from?" Daniel asked.

"I am from Rome and traveling the Jordan Valley to know this beautiful land and its people. We are planning to go to Nazareth and find our friend Jesus. Do you know of him?"

"The name Jesus of Nazareth has been mentioned many times. He is a great and righteous man. He speaks the word of God to all who will listen. Why do you seek Jesus?" Daniel asked.

"I am a friend and would like to hear his preachings in person for a better understanding of the meaning behind his message," Brian answered.

"Are you hungry?"

"Yes. We ate many hours ago. We're planning to buy supplies tomorrow for our journey to Nazareth. We have some figs, which you are welcome to. I wish we had more to offer."

"Hanna, please give our guests bread and grapes," Daniel said. Hanna stood and got a cloth pouch similar to Thomas's and went around the campfire and gave each person a piece of bread and some grapes.

Brian asked Thomas to give everybody some figs, which he did. Maya then stood up and got her bag and began to hand out almonds to everybody.

"I'll cook some meat to share with our guests," Ethan said, and then he went to his pouch and returned to the campfire with the meat on a stick and began cooking it over the fire. Brian's eyes lit up because he had not had meat other than fish for the past two days. The same was true for Martha. They welcomed a different source of meat in their diet.

After the meat was cooked, Ethan went to everyone and cut a piece of mutton from the stick for them to eat. Daniel asked, "Brian, do you have family in Galilee?"

"No. I'm just seeking Jesus, the son of Joseph the carpenter and whose mother is Mary. Do you know where I can find him?"

"No," Daniel answered, and he asked the others in his group if they knew Jesus from Nazareth.

Jeremiah answered and said, "I was passing through Nazareth a few years back and stopped at the synagogue to pray. There was a man inside praying alone and then a woman entered, and she said, "Jesus, your father, Joseph, needs your help," and they left. I will never forget that day. He seemed to have an aura of holiness about him."

"Do you remember what he looked like?" Brian asked.

"No. I was there for only a few minutes before the woman entered, and they left together," he answered.

While everybody was sitting and eating their food, Brian asked, "Daniel, is there a village north of here along the river where we can purchase food and sail on a boat?"

"Yes. You can buy food and transport in the village of Coreae in Samaria. You must travel up the river from Coreae to Scythopolis in Galilee, and then travel overland to Nazareth," he replied.

"How many days will it take if we travel that route?" Brian asked.

"Two days at most, and you'll save time and energy by traveling on the river."

"We want to thank you for being very helpful and generous with your food, and if you don't mind, we'll sleep here near the fire," Brian said to the group after he stood.

"We should all rest because we have a long day ahead us," Daniel said.

Brian, Martha and Thomas lay on the ground in the same spot where they were sitting and so did the group from Galilee. Brian awoke and saw that the campfire was dying, so he got up and went to retrieve wood to put on the fire. While he was getting wood, he remembered the dried food stored in his mantle. He reached under his outer garment and unzipped a pocket and removed the food which had become stale. He dug a small hole with a stick and buried the dried food in the desert, and then he returned to the campsite.

CHAPTER 19

It was morning and the sun was beginning to rise. The group from Galilee had left. Martha woke up and stood and saw that the Galileans had departed. She looked around but could not see them, and then she bent over and gently pushed Brian's shoulder to wake him up. When Brian awoke, he said, "Good morning."

"Good morning. Our friends have moved on. I don't see them anywhere," Martha said.

The sound of Brian's and Martha's voices woke up Thomas. Thomas stood, and after stretching his back and arms, he said, "I see the Galileans have quietly left."

"We should do the same," Brian said.

"I'd like to wash my face and hands," Martha said, and then they went to the river.

At the edge of the river they washed themselves, and after they were done, Brian said, "We must follow the trail north along the shore and when we come to a ford near the village of Coreae, we will cross it to the other side. We'll buy food there and try to arrange transport up the river by boat."

"The village is a half day's walk, and we can cross the river near Alexandrium and from there Coreae is 16 furlongs, not far from the water," Thomas said.

They returned to the path. While walking, they saw wild boars at the edge of the river drinking water. "I'd like to have one for dinner," Brian said with a wink, after seeing the boars.

Martha smiled, acknowledging his joke.

"Have you noticed how healthy and fit the people are? It must be from the organic food they eat and the exercise from walking.

Look, I see a leopard in the tall grass stalking the wild hogs," Martha said.

When the big cat moved closer to the boars, it startled them, and then the wild hogs began running south along the shore of the river as the spotted cat chased them from view. "I wish I'd kept the dagger. I hope we don't meet up with a lion. Let me know if you see a long and thick stick. I can use it as a weapon," Brian said while watching the cat chase its prey.

Thomas was twenty yards ahead of Brian and Martha. He stopped walking so they could catch up to him. When they were together, Thomas said, "We still have 40 furlongs to go before we're at Coreae."

They continued walking north and saw a group of three men traveling south on the same trail. As the group was about to pass by, Brian asked, "Is Coreae near?"

The men stopped walking and one of them said, "Yes. It's 32 furlongs from here. You'll soon come to a path that will lead you to a ford, and there you can cross the river safely and then follow the trail north."

"Thank you," Brian said. The man nodded his head in response and resumed walking south with his friends.

After walking for a while, Martha said, "Brian, look up ahead. There's a path from this trail going to the river."

Thomas was already following the path. When Brian and Martha stood next to him, Thomas said, "This is the ford where we can cross safely. The distance to the other side is about thirty yards and the current looks fairly strong."

"I'll go first. Follow me," and then he went into the water. As Thomas moved further away from the shore, the water level quickly rose above his knees to his waist because of a steep drop in the river's bed. Brian entered the water with Martha behind him as they held hands.

"This ford is wider and deeper than the one we crossed yesterday. The current is also much stronger here. Hold my hand tight and stay close to me," Brian said.

"Okay, take your time. We're not here to set a river crossing record," Martha replied.

Thomas was almost to the other side of the river when he stumbled and fell under the water, but quickly emerged. "Thomas, are you okay?" Brian shouted.

"Yes. I stepped on a rock and lost my balance," Thomas yelled back, and then he kept moving west and finally was standing on the other side of the river watching Brian and Martha cross.

Brian and Martha soon waded out of the water and stood next to Thomas.

"I can understand how you fell under. The water is murky and has many rocks on the river bed, and to make things worse the current is moving rapidly downstream, but we crossed safely," Brian said.

"Praise God the almighty. He is watching over us," Thomas said.

They were now on the west side of the Jordan River and following the path north, which led to another narrow dirt trail snaking along the river. They could see two men at a short distance traveling south and approaching them. When the men got closer, one man said, "Samarians."

"Hello. Will this road lead us to Coreae?" Brian asked.

"Yes, but Samarians are not welcomed," the man who said Samarians replied.

"I'm from Rome. Will I be welcomed?" Brian asked him.

"Yes. Is she from Samaria?" the man asked, looking at Martha.

"No. I'm also a Roman. Will I be allowed to enter the village?" Martha asked.

"I'm from Judea and they are my friends," Thomas said.

"Where are you traveling to?" the man asked Thomas.

"To Nazareth. We're not planning to pass through Samaria. We'll stop in Coreae to rest," he answered.

"My friends and I mean you no harm. We thought you were Samarians. Please accept our apology," the man said.

"Apology accepted," Thomas replied.

"Stay on this road and you will come to Coreae," the man said, and then the men continued walking south.

The village was on the left side of the road and nestled in the Jordan Valley. Here the homes were made of limestone. The stone houses did not differ in style or building material from the ones in Judea. It seemed as though a master builder had one architectural plan for the whole region. They arrived at Coreae and went to the center of the village where there was a well for water. At the well, Brian said, "After we fill our flasks, we'll find a merchant to buy enough food to last us until we arrive in Nazareth."

They filled their flasks and then walked down a narrow street looking for a shop to buy food. On the left side of the street was a vendor selling a variety of food products, where Brian bought a small quantity of bread, fruit, nuts, cooked lamb and salted fish, and he gave the food to Thomas for storage in his pouch. "Let's find a place to eat and rest," Brian said after purchasing their supplies.

"We can sit in the shade under the palm tree at the beginning of this street," Martha said, and they went to the tree and sat under it.

"We must ask somebody if they know of a person who owns a boat so we can buy passage north to the village of Scythopolis (Beit She'an) in Galilee," Brian said after they rested.

"Brian, you should ask the merchant who sold you the food. He seemed to like you," Thomas said.

"Okay," Brian said. They went to the vendor who had sold them their supplies. Brian entered the shop and approached the merchant, saying, "Hello again. Do you know a person who owns a boat that would be willing to take us north up the river to Scythopolis?"

"Yes. My friend uses his boat to fish on the river, and he sometimes ventures to the Sea of Galilee," the man answered.

"Where can we find him?"

"You must follow the road back to the water and then travel north along the western shore. You'll find him either working on his boat or trawling for fish with his net. Simon is his name, and when you find him, please let him know that Saul sent you to him."

"Thank you for the food and information. You have been very helpful. I'll mention your name to him."

"You're most welcome, and may God protect you and your friends," Saul said. Then he shook Brian's hand.

Brian, Martha and Thomas returned to the narrow dirt road that led them to Coreae and were now walking east toward the Jordan River. "There's the path Saul mentioned. I hope we can find his friend Simon," Thomas said as they got closer to the river.

"Look up the river. There's a boat," Martha said while they were walking north along the shore.

"Maybe it's Simon," Brian said.

They continued walking along the shore until they were standing in an open area parallel to the man in the boat, who was casting his fishing net into the water. "Simon," Brian shouted, but the man did not hear him, so Brian, Martha and Thomas began shouting, "Simon," and flailing their arms to get the man's attention.

The man in the boat turned and looked west in their direction and waved his right hand, indicating that he heard them shouting, and then Brian waved, signaling for the fisherman to come join them. The man pulled in his net and used a long wood pole to propel his craft on the water to where they were standing. "Is your name Simon? Saul said you could help us," Brian said when the boat was near them.

The man used his strength and pushed the pole into the riverbed to thrust his boat forward and embed it into the mud. The gray-haired, bearded man climbed out of the boat. He stood five feet ten inches tall and appeared to be in his late fifties with a muscular build and a tan complexion. He was wearing a head scarf to protect his head from the hot sun. "Yes, my name is Simon and Saul is my friend," the man said while staring at Brian.

"We just met Saul. He said you could help us travel north on the river to Scythopolis by boat," Brian said.

"Yes. I can transport you in my boat, but it will cost one shekel per person," Simon replied.

"That sounds like a reasonable price to pay. Can we leave now?" Brian asked.

"Yes. I'm ready to go if you are. What are your names?" Simon asked.

"Her name is Martha. His name is Thomas and I'm Brian," Brian answered.

Simon's boat was twelve feet long and had three planks that could seat six men. On the floor were two oars for rowing and a mast for sailing. "You'll have to climb in after I push my boat free from the mud." He pushed and freed the vessel from the mud and held it steady as Thomas climbed in first, then Martha with the help of Thomas and Brian. Brian and then Simon got into the boat. Brian sat next to Martha in the front of the boat while Thomas sat in the rear near Simon, who was standing and using a long wood pole to push off the riverbed to move the boat on the water. They were now in the middle of the river as Simon navigated northward against the current. "Simon, how long will it take for us to arrive at Scythopolis?" Brian asked.

"My guess is before the sun sets. The voyage will be long because we'll be traveling upstream," Simon answered.

"Look, there's a lion on the eastern shore drinking water," Martha said.

"Traveling by boat allows for a beautiful view of the landscape on both sides of the river. We are very fortunate to see the animals and birds in their natural habitat," Brian replied.

"I know this is an awesome view from the boat," she said, and then she gave Brian a kiss on the cheek.

"What does the word awesome mean?" Thomas asked.

Martha looked at Brian, who was smiling, and then she turned toward Thomas and said, "Awesome means amazing."

"Yes, this is an amazing journey," Thomas said with a smile.

Simon was still using his pole to push off the riverbed as he said, "Soon the water will become turbulent. I'll need to use the oars until we're in calm waters. You must hold onto something inside of the boat because the strong rapids have the potential of tossing you overboard."

An hour had passed since Simon warned them about the rough water ahead. Sitting and facing north, Brian could see the river beginning to get violent. He said, "Seems like the water is becoming more dangerous."

"Yes, it is. From this point forward, I must row with oars until we are in calmer waters. You must hold onto the boat," Simon said, and then the small boat began to bob up and down on the water as Brian,

Martha and Thomas gripped the board they were sitting on with one hand and used the other to hold onto the top of the boat's hull.

"If we capsize, we must swim to the boat and hang onto it so we don't drown," Brian said.

"That's good advice, but I don't think we'll capsize. I have navigated this part of the river many times before and never had a problem," Simon said.

Martha felt at ease because Simon had experience operating his boat in turbulent waters. As Simon rowed, the noise from the rushing water became louder and the rapids were beginning to toss them up and down and tilt the boat from side to side. Simon was working hard to keep control of the craft, and he shouted, "Hold on. We still have some distance to go before we reach calmer waters. It's going to get rougher."

The boat rocked up and down because of the violent force of the waves smashing against it. They were in the rapids and were now being lifted up from their seats due to the extreme conditions. Suddenly, a force jolted them out of the water and when they landed, Martha accidentally released her grip and was tossed overboard. The right arm sleeve of her mantle got caught on a nail sticking out of the inside top edge of the hull. Martha was partially in the river, but she was able to grab and hold onto the top of the boat's hull with her left hand. Thomas was sitting behind Martha and quickly leaned over the side and grabbed onto her clothing as they continued to bounce up and down in the water. Brian also came to Martha's rescue and held onto her left hand that was holding onto the boat and then he and Thomas pulled her back into the vessel.

"Wow, we almost lost you," Brian said.

"I know. I have goosebumps. I don't know if I'm cold or just frightened. I'm shaking all over my body," Martha said.

Simon kept rowing the boat while shouting, "You must continue to hold on. We have a little further to go before we're in calmer waters."

The river was becoming less violent, and in the distance they could see calm water ahead of them, which was a relief after their ordeal.

When they were in tranquil waters, Brian said, "Martha, imagine what the fishermen must have experienced during a storm on the Sea of Galilee."

"All boats should have seatbelts," Martha said.

"Good idea," Brian said, smiling.

"I'll raise the mast now, and we'll sail to Scythopolis. We should be there soon," Simon said. After he raised and attached the sail, they enjoyed the panoramic view of the Jordan Valley.

"I'm hungry. Let's eat now. Thomas, please remove the mutton from your bag and slice it into four equal pieces and give a portion to everybody," Brian said.

After Thomas removed the meat, he handed his bag to Brian and then cut the mutton into four pieces. Thomas gave everyone some meat while Brian distributed bread, figs and nuts to each person. Simon was sitting in the rear of the boat, steering it with the rudder as Brian handed him food. "Thank you," Simon said. After he received his share, he asked, "Brian, why are you going to Scythopolis? Do you have family there?"

"No. We're traveling to Nazareth to find our friend Jesus. His father is Joseph, a carpenter, and his mother's name is Mary. Do you know him?"

"No. There are many men named Jesus in Galilee."

"How far is Scythopolis to Nazareth?"

"It's a one-day journey. You must travel 24 furlongs from the river to Scythopolis, but the sun will be setting by the time you get there. I suggest you find a place to rest for the night and travel to Nazareth in the morning."

"I'll do as you suggest. Can we buy overland transportation in Scythopolis?" Brian asked.

"I'm sure you'll find somebody willing to be your guide," Simon answered.

Everyone on the boat was quiet and enjoying the scenery while sailing slowly north on the Jordan River. "Brian, I'm going to have a short nap," Martha said as they sailed.

Thomas saw Martha lie on a plank, and he did the same. Brian turned to the rear of the boat and said, "Simon, looks like I'll be your copilot for the rest of the trip." Simon smiled and nodded his head.

After two hours had passed, Simon said, "We are approaching the road to Scythopolis. I must now take down the mast and sail." After he took down the sail and mast and stored the equipment under the planks of the boat, he removed the long pole to navigate the boat in the water. Simon was slowly steering his vessel to the west side of the river. In the distance, Brian saw people on both sides of the shore walking on roads. "We're almost at the location where Simon will drop us off," Brian said after he woke up Martha and Thomas.

Simon kept navigating the boat north with his pole, and then he said while pointing with his left hand, "The road to Scythopolis is there. You must follow it west."

After Simon maneuvered his boat to the shore of the river, he climbed out and pulled the front of his boat into the mud to keep it from drifting away. Thomas got out of the boat first, and he helped Martha. Before Brian got out of the vessel, he removed his coin pouch and paid Simon his fee of three shekels. When Simon received his money, he said, "Thank you. You must go west from here until you come to a road. Follow it to Scythopolis."

"Thank you for the transportation and information. I wish you a safe trip home," Brian said.

"You're welcome," Simon said, and then he pushed and freed his boat from the mud and climbed in and raised the mast and sail. As Simon was beginning to sail south, he looked back and waved bye, and they returned the gesture by waving too.

Simon had dropped them off at the closest point between the river and the road to Scythopolis. Brian, Martha and Thomas began moving west in search of the road Brian had seen from the boat. In the distance, they saw people traveling west.

"Those people must be on a trail," Martha said.

"I'm sure if we keep going west, we will come to the road that I saw from the river," Brian said.

Thomas was soon a good distance from them, and he stopped and was signaling with his hands, pointing to the ground to indicate that he had found the road. "It seems Thomas has found it," Brian said.

When they caught up to Thomas, he said, "Scythopolis should be 24 furlongs from here," and then they continued traveling west. A village could be seen in the distance as the sun was beginning to set. "We should walk faster so we can arrive in the village before nightfall and find a place to rest for the evening," Brian said.

David was in his lab using the PC to surf the Internet for ancient maps of the Holy Land. He found a website that displayed a map of old cities during the time of Jesus. The map identified the village of Bethany on the east side of the Jordan River, the place where the New Testament states John preached and performed baptisms. He sat back in his chair and gazed at the map and wondered if Brian and Martha had seen or met John yet. He was beginning to feel envious because he could only monitor their movements, while they experienced the thrill of a lifetime.

Luke entered the lab and went to David, and asked, "Dad, what are you doing?"

"I found an ancient map of the Holy Land on the Internet. The last coordinates for Martha and Brian place them at Bethabara (Bethany) on the east side of the Jordan River," David answered.

"Where do you think they are now?" Luke asked.

"There's one way to know. Let's see their coordinates on Stella," David answered.

They went to Stella and saw in the tracking window longitude 35.5059 and latitude 32.5042. David removed a pen and small notebook from his shirt pocket and wrote down the coordinates and then went to the PC with Luke. At the PC, he logged on to a longitude and latitude website and, after entering the coordinates, he said, "Luke, they're in the village of Scythopolis."

David went to the chalkboard near his workbench and removed a piece of yellow chalk. He extended the dashes from Bethabara to Scythopolis. After he stepped back from the blackboard, he said, "Seems they are heading for Nazareth."

"Do you think they'll locate Jesus there?" Luke asked.

"I don't know. It's evening now for them, and they're most likely resting. I guess we should do the same." Luke left the lab while David stayed to check to see if Stella's components needed maintenance before leaving, but they were all operating fine.

Brian, Martha and Thomas arrived in Scythopolis as the sun was setting and were now searching for a place to sleep for the night. The village was larger than Coreae, but smaller than Jericho and Jerusalem and the homes were built in the same fashion as the others they had seen so far. "This street has shops and maybe there is a place selling rooms," Martha said.

"I see a wine merchant. We can ask the owner if they have rooms for the night," Thomas said.

"Lead on, Thomas," Brian said.

They followed Thomas to the shop and after entering, he went to the owner and asked, "Sir, do you have rooms for the evening?"

"Sorry, we're full."

"Do you know of a place that has room for three people?"

"Yes. Four doors down, but he could be full too."

"Thank you," Thomas said, and he walked out of the shop. After they were outside, he said to Brian and Martha, "The man told me he didn't have any vacant rooms to rent and suggested we try four doors down."

"Let's try there," Brian said.

The man had referred them to a house where Thomas knocked on the door. A man in his late twenties answered and said, "Hello. How can I help you?"

"Do you have any vacant rooms?" Thomas asked.

"Yes. I have one room available."

"How much will it cost for the three people to stay the night?"

"It'll cost you one denarius each."

Thomas looked at Brian, who nodded his head in approval, and then he said, "Fine, we will take the room."

"You must pay me first," the man said, and then Brian removed his coin pouch and paid the man. After receiving his money, the man said, "Follow me."

They entered the man's single-level home and were led to a large room that had a thin blanket for a door and four padded sleeping mats on the wood floor. The house was small, but had three large rooms in the back and one big room as you entered. "We should ask the wine shop owner if there's a place to arrange transportation on horseback," Brian said.

"Okay, let's leave now," Thomas replied.

As they were leaving, the man who rented them the room was sitting at the table. Thomas said to him, "We must leave now, but we'll return," and then they left.

Martha and Brian waited outside the wine shop as Thomas entered and approached the owner. He said, "The man you referred me to rented us a room for the night. Thank you."

"You're welcome. How can I help you?"

"Is there a place where my friends and I could buy transport to Nazareth on horseback?" Thomas asked.

"Yes. My friend owns a farm, and he has horses and provides that type of service at a good price."

"Is your friend open for business now?"

"Yes. To get to his house you must go to the end of this street and then turn right. His farm is at the end of the street. You can't miss the place."

"Thank you," Thomas said, and he went to where Brian and Martha were standing and said, "The owner has a friend who owns a farm and provides a transportation service on horseback. He gave me the directions to his house."

"Good work, Thomas," Brian said with a smile.

Thomas followed the directions the wine shop owner had given him and led Brian and Martha to the farm. The farmstead was small, consisting of a single-level home and in the back of the house was a large fenced-off area for growing crops and for animals to graze. They walked to the front door. Thomas knocked on it and an older, gray-haired man answered and said, "Hello. How can I help you?"

"We would like to buy transportation by horseback to Nazareth. Can you help us?" Thomas asked.

"Yes, and for how many people?"

"Three."

"It will cost you four shekels, one shekel per person and one for the guide."

Thomas looked at Brian, who nodded his head in approval, and Thomas said, "We accept the price."

"We want to leave tomorrow morning. How long will it take us to travel to Nazareth?" Brian then asked.

"A half day or possibly a little longer. We must rest the horses on the way," the man answered.

"Fine. We'll be here in the morning," Brian said, and then he asked, "What is your name?"

"Joseph. And yours?" the man said.

"Brian. Her name is Martha and his name is Thomas," Brian replied.

"I will see you here tomorrow morning," Joseph said and then closed his door.

Brian, Martha and Thomas returned to the home where they had rented a room for the night. Thomas knocked on the door. The same man answered and said, "Please come in. Can I offer you anything?"

"No, thank you," Brian answered, and they went to their room and claimed a padded mat on the floor to sleep for the night.

CHAPTER 20

Martha, Brian and Thomas were awakened by the sound of a crowing rooster from behind the house. They got up and stretched their arms and backs. "The padded mat made it more comfortable for sleeping," Brian said.

"My back doesn't feel as stiff this morning. I guess I'm getting used to sleeping on a hard surface," Martha said.

"Shall we leave now for Joseph's farm?" Thomas asked after he stood up.

"Yes, let's go," Brian answered.

The man who rented them the room was sitting at the table in the front room drinking hot tea. As they were about to leave, the man asked, "Can I offer you something to eat or drink?"

"Yes, that would be fine. What do you have?" Brian asked.

"I have goat's milk, hot tea, water or wine to drink and fruits, olives, bread and nuts to eat," the man answered.

"We would like to have hot tea, bread, figs and olives," Brian said.

"Please sit at the table and I'll serve you," the man said.

After Brian, Martha and Thomas were seated, Brian asked, "Thomas, how much food is in your bag?"

"Not much. We should buy some food and refill our flasks with water. We have only some figs and nuts left," Thomas answered after he looked in his pouch.

"Yesterday I saw a shop on the way to Joseph's farm that sells food and has a well to get water," Brian said.

The man returned to the table and set three wooden bowls onto it. Each one had a serving of bread, figs and olives. He then served his guests their hot tea. After eating their meal, Brian asked the man, "How much do we owe you?"

"One denarius," the man answered. After Brian paid him, they left.

"The shop I saw was on this street before we turned right to Joseph's farm," Brian said when they were outside the man's home.

Brian was leading the way to the store. When they found it, he purchased fish, bread, olives and figs and gave the food to Thomas for storing in his bag. After giving the food to Thomas, Brian said, "We should have enough food to last until we arrive in Nazareth. Now we'll get water."

Brian, Martha and Thomas found the water well and, after filling their flasks, they headed for Joseph's farm. When they were at Joseph's house, Brian knocked on the door. Joseph opened it and said, "Hello, Brian, Martha and Thomas. Please come in."

The home was larger than the homes they had previously visited, but had the same architectural design as the others. The house had a large room upon entering and four additional medium-sized rooms toward the rear. Joseph was married and had three children: a son and two daughters.

"Joseph, are these the people that you will be guiding to Nazareth?" Joseph's wife asked after she walked into the front room.

Joseph was standing at one end of the table and answered, "Yes. This is Brian. Her name is Martha and his name is Thomas. They are the individuals I told you about last night."

"Hello. My name is Dara. Our children, Levi, Sarah and Raisa, are outside and tending to the farm," she said.

"Levi is feeding the horses, and later he'll give them water. Our girls are tending to the other animals. We'll leave soon for Nazareth," Joseph said.

"We'll leave when you're ready. Are you going to be our guide?" Brian asked.

"Yes. Does everybody know how to ride on a horse?" Joseph asked.

"I do," Martha answered.

"No. I have never been on one," Brian replied.

"I know how to ride on a donkey," Thomas answered.

"I'll give Brian and Thomas a quick lesson. Thomas, riding on a horse is just like being on a donkey except the animal is much larger," Joseph said.

"I would like to ride the tamest horse you own," Brian said.

"Joseph, do you have a pony for Brian to ride?" Martha asked, smiling.

"Martha, I'm sorry, but he's too big for a pony ride," Joseph said with a laugh.

Levi entered the house through the rear door and went to the front room and announced that the horses were ready. "Thank you, Levi. While I'm away from home, you are in charge until I return," Joseph said.

"I will take care of the farm, and I'll see you when you return," Levi replied.

"Please come with me," Joseph said, and then Brian, Martha and Thomas followed him to the rear of the house and exited through the back door to his backyard, where they saw four healthy-looking horses. The horses were of Arabian breed and did not have saddles, but did have a thick riding cloth on their back and leather headgear. Joseph then mounted a horse to give Brian and Thomas a quick demonstration on how to control the animal using the reins.

"When I gently tug the right side of the strap, the animal will move to the right. When I tug the left one, he moves to the left, and to make him stop, I will pull both straps toward me. To go forward, just shake them," Joseph said, and then he dismounted his horse and gave the reins to Brian, saying, "It's your turn." Joseph untied another horse from the post and handed the reins to Thomas and said, "Think of this horse as a big donkey."

Brian and Thomas mounted their horses and took the leather straps into their hands and were now controlling their horses just like Joseph had.

"Not bad for first timers," Joseph said.

"It seems this horse likes me," Brian said.

"He's on the tamest one I own," Joseph whispered to Martha, who was standing next to him.

"You're the man," she said, smiling.

"I know we should get going," Brian replied with a smile.

"Okay, let's mount up and go to Nazareth," Joseph said, and then he and Martha got onto their horses.

After Levi opened the gate of the fence, Joseph said, "Levi, take care of your mother and sisters until I return," as he rode past his son.

"I will, Father. Have a safe trip and may God be with you," he replied.

Joseph passed through the opening in the fence and was leading the way with Brian, then Martha, and Thomas following in the rear. He said, "I'll take us to a trail that will lead us to the road going to Nazareth. The journey will take a half day because we must rest the horses along the way and give them water."

They had been riding for a short time when Joseph hollered, "There's the road ahead of us." They were soon on it and traveling northwest toward Nazareth. The dirt was compacted because of being heavily traveled and it had many rocks. The landscape was barren on both sides of the road, with rolling hills and small mountains. Looking as far as the eye could see, there were only shrubs, dirt and rocks. It was a dry skillet of a land they had to pass through. They saw people walking and riding on horses and donkeys. "We'll give the animals water at an oasis and afterward rest them at my friend Yusuf's camp. Yusuf will serve us food and drinks and provide us shade from the hot sun," Joseph said after they were riding for a while.

"Joseph, I would like to stop now so we can eat and drink some water," Brian said.

"Of course," he replied, and then he turned left off the road and led them a short distance to where they dismounted their horses.

"Thomas, please bring the food," Brian said. Thomas went to his horse and removed his bag and gave it to Brian, who handed out a portion of bread, figs and nuts to everybody.

"Thank you. Yusuf will have plenty of food and drinks," Joseph said after Brian gave him some food.

"You're welcome," Brian replied, and then he went to where Martha was while Thomas went to Joseph to chat.

"It looks like we'll soon be traveling in a sandy area of the desert. Jacob wasn't kidding when he said, 'Water can become more precious than gold in this arid land,'" Brian said as he stood next to Martha.

"I can't imagine myself traveling on foot. It would be a grueling ordeal. I'm glad we could find horses to ride. I'm sure many people have died out here because of not being prepared to travel in this harsh environment," Martha said.

"I know what you mean. Legions have passed through this perilous land, such as the Knights Templar and the Roman army. They must have lost many men due to dehydration and heat stroke," Brian said.

"I guess if you were raised in this kind of environment, you would quickly learn the skills to survive in it," Martha said.

After everybody had finished eating and drinking, Joseph said, "Let's mount our horses and go to the oasis so the animals can have some water too." They mounted their horses and Joseph guided them to the road as the temperature was getting warmer. Brian removed his mantle and draped it in front of him across his horse's back. He was becoming more fatigued and drinking a lot of water because he had never been in such an arid environment. Martha didn't feel the effects of the heat as much because she had lived in the Arizona desert. "We'll be at the oasis soon. We should see many travelers watering and resting their horses," Joseph hollered to his riders.

They rode further. Joseph turned right off the road and, after exiting, he said, "This trail will take us to the water. It's not far from here."

Joseph was still leading the way, and in the distance they saw people, horses, camels and donkeys gathered at an area in the desert. The oasis was an underground spring providing a shallow pool of water and was about five cubits in diameter with four tall palm trees that didn't provide much shade from the hot sun. Joseph selected an area away from the watering hole and dismounted his horse. Brian, Thomas and Martha dismounted their horses. Joseph took the horses to the water to quench their thirst. Brian, Martha and Thomas followed him and at the oasis splashed water on themselves to cool off from the desert heat. "When the horses have finished drinking water, we'll continue to Yusuf's camp," Joseph said. After resting a short period of time, the horses stopped drinking from the spring and Joseph said, "It seems they have had enough water." He led his horses away from the watering hole to be mounted by their riders. When everyone was on their horse, Joseph led them to the road to Nazareth and after riding for 80 furlongs, he turned his horse west, exited the road and hollered, "This is the trail to Yusuf's campsite."

They soon saw in the distance a large tan-colored tent with camels, goats and sheep nearby. They entered the campsite, approached the front entrance and dismounted their horses. The tent was made of woven goat hair and was secured with ropes fastened to wood pegs sticking out of the ground. A man came out of the tent and greeted Joseph, saying, "Hello, my friend," and the two men shook hands.

"Hi, my friend. I hope things are well with you and your family. I've brought guests. We have come to rest the horses and then continue to Nazareth," Joseph said.

"Please secure your horses and be my guests," Yusuf said, and then he went to his tent and moved the right flap to the side and said, "Please enter and make yourselves comfortable."

When Brian, Martha and Thomas entered the tent, a woman and two teenage girls greeted them. "Welcome. My name is Farhah and these are my daughters, Hafa and Karam. Please sit and be comfortable."

Martha and Brian didn't see chairs, only big pillows on the floor, and they didn't know what to do next. "Thank you," Thomas said, and then he sat on one of the large pillows and Brian and Martha did the same.

The interior of the tent was spacious, with one large room in the front for eating and entertaining. There were candles and oil lamps for light in the evening and a big handwoven carpet was on the floor in the center of the room. The tent had three additional rooms that were separated by blankets hanging at each entrance. The rooms had been sewn onto the main tent to make one large living area for the family. After Joseph and Yusuf entered, they sat on pillows too. While Farhah and her daughters were in another room, Yusuf conversed with his guests.

"Joseph, what are your friends' names?" Yusuf asked.

"This is Thomas, her name is Martha and his name is Brian," Joseph answered, while pointing to them.

"Can I offer you food and drink before you leave?" Yusuf asked.

"What do you have to drink?" Brian asked.

"I can offer you goat's milk, wine or water."

"I would like a cup of wine," Brian answered.

"I'll have the same," Martha replied.

"I'll have wine too," Thomas said.

"I'd like some wine and a piece of Farhah's delicious cheese," Joseph said.

"I can offer you grapes, nuts, figs and bread to eat," Yusuf said.

"Bread, grapes and nuts would be fine," Brian answered.

"Farhah," Yusuf hollered, and after she entered the room, he said, "Please serve our guests bread, grapes, nuts and wine. Joseph has requested a piece of your delicious cheese."

Farhah smiled and went to another room to prepare the food and drinks. Hafa and Karam returned to the main area of the tent and handed clay cups to their guests. Farhah followed her daughters with a clay pitcher and poured wine into their cups while her daughters quickly returned with three wooden bowls containing bread, grapes and almonds and set them on the floor. "Please help yourselves," Yusuf said, and they took turns removing food from the bowls.

"Joseph, as I recall, the last time you visited it was on your way to Tyre to buy horses. How did that work out?" Yusuf asked.

"I bought two horses at a good price. They are outside. Would you like to see them?"

"Later, my friend. Eat and rest. I'll have my daughters dance for us."

Yusuf then clapped his hands twice and called his children by their names. They immediately came to him, and he said, "Please entertain our guests with a dance while I will play the *oud* (one of the oldest guitars in the world) and your mother plays the *riq* (tambourine)."

Farhah entered the room and stood next to Yusuf, and he gave her the *riq*. They started to play their instruments as their daughters danced in the center of the room. Thomas stood and began dancing and when he was in front of Martha, he extended his hands for her to join them. She stood and danced while Brian and Joseph watched the performance. After the music stopped, everyone clapped their hands in appreciation. "Martha is not only beautiful, but is a very good dancer. Brian, I'll give you fifty camels for her," Yusuf said, smiling.

Brian smiled while looking at Martha and said, "Not today, but I'll keep the offer in mind."

"You're a lucky man, my friend," Yusuf said with a laugh.

"So are you," Brian said. Then he said while holding Martha's hand, "Please excuse us. We'll be outside for a few minutes," and they left the tent.

Brian led Martha away from the entrance to the tent so they could talk privately. After walking a short distance, Martha said, "So I'm worth fifty camels?"

"I'm holding out for a higher offer. How would you like to sweep the sand from Yusuf's tent?" Brian asked, grinning.

"And you can be his butler," Martha replied with a laugh.

"All kidding aside, I've been thinking about what to do with Thomas, if and when we find Jesus. If we locate Jesus in Nazareth, we still must travel to Damascus," Brian said.

"We can ask him if he'll escort us there, and if he agrees, we will thank him and pay him for his service. He's been very helpful so far and knows the culture and customs better than we," she said.

"Okay, I agree. If he decides to come with us, we'll part ways in Damascus," Brian said.

After Brian and Martha returned to the tent, they sat on their pillows and Joseph asked, "Is everything okay?"

"Yes. I needed to talk privately with Martha," Brian answered.

"Joseph, do you think the horses are rested enough to continue?" Brian asked.

"I believe so," Joseph answered. "Yusuf, we need to refill our flasks with water."

"Of course. Come with me," Yusuf said, and he exited the tent and took them to a large clay pot containing water. After Yusuf removed the lid to the pot, he said, "Please help yourselves."

They refilled their flasks and thanked Yusuf for his hospitality. They went to their horses and mounted them. "Thank you, my friend. I'll stop by and visit you on my way home. The horse I'm on and Martha's are the ones I bought in Tyre," Joseph said.

"They are healthy- and strong-looking animals," Yusuf replied.

Joseph guided Brian, Martha and Thomas east toward Nazareth again, and after riding for a while, a village appeared in the distance, nestled in the basin of a valley. It was Nazareth. As they got closer to Nazareth, Brian felt a cool chill and put on his mantle. The landscape was much greener, and the climate was slightly cooler. There were rolling hills, trees and vegetation. The land was becoming more fertile than that in Samaria or Judea. The homes in the village were made of white limestone, which stood out from the surrounding area. "Ahead of us is Nazareth. We will soon be there," Joseph hollered to his riders.

Nazareth, according to the Holy Scriptures, was the home to Mary (Jesus' birth mother) and Joseph (Jesus' stepfather). The New Testament says Nazareth was Jesus' childhood home, and at the age of thirty he traveled from there to the east side of the Jordan River to be baptized by his cousin, John, before starting his ministry. Nazareth at the time of Jesus had a small population of between one hundred and one thousand inhabitants.

When Joseph, Brian, Martha and Thomas were at the edge of Nazareth, they stopped their horses. Joseph turned his horse so that he was facing them and said, "I have a friend who owns a farm where I rest my horses for the night. You're welcome to join me. I'm sure Simcha has room for us."

"That's generous of you to offer. We could use a good night's rest," Brian replied.

Joseph turned his horse around and they headed for a farm on the outskirts of the village. They rode onto a farm that had a two-level house and a barn for animals. At the front of the home, they dismounted their horses. Joseph went to the front door of his friend's home and knocked on it. A man answered and said, "Hello, Joseph," and then they shook hands.

"Hello, Simcha. I brought three guests to spend the night, if you don't mind."

"Of course not. Any friends of yours are friends of mine."

"This is Simcha, and Simcha this is Brian. Her name is Martha and his name is Thomas. I guided them from Scythopolis to here, and I'll be returning home tomorrow morning," Joseph said as he introduced everyone.

"Please take your horses behind the house and my son, Chaim, will tend to them," Simcha said.

"I'll take the horses there now. Martha, Brian and Thomas, please go with Simcha," Joseph said.

Simcha escorted his guests into his home and hollered for his fourteen-year-old son. When Chaim entered the room, his dad said, "Please help Joseph tend to his horses," and then he left to meet Joseph at the back of the house.

"Chaim, you're growing fast. Please take care of my horses. I will be leaving in the morning," Joseph said when he saw Chaim.

"I'll make sure they're fed, watered and well rested for tomorrow," Chaim said.

"Thank you, young man," Joseph said, and then he left and joined everyone who was sitting at the table in the front room.

"Can I offer you something to drink?" Simcha asked.

"No, thank you. I would like to visit the center of the city before the sun goes down. Martha and Thomas, please come with me. We shouldn't be long," Brian said.

"I'm sure you can find your way back to the farm," he replied.

It was 11:30 a.m. and Luke was listening to music on his MP3 player while surfing the Internet on the PC in the lab. David was also in the lab at his workbench reviewing his notes for a class lecture on time travel and would occasionally monitor Stella's tracking window. Luke removed the earbuds to his music player and set the unit onto the desk and went to David. He said, "Dad, I'm hungry. I'm going to Mario's to buy a sub. Do you want something while I'm there?"

"Yes. I would like a small cheese steak sub and a soda."

"You buy and I'll fly," Luke said with a smile.

"Sounds like a fair deal to me," David said, smiling, as he gave Luke twenty dollars.

"Since you're flying, keep the change."

"Thanks, Dad," Luke said, and he put the cash into his pocket and left for Mario's Sub Shop.

When Luke entered the sub shop, he saw Mario behind the counter waiting on a woman. He got in line behind her and waited his turn to place his order. Mario leaned to his left and said, "Hi, Luke. I'll be with you in a minute."

"How are things, Mrs. Foster? I haven't seen you or your husband for some time," Mario said.

"My husband became ill a few months back and suffered a heart attack. His doctor expects a full recovery, but he has to watch his diet and exercise more. The doctors recommended more walking and less television."

"That's good news."

"While visiting my husband in the hospital, a gang used a can of spray paint to graffiti the sidewalk in front of our house. They also spray-painted the cars parked on the same street. I reported the incident to the police, and the sergeant, who was writing the report, said they were aware of a graffiti gang that is vandalizing the neighborhoods in the city. The officer said they're looking for the gang members, but don't have the resources to devote a lot of time to catch them because there are more serious crimes to deal with. This city is getting worse. I remember when I moved here twenty-seven years ago, you didn't have to lock your doors and worry if you would be assaulted or robbed after dark."

Mario handed Mrs. Foster a paper bag with her order in it, and he said, "Thank you. I hope things improve for you."

"The only way things will get better is if Jesus returns," Mrs. Foster said as she was leaving the store.

"How can I help you, young man?" Mario asked Luke.

"I'll have two cheese steak subs, French fries and two sodas to go," he answered.

Mario went to the grill and prepared Luke's order. When Luke's food was ready, he paid Mario and returned to the lab. He gave David his sandwich and soda, and they ate at the workbench.

While eating his sub, Luke said, "Dad, a woman in the store was complaining about how the crime in Salem has increased since she moved to this city. As she was leaving, Mario said, "I hope things improve for you," and then the woman said, "The only way things will get better is if Jesus returns." After I heard that, I thought about Brian and Martha bringing Jesus here. I'll bet many people feel the same way as she does, hoping that Jesus will return to make the world a better place for everyone."

"I believe you're correct. Tonight let's both say a pray for Brian and Martha's safety and also for their success in finding and convincing Jesus to visit us. I'm sure if Jesus agrees, he will renew hope in the world by reminding people that a higher power does exist and is watching them and that there will be consequences for their immoral behavior," David said.

"Where are they now?" Luke asked.

"Let's find out," David replied, and they went to Stella's tracking window, which displayed longitude 35.29556 and latitude 32.70361. After looking at the coordinates, David said, "They're now in Nazareth," and he then went to the chalkboard and removed the yellow chalk and made dashes from Scythopolis to Nazareth.

"They're getting closer to Damascus. They should be able to find a caravan route soon," David said, and then he returned to his workbench to finish eating his sandwich with Luke.

Martha, Brian and Thomas left Simcha's home to see the center of Nazareth. While they were walking, Brian said, "Thomas, Martha and I are planning to go to Damascus after we leave Nazareth. Will you escort us there?"

"Yes, for two shekels," he answered.

"That seems like a fair price to pay, my friend," Brian said. He stopped walking and removed his money pouch and paid Thomas two shekels. "I'll give you two more shekels when we arrive in Damascus."

"Thank you. I like our business arrangement," Thomas said, smiling, as he put the coins into his money pouch.

They resumed walking to the center of Nazareth. On the way they saw a store selling bread and other food items. "Let's get something to eat here," Brian said, and he bought bread, fish and figs. When they were done eating their meal near the shop where they bought the food, Brian said, "Thomas, we need to find a synagogue. Please ask the owner of the store where we can find one."

He returned to the store and approached the man and asked, "Hello. Can you direct me to the nearest synagogue?"

"Yes. You must go up this street to the end, and it will be on the left side. You can't miss it," the man answered.

"Thank you," Thomas said, and he returned to where Brian and Martha were waiting. He said, "I know where to find the synagogue. Are you ready to go there now?"

"Lead the way, my friend," Brian said.

Thomas followed the shop owner's directions, and they were now standing at the entrance to the synagogue. After Thomas, Brian and Martha entered, they saw people praying. "Brian, we should ask somebody where we can find Jesus," Martha whispered.

"Good idea," Brian whispered to her, and then he quietly said to Thomas, "We're going outside now."

"I would like to stay and pray," Thomas whispered, and Brian nodded his head okay. He and Martha left.

When they were outside the synagogue, Brian said to Martha, "I'll ask the first person I see," and just as he finished his sentence, a man was coming toward them. "Excuse me, sir. Can you tell me where I can find Jesus, the son of Joseph the carpenter and whose mother is named Mary?" he asked.

"I know two people named Jesus and their fathers are carpenters. One family lives a short distance from here and the other lives on the east side of the city with a larger family. If you walk up this street and turn left onto the next street and travel to the end, you will find somebody to show you to Joseph's house," the man answered.

"Thank you for your help," Brian said.

Thomas exited the synagogue just as the man who gave them the directions entered and he went to where Brian and Martha were waiting for him.

"We can start searching for Jesus tomorrow because it's beginning to get dark now," Brian said after Thomas was with them.

"I agree. We'll have a full day of sunlight to search for him," Martha said.

Brian, Martha and Thomas returned to Simcha's house and knocked on the front door. Simcha opened it and said, "Please come in."

"Did you find the center of the city?" Joseph asked while he was sitting at the table.

"Yes. We ate and then visited the synagogue," Martha answered.

"Do you have a place for us to sleep for the night?" Brian asked.

"Yes. Please follow me," Simcha replied, and he led them to a large room with a thin blanket hanging over the doorway and moved it aside for them to enter. The room had wood shelving on the wall, a table, one small cot, and two padded sleeping mats on the floor and three blankets. He then said, "You can sleep in this room for the night. I hope you find it comfortable."

"It's perfect, thank you. We had a long day, and we're tired. If you don't mind, we'll go to bed for the evening," Brian replied.

"I'll see you in the morning. Goodnight," Simcha said.

"Martha, you can have the cot. Thomas and I will sleep on the mats," Brian said after Simcha left.

"Thank you. That's very kind of you both," Martha said, and then they got settled into their room for the night.

CHAPTER 21

The sun was beginning to rise. Thomas woke up before Brian and Martha. Joseph and Simcha were outside in back of the house talking. Thomas went to see who it was, and at the rear of the home, he saw Simcha, who said, "Good morning." In the distance, he could see Joseph riding away. Simcha said, "Joseph left to go home. You just missed him. He didn't want to disturb you. He asked me to say bye to everyone for him."

The conversation between Thomas and Simcha woke up Brian and Martha, and they noticed Thomas was not in the room. Brian and Martha went to where the voices were coming from and saw Simcha and Thomas talking while Chaim stood next to his dad.

"Good morning. I hope you rested well," Simcha said when he saw Brian and Martha.

"Joseph just left to return home to Scythopolis," Thomas said.

"Joseph asked me to say bye for him. He didn't want to wake you from your sleep," Simcha said.

"Do you have water so we may wash ourselves?" Brian asked.

"Yes. Chaim, please get a bowl for our guests," he said, and then his son went inside the house and returned with a bowl and gave it to Brian. Chaim showed Brian to a large clay pot that contained water and removed the lid. Brian dipped the bowl into the pot, filling it with water, and set it onto a nearby wood table and began splashing the liquid on his face. When he was finished, Martha and then Thomas washed their faces.

"Can I offer you something to eat?" Simcha asked after they were done washing themselves.

"Thank you for offering, but we'll be leaving now and will eat in the city. You are very generous for allowing us to spend the night in your home," Brian answered.

"You're welcome. May you have a safe and joyous stay in Galilee," Simcha said, and then Brian and Thomas shook Simcha's and Chaim's hands, and then they left for the center of Nazareth.

Brian was leading the way to the synagogue. When they arrived at the holy site, he began to follow the directions that the man had given him yesterday to Jesus' home. As Brian, Martha and Thomas were walking down a street, they saw a woman washing clothes next to a house. Brian went to her and asked, "Hello. Can you tell me where Jesus, the son of Joseph, a carpenter, and whose mother is named Mary lives?"

"There's a family nearby that has a son Jesus and a father Joseph, but the woman's name is Sarah. They live in the seventh house on the left side of this street," the woman answered.

"Do you know of a family where there is a Jesus who has a father named Joseph and whose mother's name is Mary?" Brian then asked.

"That family lives at the edge of Nazareth," she answered, pointing northeast with her right index finger.

"Thank you." He turned to Martha and said, "That woman pointed in the same area of the city as the man did who gave us directions yesterday."

"This is exciting. We could soon be meeting Jesus," Martha said.

"I'm getting butterflies in my stomach," he said.

"You're just hungry," she said with a smile.

"You're nervous because of one man," Thomas said.

"Yes, because he's a special man to us," Martha replied.

"Well, let's go and find this special man," Thomas said, smiling too.

They went to where the woman had pointed. Brian walked to the front door with Martha and Thomas behind him and knocked on it. A man who looked to be in his late thirties opened the door and said, "Hello. Can I help you?"

"Yes. I'm looking for Jesus. Are you his father, Joseph, a carpenter?" Brian asked.

"Yes."

"Can I speak with Jesus?"

Standing in the doorway, Joseph turned toward the inside of his home and hollered, "Jesus, please come here," and then an eleven-year-old boy stood beside his father.

"Hello. You're not the Jesus I seek. He's much older than you," Brian said after seeing the boy.

"I know a Jesus on the east side of the city, and his father was a carpenter named Joseph, but his father passed on years ago," the man said.

"If I follow this street east, will it take me to his home?" Brian asked.

"Yes, and at the end turn left and somebody will direct you to his family's house," the man answered.

"Thank you for your help," Brian said, and then he, Martha and Thomas began walking east.

"Jesus should be in his mid twenties," Martha said to Brian as they were walking.

"I was surprised when the boy appeared. I hope we have better luck at the next house," he said.

"I have a feeling we are about to meet Jesus in person," Martha said.

After walking to the end of the street, they turned left as instructed and saw a man walking toward them. When the man, who looked to be in his mid twenties, was about to pass by, Brian said, "Hello."

"Hello," the man replied.

"Can you tell me where I can find Jesus whose father Joseph is a carpenter and whose mother is named Mary?"

"I am the one you seek. My name is Jesus."

Brian was staring in awe at the face of Jesus. He turned toward Martha, stunned, because Jesus did not resemble the likeness of individuals portrayed as him in holy pictures or movies. Jesus wore a white tunic with a length to just below his knees and brown leather sandals. He was six feet tall and weighed one hundred seventy pounds. He had black, medium-length hair, brown eyes and a short black beard. His skin had an olive-color tone because of daily exposure to the sun. Brian, to be sure that this was the Jesus they were seeking, asked, "Where are you going?"

"To the synagogue to pray and teach. You're welcome to join me."

"Do you have brothers and sisters?" Martha asked.

"Yes, I live with four brothers, named James, Joseph, Simon and Judas, and two sisters, Mary and Salome."

Brian and Martha looked at each other as if to say, "We found the Lord," and then Brian said, "Yes, we would be honored to accompany you to the synagogue. My name is Brian. Her name is Martha and his name is Thomas."

"Brian, Martha and Thomas, please come with me."

"How is your father Joseph and mother Mary?" Martha asked as they were walking.

"Joseph passed away seven years ago and is with my Father in his heavenly kingdom, and my mother is well," Jesus answered as they approached the entrance to God's house of prayer.

Saint Joseph is a Jewish man mentioned in the Holy Scriptures as Jesus' earthly father up to the age of twelve and then is not talked about in the Gospels thereafter. Saint Mary is a Jewish woman identified in the New Testament with the Annunciation, the appearance of the angel Gabriel telling her that she would be the birth mother of Jesus.

Jesus, Thomas, Brian and Martha entered the synagogue, which had a dirt floor and stone benches lining three walls for people to sit on. In the center of the room was a chair of honor and a separate section for only women. When Jesus entered, he was warmly greeted by men, saying, "Hello, Rabbi," and "Hello, Teacher," and others were whispering, "The teacher has returned."

Jesus responded with a smile and shook hands as he walked to the Ark that was facing in the direction of Jerusalem and contained the Torah scrolls. Hanging from the ceiling and slightly above the cabinet was the Eternal Lamp and near the Ark was a menorah with six branches.

Jesus placed both hands on the Ark and prayed in silence. When he had finished praying, he walked over and sat in the chair of honor. After Jesus sat, the rabbi, who was standing in front of the Ark, began reading from the Torah as the synagogue became totally quiet. When the rabbi was done with his sermon, Jesus stood and began preaching about a heavenly kingdom that is awaiting all mankind. He said, "I have seen this wonderful place and blessed are those who enter. Sinners must repent and change their immoral ways. My Father will forgive only those who demonstrate remorse for their sinful behavior."

After Jesus said that, the men started asking him questions about forgiveness and the acts that would be deemed appropriate to please God. Jesus had an audience of twelve men standing in front of him, and Thomas, who was standing behind the men, said, "Jesus, you speak of God's kingdom as though you have direct contact with him. How do you know God will forgive a man for his sins and allow him into his kingdom?"

"Are you a sinner?" Jesus asked.

"I've sinned, like all men have, and I ask for God's forgiveness through prayer, but I haven't received a sign from God acknowledging that my prayers have been heard," Thomas answered.

"I assure you, Thomas, my Father has forgiven you. I've seen his kingdom and blessed are those that will join him. Moses took our people to the Promised Land, as promised to Moses by God. I too promise that he who obeys God's commandments will enter his kingdom for their final resting place," Jesus said.

The synagogue became quiet and Thomas moved from the back of the audience and stood in front of Jesus. "Rabbi, I had doubts about God hearing my prayers, but after listening to you, I am now at peace. Thank you," Thomas said, and then he knelt before Jesus with his right knee and bowed his head and touched Jesus' left foot with his right hand.

"Please stand, Thomas," Jesus said.

Thomas stood and looked into Jesus' eyes, and then Jesus said, "Only true believers will make the final journey," and he put his hand on Thomas's left shoulder and smiled.

Thomas kissed the back of Jesus' hand as he was removing it from his shoulder and walked to where Brian and Martha were standing. Brian whispered to Thomas, "He's a special man."

"Yes, I'm a witness to that," Thomas whispered.

Brian whispered to both Martha and Thomas, "Let's wait outside until Jesus is done praying and teaching."

"I would like to stay and listen to him," Thomas whispered, and then Brian and Martha left the synagogue as Jesus looked toward the entrance and watched them leave.

"After Jesus has finished preaching, we should find a quiet place to talk with him and hopefully convince him to come with us to Salem," Brian said once they were outside.

"We can ask him to take us to a place where he goes to reflect on the world around him," Martha said.

"Yes. He must go somewhere to be by himself. I'll ask him," Brian replied as they sat on the steps of the synagogue waiting patiently for Jesus and Thomas to exit.

When Thomas came out of the synagogue, he went to where Brian and Martha were sitting and said, "After listening to Jesus, I had a spiritual reawakening. He is truly a special person."

"Yes, we know. We'll ask him to take us to a quiet place so we can talk to him privately," Brian said with a smile.

"He could be in there for a while. The men are asking him many questions about God's kingdom, and he's quoting the Holy Scriptures," Thomas said.

"We'll wait here for Jesus. Thomas, how much food do we have?" Brian asked.

"Not much. We should buy more," he said after looking in his bag.

"Let's find a store nearby," Brian said, and then as a man was about to enter the synagogue, he said, "Sir, can you tell me where I can buy food?"

"Go down this street and there's a shop on the left side," the man said. Brian thanked him, and they went to the shop and bought some food.

"We should return to the synagogue and wait for Jesus," Brian said after buying food.

As Brian, Martha and Thomas approached the synagogue, they saw Jesus leaving with men following him and still asking questions. While

Jesus was standing on the front steps of God's house of prayer, he said, "I answered many questions and spoke of my Father's kingdom. Go and reflect on what was said today and practice your faith. Spread the word so all will truly believe in God almighty and remind those who obey his laws, for they will be judged worthy to enter his eternal resting place in heaven." Jesus then began walking in the direction of his home away from where Brian, Martha and Thomas were, so they started walking at a quick pace to catch up to him.

When they caught up to Jesus, Brian said, "Jesus, we would like to speak with you privately. Do you know of a place where we can be alone?"

"Yes. I'll take you there now," Jesus answered.

Jesus led Brian, Martha and Thomas to a large hill outside the city overlooking Nazareth. At the top of the hill they had a panoramic view of the city and the surrounding area. Jesus went to a big rock and sat looking out toward Nazareth. "This is a beautiful place, so peaceful and quiet, with a magnificent view of Nazareth," Martha said.

"Yes, it is. I come here often to pray," Jesus said.

Looking at Thomas, Brian said to him, "Martha and I would like to talk with Jesus privately." Brian pointed at a boulder a short distance away and said, "Thomas, please wait there until we are finished speaking with Jesus. It shouldn't be long." Thomas went to where Brian had pointed and sat on the large rock and enjoyed the view.

When Thomas was far enough away that he couldn't hear their conversation, Brian said, "Jesus, Martha and I came from a different time to meet you. We are from your future and have been tasked to find and invite you to accompany us to our time."

"Where is the future you came from?" Jesus asked.

"The year 2010, which is almost two thousand years into your future," Brian answered.

"We have traveled back in time with the help of a machine that a man has created. The machine allows man to travel to the past or to the future," Martha said.

"Why do you want me to come with you?" Jesus asked.

"It would be only for a short visit, and you could return any time you wanted to. We need your help to renew hope in the world and convey the message of God you teach. The people in the future need to listen to you speak of God's kingdom and hear what they must do to be allowed in, because we don't have a charismatic leader. The people in our time must hear a divine message that will resonate to their souls and make a profound change in how God is viewed," Brian answered.

"My Father sees and hears the perpetrators of the injustices committed in the world, whether in the past, present or future," Jesus said, and then, pausing for a moment, he continued, "I will travel with you to where you came from. Only the followers of the laws given to Moses from my Father will be allowed into heaven, be it now or in the future."

"Thank you. When can you leave? We must travel to Damascus and from there we'll be transported to the year 2010," Brian said.

"I can leave today, but on the way I must stop at Capernaum and from there we can travel to Damascus," Jesus said.

Brian waved his arms to get Thomas's attention and when he did, he signaled for Thomas to come and join them. When Thomas was with them, Jesus stood and stared out looking down at Nazareth. Then he turned in the direction they had come and led them to his house. At his white limestone home, Jesus opened the front door and invited everyone to enter. The house had two levels with three small rooms on both floors and furniture made of wood. A woman came down the stairs from the second level and asked, "Jesus, who are your friends?"

"This is Brian. Her name is Martha and his name is Thomas," Jesus answered.

"Hello," they said.

"This is my mother, Mary."

"Your brothers have not returned from work yet, and your sisters are on the roof washing clothes."

"Mother, I will be traveling to Capernaum and then to Damascus. I don't know how long I'll be away, but I shall return afterward."

Jesus went to a room on the first level and returned wearing a mantle over his tunic. He was holding a six-foot-long wood staff in his left hand. Jesus kissed his mother on the cheek and said, "Woman, take care of your family and pray for them," and then they left for Capernaum.

Capernaum was a small fishing village located on the northwest shore of the Sea of Galilee. It was the base for Jesus' church and fulfilled the prophecy written in the Holy Scriptures. After starting his ministry, Jesus returned twice to Nazareth to teach, but was rejected both times. Jesus chose five of his apostles, who were from Capernaum: Peter, Andrew, James, John and Matthew.

Jesus guided them to a narrow road that would lead them to Capernaum. "How far is Capernaum?" Brian asked Jesus.

"One hundred sixty furlongs. It will take us the remainder of the day to walk there. I have a friend with whom we will stay the night, and tomorrow after I pray and teach at the synagogue, we'll travel to Damascus."

"Thank you for agreeing to come with us," Brian said.

Jesus smiled and slightly nodded his head acknowledging Brian's gratefulness. The rugged terrain they were traveling on was rocky and went through valleys traversing between large hills and small mountains. After walking for awhile, Jesus said, "We will be approaching Taricheae (also named Magdala, the village Mary Magdalene was from) on the Sea of Galilee. We'll rest before continuing to Capernaum."

They walked along the shore of the Sea of Galilee and could see the small fishing village of Taricheae in the distance as the sun was beginning to set. There were fishing boats anchored off shore with fishermen onboard preparing their gear for the next day. They also saw boats arriving at the port and men unloading their day's catch.

Walking past the fishermen who had come ashore, Brian noticed a man selling fresh cooked fish and he went to the vendor and said, "I'll have four of your largest fish." The merchant gave them a fish each and Brian paid him.

"Thomas, please give a portion of figs, nuts and bread to everyone," Brian said. Thomas handed out the food and they ate while watching the fishing boats arrive in the port.

"We will now go to Capernaum, which is 40 furlongs from here," Jesus said after resting. They continued walking along the shoreline.

It was night when they arrived at the city center of Capernaum. Jesus said, "My friend is a rabbi. I stay with him when I visit Capernaum. We'll go to his house now."

Jesus led them to his friend's house, which was northwest from the center of the city. At the front door Jesus knocked and an old man with white hair answered. He greeted Jesus with a hug and said, "Rabbi, I've been waiting patiently for you to return and so have many of your students. People keep asking me when you will come back. I tell them soon."

"I've been in Nazareth preaching the message of God to all those who will listen," Jesus said.

"Please come in and bring your friends," the rabbi said.

"Thank you, Rabbi," Jesus replied.

David was sitting at his desk in the library working on his lecture notes about how time travel has become a reality in the 21st century. He was wondering how his students and the faculty at M.I.T. would react. David knew the students and faculty members with open minds would be intrigued by the idea, while others with closed minds would think he was off his rocker. David also knew that to be credible with his claim, he would have to provide proof of such an achievement. He went to the sofa and sat and soon fell asleep.

Luke was in the lab watching the longitude and latitude of Stella's tracking window slowly change. Luke knew Brian and Martha were moving again, but didn't know where they were going. He went to the desk in the lab and picked up his MP3 player and returned to Stella and noticed that the coordinates for Brian and Martha stopped changing. Luke headed for the library to report his findings to David.

When Luke entered the library, he saw David sitting on the sofa sleeping with his lecture notes in his right hand. Luke went to David and said, "Dad, Dad."

"What is it, Luke?" David said after he woke up.

"The coordinates for Brian and Martha have stopped changing."

"Let's go see where they are," David said.

David set his lecture notes onto the library desk and they went to Stella, where David saw in the tracking window longitude 35.5750 and latitude 32.8811. He went to the PC and logged on to the Internet and entered the longitude and latitude. After he had entered the coordinates, David said, "Brian and Martha are in Capernaum, which is on the shore of the Sea of Galilee. It looks like they're moving closer to Damascus."

David went to the chalkboard and got a piece of yellow chalk and then extended the dashes from Nazareth to Capernaum. "Wow. They've traveled a long way from Jerusalem," Luke said.

"Yes. They are managing their journey well. I'll be in the library if you need me. Keep an eye on the tracking window," David said.

"Will do, Dad," Luke said, and David left the lab.

Jesus, Brian, Martha and Thomas entered the rabbi's small single-level home with four medium-size rooms.

"Please sit. I'll get another chair," the rabbi said after everyone had entered his home. He went to another room and returned with a chair and set it at the table.

"Jesus, what are the names of your friends?" the rabbi asked.

"This is Brian. Her name is Martha and his name is Thomas," Jesus answered as he looked at each person.

"My name is Peter and I'm a rabbi at the synagogue where I preach. Jesus is my teacher. Jesus, you mentioned that you were in Nazareth all this time."

"Yes. Most Nazarenes are skeptical about the message I preach for my Father. They ask many questions of doubt and disbelief, but some have seen the light, and blessed are those that follow it. Peter, after I speak in the synagogue tomorrow, I'll be traveling to Damascus. On my return to Nazareth, I'll stop in Capernaum and visit you."

"It's getting late and you must be tired. I can offer you food, but there's not enough for everyone," the rabbi said.

"Thomas, please remove the food from your bag and place it onto the table so we can all eat," Brian said.

The rabbi went to the cooking area in his home and returned with a bowl with bread and almonds. Thomas put the figs, nuts and bread from his bag onto the table. "There's enough food for everyone," Brian said.

After they were done eating, the rabbi said, "My home is small, but you are welcome to spend the night. Please find a place to sleep."

CHAPTER 22

When Martha, Brian and Thomas awoke, they saw Jesus praying. He was sitting on the floor and praying with his head bowed and eyes closed. The backs of his hands rested on the inside of each knee so that his palms were toward the heavens. "Good. I see everybody is up," the rabbi said after entering the front room of his home.

"Good morning, Rabbi. I'll be leaving now to buy food for our breakfast," Brian said.

"I'll go with you," Martha said.

Brian took Thomas's bag before he and Martha left the rabbi's home. When they were outside, he said, "We'll have to ask somebody where there's a shop."

"If we walk toward the city center, I'm sure we'll find a merchant selling food," Martha replied. After walking a short distance, they found a store that sold fish, bread, figs and olives. After buying and storing the food in Thomas's bag, they returned to the rabbi's home.

Brian knocked on the door, and the rabbi opened it. After they entered, Brian went to the table and set the bag down and asked, "Rabbi, do you have something to put the food into?"

"Yes," he answered, and he went to a corner of the room and returned with four clay bowls. The rabbi said, "I hope these will do."

"Thank you," Brian said, and then he said, "Martha, please put the food into the bowls."

After Martha filled the bowls with food and everyone was seated at the table, Jesus began to pray out loud. "Heavenly Father, thank you for the food we are about to eat. Your bounty provides the nourishment to give strength for all to live. Amen." Everybody repeated the word, "Amen," and then they took turns reaching into the bowls for food.

When they had finished eating, Jesus looked at everyone and said, "I am going to the synagogue now. Would you like to come with me?"

"Yes," everybody said, and they left the rabbi's home.

Jesus and the rabbi were walking together while Brian, Martha and Thomas followed them to the synagogue. The holy site was made of white limestone and constructed on higher ground than the one in Nazareth. There were also more people entering and exiting. They followed Jesus and the rabbi into the synagogue and noticed that the interior was also larger than the one in Nazareth. After entering, they could hear people whispering, "It's Jesus," "The teacher has returned," and "It's the rabbi."

Jesus went to the center of the room where there was a large wood chair. He sat in it and began to pray silently while the congregation watched him. The rabbi went to the Ark, which contained the Holy Torah, and began his sermon for the forty people who were there. The synagogue was completely quiet when the rabbi said, "Before I begin reading from the Torah, I want to introduce a guest who has traveled from Nazareth to be with us. Many of you know him, and the ones who don't, please welcome Jesus."

Everyone clapped their hands while Jesus sat in the large wood chair. Jesus stood and slightly raised his right hand and slowly turned to recognize the applause. After the brief applause, the rabbi began reading from the Torah. His topic was Abraham.

Abraham is considered the founding father of the Israelites. The Old Testament states that Abraham was commanded by God to offer his son, Isaac, as a sacrifice in the land of Moriah. As Abraham was about to sacrifice his son, an angel appeared and prevented him. He was given a ram as an offering instead of his son. Abraham died at the age of one hundred seventy-six.

When the rabbi finished speaking, Jesus stood and began preaching about the heavenly kingdom awaiting all who obey the laws given to Moses by God. The people in Capernaum were much more receptive to his message than those in Nazareth, and when Jesus had finished his sermon, he answered questions from the congregation. After Jesus was through teaching and answering the congregation's questions, he said, "I must leave now, but I shall return. Go in peace and practice the laws that have been handed down from God to Moses. For blessed are those who enter my Father's kingdom." Jesus then walked out of the synagogue with a few men following him along with Brian, Martha and Thomas, while the rabbi remained inside teaching from the Torah.

"We'll now go to the rabbi's house and get our belongings and then travel to Damascus," Jesus said, looking at Brian, once they were outside.

They returned to the rabbi's home, and as they were gathering their belongings, Martha said, "Brian, we must refill our flasks with water and buy more food."

"Okay," Brian said, and then he asked, "Jesus, how far is Damascus from Capernaum?"

"It's 480 furlongs. We will travel on the Via Maris road east to Damascus. It's a three-day journey on foot," Jesus answered.

"Do you know a person who provides a transportation service to Damascus?" Brian asked.

"I do not," Jesus replied.

"Thomas, please ask someone if there's a business that provides transportation on horseback," Brian said.

"I'll leave now and ask somebody," Thomas said. He left and while walking down a street, he decided to try the shop where Brian had bought food earlier in the morning. Thomas entered the store and approached the owner and asked, "Do you know of a business providing a transportation service to Damascus?"

"Yes. On the way to the Via Maris road there's a man who provides that service. His home is eight furlongs northwest from here. Just follow the road leading out of Capernaum. You can't miss his farm," the man answered.

"Thank you," Thomas said. He returned to the rabbi's home and knocked on the door. Brian opened it and Thomas entered. He said, "I spoke to a man who said there's a business eight furlongs from here that provides a transportation service."

"That's good news. Before we leave, we must fill our flasks with water and buy more food," Brian said.

They left the rabbi's home and went to the merchant where Brian had bought food and Thomas had gotten directions. At the shop, Brian purchased enough dried food to last for three days and handed the items to Thomas for storage. Then they went to a nearby well to fill their flasks. After they had filled their containers, Jesus said, "I will take us to the Via Maris road. The farm Thomas mentioned is on the way. I've seen it before." He began walking north on a main street with Brian and Martha on his right and Thomas on his left.

When they were at the edge of Capernaum, they could see a farm in the near distance. It was the same one the shop owner and Jesus spoke of. They went to the house in the center of the property and Brian knocked on the front door. A man who appeared to be in his thirties opened it and said, "Hello. Can I help you?"

"Yes. We need transportation to Damascus. Do you provide such a service?" Brian asked.

"I can transport you on my horses, but it will cost you ten shekels," the man said after he looked at them.

"That seems like a fair price to pay by people who don't own horses. I'll pay you five shekels now and the balance when we arrive at Damascus," Brian said.

"When would you like to leave?"

"Now, if you can."

"I can have the horses ready in less than an hour. Does everyone know how to ride a horse?"

They all answered, "Yes."

"Good. Please wait behind the house while I go to the barn and harness them."

The man soon returned with five horses that looked like the same breed of Arabian horse they had ridden from Scythopolis to Nazareth. "Here are your horses. By the way, I'm Isaac. What are your names?"

"My name is Brian," and then while pointing at each person, he said, "Her name is Martha, his name is Jesus and he's Thomas."

"These are fine horses. You shouldn't have a problem riding on them. I stop at two places on the way to Damascus to rest them," Isaac said while he handed the reins of each horse to its rider. Then he said,

"I must inform my wife that I'll be gone for a few days." Isaac went into his home and soon reappeared with his wife, who was holding a one-year-old child in her arms. He kissed her and the baby and went to his horse and said, "Let's mount our horses and go to Damascus."

After Isaac mounted his horse, he waved bye to his family, and his wife waved back. Isaac then galloped past his riders to lead the way. As he was passing Thomas, Martha, Jesus and Brian, he said, "The Via Maris road is a short distance from here and it will take us to Damascus. On the way, we'll stop at Hazor to rest the horses and afterward continue to Danos and sleep there for the night."

The Via Maris road was an important ancient trade route that connected to the silk and incense roads linking Syria, Anatolia, Mesopotamia and Asia. The trade route also passed along the Mediterranean coast and eastward to Damascus.

They were on a path that would take them to the trade route, when Isaac said, "There it is," and they were now traveling east to Damascus.

The road was being heavily traveled in both directions by people who were on camels, horses and donkeys, and there were carts being pulled by horses and donkeys. They also saw people walking and resting by the side of the road.

They journeyed further from the Sea of Galilee in the direction of the small village of Hazor that was 56 furlongs away. The landscape was becoming greener and the land looked more fertile for farming than in Judea. Isaac was still leading the way for Brian, Martha, Jesus and Thomas, who were in a single line behind him, and after traveling for awhile, the village of Hazor was coming into view. When they were beyond Hazor, Isaac turned his horse to the right and rode off the road and said, "We'll let the horses rest here and then continue to Danos." Isaac traveled a short distance further and dismounted his horse, and his riders dismounted too.

Brian removed his flask from around his neck and drank some water and then he asked, "Isaac, how far is Danos from here?"

"It's about 120 furlongs."

Jesus walked a short distance from them and sat on the ground facing Jerusalem. He bent his knees and crossed his legs and bowed his head and began to pray. Thomas went to where Jesus was praying and asked, "Jesus, can I sit with you and pray?"

"Yes, Thomas. God would like to hear your prayers," Jesus answered with a smile.

"Thank you," Thomas said, smiling. He sat next to Jesus and prayed too. While Brian and Martha watched them pray, Isaac tended to his horses.

"We should leave now so we can reach Danos before night," Isaac said after their brief rest. Then he handed the reins of each horse to its rider and said, "Let's mount up and get moving."

They were traveling again, east to Damascus, and their next stop was Danos, where Isaac planned to rest for the night. There were still many travelers moving in both directions. After riding for awhile, they could see a village in the far distance. "When we are at Danos, we'll stay at my friend's farm to rest," Isaac hollered to his riders as they rode.

When they arrived at Danos, the sun was beginning to set. Isaac turned his horse to the left, exiting the road for his friend's house that was on a small farm. They could see animals grazing near a barn. Isaac led them onto the farm. Near the entrance to the home, he dismounted his horse and Brian, Jesus, Martha and Thomas dismounted theirs. A man came out of the front door of the limestone home and went to Isaac. The men shook hands. "Hello, Isaac. I haven't seen you in awhile," the man said, shaking Isaac's hand.

"I know. Good to see you again, my friend. I hope things are well with you and your family," Isaac replied.

"What brings you this way?" the man asked.

"I'm escorting these riders to Damascus, and we need a place to stay for the night. We'll be leaving early tomorrow morning," Isaac said.

"This is my friend, Daniel. I stay with him while I'm visiting or passing by Danos. Daniel, please allow me to introduce my riders. This is Brian, her name is Martha, his name is Jesus and this is Thomas," Isaac said, pointing to each person.

"Welcome. Bring your horses behind the house where my sons will tend to them," Daniel said.

Daniel escorted them to the rear of his home and from there he hollered, "Eli, Moshe, come here."

Both of Daniel's teenage sons exited through the back door of his home and went to Daniel. They said, "Yes, Father?"

"We have guests. Please take their horses to the barn and give them food and water," Daniel said.

The boys took the reins of the horses and guided them to the barn for the night as Daniel opened the door to his home. Then he said, "Please enter and have a seat in the front room." They entered the room and sat at a table with chairs.

David was in the lab staring at his map on the chalkboard and was impressed with the distance Brian and Martha had traveled so far. He was following the yellow dashes from their arrival site to their present location. David glanced at Stella's tracking window and noticed the coordinates had changed to a longitude of 35.65248 and latitude of 33.24866 and were not moving, so he wrote the new coordinates on a piece of paper, went to the PC, logged on to the Internet and entered the coordinates. The results were for the village of Danos, forty-two miles from Damascus. David went to the chalkboard and extended the yellow dashes from Capernaum to Danos. He stepped back from the chalkboard and was even more impressed at how steadily they were moving along in such a short period of time. David thought they must have made it to a caravan route and knew that in a day or two Brian and Martha's trip could come to an end and, if successful, Jesus would be with them.

In the front room of the house, Brian, Martha, Jesus and Thomas sat at the table as Daniel entered carrying two wood chairs, one in each hand, and set them down at the table. After everyone was seated, Daniel said, "Isaac, you must have left Capernaum at midday."

"Yes, and we rested a number of furlongs beyond Hazor. I figure we should be in Damascus by this time tomorrow."

"My wife is visiting her friend who lives down the road not far from here. The woman had a baby a few days ago and the child is not doing well, but the mother is fine. My wife has been checking in on her and the baby daily. She should be returning home soon, and when she does, she'll serve us food."

"That would be nice. We are hungry."

Daniel's two boys entered the room. The older boy, Moshe, said, "The horses are in the barn eating and drinking. They look strong and healthy," and then the boys sat on the floor against the wall and listened to the conversation at the table.

"Where are you from? I haven't heard the name Brian before," Daniel said, looking at Brian.

"I was born in Rome. My mother is from Britain, where my father served as a Roman soldier. After serving in the military, he returned to Rome with her, and they got married," he answered.

"Will you be traveling beyond Damascus?" Daniel asked.

"Yes," Brian answered.

"Are you from Capernaum?" Daniel asked, looking at Jesus.

"I live in Galilee," Jesus answered.

"What's your occupation?" Daniel asked.

"I work as a carpenter and as a messenger for my Father," Jesus replied.

Daniel didn't realize that Jesus was implying that he was sent by God, and then he said, "He must keep you busy."

Brian and Martha looked at each other, knowing that Daniel did not know that Jesus was divine. "My Father's message is revealed in mysterious ways to those who truly believe in him. The message I bring to man is blessed from a divine being. For his kingdom is open to all, but closed to sinners who disobey his laws that were passed down to Moses," Jesus said.

"You've seen this kingdom?" Daniel asked.

He nodded his head and answered, "Yes."

The room became quiet and Daniel sat back in his chair and paused for a moment. Then he asked, "Are you a rabbi?"

"I teach the word of God to all who will listen. I have seen his kingdom and blessed are those who enter," Jesus answered.

After Luke entered the lab, he went to David and asked, "Where are Brian and Martha now?"

"They're in the village of Danos and by tomorrow this time they should be in Damascus. In a day or two we'll know if they are ready to be transported. As a precaution, I want you to go into each room and remove all the holy pictures and the crucifixion cross that's on the wall in the library and put them on my bed. We wouldn't want to upset Jesus if he is with Brian and Martha by having to explain who is depicted on the cross."

"Good idea, Dad."

"If Jesus arrives, and when it's appropriate, we can return them to their places."

"I'm getting excited just thinking about seeing Brian and Martha again, even if Jesus isn't with them," Luke said, and then he left the lab to remove all the religious symbols in the house.

Daniel's wife entered her home and saw her family and strangers sitting at the table. Daniel introduced his wife and said, "This is my wife, Leah. Leah, how is the child today?"

"Mary is doing fine, but the baby is sick and not eating. If the infant does not eat soon, it will die," Leah answered, tears welling up in her eyes.

"Where is the child?" Jesus asked.

"A short walk from here," Leah answered.

"Take me to the baby," Jesus replied.

Leah looked at Daniel. He nodded his head in approval, and she said, "Please come with me."

Jesus stood up from his chair, everyone else stood too, and then they all left the home. Leah escorted Jesus to the sick child as her family and guests followed them. When they arrived at the child's home, Leah knocked on the door. Mary's husband opened it and said, "Hello, Leah."

"I've brought a friend named Jesus who would like to visit the child," Leah said.

"Please come with me," the man said after he looked at Jesus with a sad look on his face. The man showed Jesus and Leah to where Mary was lying in bed beside her sick child, who was wrapped in a blanket. After Leah and Jesus entered the room, everyone else followed and stood against the walls. Jesus approached the bed and said, "Woman, remove the blanket from your child." Mary was crying as she uncovered her baby. Jesus said, "Woman, place your baby on top of you facing me." Mary positioned her weak, motionless infant on top of her and Jesus placed his left hand over the child's chest and stomach, closed his eyes, and turned the palm of his right hand toward heaven. Suddenly, the baby started crying, and Jesus smiled. He said, "Woman, feed your hungry child."

Mary reached out with her right hand and took Jesus' left hand and held it against her cheek and said, "Thank you."

Everyone in the room was astounded because they had just witnessed a miracle, and now the room was filled with joy. Even Mary's husband had tears in his eyes. Mary's husband held Jesus' right hand with both of his and said, "Thank you, Jesus."

"Go and be with your wife and child," Jesus said with a smile, and then he walked out of the room as Mary's husband sat on the bed hugging his wife and baby.

Leah, her family and guests left Mary's home for theirs. After everyone had entered Daniel's house, he said, "We must have a feast in Jesus' honor."

"I will prepare a wonderful meal for us," Leah said, and then she went to the area of the room that was used for cooking and gathered the ingredients for their feast while Daniel got cups from a shelf and filled them with wine for each of his guests.

Leah soon returned to the table with roasted lamb, vegetable soup, bread, goat cheese, olives and figs in bowls for her guests to share. Before they started eating, Jesus stood up from his chair and said a prayer thanking God for the food they were about to eat. When Jesus finished his prayer, he sat, and then Daniel stood and recited the prayer Birkat Ha (prayer for surviving illness). After Daniel said his prayer, he sat and everybody took turns taking food from the bowls and they enjoyed their delicious meal.

"Jesus, I hope you like my cooking," Leah said.

"God has bestowed upon you the gift of kindness," Jesus replied, smiling.

After they finished eating, Brian, who was sitting to Jesus' right, and Martha, who was to his left, asked, "Why did you save the baby?"

"It's not a sin for a child to be born into this world. The baby was pure in heart. My Father is merciful to those that are helpless at birth and blessed are those that are compassionate to the sick and disabled," Jesus answered.

"You are a very special man," Martha said.

It was getting late in the evening when Isaac said, "We should say goodnight and rest. We'll be leaving early in the morning and will travel long into evening tomorrow."

"I have two spare rooms you can sleep in," Daniel said.

"You are generous, my friend," Isaac replied.

"You're most welcome, my friend," Daniel said.

"Jesus, thank you for saving the child's life," Leah said.

"Blessed are those that see the light, because the light will guide them to heaven for eternal peace," Jesus said.

Leah took Jesus' left hand and held it to her cheek, and she said, "You are the light," and then she released his hand and left.

"You, Jesus and Thomas can sleep in this room, and Brian and Martha can have the one next to yours," Daniel said as he showed his guests to their rooms for the night.

CHAPTER 23

It was morning and the sun was beginning to rise when Brian woke up. He saw Martha sleeping and whispered her name. After she awakened, she whispered, "Is it morning already?"

"Yes. We should go to the front room and wait for the others," Brian whispered.

When Isaac awoke, he saw Jesus sitting with his eyes closed and praying as Thomas slept. Isaac then said Thomas's name, waking him, while Jesus continued praying.

"Jesus and Thomas, we'll be leaving for Damascus now. Please take your belongings to the front room. I'll check on Martha and Brian," Isaac said, and then he left the room.

Thomas got up and stretched his back. After Jesus was through praying, Thomas said, "Isaac is checking on Brian and Martha."

"Thank you. We should go now and join them," Jesus said.

Isaac was sitting at the table with Martha and Brian. When Thomas and Jesus entered the room, Isaac said, "Good. Everybody is up and ready to start the day. We'll be leaving for Damascus now. Please meet me outside behind the house," and then Isaac left to check on his horses.

Daniel was already in the barn harnessing the horses. When Isaac entered, Daniel said, "Good morning. Your horses have been fed and given water. They're ready to go. You own beautiful-looking animals, my friend."

"I bought them from a man who needed money to pay off his debts so he could keep his farm."

"I guess one person's loss is another's gain. Did you see that miracle by Jesus last night? Mary and I were up all evening thinking about it. Jesus does have a special gift for healing."

"Yes. He seems to have an extraordinary ability to heal the sick. I felt as though a divine presence was in the room," Isaac said.

"I know. Me too," Daniel said, and then Isaac took the reins to three of his horses and led them out of the barn while Daniel guided the other two animals to the rear of this home.

Brian, Martha, Jesus and Thomas got their belongings and went outside to the back of the house where Isaac and Daniel were waiting for them. "Daniel, is there water so I can wash my face and hands?" Martha asked.

"Yes. I'll bring you some," he answered, and he went into his home and returned with a large clay bowl filled with water and set it onto a wood bench next to his house.

"Thank you," Martha said, and then she began splashing the water onto her face.

Brian, Thomas and Jesus took turns washing too, and when they had finished, Isaac said, "If everybody is ready, please mount your horse and we'll go to Damascus."

They mounted their horses. Isaac was on the lead horse ready to guide them to the Via Maris road. "Isaac, I'll see you on your return trip," Daniel said, waving bye as they left his farm.

"Please tell Leah we enjoyed her wonderful meal last night," Martha said.

"I will. Have a safe journey," replied Daniel.

"We'll rest the horses twice along the way," Isaac said as they were riding east.

They were now on the road to Damascus, and even though it was early in the morning, many people were traveling to beat the heat of the rising sun. They rode past Danos, which was about 335 furlongs from Damascus, and after riding for nearly 130 furlongs, Isaac turned his horse to the right, exiting the road, and then he dismounted, and so did his riders. "We'll rest the horses here and then resume our journey. We have just over 200 furlongs to go before we reach Damascus," Isaac said.

Brian drank water from his flask, and then he said, "Thomas, please give everyone some food."

After resting, Isaac said, "We should get back on the road now. Let's mount our horses." They mounted their horses and headed east toward Damascus.

The terrain was becoming more unfriendly as they rode east. There were rocks and hills and no green vegetation because they were in the desert, and it was getting hotter. The sun looked like a big ball of fire in the sky. After traveling for another 128 furlongs, Isaac turned his horse off the road again to rest. "Damascus is 80 furlongs from here, and as we get closer to the city, we'll see many people traveling on foot," Isaac hollered as he left the road.

After they dismounted their horses, Isaac tended to his animals. Brian said, "Thomas, please help Isaac. I need to talk with Martha and Jesus privately."

Brian went to where Jesus and Martha were standing and when he looked back, he saw Thomas helping Isaac with the horses. Looking at Jesus, Brian said, "Our designated transportation point to the future is the Kisan Gate in Damascus. A man named David Solomon is tracking Martha's and my movements on his time machine. When Professor Solomon sees our coordinates at the gate, it will be the signal to let him know that we are ready to be transported to the year 2010. Martha and I had decided not to bring Thomas with us, but we would like to, if you agree."

"He's been very helpful and follows instructions," Martha said.

"Thomas is a fine young man. Have you told him that you are from a future time?" Jesus asked.

"No, but we will now," Martha answered.

"Thomas," Brian hollered, and he looked toward them and saw Brian gesturing with his right arm for him to join them.

When Thomas was with them, he said, "Yes, Brian?"

"Thomas, after we arrive in Damascus, we plan to travel very far and we will not come back. Jesus will be coming with us for a short time. We would like to know if you will accompany us too. You and Jesus can return anytime you choose."

"Where are you going after visiting Damascus?"

"Martha and I come from a time in the future. We're not really from Rome, but from a city and country that have not been discovered in your time. Tomorrow, Martha, Jesus and I will be transported through time to two thousand years from now, which is where Martha and I are from. People from our time dress and talk differently from you and Jesus."

"I'll go with you, but it will cost you two shekels," Thomas said after pausing to think about the offer.

"Okay. You are a wise businessman, my friend. I'll pay you now what I owe you and two more shekels when we arrive in the future," Brian said, smiling.

"This is a good business arrangement we have," Thomas said, grinning. Brian removed his money pouch and paid him.

"Then it is agreed. You will be traveling with us," Martha said.

Thomas smiled and extended his hand and shook Martha's, saying, "I agree to come with you, Jesus and Brian."

"It's time to go," Isaac said after the horses were rested.

They mounted their horses for the last leg of the trip. Isaac guided them back to the road, and as the sun was setting, they could see Damascus in the far distance. When they arrived at Damascus, the sun had set. Isaac said, "I have a friend who owns a farm on the edge of the city where I rest my horses. The farm is east of here, and you're welcome to join me. I'm sure he has room for all of us."

"Thank you. That's generous of you," Brian said, and they resumed riding to Isaac's friend's farm, which was southeast and just outside the city. He led them to a farm which had a barn and small animal pens on both sides for goats, sheep and chickens. The farm had a sandy-colored, two-level limestone home that was surrounded by a green pasture used for grazing and for growing crops.

When they arrived at Isaac's friend's home, he dismounted his horse and went to the front door and knocked. A man appearing to be in his forties answered and said, "Isaac, is that you? I haven't seen you in some time. You look healthy, my friend."

"Thank you. You're looking fit too. How have you been?" Isaac asked.

"I am fine," the man answered, and then he looked behind Isaac and asked, "Who are your friends?"

"This is Brian. Her name is Martha. His name is Jesus and he's Thomas," Isaac answered, pointing to each person. Then he introduced his friend to the riders and said, "This is my good friend Matthias." Then Isaac asked, "Matthias, we need a place to sleep for the night. Do you have room for us?"

"For you, my friend, always, and there is plenty of room for your friends too. Please bring the horses to the barn," Matthias said, and then they took the animals to the shelter and left them there.

"Please come with me," Matthias said, and they all went to his house. At the back door, he said, "Please enter."

They entered the house, which had four rooms on each floor, and they stood in a large entry room with a long table with six chairs. After everyone was seated at the table, Matthias's wife entered the room and went to her husband. Matthias introduced his wife as Reba. "Hello. Our two small children are sleeping in their bedroom. May I offer you something to drink? We have wine, goat's milk and water," she said, and everyone at the table requested wine.

"You must be tired. From where did you leave this morning?" Matthias asked.

"We left Danos early in the morning so we would arrive here just after dark," Isaac answered.

"You made good time. Your horses look strong."

"Yes, they are. We haven't had a problem with them."

Reba went to a shelf in the room and returned to the table and placed a cup in front of each guest. She then got a clay pitcher and filled it with wine from a small wood barrel and set it onto the table. Matthias stood and walked around the table, pouring wine into each guest's cup, and Brian said, "Thomas, please remove the food from your bag."

Matthias asked his wife to bring bowls to the table and Reba brought three clay bowls and said, "I hope these will do." Thomas put bread, figs and nuts into each bowl.

"Reba made fresh bread and cheese today. Reba, please serve our guests cheese and bread," Matthias said, and then she brought the food to the table, and they took turns taking food from the bowls.

"Matthias, in what direction is the Kisan Gate?" Brian asked after everyone had finished eating.

"The gate is north from here."

"I would like to speak with Martha, Jesus and Thomas outside for a few minutes," Brian said while looking at Isaac and Matthias.

"Please do," Matthias said, and then Isaac asked, "Is everything okay?"

"Yes. I want to talk with them privately. We will not be long," Brian answered. He stood up from his chair and said, "Martha, Jesus and Thomas, please come with me." When they were outside, Brian said, "The Kisan Gate is a short walk from here. We can go to the gate now and wait there until we are transported to the future or stay the night to rest and leave tomorrow morning."

"Since I work for you, you can make the decision for me," Thomas said.

"That's kind of you," Martha said. Facing Brian, she said, "Whatever you decide is fine with me."

"Jesus, would you like to rest for the night or leave now?" Brian asked.

"I can rest in the future," Jesus answered.

"We will leave tonight. Plus, there will be fewer people to witness our vanishing. We'll get our belongings and then I'll pay what I owe him," Brian said.

Jesus, Thomas, Martha and Brian entered Matthias's home and returned to their seats at the table where Isaac and Matthias were still sitting. "Is everything okay?" Isaac asked after they sat.

"Yes, everything is fine. We decided that we'll be leaving now and stay in Damascus for the night," Brian said, and then he removed his money pouch from around his neck and took out five shekels and paid Isaac. After paying Isaac, he said, "Thank you for providing us transportation here. It was a pleasant trip."

"You're welcome, and if you need my service again, you know where you can find me," Isaac replied.

"Matthias, thank you for the wine and food. I enjoyed meeting you and Reba. We'll be leaving now," Brian said.

"You're welcome," he said.

At the door, when Brian was about to leave, he shook Isaac's and then Matthias's hand, and he said, "Thanks again," and after Jesus, Thomas, Martha and Brian were outside, they began walking north in search of the Kisan Gate.

The ancient walled city of Damascus is more than four thousand years old and is one of the world's oldest cities. The city had seven gates for entering and exiting and was under Roman control during the time of Jesus. Damascus is located one hundred thirty-five miles northeast of Jerusalem. It is best known in the New Testament for Saul's (Saint Paul) conversion on the road to Damascus after Jesus' crucifixion. Saint Paul was struck down by a flash of lightning and then heard Jesus' voice telling him to get up and go into the city and he would be told what he must do. The Kisan Gate is where Paul made his escape from Damascus by being lowered in a basket from the ramparts.

As they were nearing one of the city gates, Brian said, "Thomas, we must find the Kisan Gate. Please ask someone after we enter."

"It shouldn't be difficult to find unless the gate is on the other side of the city," Thomas said.

"We'll soon find out," Brian said.

They entered Damascus through the Al-Saghir Gate and saw a vibrant city with people moving about in all directions. Thomas approached a man who was walking toward them and when the man was close enough, he said, "Hello. Can you direct me to the Kisan Gate?"

"Yes. It's not far from here. You must follow the street to the right, which goes along the city wall. It's the next gate. You can't miss it," the man answered.

"Thank you," Thomas said, and he went to where Jesus, Brian and Martha were waiting and said, "If we walk to the right on this street, it will be next one."

"Good work, Thomas. Let's go find the gate," Brian said.

They followed the street in the direction the man had given and saw a gate, but could not see its name. A man was on the opposite side of the street walking away from them. Thomas suddenly started running toward the stranger. When the man heard his footsteps, he turned around and saw Thomas running toward him. The man became frightened and ran away, so Thomas returned to where Brian, Martha and Jesus were. Still trying to catch his breath, he said, "I must have scared that man."

"I think so," Martha said.

They saw another man walking toward them, but on the same side of the street.

"Thomas, here comes another man. Please ask him if this is the Kisan Gate," Brian said.

Thomas walked calmly toward the man, and when the man was about to pass by, he said, "Hello. Can you tell me the name of this gate?"

"Kisan," the man answered.

"Thank you," Thomas replied, and he returned to Brian and said, "This is the gate you're seeking."

"Thanks, Thomas. We must now sit and wait there while holding each other's hands so Martha's and my electromagnetic fields will connect to you and Jesus," Brian said.

"What is an electromagnetic field?" Thomas asked.

"It's difficult to explain because it's invisible," Brian answered.

Jesus was quiet and sat near the wall with his wood staff beside him while Brian sat to his right and Martha to his left with Thomas to form a circle while holding hands.

As they held hands, Brian said, "Professor Solomon will notice our coordinates on his time machine and transport us to his home. He'll do that after he verifies that we are at this location."

"I'd guess it's about 6 a.m. in Salem, and most likely the professor is starting his day," Martha said.

"I hope he's in his lab checking Stella's tracking window," Brian said.

CHAPTER 24

David's alarm clock came on at 6 a.m., and he went for a shower and then got dressed. As he was going to his lab, he wondered if today would be the day for Brian and Martha to be transported home.

He entered his lab and went to the PC, turned it on, and then went to his time machine and checked Stella's tracking window to see the coordinates. The longitude 36.3152778 and latitude 33.5063889 were displayed, indicating that Brian and Martha were at one of the transportation sites. David became excited and immediately left the lab to wake up Luke so he could see Martha and Brian return from the year AD 29, hopefully with Jesus.

David went to Luke's bedroom and, after entering, he said, "Kiddo, kiddo! Luke!"

"What is it, Dad?" Luke asked after he woke up.

"Get up. Brian and Martha are ready to be transported home."

"I'll take a quick shower and meet you in the lab. Please don't transport them without me," Luke said excitedly.

"Will do, kiddo. Go hop in the shower and then join me in the lab. I'll be checking Stella's control panel to make sure everything is working properly," David said, and then he left as Luke hurried to the shower.

David returned to the lab. Before entering the room where the StellaPort was, he opened the metal cabinet to make sure Eve's lights were on. He next went to Stella and rechecked the coordinates being displayed in the tracking window, and they had not changed. David knew Brian and Martha were ready to be transported. Luke came into the lab with his hair still wet, carrying his tennis shoes. "That was the quickest shower I've ever seen. You have time to put on your sneakers," David said, smiling.

"I don't want to miss history," Luke said as he was putting on his shoes.

"Are you ready?" David asked.

"Yes," he answered, tying his sneakers.

David completed his final review of Stella's components, and they were all functioning fine. He turned the transport dial to the forward position, and Stella came out of hibernation mode. The light on the control panel soon became green and then went off, indicating the transportation process was completed.

Suddenly, Brian, Martha, Jesus and Thomas were sitting on the floor of StellaPort's transportation chamber. Brian looked around and realized he and Martha were home, and he said, "We've returned to the year 2010."

Brian stood up and so did everyone else. Luke went to the chamber door and, after opening it, he said, "Hi, Brian. Hi, Martha. We missed you guys. Did you bring Jesus with you?"

"Yes," Brian answered.

Luke seemed confused because neither of the two men in the transportation chamber looked like the Jesus he had seen in pictures. David went to the glass chamber as Brian, Jesus, Thomas and Martha were exiting, and Brian said, "Professor, we did it. We brought Jesus and Thomas with us."

David hugged them both and said, "I can't believe it worked. I'm ecstatic with this feat. I wish Professor Kramer were here to share this moment."

Thomas and Jesus stood outside the transportation chamber staring at StellaPort while Luke stared at them.

"Professor, please allow me to introduce you to Jesus from Nazareth and Thomas from Ein Kerem. Thomas was very helpful during our visit to the Holy Land," Brian said.

Jesus and Thomas did not hear Brian because they were mesmerized by the time machine and its lights. "Jesus, Thomas," Brian said louder, and they went to where Brian, Martha, Luke and David were standing.

"I would like to introduce you both to Professor Solomon. He invented this time machine, and this is his son, Luke. Professor and Luke, meet Jesus and Thomas," Brian said.

"Welcome to the 21st century. I hope you had a pleasant trip and that you enjoy your visit with us. You are in the basement of my home. The machine that brought you here is called StellaPort," David said.

"Can I go outside?" Thomas asked.

"Professor, can we take Thomas and Jesus to your library and answer their questions there?" Brian asked.

"Yes, of course. Let's go there now," David answered, and he shut down StellaPort and everyone left the lab. As Jesus and Thomas were leaving, they looked spellbound at all the scientific equipment.

They entered the library and David gestured toward the sofa with his right hand and said, "Thomas and Jesus, please sit." He sat in the chair near them while Luke sat at the desk.

"Luke, please bring two chairs from the kitchen so Brian and Martha can sit," David said, so Luke went and got two chairs.

"Jesus, have Martha and Brian explained why they requested you to come with them to the year 2010?" David asked after everyone was seated.

"Yes. You would like to have a person convey God's message to the people," Jesus answered.

"We need a charismatic leader to send a divine message that will resonate throughout the world so that faith in God is reinforced and to change nonbelievers into believers in a creator who is watching and hearing them," David said.

"I'll preach my Father's message to all who will listen. For his kingdom is eternal, everlasting and open to only those who obey his laws," Jesus said.

"Later today I'll meet with a man and hopefully I can convince him to come to my home for a visit. As you and Thomas will soon discover, you are in a time where man has made many technological advancements and people dress and talk differently. In the meantime, we must buy clothes for you," David said.

"Professor, can I use your shower?" Brian asked.

"Sure. You know where the showers are. Your clothes are in the spare bedroom. Luke, take Martha and Brian upstairs and get towels for them and also for Jesus and Thomas," David answered.

"Okay," Luke said, and then he went upstairs to get the towels with Brian and Martha.

"I'll bet you have a lot of good stories," Luke said while walking up the hallway stairs.

"Yes, we do," Martha said with a smile.

"We'll tell you and your dad later, but first we need to take a shower and return to the library," Brian said.

"Jesus doesn't look like the man pictured in the Holy Bible," Luke said.

"I know, but it's him," Brian said.

Luke went to the hallway cabinet and removed bath towels and gave one to each Brian and Martha.

"Someone can use the guest shower and also my dad's in his bedroom," Luke said.

"Thanks, Luke. I'll use your dad's," Martha said. Luke took them to the spare bedroom to get their clothes.

After showering and getting dressed, Brian and Martha went downstairs to the library and joined David, who was talking with Thomas and Jesus.

"Thanks, Professor. The shower felt good. We must show Jesus and Thomas how to operate them," Brian said.

"After they have showered, we need to find them clothes to wear. I have sweat pants and sweatshirts they can wear in the meantime. Brian, please help Thomas with the shower while I find clothes for them. I'll help Jesus with the one in my bedroom," David said.

Martha was sitting on the sofa in the library while everyone else went upstairs. She noticed an empty space on the wall near the desk and recalled that a cross had been hung in that spot. "Wasn't there a crucifixion cross hanging on the wall?" Martha asked after Luke entered the room.

"Yes. Dad asked me to remove all the visible holy symbols in the house just in case you and Brian brought back Jesus. He didn't want to be the one to explain who was depicted on the cross," Luke answered.

"That was a good idea, but eventually Jesus will see holy icons in his travels," Martha said.

"I know. I'm sure Dad took that into consideration," Luke said.

Upstairs, David showed Jesus and Thomas to his bedroom and removed two sets of sweat pants and shirts from his closet for them to wear. "Brian, please explain to Thomas how to use the bathroom shower in the hallway, and I'll show Jesus how to operate the one in my bedroom," David said.

David went to his bathroom shower and demonstrated for Jesus how to use the handles for the hot and cold water and the lever for turning the shower head on and off. Brian did the same for Thomas and they both understood how to use the fixtures. Jesus and Thomas were still getting acclimated to their new environment. "After your shower, you can use this towel to dry yourself. You can put your clothes on the bed and get dressed in this set of garments. When you are finished, please join us in the library," David said after handing Jesus a towel.

"Thank you," Jesus said.

Brian was in the hallway bathroom with Thomas, and he said, "After you shower and are dressed, please come to the library."

"Thank you. I'll go there when I'm done," Thomas said, and Brian left for the library.

David was at his library desk while Martha and Brian were sitting on the sofa and Luke was seated in the chair next to them. "It's 11 a.m. If you are not too tired, please take Jesus and Thomas to a department store and buy them clothes. They'll each need a suit, tie, white shirt, socks and shoes, and casual clothing," David said.

"We'll take them to a store after they come downstairs," Brian said.

"I can't believe it. I'll be shopping for Jesus," Martha said.

Thomas and Jesus returned to the study wearing sweat pants, shirts and sandals. "Luke, please gather Jesus' and Thomas's clothes and wash them," David said, and Luke left to get their clothes.

"I hope you enjoyed your shower. Martha and Brian will now take you to a store to buy clothes," David said.

"Please come with me," Brian said, and then Jesus, Thomas, Luke and Martha left the library.

Martha opened the front door. After they stepped outside, Jesus and Thomas stared in awe at their new environment. They saw paved streets, cars, telephone poles, streetlights and powerlines, and people dressed very differently. Brian went to his car, which was parked in David's driveway, and opened the passenger doors. "We call this a car. It is a big chariot without horses, but it has a machine that gives it power to move the wheels," Martha said.

Thomas and Jesus sat in the rear seats with Luke between them while Martha sat in the front seat with Brian behind the steering wheel. As Brian drove out of the driveway, Luke demonstrated for Jesus and Thomas how to use the buttons for the power windows.

After Jesus, Thomas, Luke, Brian and Martha arrived at the department store, she began shopping and the black suits she selected for them fit perfectly and didn't need alterations. Martha then chose white shirts, socks, leather belts and black shoes while Luke and Brian watched. She then picked casual dress pants and different colored button-down shirts, underwear and T-shirts. Thomas was impressed with all the products being sold in one big store. After Martha was through shopping, Brian paid for the clothes, and they left for David's home. "Brian, we should buy food for Jesus and Thomas to eat. I think they would enjoy a fish dinner," Martha said on the way to David's house.

"We'll stop at a grocery store on the way to Professor Solomon's home," Brian said.

After buying groceries, they went to David's house. When they arrived, Brian said, "Dude, please take the shopping bags along with Jesus and Thomas to the spare bedroom so they can change into their new clothes and hang up their suits."

"Please come with me, Jesus and Thomas," Luke said, and he took the store bags to the spare bedroom and set them onto the bed and hung up the suits in the closet.

Luke then selected the garments for each to wear and said, "After you change, please come downstairs," and then he left the room and closed the door.

When Jesus and Thomas entered the library, they were wearing their new clothes. Martha said, "You both look like men from this time period. Professor, we bought food at the grocery store. May I use your kitchen to prepare dinner?"

"Of course. Please help yourself. Luke, please help Martha find what she needs," David answered.

Martha and Luke went to the kitchen while Jesus and Thomas were sitting on the sofa. Brian was in the chair next to them and David was at the desk.

"Jesus, as I mentioned earlier today, I'll meet a priest and hopefully persuade him to meet with us. If things go accordingly, you'll soon have an audience with a leader in Rome. The leader is influential and has a large following throughout the world, and I'm sure when he meets with you, Rome will become your home base for delivering God's message," David said.

"Who does this leader represent?" Jesus asked.

"A religion based on your teachings and examples. The religion is called Catholicism. You have become a very important historical figure known all over the world," David answered.

"I would like to meet this man," Jesus said.

"I'll make sure you do," David said, and then he looked at his wristwatch. Then he said, "I'll go to the local church now and talk with the man. I don't know how long I'll be, but in the meantime, have your supper without me. Brian, please make sure Jesus and Thomas are comfortable." David stood up from his desk and left for Saint Peter's Church.

It was late afternoon when David entered the church through the side door as he had done before. After entering the church, he saw a few parishioners sitting in a row of pews praying. Before entering his pew row, David faced the altar and quickly knelt with his right knee and blessed himself. He stood and entered and knelt and blessed himself again and began to pray. After praying, he sat on the bench and looked around hoping to see Father Carlucci, but he didn't. He wondered if the priest was in the rectory, which was outside and behind the church. David decided to go there. At the rectory's front door, he pushed the button on the wall for assistance. A woman's voice was heard over the intercom speaker, asking, "May I help you?"

"Yes. I'm here to talk to Father Carlucci," David said.

"Is he expecting you?" the woman asked.

"No. I would like to meet with him if possible. Please inform him that Professor David Solomon is requesting a meeting," David answered.

"One moment please. I'll see if he's available," the woman said. After a minute, the same woman's voice said, "The father will meet with you," and a buzzer sounded, indicating that the door had been electronically unlocked, and he entered the rectory.

In the lobby, a woman greeted David and said, "Hello, Professor Solomon. My name is Mary. Please have a seat. Father Carlucci will be with you shortly."

David sat in the lobby and after a few minutes the priest appeared. He stood and greeted Father Carlucci with a handshake while saying, "Father, thank you for taking the time to meet with me."

"You're welcome. I was reading the Vatican's electronic newspaper, L'osservatore Romano, on the Internet. It helps me stay current on important Catholic news."

"I didn't know there was a website devoted to news about the Catholic Church."

"Yes. It's just one of the church's media outlets. We have TV, radio, newspaper and now the Internet to reach the masses and get our message out to the world."

"I'll have to go online and visit the Vatican's website. Father, can we go somewhere and talk privately?"

"Yes. Please come with me," the priest answered, and he showed David down the hall to a vacant room with a sofa, chairs and a desk. "We can talk in here," Father Carlucci said. After they entered the room, the priest closed the door and said, "Please have a seat on the sofa. It's much more comfortable than the chairs."

"Thank you," David said.

"Father, what I say here must not be repeated and must remain confidential. Do you agree not to repeat what I'm about to tell you?" David asked after they had both sat at each end of the sofa.

The priest stared intently at him and thought, "What could be so important?" and then he said, "Yes, Professor. You have my word as the Lord is my witness. I promise not to discuss what is said in this room."

"Thank you. Do you recall the first time we met?" David asked.

"Yes. It was during that terrible snowstorm."

"I asked you the question, 'What might Jesus say or do in this time of turmoil if he were here today?'"

"I remember. I thought about it for a long time."

"A scientist named Sebastian Kramer, who was intrigued with the possibility of time travel, called me one night and asked me to visit him. The evening I met with him, he explained he was ill and would like me to continue his research. He said he had to show me something. He took me to his basement and led me to a large room with a machine in the center. I asked him what the machine was for and what it did. He said it was a time machine. He knew the subject interested me. He said that he was very close to making time travel a reality, but was missing something that was slowing the movement of matter. He then explained how his machine worked and the purpose of each component. He turned it on and began to explain each component's display window. I was intrigued with what he had accomplished, and I asked him if he had tested it. He said no. He gave me the blueprints along with his research notes. We then made arrangements to have the machine moved to my home.

"After we met, I was able to invent a way to travel faster than the speed of light, making time travel a reality. The only people who know of this achievement are my son, Luke, two graduate students, Brian Soranno and Martha Valdez, Jesus from Nazareth, Thomas from Ein Kerem, and now, you."

"Jesus Christ?" the priest asked.

"Yes. Jesus in the flesh. He's at my house as we speak."

Father Carlucci looked bewildered, not knowing what to think. He glanced around the room, and then he said, "Jesus from 2,000 years ago?"

"Yes. We tested the machine with a mouse and then with a dog and the results were both successful and safe. Brian, Martha and I decided they would go to the Holy Land during the missing years of Jesus' life and hopefully find him, and if they did, to ask him to visit us in the 21st century," David answered with a smile.

"Can I meet Jesus?"

"Of course. I came here to invite you to meet him, and you can also meet Brian and Martha, who found Jesus and Thomas, a young man they met who guided them safely through the Holy Land."

"When can I meet them?"

"Is tomorrow morning at 10 okay with you?"

"That would be fine. I would meet Jesus anywhere and at any time, day or night."

"I must return home now. They looked tired. I'm sure it's been a long day for them," David said after he got up from the sofa.

The priest stood and escorted him to the entrance of the rectory. As David was about to leave, Father Carlucci said, "I'll be waiting for you at 9:45 a.m.," and they shook hands.

"Yes, Father. I will be here on time, and thank you for taking the time to meet with me," David said, smiling.

David returned home and went to the kitchen and saw that everyone had finished eating their supper. He announced, "I'll bring Father Carlucci here tomorrow morning."

"Professor, that's good news. Martha and I must go home now. What time will Father Carlucci be here?" Brian asked.

"I will meet him at 10 and then come directly here," David answered.

"Brian, please bring Murphy with you so I can play with him," Luke said.

"Will do, little dude," Brian said with a smile, and then Martha and he got up from the table to leave.

"Brian, will I be traveling with you?" Thomas asked after Brian stood.

"No. You and Jesus will sleep here tonight in Professor Solomon's house. He and Luke will answer any questions you may have. Martha and I live ten miles—er, um, 80 furlongs—from here, and we'll visit tomorrow morning," Brian answered, and then they left and got into Brian's car to go home.

After Brian and Martha had left, David was in the kitchen with Luke, Jesus and Thomas, and he said, "Luke, please clean up while I show our guests to the library. Jesus and Thomas, please come with me." After they entered the library, David gestured toward the sofa and said, "Please sit and make yourselves comfortable."

"Can I offer you wine to drink?" David asked.

"Yes," they both replied.

David left the room and returned with a bottle of wine and three glasses and set them onto the library desk. David removed the cork from the bottle with a corkscrew. Thomas was fascinated while watching David use the gadget. After the cork was pulled from the bottle, he poured them a glass of wine.

David was sitting at his desk looking at Jesus and Thomas as they drank their wine. "I'm sure you both must be tired. It's been a long day with little sleep," David said.

"After I finish my wine, I would like to retire for the day. We can talk more tomorrow," Jesus said.

"I'm also tired and want to rest," Thomas said.

"Can I offer you more food or wine?" David asked.

"No, thank you," they both answered.

"You have been very generous," Jesus said.

"You're welcome. If you need anything, just let Luke or me know," David said.

After they finished drinking their wine, David said, "Please come with me and I'll show you to your rooms." He went to the spare bedroom and said, "Jesus, you can sleep in here." When Jesus entered his room, David said, "Goodnight," before closing the door. He went to Luke's bedroom, and there he said, "Thomas, this is your room." After Thomas walked into the room and sat on the bed, David said, "Goodnight," and closed the door.

David returned to the library and poured another glass of wine for himself. Then he sat on the sofa. Luke entered and asked, "Where are Jesus and Thomas?"

"They had a long day and are tired. Thomas is sleeping in your room tonight, and you will be bunking on the sofa," David answered.

"I'm going to use the PC in the lab and surf the Internet," Luke said.

"Okay. If I'm not here, I've gone to bed," David said. Luke went to the lab while David sat on the sofa sipping his wine and reading a book about the missing years of Jesus.

CHAPTER 25

After David had finished his shower, he looked at the alarm clock on the nightstand. The time was 7:20 a.m. He got dressed and went to check on Jesus and Thomas, but their bedroom doors were closed, so he walked quietly to the library and saw Luke sleeping on the sofa. He went to his library desk and got the book about the missing years of Jesus and brought it with him to the kitchen. David made breakfast for himself and, after eating, he glanced at his wristwatch. The time was 8:05. He decided to go to his lab and read. In the lab, David sat at the desk. He set the book down. He remembered what Father Carlucci had said about the Vatican having a website devoted to Catholic news. He turned on the PC and logged on to the Internet and searched for the Vatican's website. He found a link for a site titled Vatican News Service and clicked on it. The Vatican's main media page displayed links to other pages titled Press Office, Newspaper, Liturgy Office, Radio and Television. David thought that there were roughly 1.1 billion Catholics and many must own computers and have access to the Internet, giving Christians all over the world the ability to see and hear Jesus speak. He envisioned a speech by Jesus carried on all Christian television and radio networks on both cable and satellite programs and also on all local stations. David sat back in his chair and mumbled out loud, "Only if the Holy See in Rome believes it's Jesus." If the pope was convinced it was the Lord, he would have no choice but to give him the keys to the Vatican.

It was 9:15 when Brian and Martha arrived at David's home with Murphy. Brian knocked on the rear door, and Luke opened it. He said, "Hi, Brian. Hi, Martha."

"I brought a friend for you to play with," Brian said.

Luke saw Murphy sniffing the grass in the backyard and said, "Thanks, Brian. Dad's in the lab, and Thomas and Jesus are in the library talking."

"Good morning. Have Thomas and Jesus eaten breakfast?" Martha asked.

"No, not yet," Luke answered.

"Thanks, dude," Brian said. He and Martha went to the library while Luke went outside to play with Murphy.

David heard voices and left the lab to find out who it was. He first went to the kitchen, but he didn't see anybody, so he went to the library and saw Martha and Brian talking with Jesus and Thomas.

"Good morning, Professor," Brian and Martha said when he entered the room.

"Luke let us in. He's in the backyard playing with Murphy," Martha said.

"Good morning. I hope everyone is feeling refreshed today. You must have been very tired because of your long day yesterday," David said.

"I'm ready for another trip," Brian said, smiling.

"Me too, but I prefer a vacation to ancient Egypt so I can watch Brian build the pyramids," Martha said, also with a smile.

"I'm happy to see you both are in a good mood this morning," David said with a laugh.

"Professor, I would like to make breakfast for Jesus and Thomas, if that's okay with you," Martha said.

"Fine with me. You know where things are. Please help yourself," David said. He looked at his wristwatch and said, "It's 9:30. I must leave now and bring Father Carlucci here," and he left for Saint Peter's rectory.

At the front door of the rectory, David pushed the button on the wall for assistance. A woman's voice came over the intercom speaker.

"Hello. May I help you?" she asked.

"Hi, Mary. It's David Solomon. I'm here to pick up Father Carlucci."

"Please wait, Professor. He'll be with you momentarily," she said, and then the door to the rectory opened and the priest exited wearing his black suit and a white neck collar. He said, "Good morning, Professor. You are punctual."

"I try to be. I hope you had a good night's rest. Jesus and Thomas are looking refreshed, and Martha is preparing breakfast for them. Shall we go to my home now?" David asked.

"Oh yes. Please, let's go," Father Carlucci answered.

While David and the priest were walking, David said, "Father, when speaking with Jesus, you must keep in mind that we brought him here from the year AD 29, which is one year before he starts his ministry. As you are aware, Jesus is not mentioned in the Gospels from age 12 to 30. We decided on that date so that we would not change the history of the Christian religion that is written about him."

"I understand. You carefully thought this out. It was an intelligent decision. You wouldn't want to be the one responsible for altering history," Father Carlucci said.

When David and Father Carlucci arrived at David's home, they saw Luke in the yard throwing a tennis ball for Murphy to chase. David opened the gate to his yard, and as they were walking to the rear door of the house, Luke jogged to them with Murphy. "Father, this is my son, Luke, and Murphy, Brian's dog," David said.

"Hello, young man. Why haven't I seen you at my Sunday Mass?" the priest asked.

"I go to the one at 8 a.m. on Sundays. Father O'Malley performs the Mass," Luke answered.

"Ah, a perfectly good explanation for why I haven't seen you at church," the priest said.

Luke took the tennis ball from Murphy's mouth and tossed it up into the air and Murphy caught it on the way down. "With a little more practice, Murphy could play centerfield for the Red Sox," Father Carlucci joked.

"I'm working on it, Father," Luke said with a laugh.

"It was nice meeting you and, young man, confessions are heard from 3 p.m. to 5 p.m. Monday through Saturday," the priest said.

"Father, please come with me," David said. They entered his home and went to the kitchen and saw Jesus, Thomas, Brian and Martha sitting at the table eating their breakfast.

"This is Father Carlucci, the priest at Saint Peter's Church that I spoke about yesterday," David announced, and then he introduced everybody at the table while pointing with his right index finger as he said, "This is Martha, Brian, Jesus and Thomas."

"Hello. I understand everybody had a busy day yesterday. I hope you are well rested," the priest said.

"Father Carlucci and I will go to the library now. When you have finished eating, please join us. Father, come with me," David said, and they left for his study.

After David and the priest entered the library, David said, "Father, please sit on the sofa," but before they sat, David asked, "Can I offer you something to eat or drink?"

"No, thank you. I'm fine. The man at the table doesn't look like the Jesus we have been accustomed to seeing in pictures."

"I know. That was my first thought too. Brian and Martha are certain the man sitting in the kitchen is Jesus Christ. You can ask him whatever questions you may have."

"While we're waiting for them to finish their breakfast, would you be kind enough to show me your time machine?"

"Yes, Father. It's in my basement lab. Please come with me."

David led the priest to the room containing his time machine. When David turned on the lights, the priest said, "You weren't kidding. This machine does resemble something from a science fiction movie."

David then explained the function of each component on Stella's control panel. As he was talking, Father Carlucci walked to the transportation chamber and asked, "Is this where the person is transported?"

"Yes. Shall we return to my study now?"

When David and Father Carlucci entered the library, Thomas and Jesus were sitting on the sofa while Brian and Martha sat on kitchen chairs. "Father, please have a seat in the chair next to the couch, and I'll sit here at the desk," David said.

"Is this the leader you spoke of yesterday?" Jesus asked, looking at David.

"No, but he is one of many priests representing the Catholic Church in Rome," David answered.

"I would like to meet your leader," Jesus said to Father Carlucci.

"Jesus, would you mind if I asked you some questions?" the priest asked.

"Please do, for you see the truth, and the truth shall make you free," Jesus replied.

"Nice response. The quote is in the Bible," Father Carlucci thought and paused and then asked, "Where are you from?"

"I live in Nazareth, but I'm from Galilee."

The priest asked the same question to Thomas, and he said, "I am from Ein Kerem in Judea."

"Thomas is from the same village as John the Baptist," Martha said, interrupting the conversation.

"Really? Have you met him?" the priest asked Martha.

"Yes, and so did Brian and Thomas. We all met him and were baptized by him."

Father Carlucci, looking at Martha and Brian, said, "You both met John the Baptist?" and then he asked, "Jesus, did you meet John?"

"Yes. He's my cousin. His mother, Elizabeth, is my mother Mary's cousin."

"Where were you born?"

"In the village of Bethlehem."

"Why did you agree to come with Brian and Martha to the 21st century?" Father Carlucci asked.

"I was asked to visit and preach in the name of the Lord our God in heaven. My Father's heavenly kingdom is open to all, be it in this time or in another. Only the pure in heart will enter and see the son of man sitting at the right hand of God."

The priest thought, "Wow. He sounds just like the man written about in the New Testament." Father Carlucci then said, "I have one final question. Have you performed a miracle?"

"What do you consider a miracle? A tree that provides fruit? Day that becomes night?"

Martha interrupted again and said, "Father, I believe this would be an example you're probing for. Two nights ago in the village of Danos, which is forty-two miles from Damascus, Jesus, Thomas, Brian and I, along with our guide, Isaac, stopped at a farm to rest for the night. Leah, the wife of the man who owned the farmstead, returned home from visiting her friend Mary, who had had a baby a few days earlier. The infant was sick and not eating and didn't have long to live. Jesus asked Leah to take him to the child, and she gladly did. We entered Mary's house and went to the room where she and her sick baby were lying in bed. Jesus requested that Mary remove the blanket that was wrapped around her baby and to put the infant on top of her chest facing upward toward him. Jesus then covered the baby's chest and stomach with his left hand and closed his eyes and prayed silently. Suddenly, the baby started crying and was able to receive nourishment from its mother. Father, that evening we witnessed a miracle in that room, because if Jesus had not interceded, I believe the child would have died."

"I was a witness," Brian said.

"Me too," Thomas said.

"Is that true, Jesus?" Father Carlucci asked.

"The power of prayer will heal as long as you have faith in God almighty. The soul of the child was pure in heart and saved in the name of God," Jesus answered.

"Jesus, I will be hosting a Mass at 5 p.m. today. Would you be kind enough to attend and speak to the congregation?" Father Carlucci asked.

"Yes. I would like that," he replied.

"Professor, please bring Jesus to Saint Peter's Church later today," the priest requested.

"Yes. We'll be there on time," David answered with a smile.

The priest smiled and said, "Perfect. We can talk after the Mass. I must be going now. I'll look for everybody at Mass, including Luke."

The priest stood and shook everyone's hand in the room before going to the front door where David was waiting for him. As the priest was about to leave, David said, "We'll see you soon, Father," and then Father Carlucci left for Saint Peter's rectory.

After David returned to the library, he said, "Father Carlucci seemed touched by the story of Jesus saving the baby's life. Jesus, that was a compassionate thing you did by lifting the sorrow from the hearts of the parents and filling them with joy."

"The child was born into this world with a righteous soul. My Father is merciful to those who are pure in heart," Jesus said.

David didn't know what to say and went to his chair and sat. After David sat, Thomas said, "Jesus has a special gift for healing the sick. Jesus, I believe in God's kingdom and want to enter and see you sitting at his right hand."

"I assure you, Thomas, the kingdom of God will be open to you," Jesus said.

"Thank you, Jesus," Thomas said.

Father Carlucci was in his room at the rectory sitting at his desk thinking about the conversation he had just had with Jesus and how he answered his questions and expressed himself. He was impressed and could understand how a movement could grow from his preaching. The priest wasn't sure how the congregation at his 5 o'clock Mass would react to him. He got a pen and notebook from his desk and started writing notes for his next sermon. The topic would be "It starts with just one person to ignite change in the community," and while making notes he began to wonder what Jesus would say, but knew it was going to be interesting to hear.

The time was 4 p.m. Martha asked, "Brian and Professor Solomon, may I speak with you both in the living room?"

"Yes," they answered.

"Thomas and Jesus, please excuse us. We'll be right back," David said, and then he and Brian followed Martha while Jesus and Thomas sat on the sofa. After they were in the den, Martha said, "When Jesus enters Saint Peter's Church, he'll see the large crucifixion cross."

"I'm glad you brought that up. I completely forgot about that. I was hoping not to be the one to explain who was being depicted on the cross," David said.

"I'll tell him," Brian said.

"No. I'll explain. It was my idea to transport him here," David said. After it was decided, Brian and Martha returned to the library while David went to his bedroom to get the crucifixion cross. David returned to the study and sat at his desk holding the cross.

"Jesus, as I stated before, you have become an important figure in the world. We will all die, and before our death, we pray for God's forgiveness, hoping to be allowed into his heavenly kingdom with your blessing. I know man's final fate is for God to decide. I have a crucifixion cross that is symbolic throughout the world, representing a great sacrifice made for mankind," David said.

David went to Jesus and handed him the cross. Jesus held it and looked at it, and then he said, "I know my fate, for it is written in the Holy Scriptures. My Father has sent me to preach his words to all who will listen. He has a place reserved for me at his right hand."

"There is a very large cross in Saint Peter's Church just like the one in your hands. Please don't be offended by it," David said.

"I am pleased mankind has remembered my sacrifice, but I'm saddened because man does not obey the laws given to Moses by my Father," Jesus said.

"It saddens me to say that in the 21st century, not all people follow God's commandants, and that is why you were asked to visit us," David said.

When Luke entered the library, David glanced at his wristwatch and said, "It's 4 o'clock. Jesus and Thomas, please go and change into your suits." Brian went to help them with their new clothes.

"After they have changed their clothes, we'll go to Saint Peter's Church and meet with Father Carlucci before the Mass. Luke, please wash your face and hands and change your clothes for church," David said to Luke and Martha.

Brian returned to the library with Jesus and Thomas, who were wearing their new suits, and then Luke soon entered wearing dress pants, a button-down shirt and dress shoes.

"If everybody is ready, we'll leave now for Saint Peter's Church," David said, and then they left.

When they arrived at the church, they entered through the side door and saw a vacant row of pews three rows from the front of the altar. Before entering the pew row, Brian, Martha and Luke bent their right knee before entering, and then they knelt with both knees and began to pray. Thomas, Jesus and David also entered and sat on the bench.

"Jesus, please come with me," David whispered, and then he and Jesus left to find where Father Carlucci would be preparing for the Mass. The priest was in a room behind the altar changing into his priestly vestments with the door open when he saw David and Jesus standing in the hallway. The priest went to them and said, "Thank you for coming."

"Where would you like Jesus to sit during the Mass?" David asked.

"Jesus will sit near the altar boys. I will escort him to his seat before beginning the service. Jesus, while I'm performing Mass, please stay seated until I call on you to speak," the priest said.

"Jesus, I'll leave you now with Father Carlucci and sit with the others. We'll meet you here after the service," David said, and then he left and went to the row of pews where his group was seated. David looked around the interior of the church before he sat and estimated that about one hundred parishioners were in attendance.

"Jesus, please come with me and I'll show you to your seat now," Father Carlucci said.

The priest and Jesus entered the altar area through a rear door and walked to where two thirteen-year-old altar boys, who were wearing white tops and black bottom robes, were seated waiting for the Mass to begin. There was a vacant chair next to them and Father Carlucci whispered, "Jesus, this chair is for you," and after Jesus sat, both boys glanced at him, and he smiled.

After the priest escorted Jesus to his seat, he and the two altar boys went to the front of the church to begin their procession down the middle aisle to the Lord's Table. When Father Carlucci and the altar boys were ready, the organ music began to play from the balcony, and they slowly walked down the center aisle while Jesus watched them. When they were at the altar, the priest bowed his head and made the sign of the cross and kissed the table and then turned and faced the congregation waiting for the music to stop as the boys went to their chairs and sat near Jesus. When the music stopped, Father Carlucci began Mass to celebrate the Eucharist (Last Supper). During the service and before the priest served communion to his parishioners, he started preaching about today's sermon's topic, "It starts with just one person to ignite change in the community." After Father Carlucci finished his sermon, he continued with the concluding rite, and when he was done, he said, "Today, we have a guest named Jesus. He will now say a few words. Jesus, please come and speak the word of God."

Jesus stood up and went to where the priest had been standing. Father Carlucci walked past him and sat in a large chair opposite from where the altar boys were seated.

Jesus was looking at the congregation consisting of different races and ethnic backgrounds, and he said, "Father Carlucci's sermon of how one person can make a difference to better himself and a community is true. I say hearken to the word, understand knowledge, love life, and no one will persecute you, nor will anyone oppress you, other than you yourselves. Invoke the Father and implore God often, and He will give to you everlasting life in his kingdom."

Jesus then turned and stared at the cross behind him, and he turned again to face the congregation. He said, "For God loves the world so much that he gave his one and only son so that everyone who believes in him will not perish but have eternal life. God sent his son into the world not to judge, but to save the world through him."

Jesus paused and bowed his head. He then tilted it back and lifted his arms with the palms of his hands facing upward and said, "Lord, in your name, I, your son, ask you to shine your light on me so all will see heaven on earth."

As soon as Jesus completed his sentence, he was engulfed in a visible glowing aurora around him. The congregation became completely quiet and stared in amazement at what they were witnessing. Father Carlucci looked on in astonishment and knew right then and there that this was the Lord, and he was here in the 21st century.

"Blessed are those that see the light, for the light will guide them to heaven for eternal peace," Jesus said.

There was a group of young adults sitting in the rear of the church, and they began to speak out. One person said, "Jesus is the light and the way to God's kingdom." A girl hollered, "I love you, Jesus," and then the glowing aurora that surrounded Jesus slowly diminished and disappeared.

Father Carlucci stood and went to Jesus. He reached for Jesus' right hand and held and kissed it, and then he said, "Thank you. That was a wonderful sermon."

Jesus went to his seat. After he sat, the altar boy sitting closest to him touched him to make sure he wasn't an apparition. "It's me," Jesus said, smiling, and the boy also smiled and whispered, "I know."

After Father Carlucci concluded the service, he stood at the front of the Lord's Table to greet his congregation. As the parishioners approached the altar, they looked and stared at Jesus before talking with the priest. When Father Carlucci saw that David was about to leave, he motioned with his right hand for him to wait. After the priest greeted the last person, he went to David and his group and invited them to his changing room. Father Carlucci then went to where Jesus was sitting and said, "Jesus, please come with me so we can talk more."

Jesus stood and walked with the priest through the rear door of the altar, which was near the priest's dressing room. David, Luke, Thomas, Brian and Martha met Jesus and Father Carlucci in the hallway and entered the room.

After everyone was in the room, the priest said, "I've never had a congregation get so enthused during a Mass in all my years as a priest. I will call the Archdiocese in Boston and arrange a meeting with the archbishop."

"Father, that sounds good," David said, and then he removed a small notebook and a pen from his shirt pocket and wrote his cell phone number on a page and tore it out of the book. He handed the paper to Father Carlucci and said, "Here's my telephone number. Please call me any time, day or night."

The priest took the paper and put it into his shirt pocket. Then he said, "Thank you. I hope the cardinal will be available to meet with me tomorrow morning."

"We'll leave now and wait for your telephone call," David said, and then they left for his home.

The priest removed his robe and hung it in the wardrobe closet against the wall. He left the church and went to the rectory. Father Carlucci entered his residence and sat at his desk, opened the center drawer and removed a small book. The book contained his important personal phone numbers and addresses. He searched for and found the telephone number for the Archdiocese of Boston and then sat back in his chair and thought about what he would say to the cardinal to convince him to come and visit his parish in Salem. He knew that conducting church business kept the archbishop a busy man, and to get an audience with him usually required making an appointment in advance.

A cardinal is a senior official within the Catholic Church and is normally a bishop. Cardinals are collectively known as the College of Cardinals, and they elect a new pope when a pontiff dies. All cardinals must be available to the pope when summoned, and they are the leader of the diocese or archdiocese.

The priest leaned forward in his chair and dialed the telephone number for the Archdiocese of Boston. The receptionist answered and said, "Hello. The Archdiocese of Boston."

"Hi. This is Father Carlucci calling from the Salem Parish. I would like to speak with Cardinal O'Shea."

"The cardinal is not available now, but if you leave your telephone number, I'll pass it on to him," the secretary said.

"That would be fine. Please inform him that it's urgent," the priest said after he gave his cell phone number.

"Can you be reached at this number this evening?" the receptionist asked.

"Yes. That's my cell phone number."

"I'll make sure the cardinal receives your message," the secretary said.

"Thank you and have a pleasant evening," the priest said. He ended the telephone call and sat back in his chair contemplating what he was going to say to Cardinal O'Shea.

After waiting patiently, Father Carlucci's cell phone rang. He answered it and said, "Hello. Father Carlucci speaking."

The person at the other end of the call said, "Hi, Father. This is Cardinal O'Shea. I'm returning your call. You said it was urgent."

"Hello, Cardinal. I hope things are fine with you. I called because it's of extreme importance that we meet as soon as possible. The matter concerns the foundation of the church and has profound implications for all religions."

"Can you be more specific? You know I'm busy. My time is booked solid all this week and next."

"Cardinal, this request is urgent and of the utmost importance. I assure you that when we meet, you will not be disappointed."

"Well, okay. I'll meet with you here in my office at 8 o'clock tomorrow morning."

"Thank you, but is it possible for you to come here? I believe that after we meet, you'll clear your appointments for the day and most likely for the rest of the week."

After a brief pause, Cardinal O'Shea said, "Okay, Father. I haven't been to Saint Peter's in some time. I'll be there at 8 a.m. tomorrow morning."

"Thank you, Cardinal, and have a pleasant evening," Father Carlucci said, and then he ended the call.

David was in the library with Jesus, Thomas, Brian and Martha, while Luke was in the lab with Murphy, surfing the Internet. David's cell phone rang. He answered and said, "Hello. This is David."

"Hello, Professor. This is Father Carlucci. I just finished talking with Cardinal O'Shea and he has agreed to give me an audience tomorrow at 8 a.m. at Saint Peter's rectory. After we meet, and if he agrees to see Jesus, I'll bring him to your home."

"Father, that's good news. I'm sure he'll want to meet Jesus. Please call me in the morning before you and the cardinal visit."

"I'll do that. Talk with you tomorrow. Have a pleasant evening," the priest said.

"Same to you," David said, and then they ended the call. As soon as David was through talking to the priest, he announced to everyone in the room, "That was Father Carlucci. He has a meeting with Cardinal O'Shea at his parish tomorrow morning at 8 o'clock."

"Professor, that sounds like good news," Brian said.

"Cardinal O'Shea is a very influential person in the Catholic Church. He has direct access to the pope," Martha said.

"Jesus, Cardinal O'Shea has the authority to arrange a private meeting between you and the leader of the church. When the cardinal meets with you tomorrow, I'm sure he'll set up a meeting with the pontiff," David said.

"I'm looking forward to meeting him," Jesus said.

"Professor, what is the machine called that you used to talk with Father Carlucci?" Thomas asked.

"It's called a cellular phone. The gadget allows individuals to carry the device with them to communicate with other people when you dial their contact number. There's much more technology involved to make it work," David answered.

Thomas looked confused and said, "Thank you for the explanation. I have seen many technological wonders in such a short time."

"Martha and I must leave now. We'll see you tomorrow morning," Brian said. As they were about to leave, Brian and Martha said bye to everyone. At the front door, Brian called for Murphy, and he ran to him, and then they left.

Luke was using the PC in the lab to search the Internet for a chatroom devoted to Catholics living in New England. He was curious to know if Jesus had been mentioned because of the overwhelming response he received at Saint Peter's Church. Luke found a website and slowly scrolled down the page to find today's postings. He counted twelve about Jesus and they all talked about his speech and how he glowed. One posting read, "Our Lord and Savior has returned. Jesus is at Saint Peter's Church in Salem."

After Luke read the messages, he went to tell David. After he entered the library, he said, "Dad, I just read twelve postings on the Internet about Jesus in a Catholic chat room."

David was thrilled and stood from his chair. He said, "Jesus and Thomas, please come with us to the computer in the lab."

Luke was first to enter the lab and sat in the chair at the desk looking at the website page on the monitor while Jesus, Thomas and David stood behind him staring at the computer screen. Luke was now pointing at the page being displayed, and he said, "There are twelve people already spreading the word about seeing Jesus today."

David read each posting aloud and then he said, "Soon all the chat rooms on the Internet will be talking about Jesus."

"What is the purpose of this machine and what does it do?" Thomas asked.

"It's called a computer. The machine will process, store and output data at a high speed. The person using the computer can give commands with a keyboard, mouse or by voice," David answered.

Thomas was staring at the screen in a daze as David continued, "We use the Internet to send, receive and view information. You can envision the Internet as a very long road with many other roads connecting to it, a global computer network that links other networks all over the world by satellite and telephone. It's complex and would be very difficult for me to explain so you could understand the technology."

After answering Thomas's questions, David said, "It's getting late. We should go to bed and get a good night's rest because tomorrow will be a big day," and then Luke turned off the computer and they left the lab.

CHAPTER 26

Cardinal O'Shea drove his car from the Archdiocese in Braintree and arrived at Saint Peter's rectory at 8:30 a.m. He parked his car and walked to the front door of the rectory and pushed the button on the wall.

"How can I help you?" Mary asked through the intercom speaker.

"Hello. It's Cardinal O'Shea to meet with Father Carlucci. He's expecting me," Cardinal O'Shea answered.

"Oh, yes, Cardinal," Mary said, and she buzzed the door to unlock it, allowing Cardinal O'Shea to enter the rectory. After he entered, Mary approached him and said, "Father Carlucci asked me to escort you to a room reserved for your meeting. Please come with me."

When they were at the room, Mary said, "Please have a seat and I'll inform him you're here."

"Thank you," the cardinal said as he sat on the sofa.

When Father Carlucci arrived for his meeting, Cardinal O'Shea stood and both men shook hands.

"I'm sorry for keeping you waiting," the priest said when he entered the room.

"I'm the one who should be apologizing. I'm thirty minutes late because of the traffic," the cardinal replied.

After the priest closed the door, he said, "Thank you for taking the time to come here and meet with me. Please sit."

"You said it was urgent and that it concerned the foundation of the church. I had a difficult time sleeping last night thinking of what could be so important that it would affect the core of the church," the cardinal said after sitting on the sofa.

"Cardinal, I have a parishioner named David Solomon who is a professor at M.I.T. I met with him the day before yesterday. He told me an interesting story, but only after I promised him that I would not repeat what he was about to tell me. While listening to him, I was skeptical at first, but he was sincere and seemed to be an honest man. He asked me if I was willing to meet a man at his house, and I said yes. The man had arrived at his home two days before with another young man. You must meet them. As I stated earlier, I promised the professor I would not divulge what we discussed. I'm sure he will explain everything to you as he did to me."

"Father, you have piqued my curiosity again. Let's go meet Professor Solomon."

"I'll call to tell him we're on our way." He called David to let him know that they were leaving now for his home.

David was in the library with Jesus, Thomas, Brian, Martha and Luke when he received the telephone call from Father Carlucci. After talking to the priest, he said, "That was Father Carlucci who just called. He'll soon be here with Cardinal O'Shea. Jesus, the cardinal is an important man in the Catholic Church and has great influence."

"I would like to meet the leader of the cardinal's church," Jesus said.

"I'm sure that will happen soon," David replied.

There was a knock on the front door and David said, "I'll get it." He went to the door and opened it. He said, "Good morning, Father. Good morning, Cardinal. Thank you for coming. Please come with me to my library."

"Professor, I didn't tell the cardinal what you and I had discussed yesterday. Do you think it's best to inform him before he meets your guests?" Father Carlucci asked.

"Yes. You're right. Let's go to my living room and talk there," David answered.

In the living room David asked his guests to have a seat on the sofa. After they sat, he said, "Excuse me for a moment. I'll be right back." David went to the library where Jesus, Thomas, Brian, Martha and Luke were waiting and announced, "We'll be with you in a few minutes. I'm meeting with Father Carlucci and Cardinal O'Shea in the living room."

David returned to his guests and stood facing them in the center of the room, and he asked, "May I offer you something to drink?"

"No, thank you," they both answered.

"Professor, as I said, I didn't mention our discussion to the cardinal. He is most generous in giving us an audience today."

"Cardinal, thank you for coming. I know you're a busy man."

"Father Carlucci mentioned you are a professor at M.I.T."

"Yes. I teach theoretically applied engineering techniques using nanotechnology."

"That's an interesting field. Doesn't that technology deal with the miniaturization of electronic components? I believe there are new diagnostic medical tests utilizing the technology such as swallowing a digital camera the size of a pill to view within the body without exploratory surgery."

"That's a good example. The reason you were requested to come to my home is to meet a man who is sitting in my library. Please come with me to my lab in the basement for a better understanding of what I will tell you," David said, and they left for the lab.

David took the priest and the cardinal to the room housing his time machine. When Cardinal O'Shea entered, he stood in awe gazing at the machine, and then he asked, "What is it?"

"A time machine," the priest answered.

"Yes, it's a time machine that I recently perfected. I showed it to Father Carlucci yesterday on the condition that he would keep its existence a secret. I hope I can count on you to do the same," David said.

"I'll keep the secret too. Is this the reason I was asked to come here?"

"Sort of. You will soon meet the first two time travelers, Brian Soranno and Martha Valdez, both graduate students attending Harvard University. We decided to use the machine to find Jesus during one of the years he's not mentioned in the New Testament and ask him to come visit us in our time. We chose AD 29, the year before Jesus starts his ministry, so that written history about him would not change.

Brian and Martha found him with the help of Thomas, who is from Judea and is upstairs sitting with Jesus. They began their search for Jesus in Jerusalem and traveled north to Nazareth, where they found him, and then journeyed to Damascus, and they are now in Salem."

"You're telling me our Lord and Savior is upstairs in your library?" Cardinal O'Shea asked.

Father Carlucci then said, "I was skeptical at first. I asked Jesus to say a few words during the Mass I performed yesterday afternoon. He had the congregation mesmerized and hanging on every word he said. The oddest thing happened after Jesus bowed his head and then looked up at the ceiling with the palms of his hands facing upward while saying, "Lord, in your name, I ask you to shine your light on me, your son, so all will see heaven on earth." As soon as Jesus completed the sentence he was engulfed in a visible glowing aurora around him like is seen in holy pictures. I was astonished and knew it was the Lord."

"I would like to meet Jesus now," Cardinal O'Shea said.

"Yes, of course. Please come with me," David said, and they left the lab for the library.

When David entered the library with the priest and cardinal, they saw Jesus and Thomas sitting on the sofa while Brian and Martha sat in chairs facing them. Luke was sitting in the chair next to the couch. "You met Father Carlucci yesterday. He has invited Cardinal O'Shea from the Archdiocese of Boston to meet with us. Luke, please bring two chairs here for our guests," David said.

As Luke was about to walk past the cardinal, David said, "Cardinal O'Shea, this is my son, Luke."

"Hi," Luke said as he kept walking to get the chairs from the kitchen.

David then introduced everyone in the room and said, "The man sitting to the left on the sofa is Jesus from Nazareth, and to his right is Thomas from the village of Ein Kerem."

"The same village where John the Baptist was born?" the cardinal asked.

"Yes," Thomas answered.

David then continued with the introductions and said, "This is Brian Soranno and Martha Valdez. They are the world's first human time travelers. Father, if you don't mind, Cardinal, please sit next to the sofa."

Luke returned with a chair and placed it next to Brian so Father Carlucci could sit. He then left the room and came back with another chair and set it down near the library desk and sat on it.

The cardinal was sitting, staring intently at Jesus and Thomas, and said, "Jesus, I understand you said a few words during Father Carlucci's Mass yesterday, and you asked for a ray of light to shine on you and your request was answered. Is that true?"

"I am the beacon that my Father has sent into this world. No one lights a lamp and puts it in a place where it will be hidden or under a bowl. Instead he puts it on a stand so that those who come in may see the light."

Cardinal O'Shea paused for a moment and recalled that those quotes were from the New Testament, and he asked, "Are you the son of God?"

"My Father is not from this world, but the creator of all things on it. His kingdom is not on earth and when you enter it, you will see me sitting at the right hand of God. I will tell you this: God sent his son into the world not to judge the world, but to save the world through him."

After looking at Father Carlucci and David, Cardinal O'Shea said, "Today at Holy Cross Cathedral in Boston, I will perform a service at noon. The cathedral is much larger than Saint Peter's Church and can seat sixteen hundred people. Usually there are over three hundred parishioners attending my noon Mass. Would you be kind enough to come and speak to my congregation as you did yesterday?"

"I will preach God's message to all who will listen," Jesus replied.

"Professor, I must leave now. Please bring Jesus to Holy Cross Cathedral to speak at my noon Mass," the cardinal said.

"We'll meet you in the church before the service starts," David said.

"Fine. I'll leave word with security that I'm expecting you so we can meet before the Mass," the cardinal said. He stood and looked at Jesus and said, "I look forward to seeing you again." Cardinal O'Shea went to the front door, and there he said, "I don't know if it's just me, but I felt a divine presence in the room."

"I've sensed that too since Jesus arrived," David said with a smile.

"I know I'm not the only one experiencing that feeling," the priest said as he stepped outside of David's home and headed to the rectory.

At Saint Peter's rectory, the cardinal said, "Father, I must leave now. Will you be coming to Holy Cross Cathedral today?"

"No. Jesus is in good hands with you and Professor Solomon. If the professor has to contact me, he has my private telephone number," the priest answered. After they shook hands, the cardinal got into his car and drove to his office.

After David returned to the library, he said, "Jesus, as I mentioned earlier, Cardinal O'Shea has the influence to arrange a meeting with Pope Valentine II. He's the leader of the Catholic Church and represents 1.1 billion people, but there are 2.1 billion people that consider themselves Christians in the world. Jesus and Thomas, please change into your suits, and Luke, get dressed for church."

After Jesus, Thomas and Luke left the room, Brian said, "Professor, Martha and I will be leaving now and we'll meet you in the cathedral. There will be more people at Holy Cross Cathedral to hear Jesus speak."

"I hope that's the case, and if Jesus captures the congregation's attention as he did yesterday, we'll ask the cardinal to set up a meeting between him and the pope," David said while walking to the front door with them. After Martha was outside, she said, "Professor, we'll meet you in the church," and then he closed the door and went to his study while they headed for Boston.

David was sitting on the sofa waiting for Luke, Jesus and Thomas to return to the library. After a short period of time, Luke entered and sat at the desk. When Thomas and Jesus entered the library, David said, "Brian and Martha are on their way to Boston, and they'll meet us inside the cathedral. If everybody is ready, we'll leave now," and then he went to the front door and opened it for them. After they were outside, David went to the driver's side door of his car while Luke opened the rear passenger doors for Jesus and Thomas to enter. When everyone was seated, David said, "Let's go to Holy Cross Cathedral."

"How far is the cathedral from here?" Thomas asked.

"Not far. It's about 64 furlongs. We should arrive in thirty minutes, so sit back and enjoy the scenery," David answered.

It was 11:30 a.m. when they arrived at Holy Cross Cathedral. Upon entering the enormous church, they noticed Martha and Brian sitting in the first row of pews in front of the altar to the right of the center aisle. They went to where Brian and Martha were and sat with them.

The cathedral is the largest in New England and has a seating capacity of sixteen hundred parishioners. The interior of the church has a large altar area, paintings, statues and wall sculptures of the Stations of the Cross, including side chapels and big stained-glass windows.

Brian, Martha, Luke, Thomas, Jesus and David sat on the wood bench waiting for the Mass to begin. David was looking around the interior of the church for Cardinal O'Shea, but didn't see him. He couldn't help notice the many people in each pew row praying compared to yesterday in Saint Peter's Church. After David knelt and was through saying some prayers, he said, "I'll take Jesus to Cardinal O'Shea. Please wait here."

David and Jesus went to the far right aisle walkway that led behind the Lord's Table to rooms for the clergy to prepare for Mass. One door was open. As an altar boy was about to pass by, David said, "Excuse me. Can you tell me where I can find Cardinal O'Shea?"

"He's in the room to the right of the open door," the boy answered.

"Thank you," David said.

They went to the room and knocked on the door. Cardinal O'Shea opened it and said, "Hi, Professor. Hello, Jesus. Please come in." In the room was a priest putting on his black cassock and collarino for the Mass. The cardinal was wearing a black cassock with scarlet red piping and buttons, scarlet fascia (sash), pectoral cross on a chain and a scarlet zucchetto. Cardinal O'Shea introduced the priest in the room to Jesus and David, and he said, "This is Father Smith. He will be assisting me with the service today. Father, please allow me to introduce David Solomon and Jesus. Jesus will be speaking to the congregation today."

"It's a pleasure to meet you both," the priest said, smiling, shaking their hands. The father then said, "Please excuse me. I have to ensure that the altar is prepared for Mass and greet the parishioners—just some of my priestly duties," and he left the room.

"Jesus, during the Mass I would like you to sit in a chair near the four altar boys," Cardinal O'Shea said.

David, looking at Jesus, said, "Just as you did yesterday at Saint Peter's Church."

The cardinal then said, "I'll call upon you to say a few words to the congregation."

Jesus nodded his head and said, "I will speak in the name of God to your parishioners."

"Cardinal, I'll leave Jesus with you now and join my group," David said.

"After the service, please come to this room so we can talk more," Cardinal O'Shea replied.

"I will meet you both here after the Mass," and he left the room.

After David left, Cardinal O'Shea said, "Jesus, please come with me, and I'll escort you to your seat." The cardinal then escorted Jesus to six vacant chairs to the right side and within the altar area, and there he said, "Please sit here, and I'll call upon you later to speak."

After Jesus sat the cardinal walked up the middle aisle to the front of the church, greeting his parishioners. While greeting his congregation, organ music began to play as the priest, altar boys and the cardinal assembled for their procession down the center aisle. When they were in formation, they began walking slowly toward the Lord's Table and, upon reaching it, each person went to their respective places to begin the Mass. Cardinal O'Shea and Father Smith bowed their heads and made the sign of the cross. Then they went to the white marble table and kissed it. The cardinal turned toward his congregation and began the service as the priest sat in a large chair to the left and across from where Jesus and the altar boys were sitting.

After communion was served, Cardinal O'Shea said, "I have a special guest today. His name is Jesus, and he will now say a few words to you," and the cardinal gestured with his hands for Jesus to come to where he stood. The cathedral had very good acoustics so that a clergymen's voice could be heard clearly throughout the church. Jesus got up from his chair and went to where Cardinal O'Shea had stood. The cardinal went to a vacant chair next to Father Smith and sat down.

Jesus looked out at the congregation and said, "I stand here before you, and I tell you that I am the Alpha and the Omega, the beginning and the end, the first and the last. My Father has sent me to the world to be sacrificed, his only son, so that everyone who believes in him will not perish but have eternal life. The gates to heaven are open to all that obey God's laws, which were passed down from him to Moses. You must love the Lord your God with all your heart, all your soul and all your mind. This is the first and greatest commandment."

Brian could hear a man behind him whispering, "He thinks he's Jesus Christ."

A man to the left of the center aisle stood and said, "You're quoting Jesus, our Lord and Savior, from the New Testament. Are you pretending to be him?"

"I am the Son of God, sent here to take away the sins of the world so you may have a chance to enter my Father's kingdom in heaven," Jesus answered, and he lifted his arms up with the palms of his hands facing upward and tilted his head slightly backward. He gazed out at the congregation and said, "I am the way and the truth and the life. No one comes to the Father except through me." Now Jesus was looking up at the ceiling and he said, "I am the light for all to be a witness to," and just as in Saint Peter's Church, an aurora appeared around Jesus. The congregation gasped and made muffled sounds while Jesus paused and looked around at all of them. Then he said, "I will give you the keys to the kingdom of heaven and whatever you bind on earth will be bound in heaven, and whatever you loose on earth will be loosed in heaven."

David was looking at Cardinal O'Shea and Father Smith, and he could see from their facial expressions that they were both mesmerized by Jesus. The light glowing around him slowly diminished and the congregation's whispering was becoming louder. "I believe in you, Jesus. I want to enter God's kingdom," a woman said.

A man hollered, "Jesus, you are the Lord and my light."

An old woman in the front left row who was crippled by polio slowly walked to Jesus with the help of crutches and leg braces. When the woman was standing in front of Jesus, she said, "Lord, please release me from this crippled body."

"Woman, come closer to me," Jesus said as he looked into her eyes. The elderly woman did as Jesus requested and then Jesus reached his arms out and held both of her hands. Jesus closed his eyes and opened them, and he said, "Woman, lay down your crutches and remove your leg braces."

The woman dropped her crutches to the floor and removed her braces and began walking about without the help of the orthopedic aids. The woman walked to Jesus and then took his right hand and kissed it while crying, and she said, "Thank you, Lord. I knew my prayers would be answered."

Jesus turned toward the altar to return to his chair. As he was walking past the altar boys, they blessed themselves while gazing at him. Many in the congregation began to make a commotion in the cathedral and then Cardinal O'Shea stood up and returned to the front center of the altar to face his parishioners. He motioned with his hands for them to quiet down so he could complete the Mass. When the congregation had quieted down, he announced, "We will have a special Mass at 4 p.m. today and Jesus will be the speaker." Then he ended the service by making the sign of the cross and quickly went to Jesus and said, "Please come with me."

Cardinal O'Shea quickly escorted Jesus to the room where they had been before the Mass. Father Smith, with the help of David and Brian, turned back the parishioners trying to approach Jesus. After the cardinal and Jesus entered the dressing room, Cardinal O'Shea said, "That was a compassionate act you did. The elderly woman you healed has been a member of this parish since even before I was a priest at this cathedral. She was born with polio and there is no known cure for the disease. If I didn't know that woman personally, I would have thought it was a staged event, but after witnessing what you did for her, I believe you are the Son of God. I'll be conducting another Mass at 4 p.m. today. Would you be kind enough to speak again?"

"I will convey God's message to your congregation. Professor Solomon mentioned you have the power to arrange a meeting between the leader of your church and me. I would like to meet with him," Jesus replied.

"It will be an honor," the cardinal said.

David was at the entrance to the altar and said, "Brian, I'll go check on Jesus and the cardinal. Please wait here just in case Father Smith needs your help, and keep an eye on Luke. Thomas, come with me."

David and Thomas went to the room where Jesus and the cardinal were. The door was closed and David knocked on it. Cardinal O'Shea unlocked and opened it and said, "Please enter." After they had entered the room, Cardinal O'Shea closed and locked the door.

"I didn't bring my cell phone with me, so I'll have to leave now for my office to call the pope's personal secretary to set up a meeting between Jesus and Pope Valentine. I will return to Holy Cross as soon as possible. You may wait in this room if you prefer. Jesus has agreed to speak again at my 4 p.m. Mass today. I'll have enough time to call Rome and then return here to conduct the service," the cardinal said.

"That sounds perfect, Cardinal. We'll wait here for you to return," David said.

"Before I leave, let's exchange telephone numbers in case something comes up," the cardinal said. After they exchanged cell phone numbers, the cardinal said, "I must be going now. I'll come back as soon as possible," and he left for his office.

After Cardinal O'Shea left, David said, "I'll go tell the others what he said. I'll be back in a few minutes." He went to where Brian, Martha and Luke were sitting and said, "Good news. The cardinal left for his office to call the personal secretary of the pope to arrange a meeting between Jesus and the pontiff."

"That's excellent news, Professor. Pope Valentine is in for a divine treat," Brian said.

"Dad, can I go to Rome with you guys?" Luke asked.

"We'll all travel with Jesus to Rome. The cardinal is allowing us to use one of the cathedral's rooms while we wait for him to return," David said.

CHAPTER 27

Cardinal O'Shea was in his office sitting at his desk reviewing his appointment calendar for scheduled meetings and events for the next two weeks and knew he would have to clear his schedule. He removed a sheet of paper with telephone numbers of church officials from under the calendar on his desk. The page listed the names, addresses and phone numbers of important clergy he had collected over the years. At the top of the list were the numbers for Vatican officials, including Vincenzo Fabrini, the personal secretary of Pope Valentine. The cardinal used the telephone on his desk. When the person at the other end picked up, he said, "Hello. Monsignor Fabrini speaking."

"Hello, Monsignor. It's Cardinal O'Shea calling from the Archdiocese of Boston. How are you?"

"I can't complain, Cardinal. You must come and visit us."

"That's the reason I'm calling you. I must have a private audience with the pope as soon as possible."

"He's at his summer residence and will be there for the rest of the month."

"Monsignor, I know the pontiff is a very busy man, but this request is extremely urgent."

"Cardinal, for you, I will arrange a meeting with the Holy See. When will you be arriving?"

"Tomorrow evening. We'll need a place to stay while we're visiting."

"We?" the monsignor asked.

"Yes. I'll explain when we meet. Please arrange for two cars to pick us up at the airport. I will call you after I know our arrival time."

"Cardinal, I'll reserve accommodations at the Domus Sanctae Marthae (Saint Martha's House) in Vatican City and arrange for transportation for you and your guests here."

"Thank you, Monsignor. I'll get back to you this evening with our travel itinerary," the cardinal said.

The monsignor said, "I will be waiting to hear from you," and they ended the telephone call.

Brian, David, Martha and Luke were outside the room that Thomas and Jesus were in. David knocked on the door and, after opening it, he saw Jesus and Thomas sitting on the floor with their eyes closed, praying. "Hi. Please excuse us for disturbing you," David said, and when Jesus and Thomas looked up, he said, "Cardinal O'Shea will soon be arriving to perform the 4 p.m. Mass. Can I get you something to eat or drink?"

"I would like water," Jesus replied.

"I'll have the same," Thomas answered.

David said, "Luke, go check to see if there's a water fountain or cooler in the cathedral, and if none, you'll have to make a run to the store for bottled water."

"Will do, Dad," Luke said, and he left, searching for a water fountain. While Luke was walking in the hallway, he saw a room with an open door. He went there and peeked inside the room and didn't see anyone, but saw a water cooler and paper cups. He filled two cups with cold water and returned to the room and knocked on the door. Brian opened it. Luke entered the room and gave Jesus and Thomas a cup of water and they both said, "Thank you."

Cardinal O'Shea returned to Holy Cross Cathedral and went directly to where he had left Jesus and David. The cardinal knocked on the door and opened it. After entering the room, he saw David, Luke and Brian sitting and talking.

"Where's Jesus?" the cardinal asked.

"He's with Thomas and Martha. They're viewing the holy icons in the cathedral," David answered.

"I'll go and see if they have any questions. I shouldn't be long," the cardinal replied.

"Cardinal, remember that we transported Jesus from the year AD 29 before his crucifixion and during a year that he is not mentioned in the New Testament. You must use tact when explaining the meaning behind the religious scenes being portrayed throughout the cathedral. He's aware of his final fate," David said.

"Thanks for the reminder. Hopefully, he won't have any questions for me," the cardinal said, and then he left the room to find Jesus.

Jesus, Thomas and Martha were observing the paintings on the wall near the altar and also the stained-glass windows throughout the cathedral. Cardinal O'Shea saw them viewing the beautiful artwork and went to them and stood next to Jesus.

"Cardinal, this cathedral is beautiful," Martha said.

"Yes, it is," the cardinal replied.

Thomas was walking along the walls of the cathedral, stopping at each sculpture depicting the Stations of the Cross. Martha went to him and Thomas said, "This man suffered at the hands of the Romans because of a crime he committed."

"He is a martyr because he sacrificed himself so mankind would be given a chance to get into heaven. The only crime was speaking the truth about God's kingdom and his laws that must be obeyed," Martha said.

"That martyr is Jesus."

"Yes, as I said before, he's a very special man."

"I know he's a divine being who has been sent by God to visit us."

Martha glanced toward the altar as Cardinal O'Shea was pointing to a stained-glass window that he and Jesus were standing in front of, most likely explaining the scene being portrayed in it. Martha and Thomas continued walking along the walls viewing the art while Jesus and Cardinal O'Shea moved about looking at the other stained-glass biblical scenes. Martha glanced around the cathedral and did not see the cardinal or Jesus, and then she said, "Thomas, we should now go to where everyone is," and they went to the cardinal's dressing room.

After everyone was in the room, Cardinal O'Shea announced, "I spoke with the personal secretary of the pope and he has agreed to set up a meeting with the pontiff. I told him we would be arriving tomorrow evening and that I would call him tonight with our travel itinerary. Professor, how many in your group will be traveling to Rome?

"Everyone in this room."

"Fine. I'll ask my secretary to make arrangements for our flight," the cardinal said, and then he called his secretary on his cell phone and said, "Hello, Sister. It's Cardinal O'Shea. Please make airline reservations for seven people from Boston to Rome leaving tomorrow morning. I don't have a return date scheduled yet, and please call me after you receive confirmation of the reservation. I need to know the arrival time. Thank you. Bye."

The cardinal looked at his wristwatch and said, "It's 3:45. I must get ready for my 4 o'clock Mass."

"We'll all wait here for the Mass to begin, except for Jesus. He should remain with you," David said. They left the room so the cardinal could prepare for his upcoming service.

Martha, David, Brian, Thomas and Luke sat in the first pew row, which was vacant. After sitting, David glanced behind him toward the front doors of the church and noticed a steady stream of people entering. The cathedral could seat sixteen hundred people, and at the rate the people were coming in, it would soon be full to capacity. It was now five minutes before the Mass was to begin and David again looked behind him and saw that the church was at capacity and had standing room only. David knew the parishioners who attended the noon Mass had spread the word about Jesus, and the news had traveled fast on the streets of Boston.

Cardinal O'Shea and Father Smith stood at the front of the Lord's Table along with the altar boys and saw the cathedral filled to capacity. People were standing along and against both sides of the walls. They were surprised as they gazed upon the number of people attending this special Mass. It was the largest congregation since 1964, when Cardinal Cushing conducted a Mass honoring President John F. Kennedy after his death. Father Smith and the altar boys proceeded up the center aisle to the front of the cathedral to get in formation for the procession to the Lord's Table. Cardinal O'Shea returned to his dressing room and escorted Jesus to the largest chair, which was the one in which he had sat during the noon Mass, and Father Smith would be sitting beside the altar boys.

When Jesus appeared and sat in his chair, the congregation became quiet. Cardinal O'Shea went to join the procession to the altar. As the cardinal went to the front of the cathedral, the organ music began to play and then the clergy and altar boys slowly proceeded down the center aisle. When they were standing in front of the marble table, Cardinal O'Shea and Father Smith made the sign of the cross and bowed their heads and went to and kissed the altar. The altar boys took their seats beside the priest as the cardinal began the Mass. As at the noon service, Cardinal O'Shea introduced Jesus to the parishioners near the end of the Mass. The congregation was completely quiet as Jesus was standing in the front center of the altar. The cardinal went to where Father Smith and the boys were seated and sat with them.

Jesus gazed out at the more than sixteen hundred people and said, "The word of God passes through me to you, and I'll tell you this: The only way to get into God's kingdom is through me. The Lord has sent me to this world to warn the sinners that if they don't repent, they will not enter his kingdom. You must accept the kingdom of God as if you were a child, or you will never enter it. And whenever you stand praying, if you have anything against anyone, forgive him so that your Father in heaven may also forgive you your trespasses."

Jesus slowly walked up the center aisle from where he had been standing to the first row of pews and stopped. He said, "Blessed are the pure in heart, for they will see God." Jesus bowed his head and lifted his arms up with the palms of his hands facing upward. He tilted his head slightly back and said, "Lord, our God, you are the light for all life. I ask you in your name to shine your light upon me." Suddenly, as before, Jesus was engulfed by a light shining on him.

Some in the congregation said, "Oh look" and "Oh my God."

"I am the way and the truth and the life. No one comes to the Father except through me," Jesus said while looking at the parishioners.

The woman whom Jesus had cured of polio earlier was pushing a wheelchair with an elderly woman in it down the center aisle until she was in front of Jesus, and she said, "Lord, you cured me of my disease. Please cure my friend. She believes in you and is pure in heart."

"God decides who is pure in heart," Jesus said, and then he looked at the old woman in the wheelchair who was also crippled with polio. Jesus extended his hands while the light was still glowing around him and the elderly woman in the chair held both of Jesus' hands.

"Jesus, please help me walk again," she said.

Jesus was looking down at her and said, "Woman, stand and walk. For God, thy Lord, has blessed thee and those who hunger and thirst for righteousness, for they will be satisfied."

The old woman stood and began walking. Crying, she went to Jesus and hugged him and said, "Thank you, Lord!"

Both women were overwhelmed with joy because they were cured of their crippling disease. They hugged each other and walked up the center aisle holding hands as the light around Jesus slowly diminished. Cardinal O'Shea and Father Smith stared in astonishment because they, along with some of the congregation, had witnessed a second miracle on the same day.

Jesus gazed out at the people and said, "It is more blessed to give than to receive," and then he returned to his chair as Cardinal O'Shea stood and went to the center front of the altar.

As Jesus was walking to his chair, a member of the congregation yelled out, "Jesus has returned! You are my Lord and Savior," and then someone else said, "You are my savior and light." Another parishioner hollered, "Listen to Jesus if you want to get into heaven!" and more people started saying phrases about Jesus and their faith in God.

The cardinal motioned with his hands to signal for the people to sit and be quiet. After he was in control of his congregation, he ended the Mass. As soon as the Mass was over, many parishioners started coming forward wanting to meet Jesus. David, Brian, Thomas, Martha and Father Smith blocked their way as Cardinal O'Shea and Jesus quickly returned to the cardinal's dressing room.

After Jesus entered, Cardinal O'Shea said, "Please wait here. I'll return," and then he left and closed the door and went to the altar. The cardinal stood behind David, Father Smith, Brian and Martha, who were trying to control the large crowd that wanted to meet Jesus. The cardinal raised his voice and said, "People, people, go home. The Mass has ended. You will hear from Jesus again. Come to the cathedral tomorrow."

"Will Jesus be here?" someone asked.

"Jesus is always here watching over all who believe in him. Holy Cross Cathedral will be open tomorrow morning, so please come back then," the cardinal answered.

The people calmed down and began leaving. After the parishioners had left, the priest asked the altar boys to close and lock the doors. "Jesus is waiting in my room. Professor, when the crowd in front of the church leaves, please take Jesus home with you. I'll call you as soon as I know our itinerary," Cardinal O'Shea said.

"We'll leave now. Martha and Brian, you might as well leave too. I'll call you when I know our plans," David said.

"Okay, Professor. We'll wait for your call," Brian said, and then they left through the back door.

Luke, David and Thomas went with the cardinal to the room where Jesus was and entered. When they were in the room, David said, "Cardinal, I'll leave now and will drive my car to the rear door of the church so you and Luke can help Thomas and Jesus get into my car."

David left for his car. When he was outside, he saw people still milling around the front of the cathedral. He got into his car and drove to the back door of the church and then got out. He knocked on the door and the cardinal opened it. He and Luke helped Jesus and Thomas get into the rear passenger seats. After they were seated, Luke sat in the front seat, and David drove in the opposite direction of the small crowd for Salem while waiting for the cardinal's telephone call.

When the cardinal arrived at the Archdiocese and before going to his office, he went to his secretary, and she said, "Hello, Cardinal. I just received confirmation for your flight tomorrow to Rome. Your departure time is 3:05 a.m. from Logan International Airport, and you'll be arriving in Rome at 4:26 p.m. Airport security will escort you to the plane."

"Thank you, Sister," he said. He entered his office, sat at the desk and called David.

David's cell phone rang as he was driving home. He answered and said, "Hello. David speaking."

"Hi, Professor. It's Cardinal O'Shea. I just received our departure and arrival times. We will be departing from Logan International Airport tomorrow morning at 3:05 a.m. and arriving in Rome at 4:26 p.m. I'll meet you and your group at the airport's security office, and from there we'll be escorted to our airplane. As soon as we end this conversation, I will notify the pope's personal secretary of our arrival time. Have a pleasant evening."

"The same to you. Bye," David said, and they ended the call. Then he said, "That was Cardinal O'Shea. We'll be leaving for Rome very early tomorrow morning on the red-eye flight at 3:05 a.m. and will arrive in Rome at 4:26 p.m. Luke, after we are home, please pack a travel bag for you, Thomas and Jesus." David then called Brian and told him of the departure and arrival times for the next day and that he and Martha must wait at the airport's security office for them.

When they arrived at David's house, Luke went to pack a suitcase for Jesus, Thomas and himself. After David packed his bag, he went to the kitchen and prepared supper. After the food was cooked, they had their dinner.

CHAPTER 28

Brian and Martha arrived at Boston's Logan International Airport and were standing near the airport's security office waiting for the rest of their group to arrive. Cardinal O'Shea entered the area and went to Martha and Brian, and he said, "Good morning. I see that Jesus, Thomas, the professor and Luke have not arrived yet."

"No. We've been waiting for them," Martha said, and then David, Jesus, Thomas and Luke entered the security office area and went to where Cardinal O'Shea, Brian and Martha were, and they greeted one another.

"Please wait here while I clear us with security so we can board the aircraft," the cardinal said. He walked into the airport's security office and after a brief time exited with the director of security. Cardinal O'Shea showed the director to his guests and said, "Sir, this is my party to Rome."

"Fine. Follow me," the chief said. He escorted them to a small security van with a driver who was waiting for them. When they were at the van, the chief said, "Please stow your luggage and get in."

After everyone was in the van, the chief used his radio to inform his staff that they were on the way. When they arrived at the aircraft, two pilots greeted them and transferred their luggage from the van to the airplane. After they had boarded the jet and were seated, the pilots taxied the airplane to the runway, where they waited until the plane was cleared for takeoff. Once the pilots received the go signal, they lifted into the air and headed for Rome.

The airplane landed on schedule at 4:26 p.m. and taxied to two black town cars that were waiting on the side of the tarmac. After the jet had stopped, the door to the aircraft opened. When everyone had exited the airplane they were greeted by two chauffeurs dressed in black suits. One chauffeur went to Cardinal O'Shea and said, "Good afternoon, Cardinal. I am your driver and will be taking you and your guests to Vatican City," while the pilots removed the luggage from the cargo hold of the aircraft and gave them to the chauffeurs.

After their luggage was stowed in the trunks of the cars, the cardinal said to his chauffeur, "Thank you. Please drive us to the Vatican."

Cardinal O'Shea's car with Jesus and Thomas in it approached the gate of Saint Anna for entrance to the Vatican grounds. At the gate, the chauffeur stopped and rolled down his window as a Swiss guard walked to the driver's side door with a clipboard in his hand. As the driver handed the guard his identification badge, he said, "Cardinal O'Shea and his guests have an appointment with the monsignor. He is expecting them."

The sentry looked into the car through the driver's side window and wrote something on his clipboard. After stepping back, he said, "Proceed." The chauffeur drove through the checkpoint and the second town car with Brian, Martha, David and Luke in it went through the same routine and was allowed to pass. The chauffeurs drove their cars to the Domus Sanctae Marthae residence hall.

Monsignor Vincenzo Fabrini stood outside the residence hall waiting to greet his guests as the cars pulled up to the curb. After the town cars were parked, the chauffeurs and Monsignor Fabrini opened the car doors. When the cardinal stepped out of the car, the pontiff's secretary went to him. Shaking hands, the monsignor said, "Welcome, Cardinal. I hope you had a pleasant flight. I've made arraignments for you and your guests to stay here. The staff will show you to your rooms."

"Thank you, Monsignor. Both the flight and drive were fine."

"That's nice to hear."

"After supper I would like to meet with you."

"Yes, of course, Cardinal. What time would you like to meet?"

"Will you be available at 7 p.m.?"

"Yes. We can meet in my office."

"Fine. I'll see you at 7," Cardinal O'Shea said, and then the monsignor escorted his guests to their rooms while the staff of the Sanctae Marthae residence hall took their luggage to their rooms.

After everyone was shown to their rooms, the cardinal went to David's room and knocked on the door while David and Luke were unpacking their bags. David opened the door and said, "Hello, Cardinal. These are beautiful accommodations."

"I'm pleased you like them. We'll have a meeting this evening with the monsignor at 7 in his office. I will inform the others at dinner."

"Thank you for the update. I'll see you then," David said, and he closed the door and finished unpacking his clothes as the cardinal returned to his room to rest before supper.

It was 5:30 p.m. when the residence hall staff knocked on the cardinal's and his guests' doors to announce that supper was being served and to escort them to the dining room. After everyone had finished eating, Cardinal O'Shea stood up from his chair and said, "We'll have a meeting with Monsignor Vincenzo Fabrini at 7 this evening. I'll meet you in the lobby at 6:45 and from there we'll go to his office."

The cardinal was waiting for his guests to join him. After a short time, Jesus, Thomas, David, Brian, Martha and Luke entered the lobby and Cardinal O'Shea said, "We'll go to the monsignor's office now. Please come with me."

The cardinal escorted them to Monsignor Fabrini's office. When they arrived, he knocked on the door. The monsignor opened it and said, "Ah, Cardinal, welcome. Please enter. Right this way," and then he led his guests to a large study room with a long table and twelve chairs, bookshelves and antique wood furniture. When they were inside the room, he said, "Everyone, please sit. May I offer you something to drink?"

"Water will be fine," the cardinal said.

"I'll be right back," the monsignor said. He left and then returned with a serving tray with glasses and two pitchers filled with water and he set it onto the table.

After everyone was seated, Cardinal O'Shea stood from his chair and went to one end of the room. From there, he said, "Monsignor, thank you for taking the time to handle all the arraignments on such short notice. It is greatly appreciated."

The monsignor nodded his head, acknowledging the cardinal's comment. The cardinal then continued, "I would like for you to arrange a meeting with the pontiff as soon as possible here at the Vatican."

"The pope is at his summer residence in Lazio, Castel Gandolfo, nineteen miles from here," Monsignor Fabrini replied.

"I understand, but I need to meet with him personally here."

"Yes, but can you travel to Castel Gandolfo? I'm sure he'll make time available for you immediately."

"Please call him now and ask him if he'll come to the Vatican this evening."

"Tonight?"

"Yes, tonight."

"Okay, I'll ask him."

"Thank you. If the pontiff says he can't meet with me, please give me the telephone."

The monsignor removed his cell phone from a pocket in his robe and then dialed the pontiff's personal phone number. When the Holy See answered, he said, "Pope Valentine speaking."

"Sir, it's Monsignor Vincenzo Fabrini. We have Cardinal O'Shea visiting us from the Archdiocese of Boston with his guests. He wants a private audience with you."

"I'll meet with him tomorrow afternoon here at Castel Gandolfo."

"The cardinal wants a meeting with you tonight here at the Vatican."

"Impossible. You can arrange transportation for him to come here if it's that important."

"Cardinal O'Shea would like to talk to you," the monsignor said, and then he passed his cell phone to the cardinal.

"Hello, Your Holiness. It's Cardinal O'Shea. I hope things are well with you. I must meet with you tonight here at the Vatican."

"Why is it so urgent?" the pope asked.

"If this could wait, I would not be insisting on a meeting tonight. What I have to say must be said privately and in person. So please come here now. You will not be disappointed."

The Holy See paused and said, "Okay, Cardinal. I'll come there."

"Thank you. I'll see you then," the cardinal said, and he ended the telephone call and returned the cell phone to Monsignor Fabrini.

"You were very persuasive in convincing the pontiff to come here and meet with you tonight," the pope's secretary said.

"I know, but the meeting concerns an urgent matter that he must be informed about."

"May I be of assistance in any way?"

"No, not at this time," the cardinal said, and then to his guests he said, "We should return to our rooms. The pope will be here soon. You'll be informed when he has arrived," and then they left for the residence hall.

Pope Valentine II arrived at the Vatican in a black town car. When the chauffeur parked the car where the monsignor was waiting, and after the Holy See stepped out of the car, he immediately asked, "Where is Cardinal O'Shea?"

"He's in his room resting. Should I summon him now?" his secretary asked.

"No, not yet. I must first go to my office," the pontiff answered. He went to his office, which was next to his secretary's. After sitting at his desk a short time, the pope used the telephone on his desk and called his secretary. He said, "Monsignor, please inform Cardinal O'Shea I would like to meet with him now."

"Yes, sir. I'll go now," the monsignor said, and then he ended the call and left his office.

At Cardinal O'Shea's room, the monsignor knocked on the door. The cardinal opened it and the pope's secretary said, "The pope has arrived and will meet with you now."

"Thank you. Please inform Professor Solomon, Brian and Martha that the pontiff is here and that I'm waiting for them in the lobby," Cardinal O'Shea said.

"I'll escort them to you," the monsignor said.

"Thank you," Cardinal O'Shea replied.

The pope's secretary knocked on their doors and notified them that the pope had arrived. Cardinal O'Shea was waiting for them in the entryway. After David, Brian and Martha were in the hallway, Monsignor Fabrini said, "Please come with me and I'll take you to Cardinal O'Shea."

After David, Brian and Martha arrived at where the cardinal was waiting, he said, "Monsignor, would you kindly step away for a few minutes? I want to speak with them privately."

"Yes, of course. I'll be waiting down the hall," the monsignor replied.

After the monsignor had left, Cardinal O'Shea said, "Before Jesus is introduced to the pope, you must explain to him how he was brought here."

"I'm sure that when Pope Valentine meets Jesus, there will be no doubt in his mind about who he is," David said.

"Are you ready?" the cardinal asked, and they nodded their heads yes. Cardinal O'Shea said, "Well, let's go meet the pontiff." They walked down the hall to where Monsignor Fabrini was waiting.

At the pope's office, the monsignor knocked on his door and opened it. He said, "Sir, Cardinal O'Shea and his guests are here to meet with you."

"And his guests?" the pope asked.

"Yes. Shall I show them in?"

"Yes, please do," the pontiff said as he sat back in his chair.

"The pope will see you now," the monsignor said. Cardinal O'Shea, David, Brian and Martha entered the pope's office. After everyone was in the room, the monsignor closed the door and returned to his office.

The word pope means father, and the pope is the Bishop of Rome, which makes him the leader of the worldwide Catholic Church. The term Holy See in the Catholic religion refers to the See of the Bishop of Rome, whom the church sees as the successor to Saint Peter, the leader of the Apostles. The hierarchical structure of the Catholic Church today is the pope at the head, then the bishops/dioceses (mother churches over parishes) and priests/parishes (local churches). The pope was originally chosen by senior clergymen who resided in or near Rome. The office of the pope is called the Papacy. The pope is the head of state of Vatican City, which is a sovereign city within the city of Rome. The pope's official residence is the Palace of the Vatican, which overlooks Saint Peter's Square, and is also known as the Papal Palace. Catholics recognize the pope as the successor to Saint Peter the Apostle, who was the first pontiff from AD 32 to AD 67.

After entering the pontiff's office, Cardinal O'Shea, David, Brian and Martha saw him sitting at his desk. The pope went to the front of his desk to greet his guests. The cardinal then knelt on one knee and kissed the ring on the pope's right hand and said, "Your Holiness, I would like to introduce you to Professor David Solomon."

David went to the pope and kissed his ring and then the cardinal introduced Brian Soranno and Martha Valdez. They both knelt and took turns kissing his ring. "It looks like we're all Catholics in this room," Martha said after she had kissed the pope's ring.

"That's nice to know," the pontiff said with a smile.

"Your Holiness, Professor Solomon is a professor at M.I.T. in Boston and Brian and Martha are graduate students attending Harvard University, also in Boston," the cardinal said.

"I'm Pope Valentine. I'm sure you knew that. It's a pleasure meeting all of you. Please have a seat," and then they sat in mahogany wood chairs with maroon leather upholstery, matching the pontiff's large wood desk and chair. The office walls displayed beautiful religious oil paintings that museums would fight over to display.

After everybody was seated, the cardinal said, "Your Holiness, thank you for coming to the Vatican and giving us an audience. The reason I requested this urgent meeting is because of a man who is resting in the Sanctae Marthae residence hall. I would like Professor Solomon, Brian and Martha to explain what this is about. What is discussed is the truth. Professor, please begin."

David stood in front of the pope's desk and said, "Your Holiness, thank you for allowing us an audience. The story we're about to tell you is true and involves a time machine that I recently perfected and which works flawlessly."

"A time machine?"

"Yes. The only people who know of the machine's existence are my son, who is here in Vatican City sleeping. Also, Father Dominick Carlucci from Saint Peter's Parish in Salem, Massachusetts, and everyone in your office. I am requesting that you not mention my machine to anyone outside of this room. Just imagine if my time machine fell into the hands of a rogue government or individual. History as we now know it would be changed either for the good or for the bad," David said.

The pope nodded his head, acknowledging that he understood the consequences, and he said, "Fine. I will not mention it to anyone. I do understand your concerns and the implications of such a machine in the hands of someone with sinister intentions."

"Thank you. I'll now give you a brief history of StellaPort, the name of my time machine." He began his story and said, "Many years ago a scientist named Sebastian Kramer, who was intrigued with the possibility of time travel, called me one night and asked me to come and visit him. The evening I visited, he explained he was ill and had six months to live and would like for me to carry on with his research. He said he wanted to show me a machine, and then he took me to his basement and led me to a large room with an alien-looking machine in the center of it. The machine had a circular clear glass chamber that looked like something you would see in a science fiction movie. I asked him what it was for and what it did. He said it was a time machine and that he knew the subject interested me. He was close to making time travel a reality, but was missing something that was hindering the movement of matter. He turned on the machine and began to explain each component's display window. I was awestruck and asked him if he had tested his machine, and he said 'No.' Recently, I was able to invent a way to travel faster than the speed of light, making time travel a reality." David could see by the expression on the pope's face that he had piqued his interest.

David continued, "We, I am referring to Brian and Martha, tested the machine with a mouse and the machine worked with no side effects. We experimented again using Brian's dog, Murphy, and experienced the same results. We then decided to try to bring Jesus

Christ to the year 2010 before he starts his church and during a time period during which he is not mentioned in the Gospels. We selected the year AD 29, the year before Jesus began his ministry, so that we wouldn't alter the history that has been written about him. Brian and Martha volunteered to find Jesus and, if successful, would ask him if he will come with them to visit us. Martha and Brian will now explain what happened after being transported to the Holy Land." David returned to his chair as Brian and Martha stood before the pope. They could see that the pope was intrigued by the story being told so far.

Brian said, "Your Holiness, as Professor Solomon stated, Martha and I were transported to the year AD 29 in Judea near the small village of Ein Kerem just outside Jerusalem. We hoped to locate John the Baptist at a cave that archaeologists say was used by him for performing baptisms, thinking John would be able to tell us where Jesus could be found, but unfortunately, he was not there. We decided to go to the Jordan River to find him and traveled on foot from the cave. We met Thomas from the village of Ein Kerem. He's also here in Vatican City resting. We told him we were visiting from Rome and trying to find a friend. We offered him a job as our guide, and he accepted. Thomas led us from Jerusalem to Jericho, and on the way we stopped in the village of Bethany to ask Jesus' good friend Lazarus if he knew where we could find Jesus. We found Lazarus, but he didn't know where Jesus could be because he hadn't seen him in some time, so we went to the Jordan River. There we met John the Baptist, who said he heard Jesus was living in Nazareth. Then we traveled up the river to where we found Jesus."

"You met Lazarus, John the Baptist and Jesus?" the pope asked.

"Yes, and Mary, Jesus' mother, and we were baptized by John in the Jordan River," Brian answered.

The pontiff looked at them with amazement as Brian continued, "After we located Jesus, we explained to him who we were and where we came from. We asked him if he would come with us to the year 2010 because we need a charismatic leader who can deliver a divine message to be heard throughout the world so that faith in God is reinforced and to change nonbelievers into believers in a creator who is watching and hearing them. Jesus agreed to be transported with us, and he said he would preach God's message to all who will listen and that his kingdom is eternal everlasting and open to only those obeying his laws.

"Our departure site was at the ancient Kisan Gate in Damascus. Jesus requested we travel from Nazareth to Capernaum before going to Damascus. We spent the evening in Capernaum at the home of Jesus' friend, who was a rabbi, and then we left in the morning on horseback for Damascus. On the way we stopped for the night in the village of Danos. I'll let Martha explain what happened next." Brian returned to his chair and sat.

Martha then continued the story, picking up where Brian had stopped, and she said, "Your Holiness, three nights ago Jesus, Thomas, Brian, our guide, Isaac, and I stopped for the night in the village of Danos. The wife of the man who owned the farm returned home after visiting her friend Mary, who had had a baby a few days earlier. The infant was sick and not eating and didn't have long to live. Jesus asked Leah, the farmer's wife, to take him to the child, which she gladly did. We entered Mary's home and went to the room where she and the sick baby lay in bed. Jesus requested that Mary remove the blanket that was wrapped around her baby and put the infant on top of her facing toward Jesus. He put his left hand on the baby's chest and stomach and closed his eyes and prayed. Suddenly, the child started crying and could have nourishment from its mother. Your Holiness, that evening we witnessed a miracle in the room, because if Jesus had not interceded, I believe the infant would have died."

"I was a witness and so was Thomas," Brian said.

Martha finished by saying, "In the morning, we left for Damascus to be transported to the year 2010 by Professor Solomon," and then she went to her chair and sat.

David stood, again facing the pope, and said, "That same day Brian and Martha returned to Salem with Jesus and Thomas. I went to Saint Peter's Church and told Father Dominick Carlucci about my time machine only on the condition that he would keep it a secret. After he agreed, I told him Jesus was at my home. I invited him to meet Jesus and he was more than willing to. The following day we arrived at my house. I showed him my machine and he met Jesus. Father Carlucci asked Jesus if he would say a few words at his late afternoon Mass, and Jesus said, 'Yes.' Toward the end of the Mass, Jesus spoke to the congregation. As he was speaking, he paused and bowed his head and then he tilted it back and lifted his arms up with the palms of his hands facing upward. He said, 'Lord, in your name, I, your son, ask you to shine your light on me so all will see heaven on earth.' As soon as Jesus said that, he was engulfed in a glowing aurora around him. The congregation became completely quiet and were in awe at what they had just seen. After the Mass, I asked Father Carlucci to contact Cardinal O'Shea to arrange a meeting between the two." David, looking at the cardinal, said, "Cardinal, please continue," and then he sat in his chair.

The cardinal stood and said, "Your Holiness, Father Carlucci contacted me and asked if I would come to his parish to meet with him. He stressed that it concerned the foundation of the Catholic Church and would have profound implications for all religions. The next morning I went to Father Carlucci's parish. He described meeting two men at the professor's house. He said a man had arrived three days before with another young man. He assured me that Professor Solomon would explain everything to me as he had to him. He had me curious when he said it involved the foundation of the Catholic Church, so of course I agreed to meet the men. After we entered the professor's home, he escorted us to his lab and showed us his time machine and briefly explained the function of each component. He went on to say that the machine works and that Jesus Christ was sitting in his library. At first I was skeptical about such a claim. Jesus does not resemble the man portrayed in holy pictures, as you will see. I asked him some questions, and he answered them. I was still in doubt, so I asked if he would speak at my noon Mass at Holy Cross Cathedral in Boston, and he said, 'Yes.'

"Toward the end of the service, Jesus performed a miracle. An old woman was in the congregation that I knew had been stricken with the disease of polio since before I was a priest at the cathedral.

While Jesus spoke during the Mass, she approached him and asked him to cure her, and he did. If I had not known the woman, I would have thought it was staged. After the service, I asked Jesus if he would speak at a special Mass later in the afternoon to gauge the interest of the parishioners, and he said 'Yes.' The church was filled to capacity with standing room only. Mind you, the cathedral has a seating capacity of sixteen hundred. I announced an unscheduled Mass to the congregation during the end of the service. I asked Jesus if he would speak again during the second Mass, and he said, 'Yes.' While Jesus was speaking, the elderly woman whom he had cured of polio earlier pushed an old woman in a wheelchair down the center aisle to him and asked Jesus to make her friend walk. Jesus held the hands of the woman in the wheelchair and said, "Stand and walk from your chair," and she did. I was stunned. I had witnessed two miracles on the same day, and I knew both women had developed polio in childhood. The man staying with us in Vatican City is considered a living saint according to canon law of the Catholic Church."

"Your Holiness, Jesus, our Lord and Savior, is resting on the foundation of the church which was built in his name," Martha said from her chair.

The pope was still sitting back in his chair and turned his head slightly to the right to look at an oil painting of Jesus hanging on the wall. "Your Holiness, sir," the cardinal said, and then after the pope looked toward him, Cardinal O'Shea said, "Jesus does not resemble the portrait, but I assure you, it is he in the flesh."

"I would like to meet Jesus now," the pope said.

"Should we ask the monsignor to escort him to your office?" Cardinal O'Shea asked.

"Of course not. I will go to him and ask if I can have an audience. Cardinal, please remain here with the professor until we return. Martha and Brian come with me," the Holy See said, and then he left his office with Brian and Martha.

Monsignor Fabrini was sitting at his desk and the pope said, "Monsignor, please take me to our guests." The pope's personal secretary led them to the Sanctae Marthae residence hall and then to the rooms of Jesus, Thomas and Luke.

"Thank you. You may leave now," the pontiff said at their rooms. The monsignor returned to his office. After his secretary had left, the pope asked, "Which room is Jesus in?"

Brian walked two doors down and said, "This one. Thomas is in the next room."

"Brian, can you find your way back to my office?" the Holy See asked.

"Yes."

"Good. Please take Thomas there and wait for us. We can let the boy sleep. His father can explain the evening events to him."

Brian went to Thomas's room and knocked on the door. After entering, he saw Thomas wearing his tunic and sleeping. After Brian woke him up, he said, "The pope would like to meet with you in his office. Please come with me." Thomas rose from his bed and went with Brian.

The monsignor was sitting at his desk when he saw Thomas pass by wearing his tunic. When Brian was at the pope's office door, he knocked and entered with Thomas. Then he said, "Thomas, please have a seat while we wait for Jesus, the pope and Martha to return."

Martha knocked on Jesus' door, and he opened it. She said, "Hi, Jesus. The leader of the Catholic Church is with me and would like to know if you will meet with him."

Jesus, dressed in his tunic, said, "Yes, I will speak with him," and then Martha stepped aside from the doorway, and the pope and Jesus looked at each other.

"Hello. My name is Pope Valentine. I am the leader of the Catholic Church."

"Would you like to come in and talk?" Jesus asked.

"Yes, I would like that," the pope answered, and then he looked at Martha and said, "Please excuse us. I'm sure you can find your way back to my office."

"Yes, Father. I'll go and join the others now."

After the pope entered Jesus' room, he closed the door and went to a small table with two chairs. The pope gestured with his hand toward a chair and said, "Please sit so we can talk." After they were seated, the pontiff said, "May I formally introduce myself? I am Pope Valentine II. I've been the leader of the Catholic Church for the past seven years. The church so far has had 266 leaders to date and the first pope was elected in AD 32. May I ask you a personal question?"

"Yes," Jesus answered.

"Where do you come from?"

"I'm from a kingdom not of this earth. My Father sent me into the world not to judge, but to save the world through him. I live in Nazareth, a village in Galilee."

"Do you know your fate?" the pope asked.

"Yes. I discussed this with Professor Solomon. What is written in the Holy Scriptures shall be done. I have a question for you. If you are the leader of so many, then why are my Father's commandments that were passed down from him to Moses not being obeyed?" Jesus asked.

"We live in a time of turmoil, economically, morally, socially and spiritually. We have many Christians who still follow your teachings and obey God's laws, but then there are those challenging different aspects of the Christian religion. The world you came from is much different from today's."

"Brian and Martha invited me to come with them to speak of my Father's kingdom to the people in this time," Jesus said.

"It is written in the New Testament that one day, after your death, you will return to the world," the pope said.

"What is written in the Scriptures will be fulfilled," Jesus replied.

"I understand. Shall we leave now to join the others in my office?" the Holy See asked. Jesus and the pope stood. The pontiff went to the door and opened it for Jesus, and he said, "I will escort you to my place of business," and then they left for the pope's office.

The monsignor was still working at his desk when he saw Jesus, wearing a tunic, pass by his office with the pope. When the pope was at his office, he opened the door and said, "Jesus, please come in and have a seat."

After Jesus sat in a chair, David said, "Jesus, this is the man whom I told you about. He has a following of 1.1 billion Catholics throughout the world. The land we're sitting on is considered the capital of Christianity, which was founded in your name and is based on your deeds and teachings."

"Yes, that's true. There have been many leaders of this church since its beginning," the pope said.

"Your Holiness, we asked Jesus to come here so you would allow him to reinvigorate the Lord's message using the Vatican as his platform. The Catholic Church has numerous types of media outlets to spread the word of God. I believe when people of Christian and of other faiths see and hear Jesus, they will renew their faith in God and that will have repercussions all over the planet. The Christian religion will grow dramatically after Jesus speaks to the people because he will convert nonbelievers into believers, sinners will repent and crime will decrease substantially, making this world a better place for all to live," David said.

"Jesus, would you speak at my weekly Mass tomorrow morning held outside in Saint Peter's Square?" the pope asked.

"I will speak the message of my Father to all those who will listen. We walk by faith, not by sight," Jesus answered.

The pope looked at Cardinal O'Shea and said, "We'll meet in the rear of Saint Peter's Basilica tomorrow morning at 8:45 before my 9 o'clock Mass," and they adjourned the meeting.

CHAPTER 29

It was 9:45 a.m. Cardinal O'Shea and Jesus were in a rear room of St. Peter's Basilica with His Holiness, who was preparing for his weekly 10 a.m. Mass for thousands of Christians. Jesus wore his tunic and sandals while the pope was wearing his papal vestments.

"Jesus, the Mass will be held outside of this basilica in St. Peter's Square so we can accommodate as many people as possible wanting to attend the service. I would like you to sit next to Cardinal O'Shea near the altar," the pontiff said, and then he glanced at his wristwatch. He said, "It's time to go," and they left the room.

Waiting outside for the pope, Jesus and Cardinal O'Shea were two Swiss guards along with David, Thomas, Brian, Martha and Luke. The cardinal went to where David was standing and said, "The Mass will begin in five minutes. Please find a seat and after the service return to this room."

"Okay, Cardinal. We'll meet you here," David said, and they left the basilica while the pontiff, Jesus and the cardinal were being escorted to the outdoor altar by the Swiss guards.

After Jesus, the pope and Cardinal O'Shea entered the altar area, His Holiness was pleased when he saw the large audience. The cardinal and Jesus sat next to each other while the Holy See sat in his customary place not far from the Lord's Table. The morning sky was dark, gray and gloomy and looked as though it would rain. The pontiff began the Mass on time, and after communion was served, he went to the front center of the altar. He said, "I have a special guest who will now speak to you and the world. Please welcome Jesus from Nazareth."

Jesus stood and went to where the pope was standing and, looking out at the large audience, he said, "I come to warn the sinners that if they do not repent their ways, my Father's heavenly kingdom will be closed to them. Only the pure in heart will be allowed to enter. For God loves the world so much that he gave his one and only son so that everyone who believes in him will not perish, but will have eternal life. God sent his son into the world not to judge the world, but to save the world through him. You have heard that it was said to people long ago, do not murder, and anyone who murders will be subject to judgment. But I tell you that anyone who is angry with his brother will also be subject to judgment."

The audience was quiet and listening to every word Jesus spoke while he said, "What shall it profit a man if he gains the whole world but loses his soul?" and then he raised his arms with the palms of his hands facing toward the sky while saying, "I am the way and the truth and the life. No one goes to the Father except through me." Jesus tilted his head back and looked up to the heavens, and he said, "Lord, in your name, I, your son, ask you to shine your light on me so that all who believe will know the power and the glory you bring to the world from heaven."

Jesus was still looking up toward the dark gray sky when suddenly a small ray of sunlight passed through and began to shine on him. The clouds started to part slowly, and the sky was becoming clearer. After a few minutes, the sky over St. Peter's Square turned blue, and it was now a bright and sunny morning above the Vatican. The beam of sunlight was still shining on Jesus as he lowered his arms. Looking out at the audience, he said, "Because of the increase in wickedness, the love of most will grow cold, but he who stands firm to the end will be saved. I tell you the truth: All the sins and blasphemies of men will be forgiven, but whoever blasphemes against the Holy Spirit will never be forgiven. He is guilty of an eternal sin," and then he walked forward a few steps. The light was still shining on him as he moved, and he said, "Blessed are you when people insult you, persecute you and falsely say all kinds of evil against you because of me. Rejoice and be glad, because great is your reward in heaven, for in the same way, they persecuted the prophets that were before you."

Jesus lifted his arms again and said, "Invoke the Father, and implore God often, and he will give to you. Blessed is he who has seen you with him when he was proclaimed among the angels and glorified among the saints, yours is life. Ask, and it will be given to you. Seek, and you will find. Knock, and it will be open to you," and then the beam of sunlight surrounding Jesus slowly diminished as he returned to his seat.

The pope stared at him in amazement because he knew Jesus was divine and the Lord in the flesh. The pontiff stood from his chair and went to where Jesus had been standing and made the sign of the cross with his right hand and ended the Mass. He went to Jesus and they left the altar quickly for the room in the rear of St. Peter's Basilica with Cardinal O'Shea. Some people in the audience started coming forward, wanting to meet Jesus, but Vatican security was keeping them back. Saint Peter's Square was in turmoil. People called for Jesus to return because they wanted to see and hear more from him. People were yelling, "Jesus has returned!" "Our Lord and Savior has come to us!" "My prayers have been answered," and "Jesus, please forgive us."

There were many more comments coming from the very large crowd. They had been energized just as David predicted would happen, and the Vatican was now the stage for Jesus to reinvigorate his message to the world.

David, Martha, Brian, Luke and Thomas made their way through the people to enter Saint Peter's Basilica, where Jesus, the pope and Cardinal O'Shea were. When they neared the room, two Swiss guards stopped them from proceeding further. "We are the guests of Cardinal O'Shea and the pope, and they're expecting us," David said to one of the guards, and then he pointed toward the rear of the church, saying, "We are to meet them in the basilica. Please inform them that Professor Solomon and his group are here."

"Wait here while I inform the pontiff of your presence," a guard said, and then he left in the direction David had pointed.

The remaining guard kept an eye on them and, after a few minutes, Cardinal O'Shea appeared from a short distance and was walking briskly. When the cardinal was with them, he said, "Guard, it's okay.

They are guests of the Vatican. Please allow them to pass," and then both guards stepped aside and Cardinal O'Shea escorted them to Jesus and the pope.

Cardinal O'Shea knocked on the door. The pontiff opened it and they entered. When everyone was in the room, His Holiness said, "I must call an emergency synod for all the cardinals of the Catholic Church to meet here in Vatican City so Jesus can speak to them." The pope then knelt on his right knee in front of Jesus, bowed his head and said, "Lord, I have been leading this church in your name to the best of my ability. I am your servant in life eternal everlasting."

"Stand, Pope Valentine. I am with you always until the end of time," Jesus said.

"Thank you, Lord. I will summon many representatives of the church to come here so you may speak to them. The world has been waiting a long time for this day to happen," the pope said. After standing, he turned toward the cardinal and said, "Cardinal, please escort Jesus and our guests to the residence hall and make sure they are comfortable. I'll now go and request that my secretary call an emergency synod to take place in two days," and then the pope left for his office while the cardinal escorted his guests to their dorm.

While walking to the Domus Sanctae Marthae, David asked, "Cardinal, is there a television in the residence hall?"

"Yes. It's in the hospitality room on the first floor."

"Would you kindly take us there?" David asked.

"Yes. Please come with me," the cardinal answered.

After they entered the residence hall, Cardinal O'Shea showed them to a room with a large-screen TV attached to the wall. The room had upholstered sofas and chairs and oil paintings of biblical scenes on the walls. The cardinal removed the remote control from the top of an antique chest of drawers and turned on the television and handed the control to David. "Thank you," David said, and he began changing the channels.

"Are you looking for something in particular?" Cardinal O'Shea asked.

"Yes," as he kept clicking the remote control until he saw Jesus on TV standing in front of the altar in St. Peter's Square with a ray of sunlight shining on him. "This is what I'm searching for—news stations reporting on the Lord," David said as he continued changing the channels. There were more TV stations reporting breaking news from the Vatican. "In less than an hour all the TV stations in the world will be reporting on this morning's event," and while looking at Jesus, he said, "You now have the world's attention, and with this form of media, all the people will soon be able to see and hear you."

"When can I speak to them?" Jesus asked.

"I will visit the pope and let you know. Professor, please come with me."

After the pontiff entered his office, he summoned his secretary. Monsignor Fabrini knocked on his door and then entered. When his secretary entered, the pope said, "Please sit," and the monsignor sat in the chair in front of the pope's desk.

"Yes, Your Holiness, what is it?" the monsignor asked.

"Did you attend this morning's Mass in St. Peter's Square?" the Holy See asked.

"Yes. I'm still dealing with what I saw."

"Our Lord and Savior has returned to us as prophesied. I want you to notify all 199 cardinals that I am demanding their presence. I am calling an emergency synod."

"I'll do that now. When do you want the cardinals here?" the monsignor asked.

"In two days. That should give them enough time to rearrange their schedules on such short notice. Oh, and make sure you express to them that the meeting is mandatory and I'm expecting each one of them."

"Yes, Your Holiness. I will personally call them and convey your wishes."

"Thank you," the pontiff said. The monsignor stood and left the pope's office to begin contacting the cardinals.

Outside Vatican City, in St. Peter's Square, people called friends and family using their cell phones to report on what they had just witnessed and heard from Jesus. Many TV crews were now descending on the square, and reporters were interviewing people who were at the Mass. Some people in the audience captured Jesus on their video cameras as he was speaking and saw a dark and gloomy sky over the Vatican turning into a bright and sunny day. Videos were now being uploaded onto the Internet while news crews in the square scrambled to get a copy for their station. St. Peter's Square became a media circus, and Jesus was the breaking news story for the local news channels. He would soon be the leading story on every cable and satellite TV station because of the worldwide religious importance and its implications.

The pope wanted to know what was happening in St. Peter's Square, so he went to his papal residence, which overlooked the square. After the pope entered his home, he looked out his window and saw people and many news crews wandering about. The pontiff walked away from the window and sat in a chair and began to contemplate whether Jesus should speak from his balcony later today or wait until the synod. While pondering the decision, he turned on the TV in his bedroom to view the news and started clicking the remote control. All the satellite news channels were broadcasting breaking news about Jesus from the Vatican. The pope was amazed at how quickly the events during the morning Mass were spreading worldwide. He knew many news organizations would be camping in St. Peter's Square tonight and along the wall of Vatican City hoping to be the first to get a scoop. The telephone on the pope's nightstand rang. He picked up the receiver and said, "Hello. Pope Valentine."

The person at the other end said, "Hi, Your Holiness. It's Monsignor Fabrini. The telephones are ringing off the hook. The newspapers, TV and radio media organizations are requesting interviews and an official statement from the Vatican."

"Please refer all requests to our public relations office, and have them issue a statement saying that we do not have a comment at this time. Monsignor, we'll give them a response after the synod," the pope said.

"Yes, Your Holiness. I'll get on this right away and inform PR," the monsignor said.

"Thank you," the pontiff said, and he hung up the phone. He then called the director of the Vatican's Communications Office to inquire what events were scheduled for the rest of the week.

When the director answered, he said, "Hello. This is the director of communications speaking."

"Hello, this is Pope Valentine. I want you to set up the Vatican's TV and radio equipment in the Sistine Chapel for an event in two days. You will be providing live radio and TV broadcasts simultaneously to all external media organizations. You are to allow them the capability to tap into our broadcast. Do you understand my request?"

"Yes, Your Holiness, loud and clear. I'll have my staff get to work on it immediately," the director answered.

"One more item. I want you to notify the local news, cable and satellite stations of a spectacular live event in two days that they can have access to."

"Will do, Your Holiness," the director said.

"Thank you," the pontiff said, and then he ended the call. The pope turned off the TV and headed for the Domus Sanctae Marthae to talk with Jesus and Cardinal O'Shea.

At the residence hall, the Holy See went to the hospitality room and saw Cardinal O'Shea and Jesus talking with Brian, Martha and Luke. The pope approached them and said, "I've made the necessary arrangements for the Lord to speak to all his cardinals in two days. When the Lord addresses the cardinals, it will be the most historic day for the Catholic Church since its founding and will be seen and heard on Vatican TV and radio."

The pope, looking at Jesus, said, "Lord, if you will permit me, I would like to give you a tour of Vatican City."

Jesus nodded his head in acceptance of the offer, and the Holy See said, "I'll come for you after the tourists have gone for the day." The pontiff left for his office to check if the monsignor was still overwhelmed with all the news media inquiries and whether all the cardinals had been contacted.

After the pope exited the hospitality room, David said, "Jesus, in two days you'll be speaking to many leaders of the Catholic Church and to billions of people worldwide. Even though you can't see the people, they will see and hear you on computers, TVs and radios."

"Verily I say unto you, none will be saved, unless they believe in my cross. But those who have believed in my cross, theirs is the kingdom of God," Jesus said.

"Lord, you are the way to God's kingdom, and the sinners should heed your warning of eternal damnation if they don't repent their ways," the cardinal said.

"You are spiritually whole and pure in heart. You will see me at the right hand of the Father when it is your time," Jesus said, looking at Cardinal O'Shea.

"Thank you, Lord. I am your servant for eternity," the cardinal replied.

David stood and looked at Cardinal O'Shea and asked, "Cardinal, may I speak to you for a few minutes?"

"Yes. Please excuse us, Lord," the cardinal answered, and he went with David to an adjacent room.

After they entered the room, David said, "Cardinal, as you know, we must transport Jesus back to his time. He cannot stay here. He must be returned to the year AD 29."

"I know. I wish he could stay with us," the cardinal replied.

"Please call the pope and request a short meeting with him for today—the sooner the better."

"Okay. Who will be attending?"

"Just us three. It shouldn't be long."

"I'll call him now," the cardinal said. He called the pope and arranged for a meeting at 2 p.m. in the pope's office.

After talking with the Holy See, they returned to the room where Jesus was and the cardinal said, "Lord, may I show you to a beautiful chapel named St. Martha's in Vatican City? I'm sure you will enjoy it."

"Yes, Cardinal. That would be nice," Jesus replied.

"Professor, please wait here until I return, and then we'll go to the pope's office for our meeting," the cardinal said.

The church was a short walk from the residence hall. When Jesus and Cardinal O'Shea arrived at St. Martha's Chapel, the cardinal opened the door for Jesus to enter.

St. Martha's Chapel is dedicated to Martha, the sibling of Mary and Lazarus of Bethany, and is located behind the government building of Vatican City. The chapel was built in the 16th century during Pope Paul III's reign and the interior has side chapels. The church has frescoes painted by Baciccio and Girolamo Troppa depicting scenes from the life of St. Martha. Above the altar is a painting of St. Martha by Giovanni Baglione, also an Italian painter. The chapel is not open to the public.

Jesus entered the chapel and walked to a white marble altar while Cardinal O'Shea followed him. At the altar they knelt and began to pray. After praying, the cardinal said, "Lord, I will leave you now because I must attend a meeting with the pope and Professor Solomon. I'll return afterward. I shouldn't be long," and then he stood and left the chapel.

The cardinal returned to the residence hall and entered the hospitality room and went to David. He said, "If you're ready, we'll go to the pope's office now," and then they left for the pontiff's office.

When David and Cardinal O'Shea were at the pope's office, Monsignor Fabrini greeted them and asked, "Are you here to meet with the pope?"

"Yes," the cardinal answered.

"I'll inform the pontiff that you both are here," the monsignor said. He knocked on the pope's door and opened it. He said, "Cardinal O'Shea and Professor Solomon want to meet with you."

"I'll talk with them now," the pope said.

The monsignor, who was still at the door, said, "His Holiness will speak with you now. Please enter."

After they entered the pope's office, the pontiff said, "Please have a seat," and they sat in chairs facing the pope while he sat at his desk.

"Sir, Professor Solomon has requested this meeting," Cardinal O'Shea said.

His Holiness looked at David and asked, "How may I help you?"

"As you are aware, a worldwide media storm has developed concerning Jesus. We must select a date to transport Jesus and Thomas back to the year AD 29 as soon as possible because we cannot risk changing the history written about him. I suggest Jesus be transported in three days to a place of his choosing. He will have addressed the cardinals and the people of the world," David replied.

"Cardinal, what do you think?" the pope asked as he sat back in his chair.

"I would like Jesus to stay with us as long as possible, but the professor makes a good point about altering history," the cardinal answered.

"I agree with you both. Professor, I want to accompany Jesus when it's time for him to leave," the pontiff asked.

"Yes, of course, Your Holiness. It will be a privilege and an honor to have you come to my home," David answered.

"It's settled then. Jesus will be transported back to his time in three days. Cardinal, please meet with the monsignor and make the necessary arrangements. We'll leave in the evening under the cover of darkness to elude the news organizations," the pontiff said.

"We should charter a jet in Brian's name for our flight to Boston," David said.

"I'll request my secretary to make reservations for cars to be waiting for us when we arrive at Logan International Airport," the cardinal said.

"The only obstacle is getting Jesus to the airport," the pope said.

"It will be impossible to drive him there by car. I was thinking we could all fly out of Vatican City on a helicopter and have two airplanes ready for departure, one for Boston and the other for Jerusalem, Israel," David replied.

"That sounds like an excellent plan. We can depart here on helicopters from the heliport and fly in the opposite direction of the airport while four town cars leave at the same time to confuse the news organizations. When we're a good distance from the Vatican, we'll instruct the pilots to set course for the airport," the pope said.

"Sounds like a plan that will work. As a precaution, I'll ask the monsignor to charter an airplane with a flight plan for Jerusalem. The news reporters will be tracking the jet to Jerusalem, but we'll be traveling in the opposite direction. I'll leave now and assist Monsignor Fabrini in reserving the helicopters and town cars and chartering the airplanes," the cardinal said.

"Where is Jesus now?" the pontiff asked.

"He's in Saint Martha's Chapel praying," the cardinal answered.

"I'll go and join him," the Holy See replied.

"I will return to the residence hall to be with my group," David said, and then they left the pope's office.

The cardinal went to the monsignor's office while David and the pope walked together because the chapel was on the way to the Domus Sanctae Marthae. When they arrived at the residence hall, David entered while the pontiff continued walking to St. Martha's Chapel. When the pope entered the small church, he saw Jesus kneeling in front of a white limestone sculptured statue of St. Martha. He went to the statue and knelt beside Jesus and blessed himself and began to pray. The heads of Jesus and the Holy See were bowed with the palms of their hands facing upward toward the ceiling of the chapel as they prayed. After praying, the pope stood and said, "Jesus, if it's okay with you, I'd like to take you on a tour of Vatican City."

"Yes. That would be fine," Jesus said after he stood.

The tourist visiting hours were now over, so they had the basilica to themselves, and they left for St. Peter's Basilica.

The construction of Saint Peter's Basilica was started in 1506 and completed in 1626. It was built over the Constantinian Basilica. There has been a church at the site since the fourth century. The basilica is the resting place for St. Peter (Simon Peter) the Apostle, who was put to death by Nero in AD 67. St. Peter was the first bishop of Rome and the first pope. The church has over one hundred tombs, including St. Peter's. The basilica has the biggest dome of any church in the world, which signifies it as the capital of Christianity. The enormous church also has the largest interior in the world and has a capacity of 60,000 people. The square outside the church is named Saint Peter's and can accommodate many thousands of people.

The pope escorted Jesus to Saint Peter's Basilica. After they entered, the pontiff walked beside Jesus, who looked impressed at what he saw. As they walked from shrine to shrine, the pope would explain its meaning and who designed it. Jesus suddenly walked away from him and went to the altar where St. Peter is buried and knelt and began to pray. The pontiff followed him to the altar and knelt beside him and prayed. After they were done praying, the Holy See asked, "Do you know who is entombed here?"

"One of my faithful followers. He has been rewarded after paying the ultimate price for preaching the words of God and now stands at the entrance to my Father's kingdom," Jesus answered.

"Yes. He was a charismatic leader who brought to the heart of Rome your teachings, and because of Simon Peter's sacrifice, the Catholic Church has established its home base here on this land where he died. Please come with me and we'll take the elevator to the roof and from there you can view Rome and Vatican City," the pope said.

The pope escorted Jesus to the roof's dome, where they slowly walked around the sphere. Jesus had a panoramic view of Rome and the beautifully landscaped grounds of the walled-in city. They were now overlooking St. Peter's Square. The people in the square saw them and began cheering loudly, pointing and waving. The sun was beginning to set and His Holiness waved to the crowds while Jesus just gazed at them. "I would like to show you another beautiful chapel," the pontiff said, and then he escorted Jesus to the Sistine Chapel.

The Sistine Chapel is located in the Apostolic Palace, which is also the official residence of the pope. The chapel's architecture is designed in the image of Solomon's Temple (first temple of the Israelites) described in the Old Testament. Throughout the chapel are frescoes by Michelangelo, Raphael, Bernini and Botticelli. Michelangelo Buonarroti painted the ceiling with bright colors between the years 1508 and 1512, with a mural of the hand of God giving life to Adam in the center of the ceiling. He also painted on the Sistine Chapel ceiling the ancestors of Jesus and male and female prophets. There are also nine stories from the Book of Genesis and three hundred biblical scenes of his choice that included Adam and Eve in the Garden of Eden and the Great Flood. The chapel is used for papal conclaves and is the venue for the College of Cardinals to meet for electing a new pope.

Inside the Sistine Chapel, they walked slowly while the pope explained the history of the paintings on the walls and ceiling. The Holy See glanced at his wristwatch and said, "It's getting late. I must go to my office and check on Monsignor Fabrini and Cardinal O'Shea. I'll show you to the residence hall so you can rest," and then they exited the chapel.

The pope showed Jesus to his room, and there he held Jesus' right hand and kissed it and said, "Lord, I will see you tomorrow morning. Have a pleasant evening," and then he left for his papal residence.

While David, Brian, Martha, Luke and Thomas rested in their rooms at the residence hall, Cardinal O'Shea completed their travel plans to fly out of Vatican City at 10 p.m. on two helicopters that would shuttle them to the airport. The cardinal had arranged for two airplanes to be waiting for them—one flying to Boston and the other for Jerusalem. He had also finalized plans to have four town cars reserved and ready to leave the Vatican at the same time as the helicopters.

The pope entered his home and went to a window overlooking St. Peter's Square and saw thousands of people standing and sitting. Many people were holding lit candles and praying while others held signs written in numerous languages that read, "Jesus Saves," "Our Lord and Savor has returned," "Believe in Jesus," "Jesus Loves You," "Jesus Lives" and many other personal comments. After viewing the crowd in the square, he closed the drapes over his window and went to bed. As the pope lay in bed, he was imagining how the cardinals would react when they met and heard Jesus. He was having pleasant thoughts about the upcoming sermon and fell asleep.

CHAPTER 30

By the following evening, the cardinals had arrived at the Vatican and the five-story Sanctae Marthae residence hall was bustling with guests coming from and going to their destinations. The city grounds were lively with its visitors from all over the world.

The pope was in the office of his communication director discussing the final details of a live TV and radio airing from the Sistine Chapel. After their meeting, the pope went to the residence hall to visit Jesus while the director went to the chapel to perform a system check because he didn't want a last-minute glitch that could interrupt the broadcast to the world. When the director was satisfied that the media equipment was working properly, and before dismissing his crew for the night, he said, "I'll meet you here at 8 o'clock tomorrow morning, so go home and have a pleasant evening," and then everyone left in anticipation of the big day.

The pontiff entered the Domus Sanctae Marthae and was greeted affectionately and with admiration by the cardinals standing at the entrance. One cardinal said, "Hello, Your Holiness," another said, "Good evening, Pope Valentine," and another said, "Pope Valentine, can you tell us what this synod is about?"

"You'll soon find out tomorrow morning in the Sistine Chapel," the pope answered as he kept walking to Jesus' room.

When the pope arrived at Jesus' room, he knocked on the door, but Jesus didn't answer. The pope went to David's door and knocked. David opened it and said, "Good evening, Your Holiness. Please come in."

"No, thank you. I'm looking for Jesus, but he doesn't answer his door."

"I saw him with Thomas on the first floor praying in the chapel."

"Thank you, Professor," and then he left. When the pontiff entered the chapel, he saw Jesus answering questions from the cardinals while Thomas listened to them. Jesus had them spellbound and hanging on every word when he spoke. The pope went to Jesus and said, "Lord, I see you're schooling the cardinals."

"Your Holiness, this is a remarkable man. He speaks as though he is Jesus himself," a cardinal said.

"He is Jesus and tomorrow all the clergy of the Catholic Church will listen to him speak from the Sistine Chapel. The people all over the world will see and hear from Jesus. He has returned to us, and everyone should listen carefully to his message," the pope replied.

The cardinals who were in the room then knelt before Jesus, and he said, "Stand and practice what you have learned, and go preach to your congregations the commandants given to Moses from God." They stood and each one waited his turn to kiss the back of Jesus' right hand before they left the chapel.

Jesus, Thomas and the pontiff remained in the room. After the cardinals had exited, the pope said, "Lord, please rest this evening in my home. I'll sleep here in the residence hall."

"Thank you for offering your home to me. I am comfortable being here with so many leaders of the church. It's better to give than to receive. I need only what my Father provides for me."

"I agree. It's better to give than to receive. I understand, but I feel guilty that I'm living in a much larger residence and you are my Lord."

"Be at ease. Whoever does the will of my Father is my brother and sister and mother."

"Thank you, Lord. May I walk with you to your room?"

"Yes, that would be nice of you."

The Holy See then showed Jesus and Thomas to their rooms. At the room of Jesus, the pope said, "Lord, tomorrow morning I will come here to escort you to the Sistine Chapel."

"I'll see you in the morning, Pope Valentine. Please sleep well," Jesus said, and then he entered his room and Thomas entered his room for the evening.

David was in his room when he decided to call a meeting to inform Jesus, Thomas, Brian, Martha and Luke about the plan to leave Vatican City the next night. David asked Luke to tell Jesus, Thomas, Brian and Martha that he wanted to meet with them in his room. Luke left, and after everyone was in David's room, he began to explain why he had called a meeting. He said, "We will be leaving Rome for Boston tomorrow evening and there will be two helicopters waiting for us at the Vatican's heliport. The helicopters will shuttle us to the airport where a chartered airplane for Boston's Logan International Airport will be waiting for us while another airplane is chartered for Jerusalem, Israel. Brian, the airplane for Boston is reserved in your name, while the jet chartered for Jerusalem is in the name of a Vatican official to elude the news organizations. As we are leaving on the helicopters, there will be four town cars exiting Vatican City at the same time. Pope Valentine and Cardinal O'Shea will also be accompanying us to Salem because they want to be there when Jesus and Thomas are being transported back to their time. Cardinal O'Shea has arranged for cars to be waiting for us on the tarmac when we arrive at Logan. The cars will take us to my home, and then we'll go directly to the lab and transport Jesus and Thomas back to the year AD 29. This will happen quickly because we can't risk having our history altered." Then he asked, "Does anybody have any questions?"

Nobody responded, so he said, "Let's all get a good's night rest because tomorrow will be a historic day," and then they left David's room.

CHAPTER 31

The day had finally come for Jesus to speak to the cardinals and to the people of the world. The cardinals were exiting the Sanctae Marthae residence hall for the Sistine Chapel. Inside the chapel the communications director had completed his final test for broadcasting live to all the TV and radio networks around the globe.

The pope left his papal residence to escort Jesus to the Sistine Chapel. When he arrived at the dorm, he went directly to Jesus' room and knocked on the door. After Jesus opened his door, the Holy See saw that he was dressed in his white tunic, and the pope asked, "Lord, are you ready to accompany me to the chapel to talk to the cardinals and the world?"

"Yes, Pope Valentine. I am eager to speak to them," Jesus answered, and then they left the residence hall for the chapel.

After they entered the Sistine Chapel, the pope showed Jesus to a large room where the cardinals were waiting. The room had TV cameras positioned in the rear of the room behind the cardinals and focused on the altar where Jesus would speak. All 199 cardinals were seated and were waiting for the Holy See to announce why he had called a synod. The room became quiet after Jesus and the pontiff entered and stood in the front center of the Lord's Table facing the cardinals and the cameras.

Jesus was standing next to the Holy See when the pope said, "I have called this emergency meeting because the Vatican has received a very special guest. The guest I'm referring to is standing beside me. His name is Jesus from Nazareth, our Lord and Savior. Jesus will be speaking to you and to the people around the world. He has returned to us fulfilling what has been prophesied in the Holy Scriptures."

The cardinals were still silent as the pope said, "This is a historic day, and people all over this world will remember where they were when they heard Jesus speak." He turned toward Jesus and said, "Lord, please address the leaders of your church and the world." The pontiff went to a vacant chair in the first row and sat.

Jesus stepped forward and slowly turned around and gazed at the large crucifixion cross that was displayed. After viewing the cross, he turned to face the cardinals and gazed at them, and then he said, "If any of you want to be my follower, you must turn from your selfish ways, take up your cross and follow me. If you try to hang onto your life, you will lose it, but if you give up your life for my sake and the sake of good news, you will save it. Remain in me, and I will remain in you. No branch can bear fruit by itself. It must remain on the vine. Neither can you bear fruit, unless you remain in me. Invoke the Father, implore God often, and he will give to you. Blessed is he who has seen you with him when he is proclaimed among the angels and glorified among the saints. Yours is life."

Jesus had the attention of everyone in the chapel and, pausing, he said, "Watch and pray so that you will not fall into temptation. The spirit is willing but the body is weak. Be perfect, therefore, as your heavenly Father is perfect. For we walk by faith, not by sight. There is only one love that loves unconditionally: the love of the divine. Blessed are those who hunger and thirst for righteousness, for they shall be satisfied. Come be my disciples, and yes, I am with you always, until the end of time."

Jesus stepped back and stood on the front center step of the altar. He looked into the television cameras and said, "I am the Alpha and the Omega, the beginning and the end, the first and the last. I am the way and the truth and the life. No one comes to the Father except through me. God sent his son into the world not to judge the world, but to save the world through him."

Jesus tilted his head backward slightly and raised his arms with the palms of his hands facing upward. He then said, "Father, please shine your light on me so that heaven can be seen on earth for all the people of this world," and, just as before, a beam of light passed through the ceiling and was shining on him. The cardinals in the room gasped and looked on in amazement. Jesus lowered his arms and continued looking into the TV cameras and said, "You have heard that it was said to people long ago, do not murder, and anyone who murders will be subject to judgment. But I tell you that anyone who is angry with his brother will also be subject to judgment. What shall it profit a man if he gains the whole world but loses his soul? Is anything worth more than your soul? Repent, for the kingdom of heaven is at hand."

Jesus paused again for a moment while still looking into the camera, and he said, "My Father passed the following laws to Moses for all people of this world to obey, and they are:

1. I am the Lord your God.
2. You shall have no other Gods before me.
3. You shall not make wrongful use of the name of your God.
4. Remember the Sabbath and keep it holy.
5. Honor your father and mother.
6. You shall not murder.
7. You shall not steal.
8. You shall not bear false witness against your neighbor.
9. You shall not covet your neighbor's wife.
10. You shall not covet anything that belongs to your neighbor.

After Jesus reminded the people of the Ten Commandments, he said, "A new commandment I give unto you, that ye love one another as I have loved you, that ye also love one another. By this shall all men know that ye are my disciples, if ye have love one to another. Judge not that you be not judged. For with judgment you pronounce you will be judged, and with the measures you use, it will be measured unto you. Blessed are the peace makers, for they shall be called sons of God. You must love the Lord your God with all your heart, all your soul and all your mind. This is the first and greatest commandment. So whatever you wish that others would do to you, do also to them, for this is the law and the prophets. If you can believe, all things are possible to him who believes."

Jesus stepped forward from the altar and said, "I must return to where I came from. I will always be with you. Don't worry about tomorrow, for tomorrow will worry about itself. Each day has enough trouble of its own."

The light shining on Jesus was slowly diminishing and the pontiff stood up from his chair and walked to where Jesus was standing. The pope looked out at his clergy, who were still silent and awestruck, and he said, "Please remain here and reflect on what Jesus has said. I must leave now and give an official statement from the Vatican," and then he went to the Vatican's public relations office while Jesus remained in the Sistine Chapel.

David, Luke, Brian, Martha and Thomas were in the hospitality room of the residence hall watching Jesus live on the Vatican's TV network. When Jesus was done speaking, Brian said, "Jesus is a great orator. I wish we could see the facial expressions of the people as he spoke."

"I know countless nonbelievers in God just became believers and now know there is a higher power that is watching them," Martha said.

After Jesus had finished speaking, David began changing the channels to gauge the reaction of his speech in other countries. All the foreign news stations had positive comments about Jesus and were reporting how Jesus had returned from heaven as prophesied in the Holy Scriptures. "In a few days church attendance will increase dramatically, and crime will take a deep plunge. Countries at war will put their differences behind them and make peace. People will reflect on what Jesus said and change their sinful ways. The world has just become a better place to live," David said.

After the pope entered the Vatican's public relations office, he walked into the director's office. The director was sitting at his desk, and the pope said, "I want you to issue the following official statement":

Jesus has returned as written in the Holy Scriptures. He has come to his church to warn people that a higher power is watching and hearing them. Sinners must repent or face eternal damnation. The Vatican is issuing a proclamation that today is a Holy Holiday to be observed and celebrated annually from this day forth.

"Please release this immediately," and then the pope left to return to the Sistine Chapel to be with Jesus and the cardinals.

When the pontiff entered the chapel, he saw Jesus standing in front of the altar answering questions from the cardinals. The pope went over and stood next to Jesus. A cardinal stood and asked, "Lord, what good deeds must I do to achieve eternal life?"

"Why do you ask what is a good deed? There is only one deed you must perform if you want to be given eternal life, and that is obeying my Father's commandments," Jesus answered.

Another cardinal stood and asked, "Lord, do you judge who is greater serving in the name of God?"

"For who is greater, the one who is at the table or the one who serves? Is it not the one who is at the table? But I am among you as one who serves," Jesus replied.

Another cardinal stood and asked, "Lord, we live in a time when people seek and pray for a sign from God acknowledging that he is listening to them. Why haven't their prayers been answered until today?"

"Why do generations ask for a miraculous sign? I tell you the truth: No sign will be given to it," Jesus said after sighing deeply.

After Jesus answered the last question, the pope said, "Our Lord and Savior has come to us and must return to where he came from. Please go and preach what has been said by Jesus to your parishioners," and then looking at Jesus, he asked, "Lord, would you like to add anything?"

"Yes. Every kingdom divided against itself will be ruined, and every city or household divided against itself will not stand," Jesus answered.

"Jesus, please come with me," the pontiff said, and he escorted Jesus to his papal residence while the cardinals remained in the Sistine Chapel talking among themselves.

David was still in the hospitality room watching events unfold on television. He was watching the news with Brian, Martha, Luke and Thomas, and it seemed like every TV station was broadcasting live during and after Jesus' sermon. News reporters were interviewing people outside the Vatican in Saint Peter's Square, where there was a jumbo TV screen, to get their reactions on what they had just witnessed and heard from Jesus. The response was overwhelmingly positive. It was as though the earth stopped turning and started again with a new beginning. David said with a smile, "We have accomplished what we set out to do, and that was to revive the fear of God in the people on this planet. They witnessed a higher power returning with a warning to repent their sinful ways or face eternal damnation. We now have one last task, and that is getting Jesus to StellaPort so we can send him and Thomas home."

The pope had gone to his papal residence with Jesus. When they were inside, the pontiff said, "Lord, please wait here while I get Professor Solomon and his companions," and then he left his home and went to the hospitality room where David and his group were watching replays of Jesus' sermon.

The Holy See entered the hospitality room, went directly to David and said, "Professor, please accompany me and your party to my residence. Jesus is waiting there. I'll be sending for Cardinal O'Shea to join us."

David, Thomas, Brian, Martha and Luke followed the pontiff, and as they were walking, the pope called Monsignor Fabrini on his cell phone. "Hello, Monsignor. It's Pope Valentine. Please bring Cardinal O'Shea from the Sistine Chapel to my residence now."

"Yes, Your Holiness. I'll go find him now," the monsignor said and ended the conversation.

They arrived at the pontiff's residence. After everyone had entered, they could see Jesus standing on the balcony overlooking St. Peter's Square, which was overflowing with people. Jesus saw himself on the huge jumbo television screen while the many news organizations had their cameras focused on him. The large crowd was silent and waiting for Jesus to speak as the pope remained from view so the people in the square would not see him. Jesus looked out at the enormous crowd and said, "I stand before you to give a warning. If sinners do not repent, they will never be allowed into the kingdom of God. Therefore, I tell you that whatever you ask for in prayer, believe that you will receive it, and it will be yours, and when you stand praying, if you hold anything against anyone, forgive him, so that your Father in heaven may forgive you your sins."

The crowd was silent and many were on their knees praying and looking up at Jesus as he raised his arms and said, "Many of you seek a sign from heaven. Well, here I stand before you, the son of man. For God loved the world so much that he gave his one and only son so that everyone who believes in him will not perish but have eternal life. God sent his son into the world not to judge the world, but to save the world through him."

Jesus looked upward to the clear blue sky and loudly said, "Father, they are like sheep and need a sign to be led from temptation. I ask you to send a sign in your name to the sinners of this world who have committed a mortal sin." Suddenly an explosion was heard in the sky, and then a lightning bolt struck the top of the dome of Saint Peter's Basilica. The crowd gasped and became frightened, and one by one everyone in St. Peter's Square knelt before Jesus.

"What comes out from a man is what makes him unclean. For from within, out of men's hearts, comes evil thoughts, sexual immorality, theft, murder, adultery, greed, malice, deceit, lewdness, envy, slander, arrogance and folly. All these evils come from inside and make a man unclean. Blessed are the pure in heart, for they shall see God and me, his son, sitting at his right hand. So pray always that you may be counted worthy to escape all these things that will come to pass and to stand before the son of man. Haven't you read that at the beginning the creator made them male and female? For this reason, a man will leave his father and mother and be united to his wife and the two will become one flesh so they are no longer two, but one. Therefore, what God has joined together, let man not separate," Jesus finally said, and then he walked into the pope's residence.

The crowd was calling for him while the pope closed the doors to his balcony. He said, "Lord, as you know, you must return to Galilee."

"Jesus, which village would you like to be transported to?" David asked.

"I would like to go to Capernaum, which is my favorite village along the Sea of Galilee," Jesus answered.

"It will be done, and Thomas, what about you?" David asked.

"I'll follow Jesus," Thomas answered.

"I'll send you both there as soon as we arrive at my home," David said.

After Cardinal O'Shea entered the pope's residence, he said, "Your Holiness, you requested my presence. I'm sorry I'm late. I was watching Jesus speak on the TV from your balcony."

"Cardinal, in the evening we will be leaving for Boston and then travel to Professor Solomon's home. I must go now and help the monsignor cope with all the news organizations seeking statements and interviews. Please confirm our travel plans, especially for getting to Rome's airport. It must work without a glitch," the pontiff said.

"I'll do that immediately," the cardinal replied, and then he left for the monsignor's office.

The pope said, "Everyone, please remain here and make yourselves comfortable. I'll return as soon as possible," and then he left for his PR office to check on how things were going there.

At the public relations office, the pontiff met with his chief to have him write another statement regarding the afternoon speech by Jesus.

"Your Holiness, the server for the Vatican's website has already crashed twice today because of the volume of incoming emails. The emails just keep coming. There seems to be no end in sight, and the phones keep ringing," the director said.

"Just do the best you can. We must issue another brief statement concerning Jesus' speech from my balcony," the pontiff said.

"Your Holiness, what would you like the communiqué to say?" the director asked.

"You must incorporate into our response that Jesus has returned with a message of hope and warn the sinners of the world that a higher power exists and is watching them. God hears their prayers, and if they don't repent, justice will be served, either now or later," the pope answered.

"I'll do that right away and send it out immediately," the director said.

"Thank you for your hard work," the pope said.

After the pontiff left the PR office, he went to the Vatican's communication office in the same building and greeted the director and thanked him for a job well done. The pope then went to the monsignor's office and congratulated him for coordinating a successful synod on such short notice. "Monsignor Fabrini, please help the cardinals make arrangements to get to the airport so they can return to their parishes," the Holy See said.

"Yes, Your Holiness. I'll see to it."

"Excellent work, Monsignor."

"Thank you, sir."

"Oh, did Cardinal O'Shea stop by?" the pontiff asked.

"Yes. After he made some phone calls, he left," the monsignor answered, and then the Holy See left for his home.

When the pope arrived at his residence, he saw Cardinal O'Shea and his guests watching the international news that was being televised live from the Vatican. "The cardinals are now leaving to return to their parishes and repeat the Lord's message. I'm sure all the local churches will experience a significant increase in parishioners. This evening we'll depart for Boston but, before we leave, I will have my staff prepare and serve us a last supper with Jesus," the pontiff said.

The pope called the papal residence chief of staff to request a dinner for eight people to be served in his formal dining room. As he was talking on the phone, Martha said, "Excuse me, Your Holiness."

The pontiff stopped talking, looked at her and said, "One moment please. Yes, Martha?"

"Please request your chef to prepare dishes of fish, figs, nuts, garden salad, lentil soup, artichokes and wine to drink," Martha said, and then she glanced at Luke and said, "and milk."

"Is there anything else?" the pope asked.

"No. We prefer fish to eat, especially Brian," Martha said, smiling.

The pontiff relayed Martha's dinner menu request to his chief of staff, and the chief said, "Your supper will be served shortly."

"Thank you," the pope said. After ending the call, he invited everybody to his hospitality room while waiting for dinner to be served.

Two members of the papal staff entered the dining room and began to set an elegant table using a silk tablecloth linen, silverware and crystal glasses. After the table was set, the chef and his staff brought the food. The chief of staff went to the hospitality room and informed the Holy See that supper was being served. The pope and his guests went to the dining room and toward the end of their dinner, the pontiff stood from his chair with a glass of wine in his right hand and said, "I would like to propose a toast to our Lord and Savior, and to Thomas." The pope raised his glass and, looking at Jesus, said, "Lord, you are the light for all to see and worship. We are forever in your debt, and because of you, man will live forever more." Then the pontiff looked at Thomas and said, "I know we have not spoken much since you arrived here. I wish you a long and happy life. The Lord can use a person with your character to assist him in his travels, and thank you for safely guiding Brian and Martha through the Holy Land." The pope paused briefly, and then he said, "Everyone, please stand except for Jesus and Thomas." When they were standing, the pope lifted his glass higher and then drank his wine and so did all his guests, except for Luke, who drank milk.

After the toast, the pontiff said, "Cardinal, please escort our guests to the Domus Sanctae Marthae to gather their belongings. Jesus will remain here with me. We will meet everybody at the heliport at 9:30 p.m."

"Your Holiness, we'll meet you there," Cardinal O'Shea said, and the cardinal exited with everyone except Jesus to pack for the return trip to Salem.

It was time to leave and Cardinal O'Shea knocked on each of their doors and said, "It's time to go. I'll be in the lobby." After everyone had assembled in the lobby, they went to the heliport that had two helicopters on the pad with pilots sitting in them. The pope and Jesus then arrived with Monsignor Fabrini, who had a handheld radio he was using to communicate with the helicopter pilots.

Outside Vatican City, there were people trying to get into the city by climbing over the wall that surrounded the Vatican. The Swiss guards were positioned throughout the grounds and had their hands full. They ran from one section of the wall to another, responding to security sensors that sounded alarms indicating intruders. It was chaos both inside and outside Vatican City.

"Cardinal O'Shea, I will have my secretary order the town cars to leave the Vatican as the helicopters are taking off. The chauffeurs have been driving the cardinals to the airport all day, and the news media are stopping every car looking for Jesus," the pope said.

Monsignor Fabrini was standing between and in front of both helicopters and using his radio to instruct the pilots to warm up their engines. The rotor blades of the two black helicopters started twirling and making a loud noise. "Pope Valentine, the pilots have informed me they are ready for departure," the monsignor said.

"Good. We'll get on board now. Cardinal O'Shea, Jesus, Thomas and I will board one helicopter and Professor Solomon, Luke, Brian and Martha will get on the other," the pontiff said.

"I'll go and inform them now," the monsignor said, and then he went to David and shouted directions to him because of the noise being made by the helicopters.

"Professor, you, your son, Brian and Martha will travel on this helicopter, while Jesus, Thomas, the pope and Cardinal O'Shea will ride on the other aircraft," Monsignor Fabrini said, and then he helped David and his group board their helicopter. After everyone was seated, he closed the door.

The monsignor then went to the pope's group and helped them onto their aircraft. After they were seated, he closed the door. After both helicopters had their passengers on board, the monsignor used his radio and instructed the town cars to begin leaving Vatican City. He then ordered the pilot of the helicopter with Jesus on board to take off first, and after it was at a safe distance, he gave the green light for the remaining aircraft to depart.

As the four town cars began leaving Vatican City, they were each being stopped by news crews, but when the helicopters started departing, all eyes were focused on the dark sky, watching them take off from within the city walls. The many news crews had their TV cameras focused on the helicopters while the reporters were announcing their guesses as to where they were going. Most news organizations reported that the helicopters were flying to the pope's summer residence or to Rome's international airport. When they were far enough away from the Vatican, the pilots set course for Rome's airport. Upon arrival, both helicopters hovered above the tarmac close to the two chartered jets and then landed. The pilots of each plane greeted the pope and escorted him and everyone else to the jet that was headed for Boston. After everyone had boarded and was seated, the pilot closed and locked the door. The helicopters then took off as the plane that was chartered for Jerusalem taxied onto the runway and was cleared for taking off to Israel. After the airplane was in the air, the aircraft with Jesus and everyone else aboard taxied to the runway and was cleared for departure for Boston's Logan International Airport.

When the pope, Cardinal O'Shea, Jesus, Thomas, David, Brian, Martha and Luke arrived at Logan International Airport, there were four cars waiting on the tarmac for them. After the airplane came to a stop, the pilot unlocked and opened the airplane door. They exited and went to the chauffeurs that were stowing their bags in the trunks of the cars. After everyone was seated in their car, they were driven to David's home. When they arrived, the drivers parked their cars in front of his house. After they entered David's home, they went directly to StellaPort. David turned on the lights to the room. When the pope saw the time machine, he looked at it in awe and said, "This looks like a machine that only God could bestow the wisdom to be built."

"Pope Valentine, it's time for Jesus and Thomas to return to the year AD 29. Jesus, do you still want to be transported to Capernaum?" David asked.

Jesus nodded his head and said, "Yes."

"Thomas, the same place for you?" David asked, looking at him.

"Yes," he answered.

"Brian, please help Thomas and Jesus into the transportation chamber and have them each stand on a Mollie," David said. Brian escorted Jesus and Thomas into the chamber, where they stood on a platform.

"Jesus, would you like to say something before leaving?" David asked.

"But of that day and hour no one knows, not even the angels in heaven, but my Father knows," Jesus said.

David went to Eve and turned on his mini supercomputer and then each of Stella's components. David was at Stella's control panel. He began to use the keypad to enter longitude 35.5750 and latitude 32.8811, the location for Capernaum, and the date of May 7, 0029, and 5 a.m. as the time of arrival. The coordinates, date and time were now set, and David started the process to return Jesus and Thomas to the Holy Land. Mollie and Eve went into action calculating the amount of energy required to transport them. Eve calculated the energy and transferred the data to Mollie. The numbers in Mollie's display window stopped changing, and a green light appeared next to the window, indicating that the power needed had been calculated. David turned on the laser lights and then the antigravity machine, and they began to rise. David introduced the electromagnetic waves and turned the transport dial to the backward position. A vortex now appeared above them in the glass chamber and started to move in a counterclockwise motion with increasing speed. Suddenly, they vanished. The subject tracking unit signaled that it was locked onto Jesus and Thomas because the longitude of 35.5750 and the latitude of 32.8811 were being displayed in the window, indicating that they both had arrived at Capernaum. David then shut off the antigravity machine, the laser lights and the electromagnetic wave inducer.

CHAPTER 32

Jesus and Thomas suddenly found themselves standing in a grassy field near the outer village limits of Capernaum, facing in the direction of the Sea of Galilee. Thomas turned and looked behind him and said, "There's Isaac's farm. We're home. Our time is less complicated than the time of Brian and Martha. They have made many technological advancements, but it seems their machines are controlling their lives."

"God has given them the wisdom to overcome obstacles to achieve their dreams, either for the good or for the bad. We live in a time when man is still finding his way in the world with primitive means compared to man in the 21st century," Jesus said.

"Where are you going now?" Thomas asked.

"I'm going to visit my friend the rabbi, whom you met. I will give a sermon to his congregation and then return home to Nazareth."

"I'll accompany you, and after I hear your sermon, I'll go home to Ein Kerem to help my father with his business."

When Jesus and Thomas arrived at the synagogue, they entered and saw thirty men praying. Thomas sat with them and prayed while Jesus went to the rabbi, who was standing in front of the Ark, and greeted him with a smile while shaking his hand. The rabbi smiled and introduced him to the congregation and Jesus began his sermon. After Jesus was done preaching, he walked out of the synagogue with Thomas and they traveled along the western shore of the Sea of Galilee. When they arrived at the small fishing village of Taricheae, Thomas said, "Jesus, I must leave you now. I'm traveling south to Jerusalem and from there to my home. You are a divine being, and I've been blessed with the opportunity to meet such a great leader of men. I will speak your name to my family, friends and strangers telling them of the work you're doing for God."

"Thank you, Thomas. You are a righteous man and one day you shall see me sitting at the right hand of God. As you live, obey the laws of God and warn the sinners that they must repent before being allowed into my Father's kingdom," Jesus said.

"Bye, Lord. I hope to meet you again in this world. If we had cell phones, we could stay in touch," Thomas said while hugging Jesus. Jesus laughed and then he continued walking west to Nazareth while Thomas headed south toward Jerusalem.

After Jesus and Thomas disappeared from the transportation chamber, David, Pope Valentine, Cardinal O'Shea, Luke, Brian and Martha were still in the room that housed StellaPort. David looked again at the subject tracking window and said, "The longitude and latitude coordinates for Jesus and Thomas are slowly changing, indicating that they are now in the Holy Land. I'll turn off all the components to StellaPort and sever the electromagnetic wave that is still connected to them." After David turned off his time machine, he said, "Let's all go upstairs to my living room, but first I must conceal this room so my machine will be kept a secret from the world. I will join you in a minute," and then they left him alone.

After everyone was gone, David softly said, "Stella, you made my dreams come true. We did it," and then he turned off Eve and pushed the cabinet against the wall and removed the key from the secret compartment in his wallet. David inserted the key into the locking mechanism and secured the cabinet to the basement wall. After his time machine was hidden, he turned off the lights to the lab and went to his living room.

When David entered the living room, he said, "I'll turn on the television so we can see what's been happening in the world." All the major U.S. networks were reporting from the Vatican, including many foreign countries, and they were announcing that people had been flocking to their local church to pray. The scene was still chaotic outside Vatican City, and many international news organizations were at the Jerusalem Airport waiting for the aircraft to land and hoping to get a glimpse of Jesus.

"Good work, everyone. Our plans went off without a glitch. I must return to Rome immediately to personally make a statement," the pope said.

"I'll have my secretary make the necessary arrangements. When would you like to leave?" Cardinal O'Shea asked.

"As soon as possible," the pope answered.

Cardinal O'Shea then used his cell phone and called his secretary to ask her to charter an airplane for immediate departure for Rome and to inform him when the pope's travel plans were completed. After a few minutes, the cardinal's secretary called him and said, "Cardinal, the jet that you arrived on is refueling and will be departing from Logan in two hours for Rome."

"Perfect. The pope will be on it. Thank you," the cardinal said and ended the call. Then he said, "Your Holiness, your airplane will be leaving in two hours from Logan International Airport."

"Thank you, Cardinal. We should leave now," the pontiff said. Then he went to David, and while they shook hands, he said, "Professor, that was a wonderful thing you did for mankind. I believe you made the world a much better place to live and increased daily church attendance."

The pope then turned to Brian and Martha, smiling, and when he shook their hands, he said, "Thank you for risking your lives to find Jesus and bring him safely to us. Without your valiant efforts, this historical event would not have been possible."

"You're welcome," Brian said with a smile, and then he asked, "The next time I'm visiting Rome, will you give me a personal tour of the Vatican?"

"You've got it, son. It would be a pleasure, and don't forget to bring Martha with you," the pope answered.

"Thank you, Pope Valentine. We could be in Rome next year at this time," Martha said, and after smiling at Brian, she asked, "Do you perform wedding ceremonies?"

"No, but for you two, I'll make an exception," the pope answered, still smiling and looking at Brian. The pontiff began walking to the front door, and as he was about to pass by Luke, he stopped, gently patted him on the head and said, "Young man, we didn't talk in Rome, and I guess it's the same here. But I'll say a prayer for you during my next Mass in St. Peter's Square, and I'll mention your name to the people."

"Thanks, Pope Valentine. That sounds cool," Luke said.

David escorted the pope and Cardinal O'Shea to the front door and opened it. When the cardinal was about to leave, he shook David's hand. After their handshake, the cardinal continued holding his hand and said, "Professor, that was an unselfish deed you did. I know you could have used your time machine for personal gain, but instead you chose to use it to help humanity in a time of crisis. God bless you, Professor." The cardinal then joined the pope, and they went to their cars, where the pope was to be driven to the airport.

David closed the door and he returned to the living room and sat with Brian, Martha and Luke, who were watching the news. Then Brian said, "All the excitement for us has seemed to have calmed down. Martha and I must return our biblical clothing."

"Luke, please bring Brian's and Martha's costumes from the spare bedroom," David said. Luke went upstairs and soon returned to the living room with two boxes and gave them to Brian.

"We must stop at the handcraft store on the way to the costume shop to have the seamstress remove the pockets on the inside of the mantles. She'll also have to repair the tear on the sleeve of my garment," Martha said.

"How did you tear it?" Luke asked.

"Do you recall when Martha said she wanted to come with me to the Holy Land in case I needed to be bailed out of a jam?" Brian asked.

"Yes," Luke answered.

"Well, she's the one who got bailed out. We rented a small fishing boat to take us up the Jordan River on the way to Nazareth. We were in rough waters and Martha was tossed from the boat. As she was being ejected, the right sleeve of her mantle got caught on a nail that was protruding from the inside of the craft. Thomas rushed to her rescue and so did I. We pulled her back in while Simon kept steering the boat. Martha was almost a goner."

"Brian and Thomas are my heroes," Martha said.

"Wow! I wish I had been there to see that," Luke replied.

Brian and Martha stood up from the sofa and went to the front door. As they were about to leave, David said, "We should have a picnic this Saturday at Christopher Columbus Park in Boston."

"That sounds like a nice idea," Martha said.

"Brian, please bring Murphy," Luke said.

"That would be fine. What time should we meet you at the park?" Brian asked.

"We'll meet you there at 11 a.m., and we'll bring the food and drinks," David answered.

"Dude, I'll bring Murphy with me," Brian said, and they left for the handcraft store.

David returned to the living room and sat with Luke on the sofa holding the remote control while they watched the news. As David was changing the channels, the reporters from the many different networks were reporting a dramatic decrease in crime compared to the week before. It seemed the return of Jesus scared many deviants into becoming law-abiding citizens. David continued watching the news and was pleased because his plan turned out just as he had envisioned.

Brian and Martha drove into the parking lot of the handcraft store. They went into the store carrying their garments and approached the clerk at the checkout counter. "May I speak with the seamstress?" Martha asked at the counter.

"Yes. I'll go get her," the store assistant answered. The clerk entered a room in the rear and soon reappeared with the seamstress.

When the seamstress was with Brian and Martha, she said, "Hello. I remember you. How may I help you?"

"Would you be kind enough to remove the pockets you sewed on the inside of these two garments and also fix the tear on the sleeve?" Martha asked.

"Yes. I can do that. It shouldn't take long, and you're in luck. I have the same color thread as the torn garment," the seamstress answered.

"Can we wait while you work on them?" Martha asked.

"That will be fine. I'll get to work on this now," the woman answered, and then she returned to the rear room in the store.

After they had waited for a short time, the seamstress returned with the two garments draped over her arms and set them down onto the counter. Brian and Martha went to the counter and the woman said, "They're ready."

Martha examined each garment and said, "You did an excellent job on the tear and removing the pockets."

"Thank you for the kind words. Oh, in one of the pockets was this wool bag and gold jewelry," the woman said.

"Thank you. We forgot about those items," Martha said.

The seamstress handed Martha the garments, pouch and the jewelry. Martha paid her and then they left for the theater supply shop.

Brian drove to the theater district in Boston and parked his car in front of the shop where they had rented the costumes. They entered the shop, each carrying a box containing their garments and accessories, and saw the gentleman who had rented them the clothes at the checkout counter helping a customer. After the gentleman was done assisting the customer, they approached him and he asked, "How may I help you?"

"We would like to return these costumes and accessories," Brian answered.

The man removed the garments from each box and examined them, and then he said, "The sandals seem to have some miles put on them."

"Yes. We had to travel a good distance to complete our mission ... I mean, roles," he replied.

"I hope you both get the roles you auditioned for."

"Thank you. We do too," Brian said as he shot a smile at Martha.

After they left the shop, Brian drove Martha to her apartment. When they arrived, he said, "I'll call you later this evening," and then he gave her a kiss before she got out of the car, and then he drove home.

CHAPTER 33

It was Saturday morning and David was sitting at the desk in his basement lab reading a book on the possibility of time travel. Miriam was standing at the entrance to the lab and said, "David, we're just about packed for the picnic. We should be leaving now for the park."

"I'll be there in a minute," David said.

David set the book down onto the desk and on his way out of the lab, he turned off the lights and went to the kitchen where Luke was helping his mother pack the two ice coolers with food and drinks. "Luke, I'll take over in here. Go to the garage and bring the charcoal and lighter fluid to the car," David said.

When they finished packing, David carried the two coolers to his car and put them into the trunk. After the trunk was packed, they drove to Christopher Columbus Park to meet Brian and Martha. While David was driving, he began smiling because he was visualizing Brian's and Martha's facial expressions when they would be introduced to Miriam. After arriving at the park, Luke saw Brian throwing a Frisbee and Murphy chased it on the grass field while Martha sat on a picnic table bench watching them. "There they are," Luke said. David parked his car, and they brought the ice coolers and supplies to where Martha was sitting. David, Miriam and Luke set the picnic items onto the table as Brian jogged with Murphy to them.

"Hi, Professor. Hi, Luke," Martha said.

Brian was quick to arrive with Murphy. When he did, David said, "Hi, Martha. Hi, Brian. This is my wife, Miriam. Miriam, this is Martha and this is Brian. They are the graduate students I told you about."

Martha and Brian took turns shaking Miriam's hand. When they did, each said, "It's a pleasure to meet you."

"It's also a pleasure meeting you both. David has been speaking highly of you. He mentioned you like to travel to exotic places," Miriam said. Brian and Martha looked at each other and then at David with surprise on their faces.

"Hi, Brian. Hi, Martha," Luke said, and then he threw a green tennis ball toward the waterfront. Murphy chased it while Luke ran after him.

"Miriam, please excuse us for a few minutes. I need to talk with them. We'll be right back," David said.

"I'll set the picnic table in the meantime," Miriam said, and then they walked a short distance, far enough away from her so she couldn't hear their conversation.

"I know you have the question, how?" David said.

"Professor, I thought your wife died during childbirth," Brian said.

"The day we returned from Rome, after you and Martha had left my home and later that day when Luke went to the movie theater with his friends, I was alone in my basement lab and saw the shoebox in which we sent Harry to visit me in the past. I thought, what if I left a message to myself the day before Luke was to be born warning that if a cesarean section was not performed, Miriam would die because of childbirth complications. I did just that and now Miriam is with us," David replied.

"Professor, you used your time machine to play God," Martha said.

"Before I made the decision, I recalled the story you told of Jesus saving the baby's life in Danos. Jesus saved the child's life because his Father in heaven had given him the ability to heal the sick. I also thought about the last words Jesus said to us before being transported, and they were 'but of that day and hour no one knows, not even the angels in heaven, but my Father knows.' My time machine was created because God bestowed upon me the wisdom to build such a machine. I decided to use God's gift to me to save a life by using my time machine," David said.

"You're not Jesus," Brian said.

"I didn't say I was. I did not save Miriam's life in God's name with the help of divine intervention. I saved her life using God's wisdom that he blessed me with. If God did not trust me, I would not have been the man who made time travel possible. StellaPort is now securely hidden and will not be used again," David said with a smile, and then he said, "unless the world needs two heroes to save mankind."

"Professor, you are truly a unique man," Martha said.

"Thank you for saying that," David said. Then he looked toward Miriam, and the picnic table was ready for enjoying the day at the park.

Luke was playing with Murphy near the waterfront, throwing a green tennis ball which Murphy would retrieve. After Luke tossed the ball, a man approached him and said, "Hello, young man. You must keep your dog on a leash."

"I didn't see a warning sign," Luke replied.

"I was a park ranger years ago and this park was my beat. I've been retired for many years now, and I know that when I worked as a ranger, dogs had to be kept on a leash for the public's safety," the man said.

"I'll put Murphy on one now."

"Did you say your dog's name is Murphy?"

"Yes, that's his name."

"I remember, years ago, a boy close to your age had a dog named Murphy who wasn't on a leash. I gave the boy a warning because it was his birthday, and today you'll get a break because I'm retired."

Brian was at the picnic table and noticed Luke talking to the man who was gesturing toward Murphy with his hand. Brian grabbed Murphy's leash from the table and jogged over to where Luke and the man were talking. When Brian arrived, he attached the leash to Murphy's collar.

"Thanks, Brian. This man was a park ranger, and the law says we must keep Murphy on a leash in the park," Luke said.

"Your name is Brian and this is your dog?" the man asked.

"Yes. I've owned him for a few years now," Brian replied.

"I was telling this young man about a boy named Brian I met in this park many years ago. He also had a dog called Murphy. What a coincidence to find a person named Brian who owns a golden retriever named Murphy in the same park."

"I know. I wonder what the odds of that would be," Brian replied. Then he said, "Dude, we should return to our picnic area now."

"I enjoyed meeting you both. Have a pleasant stay in the park," the man said, and then he walked away.

Luke, with Brian holding Murphy's leash, began walking to the picnic table. While they were walking, Luke asked, "Brian, do you think he's the park ranger you met when Murphy was transported back in time to find you?"

"I believe so," Brian answered with a smile, and then they enjoyed the rest of the day in Christopher Columbus Park.

Would you like to see your manuscript become a book?

If you are interested in becoming a PublishAmerica author, please submit your manuscript for possible publication to us at:

mybook@publishamerica.com

You may also mail in your manuscript to:

**PublishAmerica
PO Box 151
Frederick, MD 21705**

www.publishamerica.com

CPSIA information can be obtained at www.ICGtesting.com
Printed in the USA
BVOW08s2142150114

342004BV00001BA/68/P